Praise for LINNEƎ SINCLƎIR

"Fun, fast and sexy! Linnea Sinclair always delivers a great read." —Robin D. Owens, author of *Heart Thief* and *Heart Duel*

"With her trademark snappy dialogue, smart characters, and sizzling romance, Linnea Sinclair has readers flipping the pages at light speed." —Susan Grant, author of *The Legend of Banzai Maguire* and *Your Planet or Mine?*

"One of the brightest new voices in science fiction romance." —Catherine Asaro, author of *Schism* and *Skyfall*

"[Linnea Sinclair] has the knack of intriguing with romance and delivering a solid story too." —Jacqueline Lichtenberg, author of *Dreamspy* and *Those of My Blood*

"Linnea Sinclair brings her own dimension to the world of sci-fi/fantasy romance. Her richly textured novels are to be cherished first page to last." —Patricia Waddell, author of *Whispers in the Stars* and *True Blood*

Praise for FINDERS KEEPERS!

Award of Distinction for Exceptional Merit from *Heartstrings Reviews*

Winner of the CataRomance Reviewers Choice Award for Single Title Sci/Fi, 2005

Finalist for 2006 RITA Award for Best First Book

Finalist for the 2005 RIO Award for Best Sci-Fi/ Fantasy Romance

"Has the 'wow!' factor in spades... The plot and characterizations are detailed, dynamic and deeply immersive and make this super-charged sci-fi release twice as interesting as anything this reviewer has come across before... Well-developed and wonderfully imaginative, *Finders Keepers* has 'exceptional merit' written all over it." —*Heartstrings*

"*Finders Keepers* is a great ride from start to finish... A delight to read... Sinclair delivers a story balanced nicely between space opera adventure and emotion-centered romance—not the easiest thing to find anymore. Thanks, Linnea!" —*Speculative Romance Online*

Praise for GABRIEL'S GHOST

Winner of the 2006 RITA Award for Best Paranormal Romance
2003 Prism Award, 2nd place (tie with *An Accidental Goddess*), for Best Futuristic Romance
2003 RWA Windy City Choice Award, 2nd place, for Best FF&P Romance
Winner of the 2002 Affaire de Coeur Award for Best Futuristic Romance
2002 Sapphire Award, 2nd place (tie with *An Accidental Goddess*), for Best Speculative Romance Novel
2002 PEARL Award Honorable Mention for Best Science Fiction Novel
Romance Reviews Today Perfect 10 Award
WordWeaving Award of Excellence

"Readers have come to expect the extraordinary from author Linnea Sinclair, but *Gabriel's Ghost* still exceeds all expectations! With the vision and texture of a poet, the heart of a warrior, and the skill of a master, Sinclair creates a world of psychic gifts and shape shifters, of dangers beyond imagination and love beyond question... A tale so entrancing, so mesmerizing that readers will be absolutely blown away."
—*Midwest Book Review*

"Sinclair writes an intriguing blend of science-fiction and romance, with lots of action-adventure, great dialogue, a sneaky sense of humor that won't quit... A much richer, more emotionally demanding tale of suspense that... starts off fast and furious and never lets go." —NoveLists.com

"*Gabriel's Ghost* may be the best synthesis of science fiction and romance fiction yet, appealing to two readerships that once seemed to have nothing in common. Both the dramatic tension and the sexual tension are there from the first chapter, and they never let up... The whole novel combines grittiness of character with grittiness of science fiction background in the tradition of C.J. Cherryh." —John J. Pierce, author of *Imagination and Evolution*

"A non-stop thrill ride with a pace that never slows down, *Gabriel's Ghost* is enthralling...The sexual tension crackles and the love scenes are positively incinerating. Combine all of this with fascinating supporting characters who are never quite what they seem and a hard look at prejudice, genetic engineering and the ease with which the truth can be twisted, and you have an intellectually and emotionally satisfying book." —*Sime-Gen Reviews*

"How can a review do justice to a book that sweeps you away from the very first page?... *Gabriel's Ghost* is a phenomenal book and one that deserves its place on keeper shelves all over the world...Linnea Sinclair has managed to mix religion, politics, adventure, science fiction and romance into one of the best reads of the year. A true winner!" —*Interludes Magazine*

"An adventure a minute, with one revelation after another developing and deepening the relationship between hero and heroine, even as they threaten to tear them apart. I don't know if there are any more stories in this universe, but I'd sure like to read them if there are." —Gail Dayton, author of *The Barbed Rose*

Praise for
an accidental goddess

Finalist for the 2005 RIO Award for Best Sci-Fi/ Fantasy Romance
Winner of the 2003 RWA Windy City Choice Award for Best FF&P Romance

"Proves once again why Sinclair is one of the reigning queens of science fiction romances . . . This is a book readers can hand to non-SF fans and say, "Try it. You'll like it." And they will . . . provided they enjoy bright, attractive characters, an interesting plot, action, adventure, humor and romance." —*Starlog*

"A quirky, humorous, fast-paced saga of deception, passion, trust, and risk . . . Linnea Sinclair's innovative and entertaining story will captivate the reader and provide hours of laughter, suspense, and adventure." —*Fantasy Book Spot*

"A great, great story with a fabulous romance and I loved every minute of it. No wonder Ms. Sinclair is a double RITA finalist with *Gabriel's Ghost* and *Finder's Keepers*." —Gail Dayton, author of *The Barbed Rose*

Praise for GAMES OF COMMAND

"Linnea Sinclair just gets better and better! *Games of Command*, her latest science fiction romance, features not one but two sexy, dangerous heroes, along with two strong, capable women and two fabulous furry furzels. Sinclair whips her characters through a story that is as exciting and action packed as it is passionate. *Games of Command* is not to be missed!" —Mary Jo Putney, author of *Stolen Magic*

ALSO BY LINNEA SINCLAIR

Finders Keepers
Gabriel's Ghost
An Accidental Goddess

GAMES OF COMMAND

LINNEA SINCLAIR

BANTAM BOOKS

GAMES OF COMMAND
A Bantam Spectra Book / March 2007

Published by
Bantam Dell
A Division of Random House, Inc.
New York, New York

The characters and some scenes in this novel were originally part of
Command Performance (NovelBooks, Inc., 2002) and several short
stories that were part of the *Alliance Command* series.

ISBN: 978-0-553-58963-4

www.bantamdell.com

OPM 10 9 8 7 6 5 4 3 2

This bit of space opera romance silliness
is dedicated, with thanks, to:

Janie Blankenship, RN, DON, aka Doc Eden, who
kindly and with much encouragement let me reinvent her
real life into an intergalactic adventure (and borrow one of
her cats for the story as well);

Commander Carla Arpin, my publicist, who graciously
permitted me to up her to the rank of admiral in the U-Cee
Fleet;

My readers and fans at the Intergalactic Bar & Grille,
who constantly pestered me for a resolution to Sass and Kel-
Paten's story and were patient—and faithful—for its return;

Intergalactic Bar & Grille regular and creative partner
April "Cosmic Wench" Koenig for the "discovery" of
McClellan's Void (also known as Dreehalla):

> *The Danvari call it Dreehalla, the mother of the
> universe. The Krylle's word for it is simply a popping
> sound, which literally translates to "devourer of all
> that is good and evil." The Rebashee don't give it a
> name but when speaking of it make an odd symbol
> with their fingers to protect them from its taking no-
> tice of them. Us? We call it simply McClellan's Void,
> McClellan's Lie, McClellan's Folly . . . named after the
> fleet captain who went in and lived to tell the tale—or
> so he claims.*

And the following Bar regulars for their creative assistance with naming the following: Degun's Luck (Gerard
Gourion), Crylocs (Mo Boylan), Morrassian Mists (Ken),
and Asterion (Linda Durkin).

My crit partners, author Stacey "Silver Spoon" Klemstein and Lynne "Liberrry Lady" Welch; and readers Donna Kuhn and Michelle Williamson, who put up with my mad rambling e-mails and desperate pleas for feedback with such panache;

My editor, Anne "Gemstone" Groell, and my agent, Kristin "Let's Try That Martini Next" Nelson, for not letting me give up;

My husband, Rob Bernadino, who after twenty-six years still finds me amusing;

And to Daiquiri, my real-life Tank the Furzel, and his little buddy, Miss Doozy, who perhaps will get her own book someday....

GAMES
OF
COMMAND

PROLOGUE

CAPTAIN'S OFFICE: UNITED COALITION HUNTERSHIP *REGALIA*

"You might want to sit down." Admiral Cayla "Ace" Edmonds's countenance on the *Regalia*'s comm screen was serious. But Sass—Captain Tasha Sebastian—had known the admiral since Ace was a captain with the U-Cee Fleet and Sass was a fast-talking rim runner with questionable associations and excellent reflexes. That was sixteen years ago—long enough to recognize a slight twinkle of mirth in the older woman's dark eyes.

So it wasn't something galaxy-shaking serious. With a half shrug, Sass sat behind her desk and played along. "The Triad rescinded the peace agreement?"

Alarm flared briefly in Ace's eyes. Then the admiral clasped a hand over her heart, obscuring the United Coalition insignia on her khaki uniform. "Don't do that to an old woman. Not after what we've just been through."

Grueling was a good word to describe *that*. There were times Sass wondered how she and Ace had survived four months of negotiations with the United Coalition's one-time enemy—negotiations that were taxing to diplomats and senior military personnel on both sides. But peace and cooperation were things the technologically superior Triad said they wanted, even more than the rich U-Cee resources they'd chased for years. The U-Cees agreed: the Illithians were a growing threat neither of them could handle, and an alliance with the Triad was preferable to the annexation the Rebashee suffered more than sixty years before.

"So what's the gossip?" Sass asked.

"Not gossip. Fact. I've put my official signature to it."

"Then we are talking about the Triad? Or the new Alliance?"

"The Alliance. And I'm pleased to report you've been demoted." Ace grinned broadly. "Commander," she added, stressing the title.

A spike of fear flashed through Sass's gut but quickly subsided. Hell, Ace was probably more responsible for the existence of Tasha Sebastian than Sass was. And that was a secret both would take to their graves. So this wasn't a demotion due to the lies that created a U-Cee officer named Tasha Sebastian out of a rim runner named Sass. This was something else. Another one of Admiral Edmonds's secret missions?

"So I'm demoted. What else am I?"

Ace paused for a half a breath, then: "The new first officer on the *Vaxxar*."

Sass jerked upright in her office chair. "I'm *what*?" Her voice, much to her consternation, squeaked.

"New first officer, reporting directly to the Tin Soldier himself. If you behave, in six months—maybe less—you'll have your rank of captain back."

"You're transferring me to the *Vax*?"

"Admiral Kel-Paten specifically requested your transfer as part of the Alliance Personnel Integration Program. You know he's still acting captain on board? I gather it was a nonnegotiable issue. What I did negotiate is fifteen of your officers to be transferred within two weeks of your arrival."

Sass leaned back in her chair and clamped her lips shut before her mouth could continue its fish-out-of-water imitation. The *Vaxxar* was more than just Kel-Paten's flagship. It was arguably one the best hunterships on either side of the Zone. Her wildest dreams during the war included its capture so she could explore its technical perfection. But she figured the chance of that happening ranked right up there with her personally solving the mystery of McClellan's Void—that mythical location that down-on-their-luck spacers used to cadge a free drink.

Now she was actually going to be on board the *Vax*. But her thrill of anticipation wavered as the impetus for this windfall registered. Admiral Kel-Paten—the Triad's *biocybernetic* admiral—had requested her transfer. Requesting her head on a platter would make more sense. Had he guessed that the mercenary Lady Sass wasn't really dead? Ace would never take that risk. Yet, last she heard, the APIP hadn't reached the final stages. Why did Kel-Paten want her on board, and ahead of schedule? What game was her former nemesis playing?

"My choice of officers. He agreed to that?" she asked warily.

"I've already logged in Doc Fynn, Cisco Garrick, and Perrin Rembert."

"And Tank. I'm sure Kel-Paten has a dozen regulations prohibiting pets on board, but Tank goes or I don't." She didn't anticipate a problem with the others. Eden Fynn, the *Regalia*'s chief medical officer and Sass's closest friend, was a top-notch Healer. Garrick was one of the sharpest chiefs of security she'd ever worked with, and Remy was a science officer so thorough that she felt even the Triad's biocybe admiral would be hard-pressed to find fault with him.

But Tank was her furzel. Fidget, really, as he was not yet full grown. A ten-pound fluffy bundle of long black and white fur with an unstoppable curiosity, an insatiable appetite, and a heart full of unconditional love.

"Already approved."

Kel-Paten approved a furzel on board? Warning bells blared through Sass's mind. "This is not a good idea, Ace."

The admiral's grin widened.

"We'll end up killing each other," Sass continued, "if he doesn't dump me out in McClellan's Void first. Gods' blessed rumps, he eats, lives, and breathes regulations. Plus, if he ever finds out I'm—"

"It's been seven years since Lethant. He won't." On the comm screen, Ace waved one hand dismissively. "Look at the positives. You, my dear, will have one of the Triad's best hunterships at your fingertips. There are things that ship can *do* that our best intelligence agents could never confirm. All the pretty talk of this new Alliance aside, I never thought we'd get even a U-Cee *ensign* on board the *Vaxxar*. Then I get this." Ace held up a thin datadisk. "Your transfer, scheduled for three weeks from today. Kel-Paten obviously has no idea who you are, what you can do, or he'd never let you on board."

Actually, he did know what she could do, though it was almost twelve years ago, just before the war . . .

Twenty-four-year-old Lieutenant Sebastian sits at the helm on the Sarna Bogue *under command of Captain Rostikov. Both captain and ship are years past their prime, relegated now to patrolling the Far Reaches and hauling supplies to places no decent U-Cee crew wants to go. But for Sass, it's the best chance she's had. Reinvented with the help of a crafty U-Cee captain named Edmonds almost four years prior and legitimized by the United Coalition Intelligence Division, she's working her first shipboard posting as Lt. Tasha Sebastian. She covers for Rostikov when he's too drunk to make it to the bridge, tweaks illegal patches into the faltering drive systems, learns to play a mean game of Starfield Doubles from the leathery-faced Tsariian chief engineer.*

Then the Vaxxar shows up on short-range scan— the long-range gave its last gasp only an hour before—and all hell breaks loose. Sleek, fast, and deadly, the Imperial huntership is universally feared. But despite its superior tech and its subjugation of the

Rebashee's Danvaral sector, the Keltish Triad is running out of resources. And with both sides battling for possession of the Staceyan asteroid belt, U-Cee supply freighters are a favorite Triadian snack.

The Bogue is apparently on the menu, but Captain Rostikov is deep in a bourbon fog and snoring. The two techies are green ensigns fresh out of the academy. One wets his pants when the red-alert siren blares and the comps ID just who is on the Bogue's tail.

She catches the look in the chief's yellowed eyes—a mix of hopelessness and anger.

"We can't outrun the Vaxxar, Tasha."

"I know that, Chief."

"Can't fight 'em neither. Starboard lasers are locked up. I can get ya maybe half power on the port ones, but it's just pissin' in the wind against that one."

The remaining techie shivers at the comm panel. He dutifully sent out the SOS and dutifully reported back an ETA of one hour for the rescue team from Garchan-3. "But we're being hailed by the"—he gulps—"Vaxxar." He says the Triadian huntership's name in a hushed voice. Maybe hoping if no one hears him, it'll go away.

She gives the techie the order to open the comm and—for what will be the first of many times to come—hears the voice of Captain Kel-Paten. The Kel-Paten. But only his voice. Visual's out. In order for short-range scan to function at all, it has to be.

"Sarna Bogue, this is Captain Kel-Paten of the Vaxxar. Cut your drives immediately or you will be fired upon. Prepare to be boarded."

With a nod to the chief, she seats herself in the

command sling, takes a deep breath, and activates the comm mike: "Vaxxar, *this is the* Sarna Bogue. *Fuck you and the equinnard you rode in on. Sebastian out.*" *She slaps the mike off and turns to the chief, ignoring his wide-eyed expression.* "We've got work to do."

She knows from personal experience what Kel-Paten needs: maximum haul, minimal time. You board a U-Cee supply freighter, it's all there at your biocybernetically enhanced fingertips. Logs. Manifests. Locations and entry codes. Scan the data, locate the desired cargo, compute location coordinates, and transbeam the stuff out. Simple. Easy. Efficient. Quick.

Lady Sass's raids always were.

So she tweaks everything—the comp codes, the nav codes, the security locks. Hell, most of the stuff malfunctions as a matter of course. All she really does is let the Bogue *be herself.*

We can't outrun you, but we *can* slow you down.

She comes back to the bridge just moments before the Bogue *is jolted by unfriendly laser fire. Her drives are dead. Garchan-3 rescue sends word they're thirty minutes out.*

She lets her acknowledgment of Garchan-3's ETA go through the unsecured comm. Just in case the Vaxxar's high-tech descramblers weren't listening the first time.

Transbeams slice through the hull, setting intruder alarms wailing. She leans back in the sling, crosses her legs, and watches a wide shimmer of light coalesce in front of her. Four Triadian crew—no, three crew and one cybernetically enhanced captain, aloof in demeanor yet oddly handsome, disconcertingly so. She expected someone—something—less human in that black uniform and trademark black gloves. And definitely not as male.

She stares into a pair of ice-blue eyes, notes his slight frown of confusion. He scans the bridge quickly and she knows what he sees: two young pimple-faced boys shaking in their seats; one grizzled, balding old Tsariian with rheumy eyes and stooped shoulders; and one pint-size female whose short-cropped blond hair is partly covered by a ratty-looking red cap bearing the logo of a Kesh Valirr nighthouse.

He steps toward her, his gaze briefly on the single bar above her name patch. It's the only part of her attire that's remotely regulation. When he speaks, there's clearly a warning tone in his voice: "Lieutenant Sebastian."

She doesn't need to see the three diamond-studded stars affixed to the gold lightning insignia. She acknowledges him without a hint of emotion: "Captain Kel-Paten."

Twenty-nine minutes. Twenty-eight...

With six minutes to spare, the tall, dark-haired biocybe captain turns away from the Bogue's data station, the only evidence of his frustration in the clenching and unclenching of one gloved hand. As his officers stand rigidly beside him, he wastes an entire minute with his gaze locked on her.

"Sebastian," he says, but nothing more. Just a pause. An intense, heavy pause.

"Kel-Paten," she replies, and then—knowing she

courts his wrath by doing so—lets her mouth curve into the barest of smiles.

When the boys and girls from Garchan-3 arrive, the Vaxxar *has gone away, empty-handed—but the image of Kel-Paten's heated gaze stays with her for many years to come . . .*

I'm the new first on the Vax. *Oh, bloody damned hell.* Sass watched the triple ovoid rings of Triad Imperial Station 12 grow larger on the transport's small screens and felt the hand of destiny tighten around her throat. A black-gloved hand . . .

In spite of her fascination with the ship, she didn't see this whole thing as quite the coup that Edmonds did. More likely this was Kel-Paten's expertly crafted revenge for not only the *Sarna Bogue* but all the other run-ins she'd had with him since: more than fifty intercepts in the Far Reaches, another twenty off the Staceyan Belt. And in the Zone . . . she'd lost count.

If you behave, in six months—maybe less—you'll have your rank of captain back, Ace had said in that fateful conversation three weeks ago. Didn't the woman realize Kel-Paten's definition of *behave* was vastly different from Sass's?

Case in point: her arrival on IS-12 via transport shuttle, not via the *Regalia*. The last thing she wanted was the pomp and circumstance of an official send-off with herself and her crew in their starched tan U-Cee dress uniforms. Starched uniforms played hell with a hangover.

Sass only half-listened as IS-12's traffic control acknowledged the transport's approach. Yuri—Captain

Yuri Ettoran, an old friend from her days working the rafts around Kesh Valirr—answered with the standard verbiage. Red docking lights flashed to life around the black maw of Shuttle Bay 27.

Sass had never been to IS-12, but she'd listened to the gossip from itinerant freighter crews who held no political allegiances but went where the money was.

All spit and polish—pure function. Don't find no potted ferns prettyin' up the corridors there.

So she was prepared for that.

But not for him.

Admirals—especially Triadian admirals, even if they were acting captains—didn't serve as official greeters to arriving crew, even if the arriving crew was the new first. That's what the gods made lieutenants for.

But his presence was just another preemptive move in whatever game he was now playing with her and the U-Cees. A familiar ice-blue gaze sized her up as she stopped in the rampway's airlock. She knew what he saw: the *Vaxxar*'s newest officer in civvies, half-empty wine bottle stuffed haphazardly into her knapsack, and a furzel kennel on an antigrav pallet riding close to her left hip.

Footsteps thudded behind her. She glanced over her shoulder as the transport pilot sauntered down the ramp. Oblivious to the Tin Soldier's presence, Yuri affectionately slapped her on the rump for luck. "Give 'em hell, babe." He tugged at the brim of her ratty red cap—newer but with the same nighthouse logo—then, whistling, headed down the corridor.

The Tin Soldier's gaze never wavered. His only response was one word, a warning tone in his voice: "Sebastian."

She stepped off the ramp. The three diamond-studded stars had recently been topped by two more; five stars in all riding the slash of gold lightning on his impeccable black uniform. She presented him with her cockiest stare, waited the requisite pause, then let her mouth curve into the barest of smiles: "Kel-Paten."

Let the games begin.

1

SHIP'S GYMNASIUM, TRIAD
HUNTERSHIP *VAXXAR*

"Captain, we have a problem."

It took a moment for Sass, toweling the sweat off her face, to acknowledge the comment voiced by the tall woman striding down the locker room aisle toward her, her black and tan Alliance uniform partly obscured by a blue lab coat, her shoulder-length blond hair uncharacteristically mussed.

Captain. Gods' blessed rumps, after five and a half months of being called "commander," she finally had her rank back. That was the only good news Admiral Branden Kel-Paten gave out during the senior staff meeting earlier—though the definition of "captain" on board the *Vaxxar* was, in Sass's opinion, still up for grabs.

However, Sass had a feeling that the admiral's

announcement—at that same meeting—of the *Vaxxar*'s departure from Lightridge Station within the hour was solely responsible for the grim expression on Doc Eden Fynn's face.

"You've given Lightridge some decent leads—"

"Leads?" Eden came to a halt in front of her, then flung her arms wide in exasperation, narrowly missing smacking her hand on a metal locker door. "People are dying of *fright* in the space lanes, Tasha. No one knows how or why. And now we have eighty-seven more dead bodies exhibiting abnormally high levels of dopamine and serotonin."

The deaths on the freighter *Degun's Luck* were the sixth such incident in Triadian space in the past four months. Lightridge had promptly alerted Alliance HQ, requesting a forensic medical team. The *Vaxxar,* chasing down reports of an Illithian mother ship in the sector, had been diverted to Lightridge, pending the team's arrival. But only temporarily.

Sass draped the towel around her neck. Three of the dead were Zingarans, Eden's people. That only made the incident worse for the CMO. "The med team from HQ arrives in ten hours. They're best equipped to handle this. We're a huntership, Eden. We need to be out there stopping the Illithians from breaching our borders, not sitting on station performing autopsies."

Eden didn't seem to hear her. "I'm the only empathic doctor to come on scene in the first thirty hours after one of these incidents. There are still emanations. But I need time to work with them. Only now *he* pulls us off Lightridge. All because some damned pirate-turned-informant decided to go on an unscheduled vacation!"

"That damned pirate was gathering intelligence on the Illithians," Sass pointed out. "HQ and the admiral feel it's imperative we locate him." Border breaches and a missing undercover operative did not make for a happy Admiral Kel-Paten. Sass figured that was why he denied Eden's request to stay behind on Lightridge. He needed Eden's expertise when they captured Jace Serafino. Sass just wasn't sure if he was referring to Eden's empathic talents in discerning falsehoods or her medical ones in putting Serafino back together after the admiral wiped the floor with him. Their mutual animosity went back years.

It was years as well since Sass had seen Serafino. He was a charming rogue, always hip-deep in some kind of trouble. According to the staff briefing, he had changed little.

But Tasha Sebastian—the woman Serafino knew as Lady Sass—had changed. Though she *prayed* he wouldn't remember her. She didn't need Admiral Edmonds's warning ringing in her mind to know that there were parts of her past that the Triad—and especially Kel-Paten—must never know.

"Since he won't grant the medical investigation critical-mission status," Eden was saying, "then I'm asking for a two-week leave of absence. It would take me only six hours to get back there by shuttle."

They were still in the inner-system lanes and at sublight speed. A shuttle launch would slow them down twenty, thirty minutes at most.

If Kel-Paten agreed to it. And he might, if Sass couched it in the proper terms. For all of Kel-Paten's aggravating qualities—and they were legion—he encouraged her input. Sass enjoyed testing the depths of his cybernetically perfected mind. His cybernetically perfect form wasn't half bad either, she grudgingly admitted. Except for his attitude and that damned perpetual scowl...

But she'd brave that for Eden, even though she wasn't thrilled with the idea of losing her CMO—and closest friend—for two weeks. "Let me see what I can do." Her comm link trilled as if to punctuate her words. It took her a moment to find it under her towel, clipped to the neck of her pink workout shirt. "Sebastian."

"My office. Five minutes." The admiral's familiar deep voice brooked no argument. She wondered what crisis he uncovered—again—to occupy what was left of her free time.

But, hell, she'd just agreed to talk to him on Eden's behalf.

"By your command, sir." Sass clicked off the link and caught Eden's wry grin. "What?"

"Good shirt."

Sass looked down. *My name's No, No, Bad Captain! What's Yours?* was clearly visible now that she'd removed her towel. She grinned back as she tossed the towel into a nearby hamper, remembering the day her officers on the *Regalia* gave her the pink T-shirt. Remembering more the wide-eyed expression on Kel-Paten's face the first time he saw her wearing it as she left the *Vax*'s gym. Gods, she so enjoyed rattling his cage.

"Want to try double-teaming him?" she asked, heading for the door.

Eden fell into step with her. "He can dock my pay for the cost of the shuttle fuel if—"

The red-alert sirens erupted as the corridor doors slid open, stopping Eden in mid-sentence.

Damn. What now? Sass flicked on her comm link. "Sebastian to bridge. Status, Mister Rembert."

"Incoming interstellar thermal wave. Eight-point-two on the Graslan scale. McAbian residue readings—"

"On my way! Sebastian out."

Sass bolted down the wide gray corridor for the lifts, her heart pounding. She didn't have to hear the residue reading figures. An 8.2 Graslan wave was more than enough to tear a huntership the size of the *Vaxxar* apart.

Oh, gods. Tank. She stepped into the lift, gave the command for the bridge deck, and tapped her comm link again. "Sebastian to captain's quarters. Tank. Kennel, now!"

She knew her voice would sound in her quarters. She prayed her black and white fidget wasn't sleeping so deeply he couldn't hear it. No, he'd be awake. The sirens would have accomplished that. Chances were good he'd clambered into the small safety pod even before she barked out the order. The pod was rigged to dispense one of his favorite treats when it sensed his presence inside. The fidget might not understand emergencies, but he was never one to miss a meal.

"Bridge," the tinny autovoice announced.

She lunged out of the lift, almost colliding with a tall, dark-haired man in a black Triad uniform. Kel-Paten. He slanted her one of his infamous scowls before guiding her through the double sliding doors that led to the upper level of the bridge.

The two-tiered, U-shaped command center of the huntership was already frenzied with activity, black-uniformed senior officers moving efficiently from station to station, specialists glued to their chairs but swiveling quickly as new information downloaded to a nearby screen. Voices were terse, commands clipped. Every screen streamed with data.

Kel-Paten released her arm. "You're out of uniform."

She was also off duty, but the possibility they were at death's door prevented her from reminding him of that fact. She offered him a brief "noted" as she headed for the closest scanner station to check incoming data.

What Sass saw on the screens wasn't pretty, but they had time. Five, maybe ten minutes to try some fancy dancing that could either save their lives or send them to their graves in infinitesimal pieces. She glanced over her shoulder. Kel-Paten slid into the left command seat. She watched as, with a practiced familiarity, he thumbed open a small panel covering the dataport in the armrest and linked into the ship's systems through the interface built into his wrist. He frowned slightly, then his eyes flared with that eerie, luminous hue that signaled his cyber systems were at full power. He was spiked in, as much a part of the huge huntership as the drives, scanners, and bulkheads.

Except, unlike the drives, scanners, and bulkheads, he could talk.

She turned back to her console, knowing he could hear her just as well from there as if she were seated next to him.

"Admiral, my data shows a major energy distur-bance at oh-five-seven-point-four."

"Oh-five-seven-point-four-three-two," the voice through her comm link stated. "No damage from preliminary residual shock waves. Ship integrity is sound. Secondary waves—"

"Damn!" Sass swore as she was thrust abruptly sideways. She clung to the wide console with both hands and considered sitting down and strapping in.

"Forward shields down to eighty-five percent," a crewmember's voice announced below her.

She opted to remain standing, working at the con-sole. Kel-Paten was no doubt eons ahead of her calcu-lations in his inner journey through the data, but he looked for the known, correlating and synthesizing, while she looked for the unexplainable. Granted, his cybernetically enhanced thought processes were a million times faster than hers, but he was linear, where her analysis tended to do pirouettes and som-ersaults.

"Tell me what we *don't* have, Kel-Paten," she said tersely under her breath, forgetting for a moment that—spiked in—he could hear her. The huntership shuddered as another line of shock waves impacted its shields.

"Energy signature is not indicative of ionic-storm formation," he replied. "No indication of interstellar gas cavity. No known binary-collision region in this sector." And no comment as to the inappropriateness of her sarcastic tone.

"Space–time rift?" she ventured, her fingers rap-idly tapping instructions into the sensor pads.

"Highly improbable, with no previous black-hole activity recorded in this quadrant."

"We might just be making history, then," she quipped, scanning the results of her latest data request. She frowned. "We have abnormally high levels of McAbian particle residue."

The *Vax* heeled hard to port, and Sass's stomach made a corresponding lurch to starboard. "Admiral, look at those levels!"

The few seconds of studious silence from the admiral were filled by the sounds of voices around her: reports of minor hull damage on Deck 7, another fluctuation in shield integrity portside, two crewmembers with broken arms on Deck 10. Down in sick bay, Eden would be up to her eyes in contusions and broken bones. After this, they'd both need a pitcher of iced gin.

"McAbian levels are increasing at the rate of seventeen parts per nanosecond," Kel-Paten reported. "Probability of vortex formation is eighty-seven point six-five percent in the next ten minutes."

At his words, a chill surged up Sass's spine. A vortex—a hole violently torn in the space–time continuum. It could be anything from the universe farting to the birth of a major black hole as the result of a dark-star implosion perhaps hundreds of thousands of light-years away. But there were always warnings. For a vortex to just suddenly appear was...impossible. Yet there it was. And here they were, stuck at the wrong place at the wrong time with nowhere to go but down the galactic shitter.

And no time to figure out the whys and hows.

"Can you spike out? We have to do some fancy dancing. I need you at the con."

"Agreed. Acknowledged."

"Remy!" She called to the lanky, amber-skinned man—the *Regalia*'s former science officer—two consoles down. "Monitor this station—we've got a rift coming."

She took the seat next to Kel-Paten, raked a safety strap across her chest, then stabbed at the intraship comm link on her seat's armrest.

"This is the captain. Secure all decks. We're on a rift horizon. Sebastian out." She turned to him. "Shields were down to eighty—"

"Corrected." His pale eyes were losing their eerie luminescence. "They're back at optimum."

"Well, praise the gods and pass the peanut butter," she said, noting the undisguised superiority in his tone. "Remind me to tell you how much I love you, Kel-Paten. *If* we live through this."

The ship lurched sickeningly again. Alarms wailed. Data on her screen relayed everything she didn't want to know. This was a different kind of reminder, a deadly one.

One that stated that when huntership met vortex, vortex usually won.

CAPTAIN'S CABIN

Friend? Friend? Tank hunkered in the rear of the kennel-pod and called out plaintively to the older furzel a few cabins away. The alarm—what he termed "Loud High Noise"—blared constantly, making his furry ears twitch. Big Ship shuddered and pitched. He was in Small Safe Place and shouldn't be worried, but worried he was. And it wasn't because of the way Big Ship moved. *Friend? Bad Thing here!*

Friend. Reilly's mental contact was reassuring to the fidget. *See. Smell. Know. Have time. Be safe.*

Go Blink now?

No Blink now.

We stop Bad Thing?

A sense of pride filtered through his mind. *Our job. We protect.*

Big Ship shimmied and Tank bumped against the pod's side. *Protect MommySass.* He paused. *Thirsty.*

A mental sigh sounded in his mind, then an image of two small glowing circles. *Remember! Blue light, blue light water,* Reilly instructed. *Blue light, yellow light food.*

Tank ducked his head slightly, even though he knew Reilly couldn't see. Remember! So much to remember, and he was only a fidget.

Standing a bit unsteadily, he found two blue lights on the side of Small Safe Place, then recognized the pattern of sticklike markings above it: WATER. There was a small round spot. He nosed it and a slender tube slid down. The tube dripped a cool wetness onto his tongue.

Thirst quenched, he closed his eyes, ignored Loud High Noise, and reached carefully through the neverwhen.

Yes, there it was with its ugly smelly light. Bad Thing. Bad Thing was here.

When Reilly gave the word, Tank would be ready.

2

Remind me to tell you how much I love you, Kel-Paten.

Something in Kel-Paten's chest tightened sharply at her quip. He had wanted to hear those words for so long that even now—laced with sarcasm and in the midst of an emergency—they still had the power to send a wave of heat rolling through his body.

He automatically locked down emotions Psy-Serv would dismantle him for experiencing and forced his gaze away from the woman next to him. The data on the screen on his left showed him that Tasha had already dropped power on the sublight engines.

Good girl. The mistake most novice—and nervous—captains made when encountering a rogue energy field was to buck it full bore. It was better to ride the field, navigate the energy waves. But that took very delicate handling.

Civilized space was littered with debris from ships

whose captains had tackled Lady Nature head on. His ship, he knew with complete certainty, would never be one of them.

Not as long as either he or Tasha Sebastian was in command.

He checked the status in engineering on the wide command monitor angled out from his armrest. "Fifty-five seconds to primary flare."

"Great," Tasha intoned, following the same data on her monitor. "The galaxy decides to fart while we're sharing its undies."

A ripple of nervous laughter sounded from nearby crewmembers seated at the navigation, engineering, and defense stations ringing the upper bridge. He wondered if he should chance a commiserating smile, but she'd already swiveled around to nod at several officers in Triad black and Alliance black and khaki.

"I love you all, you know that," she announced blithely.

"Yes, ma'am!" came back several replies.

A high-pitched beep returned his attention to his screen. "Thirty-five seconds." He glanced again in her direction, opening that hidden part of his mind that her presence triggered, letting technologically impossible emotions spill forth. She regarded him questioningly. The words he ached to say died in his throat. He turned back to his comp screen and wondered, not for the first time, if he was going to die without ever being able to tell her how he felt.

"Ten seconds," she reported.

"Switching helm control to manual." He keyed in his clearance code.

She finished hers, nodded. "Helm control on manual. The admiral has the con. Hang on, boys and girls. It's going to be a rough ride."

He watched the primary flare explode on the ship's forward viewscreen like a thousand suns colliding in some crazed dance, streams of energy suddenly spiraling outward. Without thinking, he grasped her hand and, when she turned to him, called up all his courage and said her name. "Tasha, I—"

The *Vaxxar* collided with the full force of the expanding vortex. His words—and grasp on her hand—were lost in the wailing of alarms and groaning of metal bulkheads straining under impact as the ship lurched violently, first to port, then to starboard.

Bridge lights flickered and went out, though it was only microseconds before auxiliary emergency lighting kicked on, bathing everything in a murky green glow. The ship lurched again; two crewmembers went sprawling across the deck. A pressure vent ruptured in a lower bulkhead panel, sending a mushroom of hot, moist air across the upper bridge.

Kel-Paten coaxed the huntership through a series of snakelike maneuvers.

The *Vax* seemed to glide for a moment before another shock wave sent her careening to port.

"Damn it!" Tasha swore. Her safety strap had just enough give that she bounced against his shoulder. For the second time he grabbed her, and for the second time what he wanted to say refused to pass his lips.

"Sir?" she asked with a slight frown.

He released his hold on her arm. "I want to try feathering the aft braking vanes."

There had to be forty different edicts prohibiting

the feathering of braking vanes in the Triad Fleet's operational manuals. He had probably authored thirty of them. Feathered vanes were known to shear off, taking sections of the hull with them. Or create vibrations that threatened the stability of a ship.

At least that's what they did under normal circumstances. But the eye of a vortex was not a normal location.

"Retract forward vanes," he ordered.

"Vanes retracted," she replied, and the ship began to shimmy in response.

Immediately, reports of structural slippage were heard around the bridge. Kel-Paten ignored them.

"Invert aft vanes, fifteen percent."

She tapped at her screen. "Fifteen."

"Start with a five percent pitch, Sebastian, then give me a two percent increase on my marks."

"Affirmative, Admiral. At five."

He watched twenty seconds click by on his vision field.

"Mark."

"At seven."

Twenty more seconds.

"Mark."

"At nine. Must be jelly 'cause jam don't shake like this," she added.

At nineteen percent, the shimmying noticeably subsided. He could feel the helm responding to his commands. At twenty-seven percent, the *Vax* seemed to find her space legs again. Overhead lighting flickered back on, and at least five of the fifteen-odd alarms ceased to wail.

It was an encouraging sound. Almost as encouraging as ... Well, he'd think about her words later. Right now he had an illogical appearance of a vortex to decipher, a damaged ship to deal with, and two of his engineering officers requesting his input. All on top of more reports from First Fleet captains detailing Illithian attacks in the Zone, and the threat of yet another Rebashee uprising in Danvaral.

He pushed himself out of his seat and headed for the lower bridge. They had lived through the worst of the vortex. He took it as an omen to mean he had time yet to tell her how he felt. And time yet for her to say the words he had waited almost twelve years to hear.

She was on his ship. With him. For the rest ... there was time.

UPPER BRIDGE, COMMAND SLING

It took almost two and a half hours for operations on the bridge to return to some semblance of normalcy, with only the never-ending litany of damage reports hinting at the severity of the encounter. What they'd experienced—a rogue vortex, for the lack of any more-accurate classification—Sass left to Kel-Paten and the science team to unravel. The ship and her crew were things she could contend with.

"Sebastian to sick bay. Come up for air yet, Doc?" Sass could almost see Eden's responding grimace to her question.

"I think we'll make it," said Eden's disembodied voice over the command-sling comm. "Briefly, we have four concussions, fifteen broken arms, eight broken legs, and more bumps and bruises than I have space in my medical logs to record."

"And the furzels?" she asked, lowering her voice.

"Cabin monitors show them back to their usual mischief."

Knowing Tank, that could be good or bad news. Sass allowed herself a small grin. "Sounds like you earned this week's pay. Keep me informed. Sebastian out."

She flicked off the comm, leaned back in her seat, and let out the sigh she'd held in for she didn't know how long. The sound must have drawn Kel-Paten's attention. He turned from where he stood near the upper-bridge railing.

"I'd like to do a physical inspection of ship's damage," he told her after a lengthy moment of silence.

Why not? she thought. Hell, it was only 0145 in the morning. She glanced down at her pink sweatpants and realized she still wore her *No, No, Bad Captain!* shirt. A hands-on of the ship would probably take another two hours. After that she could fall directly into bed and wake up two hours later for her ritual workout with Eden Fynn. Still in her sweats. How convenient! She grinned in spite of the dull ache between her shoulder blades.

She pushed herself out of her seat. "Want to start in engineering?"

He was silent for a moment, his expression unreadable. "Sick bay. Engineering after that."

The suggestion surprised her, though she said nothing as she followed him down the corridor to the lifts. Sick bay was where she started after any trauma on board the *Regalia*. But Kel-Paten...it was well known he rarely showed up in sick bay except under the direst of circumstances. Maybe, she mused, all that shimmying finally shook some compassion into that cybernetic system of his.

If it did, he might be willing to give credence to Eden's request to take a shuttle back to Lightridge. They may have bested a vortex, but those unexplained deaths still worried her. If only they didn't have that damned runaway pirate to find.

SICK BAY

Eden Fynn was too tired to hide her surprise when Kel-Paten showed up in her ER. His dislike of medical facilities was well known. She didn't blame him. If someone had cut off her arms and legs when she was a teenager and replaced them with biocybernetic limbs, she wouldn't have pleasant memories of the place either. However, any comment she might make was preempted by an emergency call from the bridge.

Again.

Kel-Paten swung around to the intraship vidscreen on the nearest bulkhead, with Tasha only steps behind him.

"An unidentified ship, sir," Commander Kel-Faray informed him, his dusky face creased with concern. "Seems we dragged her out of the vortex with us. She's badly damaged and breaking up."

"Life forms?"

"Four humanoid, and one's fading fast," the *Vax*'s

new first officer said. "But it won't matter if the ship—"

"Transport all survivors to sick bay. And send a full security team." He glanced to his left. "You're about to have a few more visitors, Doctor."

"We can handle it" was her professional reply. Already her med team angled equipment into position.

Four broad beams of light coalesced into human forms on top of the emergency diagnostic tables. Blue-coated personnel swarmed around them, with Eden heading her own team at the first diag bed. She ran the medicorder briefly over the still form of an elderly man who had died from his injuries minutes before being transported. Real injuries, not fear. Nothing like *Degun's Luck*.

She recorded time of death and moved automatically to the next bed, her scanner parading the important data before her eyes: Male. Humanoid. Approximately forty-one years of age. Six foot three and one-half inches. Two hundred twenty-two pounds. Respiration was rapid but not life-threateningly so. Blood pressure elevated.

The medicorder categorized his injuries: concussion, broken left wrist, some minor internal bruising to the left side. She was about to move on—he'd make it on his own for now—when her patient stirred and groaned softly.

Immediately she reached out and laid her hand gently against his face, which felt stubbly from several days' growth of beard.

"Shhh," she crooned. "You're safe. You're on board the Alliance ship *Vaxxar*."

Jet-dark lashes fluttered against bruised cheek-bones.

"Admiral." Kel-Faray's voice filtered through the vidscreen behind her. "We have a positive ID on the ship that broke up."

The lashes parted, revealing startlingly deep-blue eyes. Not pale like the admiral's, but dark like the jeweled waters of the Isarrian Ocean.

Something buried under several layers of professional medical training exclaimed, *Damn, but this guy is gorgeous!* Right from the tips of his scuffed boots to the gray pants that hugged well-muscled thighs, to the torn shirt that revealed a flat, hard stomach, to the square jaw with that damnably attractive cleft, to his night-dark long hair that escaped its careless tie and now lay against his shoulders—he was unequivocally gorgeous.

Quickly, she shook herself back to reality and mentally readjusted her "doctor's cap." "Just lie still. You've been injured—"

"The *Vaxxar*?" the man's voice rasped painfully. He licked at dry lips.

"Go ahead, Kel-Faray," Kel-Paten said from where he stood at the screen.

"You're on the *Vaxxar*," Eden repeated calmly.

The man's gaze seemed centered on her chest. Eden belatedly realized her lab coat hung open and the front zipper on her black and tan Alliance uniform jumpsuit had somehow snaked down, revealing the sheer blue lace of her bra. She hurriedly yanked on the zipper's tab.

"We believe the ship destroyed was Captain

Serafino's ship, the *Novalis*," Kel-Faray's voice informed sick bay.

Kel-Paten turned, and a low, bitter expletive escaped his lips. The sound drew the man's attention, and slowly, painfully, he turned his head in Kel-Paten's direction.

The admiral cut through the throng of med-techs and strode up next to Eden. "Serafino." He spat out the name, anger tingeing every syllable.

Jace Serafino responded with a cocky, lopsided grin. "It's good to see you too, Tin Soldier. And you are ... ?" He grasped Eden's hand and brought it to his lips.

Eden stared in shock. *This* was the damned pirate? The agent gathering intelligence on the Illithians? The staff meeting outlining the mission to find him had clearly detailed all his sins and the specs on his ship— but hadn't provided, she realized with a start, one clear holo-image of the man. She wasn't sure even a clear one would've done him justice.

She drew her hand away immediately as Tasha stepped up next to her. "I'm Dr. Fynn, Chief Medical Officer."

He laughed softly at her discomfort, then coughed from the effort.

"Captain Serafino," Eden said sternly, "you really must—"

"Wait. Don't trank me out yet, sweetling," his voice rasped. *"No, No, Bad Captain!"* he read out loud. "Of course. This has to be Sebastian." He winked at her.

It was Tasha's turn. "Captain Serafino—"

"Damn, Kel-Paten, I really have to compliment

you," he said, turning away from her. "A truly creative and inspiring choice of uniforms for your officers."

And with that pronouncement, Jace Serafino promptly passed out.

CORRIDOR, SICK BAY DECK

Sass lengthened her stride in an attempt to keep up with Kel-Paten, who barked orders into his comm link on their way back to the bridge.

"I want every bit of debris you can find. Do you understand me, Lieutenant?"

They turned the corner. Two black-clad maintenance crew dove out of their way.

No need for my morning jog with Eden, Sass thought as she trotted alongside, listening to the salvage-crew lieutenant try to reason with Ol' No-Excuses Kel-Paten.

"I don't care what the current equipment limitations are. If you have to, Lieutenant, you get *out* there with every godsdamned sieve from the godsdamned galley and bring me everything that may have been even remotely connected to the *Novalis*!"

She understood his insistence, even if she didn't much like his method. Illithian border breaches had become more plentiful of late, casting serious doubts on the efficacy of the Fleet—something Kel-Paten took personally. Serafino's mission could have provided answers to that problem. But Serafino had turned the tables or turned tail, she wasn't sure which. Whatever answers Kel-Paten couldn't wrench out of "the damned pirate" might be found on his ship—or what was left of it. Sadly, a sieve might be the only useful tool.

They reached the lifts, breathing hard. Sass considered taking her pulse and jogging in place. She certainly was in appropriate attire but doubted that Kel-Paten, standing with his hands shoved in his pants pockets and scowling fiercely at the closed lift doors, would find her actions the least bit funny.

That she found them downright hysterical only told her how bloody tired she was.

And relieved. *Sebastian,* Serafino had called her. Not Sass and, thank the deities, not Lady Sass. So he didn't recognize her. At least, not in his semiconscious state. There was always the chance he might when his injuries healed. She hastily threw together a few facts—and a handful of rather pretty lies—that would work as a cover story for the dealings she had had with him when she was part of Gund'jalar's mercenary cell and working arms runners like Serafino had been her job for the UCID. If she was lucky—and she prayed she wasn't over quota on luck this week—she wouldn't deal with him again. She'd gladly relegate that duty to Kel-Paten and knew the admiral would have it no other way, not after the embarrassment

Serafino and the *Mystic Traveler*—his ship back then—had caused Kel-Paten years ago out by Fendantun on the *Vaxxar*'s shakedown cruise. The sneak attack had not only taken out the *Vax*'s aft shields but launched a jammer drone up a missile tube, rendering all on-board communications systems useless. More annoying than dangerous, had there not been three top Fleet admirals on board. Ever since then, Serafino was Kel-Paten's personal nemesis. His attitude in the staff meeting had made that abundantly clear.

Still, she didn't want to stir up old memories. She had no desire to spend the next few weeks in the *Vaxxar*'s brig if someone like Kel-Paten started poking holes in her past and realized that Sass wasn't the simple derivative of Tasha that people often assumed it to be. It was the only name she had for the first twenty years of her life and—for a period of time after that—it had acquired a small bit of notoriety.

Notoriety that could put her career—and her life—in serious jeopardy if the Triad found out that the new captain of the *Vax* had started hijacking Triad supply ships when she was sixteen. That was one of the many things Gund'jalar had taught her.

The deck numbers on the lift panel before her crawled by. She propped herself up against the wall next to the doors. The metallic sheeting felt pleasantly cool through her thin T-shirt. She closed her eyes, longing for five seconds of peace and quiet. Well, as much peace and quiet as one could expect after what the *Vaxxar* had just gone through. But after all her years in space, the continuous chatter over shipboard comms—requesting *Lieutenant So-*

and-So to report to *Such-and-Such* or advising *Team Whatever* that the *Who-Gives-A-Lubashit Drill* was about to commence—no longer registered in her mind.

Kel-Paten's deep voice did.

"Hypothesis, Sebastian, since I gather you do not find the sudden appearance of the *Novalis* disturbing."

Sass opened one eye and peered up at him. His gloved hands were crossed over his chest. Classic defensive posture. *My, we're a bit testy this morning, aren't we?* And gods, it *was* morning—about 0230 or later if the aches in her body were correct.

She closed her eye. "I find," she said, after a deep breath and the requisite counting to ten that was supposed to help but never really did, "the sudden appearance of the *Novalis* and Captain Serafino to be just one more damned thing to deal with."

"Sebastian—"

Pause.

There was always the pause after her name. The glare. It was a small ritual she'd most times found humorous, almost endearing. But right now it only fed her annoyance.

Reluctantly, she shoved herself away from the wall. "With all due respect, Admiral, the appearance of Serafino at our doorstep certainly saves us the time and expense of going to look for him. Do I find that a bit odd?" She rephrased his question. "Yes. But disturbing?" She shook her head. "Not yet, not without further information."

"You don't find it disturbing that, within twenty-four hours of when we were commissioned to find

Serafino, he suddenly shows up, along with an inexplicable vortex?"

No, I don't have your paranoia, she thought. A second later she chastised herself. Just because their leadership styles were different—vastly different— and she was at the moment tired and cranky, didn't mean she had to be so critical. She understood the pressure he faced to recover Serafino. It wasn't so much the two hundred fifty thousand credits that Serafino had allegedly absconded with. It was the fact that those two hundred fifty thousand credits were part of the Alliance's payment to him for undercover services that apparently were never rendered. The Triad Ministry of Intelligence was having furzel fits over it. No doubt they'd want Serafino delivered for interrogation and prosecution, most likely to Fendantun or Panperra. That meant, again, going in the opposite direction of the *Degun's Luck* mystery on Lightridge.

Eden wouldn't be happy. But Sass suspected an unhappy Doc Eden was easier for Kel-Paten to deal with than an unhappy Ministry of Intelligence.

The lift signal pinged.

Kel-Paten allowed her to enter the empty lift first. He gave the voice command for the bridge as the doors closed, then glanced down at her, probably wondering if she was going to answer his question.

She sighed. "I will not jump to conclusions before I have all the facts. If you're suggesting that Serafino or his ship somehow caused that vortex, I can't even guess how that would be possible. Unless the Triad has some kind of secret weapon project you've decided not to share with us."

Dark brows slanted down. Pale eyes narrowed. Hmm, he didn't like that suggestion one bit.

"Okay, okay. Hypothesis withdrawn." She gave a tired half wave of one hand. "So let's look at the facts. We *are* in a quadrant Serafino is known to frequent, according to HQ's report. You suggested at the staff meeting a few hours ago that it was your opinion we weren't far behind him. Actually, it seems we were in front of him, because somehow he got piggybacked to our—oh, never mind." He was giving her one of those sideways warning looks. She decided to ignore him before her tired mind fueled her temper.

She was still ignoring him when the lift pinged again to signal they'd reached Deck 1. She barged past him and strode down the corridor.

"Sebastian!" he called after her.

She stopped just short of the bridge doors and turned. Was that a glimpse of a smile just now leaving his face? She must be more tired than she thought. Ol' No-Excuses Kel-Paten never smiled.

"Let's get some coffee," he offered. "I need to do some thinking aloud about how the Illithians are getting past our patrols. You know I work better if you're there to punch holes in every hypothesis I come up with."

"Sure," she said, unable to hide the note of surprise in her voice at his sudden change of tone. "I desperately need coffee right now."

He activated the comm link clipped to his shirt. "Kel-Faray, the captain and I will be in my office. I want an update on all damage reports in fifteen minutes. And everything and anything that salvage comes up with on the *Novalis* as soon as you hear from them."

ADMIRAL'S OFFICE

Tasha had her back to him, leaning one hip against his office wall while she waited for the galley panel to kick out two cups of coffee. Kel-Paten permitted himself a few moments of pleasurable indulgence at the sight, then clicked open the comm link on his console before he totally forgot why the Triad bestowed the rank of admiral on him. "Dr. Fynn, what's the status on Serafino?"

"He regained consciousness briefly," Fynn told him, an undercurrent of exhaustion in her voice. Sass pushed a steaming cup across the desk toward him, then sat. He nodded and focused on the CMO's report. "I'm not totally happy with some chemical changes in his bloodwork. But he's resting comfortably. His injuries are serious but not life-threatening."

"Good. Your orders, Doctor, are to keep him alive, but that's all. Just keep him alive long enough so I can have the pleasure of killing him. Kel-Paten out."

He sifted through a short line of messages from various division commanders that blinked on his screen just as he finished with Fynn. He could've spiked in through the interface in the armrest of his chair and downloaded the information directly into his memory, but Tasha was there, sitting, sipping coffee, watching him.

He knew what he was. *She* knew what he was. But he didn't like reminding her of it. Spiked in on full 'cybe power, his eyes would take on a luminescent hue. He had no choice on the bridge earlier, when they encountered the threat of the vortex. But he had a choice here.

Damage reports were encouraging. Reports on the vortex and Serafino's appearance—both unexpected and illogical—were less so. Tasha's offhand suggestion of a Triad secret weapon hovered in his mind. Leave it to her to come up with something so wildly crazy it just might be true. Except that, if it was, he would more than likely be involved with the project, and he wasn't.

Unless...He brought up one of the mental filters he'd created years ago to circumvent what Psy-Serv programmed into his mind and made a note to do some discreet poking around later. He couldn't chance—during his routine uploads and downloads when spiked in—that Psy-Serv wasn't also doing some less-than-routine poking around in his personal databases at the same time.

He cleared his screen, then turned away, reaching for his coffee. "I apologize for the delay. But there were a couple—" and he hesitated, stopped in his mental and verbal tracks by the enigmatic grin on Tasha's face.

The grin faded and Tasha pulled herself upright in her chair. "Oh, sorry. When I'm tired, the mind wanders."

"A new hypothesis?" The look on her face was absolutely blissful—like a furzel licking fresh cream off her whiskers. He hoped her mental wanderings had nothing to do with the security officer who often partnered her in racquetlob. He'd be duty-bound to kill the man. Or at the very least transfer him to the farthest reaches of the galaxy where nothing, human or otherwise, would ever wish to be.

And while he was at it, he'd send that bastard Serafino with him.

Serafino. A thought occurred to him, so chilling that even the mouthful of steaming coffee he took did nothing to melt the rock-hard feeling that suddenly lodged in the pit of his stomach.

Had Tasha been thinking of Serafino?

Serafino's effect on women was legendary. Kel-Paten hadn't missed the wink Serafino gave her, saw the way Serafino's gaze raked over her half-naked form. . . .

He didn't realize he'd spoken the name aloud until he heard Tasha's voice.

"What about Captain Serafino?" she asked. "Besides the fact that he's here and our house guest for a while."

House guest? He'd prefer to see him an occupant of the morgue. He tapped at his screen, bringing up a series of folders Triad Intelligence had gathered on the man over the last decade.

"Just what do you know about Serafino? Not," he touched the screen, "what's here. But what do *you* know?"

She shrugged. "What makes you think I know anything more than you do?"

He answered with a narrow-eyed stare. "You've worked the Zone almost as long as I have."

"And the *Regalia*, under my command, was a warship. Small time smugglers are handled by local patrols."

He knew that. But that's not what he was asking, and he told her so.

Something dark and tense flickered briefly through her eyes. He saw it not so much because he'd been progr—was skilled in detecting human facial nuances. He saw it because he spent years memorizing every line of her face, the curves of her mouth, every light that danced in her eyes. The lights had stopped dancing. Something about Serafino bothered Tasha Sebastian. Then, just as quickly, it was gone. She ran one hand absently through her short hair.

Was she just tired or was it something more?

"Our paths may have crossed," she said finally, with a casual shrug.

"You've met before."

"My life's full of interesting characters. It's part of my job description."

"You find Serafino interesting?" He steepled his fingers in front of his mouth and peered at her from over their black-clad tips.

She sighed. "I thought you wanted my hypothesis on the Irks?"

"I do. But first tell me why you find Serafino interesting."

"Why not? You find him disturbing," she challenged. "I think interesting might fit right in there. Especially when you consider the circles he's run around the Triad and the U-Cees when we've tried to stop his smuggling operations. Then there was that double cross he pulled on the Irks over that shipment of Zonn-X rifles six years ago. In some ways, I admire his creativity."

He closed his eyes briefly. Creativity? Unorthodox

methodology was more like it, and not unlike his own Tasha in that. But past associations with a known smuggler wouldn't sit well with Fleet HQ on Prime. Better he find out before they did.

"Where did you first meet him?" He fired the question at her. "And how well did you know him?"

Anger flared in her eyes. She sat upright. "You think that because the *Novalis* shows up right after we're ordered to find him that I leaked that information to him somehow? So he could stage a repeat performance of his infamous ambush on the *Traveler* out by Fendantun?"

Before he could reply, she rose and pointed her finger at him. "That's what you meant when you said you found his 'sudden appearance disturbing,' isn't it?"

He tamped down his annoyance at the mention of Fendantun. That wasn't at all the issue here. "Sebastian—"

"Why would I do that," she continued, leaning her hands on his desk, "and drop him oh-so-pretty in your lap, if I were working with him? That would make no bloody sense!"

"Sebastian—"

"Do you really think I'm that stupid?"

No, but he began to wonder about his own mental faculties. Somehow he'd lost control of this discussion, and he wasn't quite sure how or where. His meetings with Tasha often contained heated exchanges, though not the kind of heat he'd have liked. They had clashed, amicably, for years. Yet there was something different in her forcefulness this time. An element of hurt or fear?

"I don't think you're stupid. Sit down."

She sat, though he could tell by the way she folded her arms across *My name's No, No, Bad Captain!* that she was none too happy about it. Or with him.

"I need to know how you know Serafino. In case HQ questions me about it."

"From Sookie's" came the tense answer after an equally tense silence.

The name had a faint ring of familiarity but he couldn't place it. "What's Sookie's?"

"Sookie Tawdry's. A nighthouse and casino on Kesh Valirr." She leaned back in her chair. "Don't look so shocked, Kel-Paten. I spent two years with UCID doing undercover work."

He knew about her stint with the United Coalition Intelligence Division. He'd damned near memorized her personnel file.

"And Serafino was..."

"A player. I doubt he remembers me. That was years ago. Plus, even if he did, he wouldn't remember me as Sebastian. No one—" And she stopped, gave her head a small shake. "We used nicknames. You know how covert work goes." She drew a deep breath. "Have we cleared up any possible charges of treason against me? Or should I anticipate spending the night in the brig, just to be safe?"

"I don't think the *Vax*'s brig could hold you," he answered truthfully. He'd never doubted her loyalty to the Alliance or her crew for a moment. It was her allegiance to himself that had him worried.

But his comment finally evoked a small smile from her. "Not for long," she agreed. "Now, are you finally ready to give me your theories on the Illithians?"

He shook his head, closing his eyes briefly. Those damned yellow numbers still glowed in the lower left corner of his vision: 0342.15.20. No matter how many numbers were attached, it was still very late. Or very early.

He always had the option of switching to his surplus power supply to stay awake for another thirty-six to forty-eight hours. Under normal conditions, he rarely slept for more than four hours a night.

But Tasha had no auxiliary cybernetic power supply. And he could tell from the shadows under her eyes that any productive time for discussion had long passed.

"It's late, Sebastian. Your temper's sharp and my mind is not right now." He waved her off. "Get some sleep."

"You sure? I'm sorry I popped off at you like—"

"I doubt it," he said, and forced his mouth into what he hoped looked like a smile. It wasn't an expression he was used to wearing, and it felt as if his mouth fought him every time he tried. "If you ever stopped arguing with me, I'd know there was something wrong."

She eased herself up out of the chair and headed for the door. "We'll pick up where we left off tomorrow morning—today. Morning. Hell, you know what I mean."

"Oh-eight-thirty, this office," he told her as the door slid open.

"Oh-eight-thirty?" she squeaked.

"Oh-nine-thirty, then. In uniform. And on time."

"Who, me?" she asked in mock innocence, then

saluted him, hand over her heart. "By your command, Admiral."

"Dismissed," he replied, and then, ever so softly and only after the door had closed, added a gentle benediction: "And may the gods keep you in their care."

That had been his private blessing to her for years, so much so that it was almost automatic, though rarely spoken out loud. Yet this time he added extra energy to the plea. Something about Serafino's appearance troubled Tasha. Something more than just the fact that the man was a pirate, a rogue—and a decidedly romantic figure.

Therefore, that same unknown something about Serafino troubled him deeply. He steepled his hands in front of his mouth and tried to identify the source of both their disquiet.

He couldn't. And that troubled Admiral Branden Kel-Paten, the infamous Tin Soldier, even more.

He pulled down the wrist flap on his glove and lined up his hand with his chair's dataport, spiking in. Data pathways—Triad, U-Cee, Psy-Serv—scrolled through his mind. He accessed Tasha's personnel file. Maybe it was time he reviewed her undercover assignments again. Sookie Tawdry's. Yes, there it was. He merged with the data and looked for things he might have overlooked before. Things that perhaps the U-Cees, and especially UCID, might not want the Triad to know.

SICK BAY

The ship was twenty-eight hours out of Lightridge Station, not quite twenty from Serafino's unexpected arrival. During that time period, Kel-Paten twice denied Eden Fynn's requests to return to Lightridge and her work on the *Degun's Luck* investigation. Serafino's capture did not mean the mission was completed. It was, in fact, only just beginning.

And, no, she could not take a shuttle and return to Lightridge alone. "Depending on how Serafino responds to interrogation, your services, Doctor, might be needed."

Eden was about to point out that her medical team was quite competent in dealing with whatever torture Kel-Paten chose to inflict on his prisoner, when she realized it wasn't her medical but her empathic expertise Kel-Paten wanted. She was the only certified empath on board. She'd function as an unerring lie detector when Serafino was questioned.

So, yes, she was, uniquely, needed.

Eden left the admiral's office and found Tasha in the corridor outside her ER doors. Meal break—dinner for them—was in less than an hour.

"Said no again, did he?" the captain asked.

"Won't play Truth or Lies without me."

"Ah. How are our house guests?"

"Come into my office and I'll show you the latest reports. Then we can get a bite to eat."

Tasha followed Eden to her glass-fronted office and sat, reading quietly while Eden uploaded a copy of her report to Kel-Paten's in-box. Well, perhaps reading quietly wasn't quite accurate. Eden came to the conclusion that there must be a racquetlob game going on somewhere in sick bay. A *silent* racquetlob game, which only Captain Tasha Sebastian could see.

The booted foot propped against the edge of Eden's desk rocked the captain's chair back and forth, back and forth. It was a motion, Eden noted, that was in direct relation to the sound of sick bay's doors opening:

Phwoosh.

Tasha tilted back, head turned slightly for a second.

Thwip. The doors closed and Tasha sat forward.

Phwoosh.

Tasha tilted back.

Thwip.

Tasha sat forward.

Given the amount of traffic through sick bay on a normal day—and they were less than twenty-four hours after the vortex-rift incident—there was always a lot of *phwoooshing* and *thwipping*. Most of which Eden long ago learned to ignore.

But after all the stress of the day before and the disappointment at Kel-Paten's final refusal, the captain's seesawing movements were just a bit more than Eden could take. But she at least waited until Tasha was in the *thwip* stage before she reached over her desk and grabbed the older woman's boot.

Startled, Tasha almost went ass over teakettle right out of Eden's office.

"Hey! What are you—"

"What are *you* doing?" Eden chimed in. "Are you rocking yourself to sleep down here? Or am I missing Fleet finals in racquetlob in my ER?"

"I'm—Oh, sorry." Tasha grinned sheepishly and dropped her foot to the floor. "It's *him*." An upward wave of her hand delineated something larger and taller. "If I go down to engineering, five minutes later there he is. If I'm in the wardroom having coffee, he shows up. But today he's driving me—how do you like to put it? Nucking futz?"

"This is something new?" Eden asked in obvious disbelief.

The answer was preceded by a sigh. "No, just worse. Or maybe I'm just getting less tolerant." She tossed the report back on Eden's desk, then rubbed the heels of her hands over her eyes. "I really popped off at him last night. This morning. That was unprofessional. But he seems to feel that being captain is a two-person job: his and mine, together. You know that's not SOP. He's admiral of the First Fleet. I'm captain of this ship. Granted, he's technically, mechanically, part of this ship, and he's certainly

capable—being what he is—of handling both respon-
sibilities. But then," and she hesitated, frowning, a
dark look in her eyes, "why am I here? If I'm not to
function as captain, then what kind of game—" She
shook her head. "Never mind. I'm rambling. His
paranoia is getting to me."

"Paranoia?"

"Questioning everything I do, everyone I talk to.
As if I'm going to wholesale Triadian secrets to the
Cryloc Syndicate or some such lubashit."

"Like what?"

"Like what?" Tasha repeated. "I don't even know
what secrets the Syndicate would be interested in. Or
don't already know."

"Not that. What makes you think Kel-Paten is
paranoid?"

"You mean besides the fact that he insists on personally reviewing just about every damned report I
write? Or tries to fill up what little spare time I have
doing this-that-or-the-other-thing with him where—
and I know this is true—he can keep an eye on me?"
She raised her gaze in a pleading gesture. "Like yesterday after the staff meeting. 'I'll require your attention for a moment longer,' " she mimicked, lowering
her voice in a bad imitation.

Eden chuckled, but she understood Tasha's frustration. She also had theories about Kel-Paten's behavior, derived from watching him over the past few
months. But she so rarely had a chance to focus her
empathic talents on Kel-Paten without others' emotions swirling around as well that she wasn't confident enough to voice her theories. It could be, as

Tasha surmised, a basic but expected distrust of anything U-Cee. But a few times she felt something that—if true—might require her as chief medical officer to file a Section 46 on him. She didn't think that would go over well in the Triad part of the Alliance. Then the puzzle of how—and why—the freighter crews were inexplicably frightened to death would be the least of her problems.

"Then when he found out I knew Serafino—"

"You *know* Serafino?" The information surprised Eden.

"Gods, not you too!" Sass groaned. "Yes, I knew Serafino. Past tense. I worked at Sookie's, years ago, remember?"

"And Kel-Paten knows this?"

Sass glanced quickly over her shoulder, then turned back, dropping her voice. "He does now. I figured I better bring it up in case Serafino says something... stupid. It's in my personnel file as an undercover assignment. As long as no one goes poking further, it shouldn't be a problem."

"I didn't know Serafino worked for the U-Cees."

"He didn't. He was a player at Sookie's with armsrunning connections that UCID and Gund'jalar wanted information on. We had some minor dealings—even played a couple hands of Starfield Doubles."

"Would Serafino remember you?"

"Maybe. Why?"

"I'm a little worried about his condition," Eden admitted. "He should be fully conscious by now or at least be showing signs."

"You don't ride through a vortex flare and come

out smelling like a blossom," Tasha pointed out. "And the *Novalis* wasn't the *Vax*."

"True, but—"

"But what?" Tasha leaned forward. "You've picked up something and you don't like it. I've known you too long, Doc. What do we have here?"

"It's nothing I've encountered before," Eden said truthfully, folding her hands. "But whatever it is, it's keeping him unconscious. I just thought that if he heard a familiar voice, it might draw him out."

"I could stand next to him and say, 'Place your bets, please,' but I don't think that's going to help."

"Probably not," Eden admitted. "I—Uh-oh." She reached for a stack of reports to her left and quickly dragged them to the middle of her desk. Her voice, when she spoke, was a bit louder than normal and almost authoritative. Eden did many things extremely well. Acting was not one of them.

". . . and I think that if we can make the crew understand the importance of proper nutrition—oh, hello, Admiral. Can I help you with something?" For a moment, hope blossomed. Maybe he'd reconsidered and would let her take a shuttle back to Lightridge.

"Doctor."

He spoke her title but didn't look at her. He watched Tasha, or more accurately, the back of the captain's head.

Seeming to realize she was the object of scrutiny, Tasha raised her eyes in a pleading gesture before turning in her chair.

"Sebastian," Kel-Paten said. Pause. "I didn't realize

the doctor needed to report to you on the crew's nutritional requirements."

"We were covering a number of topics," Tasha told him blandly.

Eden quietly replaced the report in the stack. There was no way the admiral could have overheard their conversation—the noise level in her sick bay was too constant. But his appearance seemed anything but coincidental. Tasha was right; he was following her, but was it because she was U-Cee or something else?

"You'll be off duty shortly, Doctor." It was a question, but as with many questions posed by Admiral Kel-Paten, it was issued in the form of a statement.

Eden glanced at her watch, using the movement to give her time to open her empathic senses. It was just the three of them in this relatively small area of her office. This was her best chance to try to read Kel-Paten's aura—if a biocybe could be accurately read by an empath. Damn, she hadn't considered that. "Shift ends for me in half an hour, sir."

"Then I'm sure you have things to attend to before leaving."

"Actually, the captain and I were—"

"I'm afraid I'll be requiring"—and at this point Tasha turned her head, so only Eden could see, and exactly mouthed Kel-Paten's words—"Captain Sebastian's attention at this time."

Tasha's glib action caught Eden by surprise, and she tried to cover her gurgle of laughter with a coughing fit.

Tasha winked, then turned and faced Kel-Paten. "I don't suppose it can wait until after dinner? I made plans to—"

"You'll have to cancel those plans. I'll have something to eat brought to the ready room."

Tasha sighed theatrically as she stood. "Dining by starlight, Admiral?" The *Vax*'s ready room had large floor-to-ceiling viewports set into the outer wall. "How can I resist such an invitation?" And with that she waltzed out of the office.

The mask dropped. Eden—waiting for something exactly like this—saw it and felt it. Kel-Paten's usual impassive expression blurred into something heavily tinged with emotion when Tasha coquettishly turned her face up to his. And Eden saw an aura that only she or another empath like her could see.

Kel-Paten's aura pulsed with an intensity not unlike the hot flare of the vortex he fought yesterday. He was fighting a surge of emotion, Eden realized. But was he fighting to suppress it or fighting whatever was keeping him from experiencing it?

Either way, it was a problem. A properly functioning biocybe was not supposed to experience emotions.

He looked back at Eden for a brief moment as if he were about to say something, then caught himself as if he knew what she was thinking: Section 46.

The mask fell back into place.

"If you'll excuse me, Doctor." He inclined his head slightly.

"Of course."

Eden leaned back in her chair after he left and tried to analyze what had happened. Something about Tasha Sebastian sparked a change in Kel-Paten. An emotional change. She wondered who put it there: Kel-Paten himself—responding to years of games with the

U-Cee captain—or Sellarmaris Biocybernetics and Psy-Serv, looking to add another layer of complexity to their cybernetic creation now that the U-Cees were part of the Alliance?

Either possibility was valid. And both could very well be dangerous.

EDEN FYNN'S QUARTERS

Issues other than Tasha's continual run-ins with Kel-Paten gnawed at the back of Eden's mind all through dinner with navigation officer Dannar Kel-Minra, but she couldn't quite place what they were. It wasn't Dann's obvious interest in her. He'd never made her feel uncomfortable.

But he didn't make her feel anything else either. She couldn't truly remember a man who had in the years since her divorce. She prowled about her quarters after dinner and wondered if that was why she felt so restless. Her life was fulfilling in all areas except one: romance.

But then, she didn't sign on with Fleet because she was husband-hunting.

She thought about taking a sedative—she had the night before because of sheer exhaustion. But tonight, other than that odd restlessness, the usual aggravations of a huntership CMO were her only concerns. The comfort of Reilly, her large black furzel, nestled against her was all she needed. She fell asleep shortly after her head touched the pillow.

Or she thought she did.

Over the years, she'd tried to figure out if the space

she now occupied—this gray, hazy, yet palpably solid space—was real or just a dream.

It never felt like a dream. It felt as if she stood in a large, dimly lit room. She had no sense of walls, but she had a definite sense of floor, and, as she did for years, she took a few steps forward once she realized where she was.

She wasn't afraid. This was a place of immense peace. It calmed her mind. Often, when she was troubled before sleep, she would wake—if that's what she did—to find herself here. And she knew that if she waited long enough, the thoughts or images needed to solve her problem would come into her mind. She wouldn't physically see them—she never physically saw anything here except for the soothing gray mists.

Except now.

She stumbled over him in the fog, sensing his presence only moments before they collided—she, moving dreamily forward, and he, just rising from his seat. And then there was the warm and very reassuring pressure of his hands on her arm and about her waist as he drew her against him, then back down to the bench.

A bench. A stone bench.

And a man.

Jace Serafino.

"I'm sorry, I—ohmygods!" she gasped. She had to be dreaming. But her hand, now pressing against the soft fabric of the shirt covering his chest, felt the presence of a heartbeat.

He studied her face. "I...know you." Like Kel-Paten—it was a question yet a statement.

She nodded. "Dr. Eden Fynn, CMO on the

Vaxxar." And winced when she heard the formality of her own tone. *Why the hell didn't you just add "reporting for duty"?* she chastised herself mentally.

Jace was smiling at her. "Why didn't you?" he asked.

"Why didn't I—" And she stopped, frozen by the realization that he heard her thoughts.

You're a telepath. She whispered the words in her mind.

Yes. Like you.

Like me? I'm not a telepath. To be a telepath meant you were either a government agent with TelTal or Psy-Serv, or you were declared—based on the Intergalactic Psychic Concordance and Protection Statutes enacted when she was a child—legally insane. *I'm a Healer, an empath.*

You're here, aren't you? His question was as gentle as the hands that now rested against her waist. She knew she should object to this sudden familiarity, except that it didn't seem all that sudden. The way he held her, the way he guided her to the bench, even the way he now used that light, teasing tone in his voice—his mind voice—seemed so natural, so normal.

Here? she questioned.

In Novalis.

She shook her head. *That's not . . . the* Novalis *was your ship.*

Novalis is a place. This place. I named my ship after it.

How did you know the name? Did you name this place?

His soft chuckle was audible. *The ancients named*

this place, I think. Or maybe the gods did. It depends on which legend you're taught. Don't your people have songs about it?

Not that I remember. But I wasn't raised . . . my father was human.

Ahhh. He touched his fingers lightly on the left side of her face, first at her temple, then twice on her cheek, about an inch apart. His thumb came to rest under her chin.

She was trembling. She knew what he'd done and she suddenly knew who—no, *what*—he was. She felt his touch beyond her mere physical existence, though the physical sensations were admittedly pleasant. It was an ancient benediction, a blessing of a Nasyry warrior–priest that denoted safekeeping. *May the gods keep you in their care* were the words that often accompanied it.

Innocuous words, but said by a Nasyry, they carried power.

A power that, decades before, severed relations not only with the U-Cees and the Triad but with the empathic Zingarans who worked with them. *Sajoullum,* they termed her mother's people. Consorts of dead minds, a damnation against an empathic people who willingly associated with non-telepaths.

"Who are you?" She spoke out loud now, afraid what her thoughts would reveal. More afraid of how he might judge her, half Zingaran, half *oullum*. Dead mind.

He looked at her quizzically and withdrew his hand from her chin. "I'm Jace Serafino, last time I checked."

"But you're Nasyry."

His eyes narrowed for a moment. "Your studies have not been totally lacking, Doctor."

"There were things I wanted to know." Her father never encouraged her interest in her deceased mother's Zingaran heritage. It took her years to learn the little she had.

"Self-taught, Healer?"

Was he reading her thoughts? "Mostly, yes."

His hand was back, cupping her face. She felt his feather-light touch in her mind, the sensation almost soothing if it weren't for the fear she kept tamping down. But that was silly. This was only a dream.

Relax. Jace's voice was soft. *I won't hurt you.*

"But you're a telepath."

So are you, came the answer, still in her mind. *A touch telepath, Doctor. At least, you are with me. You can link to my thoughts by touching me.*

I'm an empath, she repeated.

He seemed amused by her stubbornness. *The two aren't mutually exclusive. You experience your strongest empathic readings when you touch your patients, don't you?*

It was something she always knew but never admitted, not even to her examiners in med school. Especially not to her examiners. *But in sick bay, I tried with you. There was nothing.*

A small smile. *You underrate yourself. Especially in that delightful outfit—do you always work half undressed in sick bay? I found that touch of blue lace rather memorable. . . .*

Eden saw what he'd seen as he flashed the mental image to her: her less-than-cooperative uniform zipper and the blue lace—gods, that bright blue bra of hers!

That's not what I meant!

You blush beautifully. I'll have to keep that in mind.

Captain Serafino—

Jace. There was a firm but friendly insistence in his tone.

She sighed. *Jace, I received no telepathic readings from you in sick bay.*

A waft of negative emotion now; a slight tension from him that quickly faded. *That's courtesy of Psy-Serv.*

Psy-Serv? You're an agent for them? The fear that abated from his light teasing returned full force.

No! His answer was emphatic and, she knew through her empathic senses, the truth. *May the gods strike me dead if I ever . . .*

He drew her against him, fitting her against his chest, his face resting in her hair. She could feel the warmth of his breath on her neck, and it was calming, reassuring, like the gray mists around her.

And there was something else: safety, protection. Eden imagined that she couldn't feel more protected were one of the gods to suddenly come down and cup her in his hand. There was a tremendous power in this man called Jace Serafino. And a tremendous benevolence.

Suddenly he tensed, his breath catching hard as sharp pains, thin and cutting as microfine wires, laced through his body. He thrust her from him, but she grabbed for his hand.

"Eden, don't! It might kill you," he rasped.

"What's wrong?" Where they touched, her flesh stung and tingled like a thousand insects dancing a fandango of death on her skin.

He managed a pained smile. "Psy-Serv. Four years ago." He gulped for air. "An implant. There's an implant. It inhibits telepathy. That's why you can't—"

He slid to the ground, his body shaking. "Oh, gods. Eden—!"

Then he disappeared.

She bolted out of her bed, rudely dislodging the sleeping furzel. She pulled on her uniform, fumbling with the zipper, then grabbed for her boots and comm link. It trilled just as she exited—still in her stocking feet—into the corridor.

"Sick bay to Fynn! We've got a Code Red on Captain Serafino!"

"I know, gods damn it, I know!" she barked back at the tiny transmitter. "I'm in the lift and on my way!"

SHIP'S GYM

Sass was upside down, grasping her ankles in a spine-popping stretch, when she saw Eden walk into the gym. Well, perhaps *walk* wasn't the right word. Even from Sass's inverted perspective, the CMO's method of perambulation was better categorized as *trudge*.

A tall, full-figured woman of a comfortable beauty, Eden Fynn had sparkling blue eyes, honey-gold hair, and, as heard more than once from the lips of various male crew, "legs that don't quit." But that reference had nothing to do with the act of walking—an act that Eden wasn't performing with her usual bright gait. Especially not at 0630, when she normally bounded in to the gym to accompany Sass on their morning jog.

"Captain, we need to talk," Eden said as Sass slowly straightened out of her stretch.

Sass took an intuitive leap based on the fact that Eden was still in her sick-bay scrubs: "Serafino."

A confirming nod.

"He's still alive?"

"Don't ask me how or why, but yes."

"Kel-Paten didn't—"

"This has nothing to do with Kel-Paten. At least, not at this point," Eden said with a tired sigh.

"Then what does it have to do with?"

Eden's answer was barely audible. "Psy-Serv."

"Oh, damn." That wasn't a term Sass wanted to hear. Psy-Serv was—in her opinion—a vicious, insidious, power-hungry agency that was far beyond the control of any rational governmental authority. Its proponents lauded it as the great protector, an eradicator of the unscrupulous. Sass doubted any Psy-Serv agent would know a scruple if it bit him in the ass. She grabbed her friend by the elbow. "My office. No. My quarters." The latter was the only place she could be sure Kel-Paten wouldn't barge in to unannounced.

Sass pulled a bowl of lushberries from her small galley's refrigerator as her cabin door closed behind Eden. A plaintive cry sounded at her feet. She glanced down into a pair of pleading golden eyes. "You've already been fed," she told the long-furred fidget, hearing Eden chuckle knowingly.

The golden eyes didn't waver.

"Oh, all right." Sass filled a small saucer with sweet cream and put it in its usual place on the counter. The fidget stretched his pudgy body against the tall stool and made several snuffling noises.

"Still can't jump that well, can he?" Eden asked as

Sass put down the bowl of lushberries and picked up the soft creature, placing him in front of the saucer.

"Not when there's someone around to save him the trouble." Sass retrieved the bowl of fruit and plopped it in the middle of her dining table. "Start from the beginning," she said. Then she sat, hands folded, and listened to Eden's recitation: her inability to use her empathic senses to diagnose Serafino, her nagging feeling of something being very wrong, and her inexplicable encounter with Jace Serafino in a place called Novalis and, no, it wasn't on his ship.

"This isn't just a dream?" Sass asked.

Eden plucked one of the plump lushberries from the bowl in front of her. "I guess you could liken it more to an out-of-body experience. You'd have an existence there. You can touch and feel things."

Sass sat back in her chair, popped a large purple lushberry in her mouth. She chewed thoughtfully. "And you can access this dream place because you're Zingaran. Makes sense. How did Serafino get there?"

Eden didn't reply until Sass swallowed the berry. "He's a Nasyry telepath."

Sass felt her jaw drop open. "Oh, damn."

"I know."

"But the Nasyry don't associate with us. With non-telepaths. What's he doing here? Other than the fact that we found him, that is."

"I don't quite know yet."

"You mentioned Psy-Serv." Sass's words came quickly, her brain pumping out worried thoughts even faster. "If Serafino's a telepath and the Triad—I mean, the Alliance—ostensibly hired him for the Illithian mission, that means he's on their payroll, which means he's also on Psy-Serv's payroll . . . Am I right on this? Are you following me?"

"Yes. I mean, no, he's not on Psy-Serv's payroll. He's on Psy-Serv's shit list."

The proverbial light of knowledge clicked on in Sass's brain. "A rogue telepath." The very thing the Intergalactic Psychic Concordance and Protection Statutes were designed to hunt down. The illegal use of telepaths to acquire inside information in the business and legal sectors had wreaked havoc in the trade markets and the courts in both the Triad and the Coalition. The Concordance ensured all telepaths were identified, properly trained, and monitored. The Protection Statutes went after those who weren't.

Serafino's rogue abilities were probably one of the reasons—now that she thought about it—why he was so damned lucky over the years, always one step ahead of the competition or the law. Or the card dealer.

"I think that's probably correct."

"You *think*—?" Sass asked as a *thump-thump-thud* behind told her Tank had finished his cream and jumped down from the counter with his usual lack of grace.

"We weren't that far into an explanation when his physical body had a seizure. There's an implant in his brain, courtesy of Psy-Serv. It doesn't show up on any of my med-scans—that's how treacherous it is. I had to use resonance imagery to find out what little I know."

"But how could he meet you in this Novalis place if he has this implant?"

A sigh of frustration blew through Eden's lips. "He

seems to be able to override it for short periods of time."

"It could be a behavioral implant. They've been used with homicidal psychotics."

"That was outlawed over sixty-five years ago. I checked my medical journals."

"Lubashit." Sass held Eden's gaze with her own for a moment, then looked away. "There were cons on Lethant with them. You know what I went through there."

"Ten months of hell," Eden said quietly.

Hell it was—a desolate, lawless wasteland populated by what the legal system adjudicated to be human filth. Even now, years later, it wasn't easy to talk about.

"Were they recent implants?" Eden asked, bringing Sass's thoughts back to the present.

Sass smiled thinly. "If you consider seven years ago recent, yes. They have a med facility on Lethant."

"I don't suppose they'd risk doing them on Varlow," Eden mused.

"Right next door to HQ? The public outcry would topple the government faster than a fleet of Triad hunterships. Oops, sorry. I forgot; we're one of them now. But where were we?" she asked, her fingers pinching the bridge of her nose for a moment. Talking about Lethant invariably gave her a headache.

Something soft and warm brushed against her pants leg. She reached down and ruffled Tank's furry ears, her headache receding. "Oh, yes. Serafino. Are we sure we're not dealing with some serious psychosis here? I take it you want to remove the implant."

"I think if I don't, it'll kill him."

"Are you sure if we do, he won't kill us?" Sass challenged.

"At this point, relatively sure."

"Kel-Paten's not going to like 'relatively,'" Sass said as Tank butted his head against her shin.

"Kel-Paten... Sass, I need a favor." Eden leaned over the table toward her. "I don't want the admiral brought in yet."

Someone else wanted a favor. Fat paws poked her thigh. "I understand your concern, but he despises Serafino pretty thoroughly already," she said, drawing the pudgy fidget up into her lap. "I don't see how telling him Serafino's a telepath will add to that."

"It's not just Serafino," Eden answered quietly. "I'm a telepath too."

This time Sass's mouth gaped all the way open. "How?" she finally managed. Granted, TelTal—the U-Cee's Telepathic Talent Regulatory Agency—wasn't as overzealous as the Triad's Psy-Serv. But they still routinely scanned the populace, starting in grade school, for the slightest twinge of telepathic ability.

If there were rogue telepaths—and there were always rumors—it was because they grew up on desolate rim worlds and were never exposed to formal schooling. Or regular medical exams.

Sass knew what that was like. But Eden didn't. "You're from Glitterkiln, not the Far Reaches. Do you mean TelTal never scanned you?"

"Same as my classmates, yes," Eden said. "But I was recognized as an empath when I was still small. Whatever they sensed from me they probably just chalked up to empathic talents.

"Plus, I don't really remember experiencing what Serafino calls Novalis until I was in my teens. The telepaths I heard about developed their talents much younger, around four or five."

"But when you went for your Fleet physical, didn't they scan you again?" Sass asked as Tank, after much insistent kneading, finally curled into a ball and sought sleep.

"Yes. But it appears my telepathy is touch-induced. That might be something they couldn't detect as easily."

"But you're sure?"

Eden nodded slowly. "Gods help me, yes I am. Though obviously not well trained, or I wouldn't be running into the problems I have now."

"With Serafino."

"I'm hoping I can contact him again. I'm hoping he may have the answer to the implant."

"What do you need me to do?"

"Keep Kel-Paten out of sick bay as much as possible, for one," Eden replied.

"That means you won't be seeing much of me. Where I go, he goes these days. What else?"

Eden took a deep breath. "As you said, Kel-Paten may be the Triad's most loyal officer, but he has no great love for Psy-Serv. I have reason to believe he has an extensive personal library on Psy-Serv. I need access to it."

"You think it might hold the answer to Serafino's implant?"

"Maybe not Serafino's specifically, but at least its medical pedigree."

Sass pursed her lips and regarded her friend

carefully. Her fingers absently stroked the fidget's soft fur. "You're asking me to break into the admiral's secure locked datafiles. Files that are probably loaded with every defensive hacker trap he could create with his megamillion-credit mind. Files that probably have more security devices, hidden alarms, and fail-safe programs than anything else in civilized space, Psy-Serv's own databanks included."

"Yes."

"Files that are located in his quarters, which are again no doubt the most secure location on this ship—hell, probably in this Fleet."

"Yes."

Sass shrugged. "Piece o' cake. Anything else?"

"If you get caught we'll both be court-martialed, you know that."

"No," Sass replied. "*We* won't be court-martialed. If I get caught, I go down alone."

Eden shot her a look that clearly stated she disagreed. "It's not an issue," Eden said, "because you won't get caught, right?"

At the optimistic pronouncement, Sass grinned broadly.

"And number two, if you are, I bet you Kel-Paten won't tell a soul."

Sass burst out laughing, eliciting a *murrupf* of annoyance from Tank. "Lubashit! He'd be so righteously pissed that my biggest problem would be talking him out of jettisoning me into McClellan's Void just so I could be formally court-martialed."

"I think you're wrong," Eden countered with a grin.

"You're right. I am. Ol' Rules and Regulations Kel-Paten would definitely opt for a court-martial. If for no other reasons than to prove to us U-Cees how far superior the Triad military justice system is to our own."

EDEN FYNN'S QUARTERS

Eden trudged a little less wearily back to her quarters. Sass—Tasha—would find the answers. She had faith in her friend's unorthodox talents and knew that when Tasha put her mind to something, that something inevitably cooperated.

But Kel-Paten—now, there was a puzzle. Focused on Serafino, she didn't have time to chase down any gossip concerning recent emo-program changes to the biocybe admiral. Still, her gut—and her empathic talents—suggested that the first thing that would come to Kel-Paten's mind upon finding Tasha in his quarters would have nothing to do with the mythical void. Whether by accident or design, he had a measurable, almost palpable emotional response to Tasha's presence. Almost...romantic?

Not a court-martial but a formal courting? Or perhaps not so formal if he found Tasha in his quarters. Maybe...

No, No, Bad CMO! she chided herself. Her tired mind was producing silly speculations. She glanced at the clock on her nightstand and told the computer to wake her at 1330 hours. That would give her about six hours. And with Serafino sedated, she felt safe that she wouldn't be meeting up with him in Novalis.

They both needed a good night's sleep—even if it wasn't technically night.

The last thing Eden remembered was Reilly snuggling against her arm, purring loudly. Then Jace was rising from the stone bench, hand outstretched to greet her.

"I hoped you'd be here." He took her hand in his as they sat down. "I thought I might have scared you away." He smiled, but it was a smile touched with a nervous tension.

"You shouldn't be here. I don't know if I can pull you back from another seizure."

"I overstayed my limit last time, I'm sorry. But—"

"Your limit?" Then he did have a way of temporarily bypassing the implant.

He nodded. "Twelve minutes and fifteen seconds is the max at the moment. I try to keep an internal clock running, but it got away from me last time. It's just been so long." He closed his eyes briefly. "I have so much to tell you. I don't know if there's time."

A feeling of deep loneliness emanated from him, as well as a sadness over the injuries—and loss of life— his crew had experienced battling the vortex.

"You haven't been in touch with another telepath in quite some time." It wasn't a guess. She was primarily an empath.

"Not since Bianca and Jorden."

"Bianca?" she questioned, and immediately an image flashed into her mind: a woman, dark-haired and beautiful. She recognized the azure-blue eyes. They were like Jace's. She felt the bond of strong affection he had for his older sister and her young son. And she also realized how much more could be transmitted telepathically than through words.

And then she felt Jace's fear and his anger and knew that the implant had something to do with Bianca.

"It was a trade," he said out loud. "Psy-Serv made it clear. My life, or my talents, for hers and Jorden's. He's a lot like me, you know," he mused sadly. "Scares the hell out of her sometimes, she used to say."

"Used to?"

A feeling of loss. "I haven't seen her in more than four years. I don't even know if she's alive, although I was promised as much. No one dictates to Psy-Serv. Not even Captain Jace Serafino." He squeezed her hand, and she knew he needed just to feel her warmth right now.

She squeezed back. "You said you needed my help. What can I do?"

"In eleven minutes? Oh, Eden, I do need your help, but you may have to take a lot of furzel-naps to get the whole story."

"Couldn't we talk in sick bay? The seizure was serious, but unless we mistime this meeting now, the implant shouldn't activate again. I hope to have you responsive by tomorrow."

A sad smile crossed his face. "The implant does more than just prohibit telepathy. It blanks parts of my conscious mind. The Jace Serafino you have in sick bay is only part of the person I am. And he's not my better part." He brought her hand to his lips and lightly brushed them across her knuckles. "Gods, woman, you are a gorgeous creature. I think I've told you that, haven't I? And, yes, you are blushing beautifully again.

"The man you know out there as Captain Serafino," he continued, with an upward nod of his head as if sick bay were off somewhere in the distance, "is a rake and a scoundrel, who has only one use for beautiful women— and it's not friendship. And right now I really need a friend. I just wish you were ugly. It would make dealing with you so much easier."

"Captain Serafino," she said, gently withdrawing her hand from his, "we are both professionals. There's no reason we can't work together in that atmosphere."

"No, of course not." He laughed. "You underestimate yourself, Doc. But then, you probably have a fleet of men who tell you that daily."

"Jace."

"All right. Back to business. We have seven minutes. I'll talk or transmit, whatever is easier. You listen."

She nodded.

He was, as Tasha had termed it, a rogue telepath. He and his sister were the products of a liaison between a Nasyry priest and a rebellious daughter of a wealthy Kel family.

Why aren't you with your father's people? Couldn't they help you?

A twinge of anger mixed with shame. *We were, for many years. But the Nasyry have no love of weakling half-breeds.* Saj-oullum, *we're called.*

She recognized the term. Consorts of dead minds. It startled her to realize that Jace was very much like her.

Then you and Bianca—

She's all I have. She and Jorden. He has my talent, by the way—his mother doesn't. To the Nasyry, she's oullum. *An outcast. Which may be how Bianca made the one big mistake in her life: her Psy-Serv lover, Galen Kel-Rea. Jorden's father. That's how this whole thing started.*

Eden saw and felt how the quiet, methodical woman, living with her mother's family on Sellarmaris, was totally unprepared for the handsome Psy-Serv agent who'd swept her off her feet—solely to gain access to Jace. It had taken the agent ten years of pretending to love Bianca for Bianca to trust him enough to arrange for him to meet with her brother, who by then had already established a reputation for himself as a daring mercenary.

Jace had hated the man on sight and later blamed himself for Bianca's marriage. He'd spent little time with his sister over the years, the nature of his career keeping them out of touch for long periods. The first time he ever saw his nephew was the first time he met with Bianca's husband. The agent's talents were so strong that Jace didn't pick up on the fact that he was a telepath. Not until it was much too late.

And then he learned something else: the Psy-Serv agent was an officer on the *Vaxxar* and was recommended for the mission by Captain Branden Kel-Paten.

The agent gave Jace the choice—work with us, permit the implant, or your sister and her son will die.

That was a little over four years ago. Jace made the only choice he could.

You're the only non-Psy-Serv telepath I've found since that time, he told her. *There is so much you need to know. It's almost providential you're on the* Vaxxar, *on his* ship, *and that you have access to everything this ship can do.*

Did the admiral...was it on his orders that this agent seduced your sister? Military personnel follow orders, often not knowing the end result of their acts. Eden knew that was possible in this case, and yet the fact that Kel-Paten was party to Bianca Kel-Rea's betrayal sickened her.

I don't know. But it's no secret he has a lot of influence at the Ministry of Intelligence and has been the brains behind a number of their operations. It's also no secret I've been on his hit list ever since I made a fool of him out by Fendantun.

I do know that because of him, someone I love has been hurt. As much as I'd like to make that my sole focus, though, I can't. There are bigger problems here. That's why I had to take the risks I did. I need your help, or else more than just the Triad and this new Alliance will suffer.

She felt his pain, but she also felt his sincerity.

He raised her hand to his lips, then spoke out loud. "I'm about at my limit here. Trust me, Eden, but keep your bedroom door locked. My evil twin, you know." He grinned wryly.

"I've asked Sebastian to help," she said, ignoring the pleasurable little chills that ran up her spine at his touch.

"Excellent decision."

"I think Kel-Paten has some med-files from Psy-

Serv. They may give me some insight into your implant. Do you have enough time to tell me what you know about it?"

In a microsecond, an image of a small red and silver device flashed into her mind along with the words: *That's all I know.*

It's a start, she told him encouragingly.

He drew a deep breath. *I have to go.* His lips brushed against hers in a feather-light kiss just as he disappeared.

Next to her, Reilly shifted his considerable furry weight, demanding space that she automatically granted him. He rubbed his soft face against her arm, sensing that his mommy was not quite asleep and not quite awake. If he nudged her a bit more, perhaps a can of food might appear.

But she only sighed and settled deeper into the coverlet. Reilly sighed also, purred for a while, and snuggled closer, only to be dislodged a bit later.

Mommy up?

No, Mommy wasn't up. But something . . . something was. Golden eyes narrowed, searched the shadows of the cabin.

Bad Thing, sending out tendrils.

He couldn't permit that.

Protect Mommy. Must protect Mommy.

He sent a small stream of energy back. Just a little Blink. Not a lot. It wasn't time yet to let Bad Thing know he was here. Too dangerous. Reilly had much to learn before he could help.

The ugly, smelly light coiled back in upon itself.

Good.

Reilly slept lightly after that, furry ears alert, twitching.

Must protect Mommy.

ADMIRAL KEL-PATEN'S OFFICE

Eden disliked being called into the admiral's office, especially when it was only a half hour after she'd awakened. Especially when she hadn't finished her mid-shift version of breakfast yet. And most especially when she plotted with two captains against him.

At least, that was the way Eden's overactive conscience viewed the situation. It made a private meeting with Kel-Paten almost qualify as a nail-biter.

She spotted Timmar Kel-Faray exiting the admiral's office just as she arrived. He nodded in greeting, his voice dropping to a hushed tone. "He's not happy over something. Sorry."

Eden's stomach plummeted. Oh, damn. He found out that Serafino was a Nasyry telepath. He found out that *she* was more than just an empath. No, worse. He found out that she'd asked Sass to break into his quarters and pilfer his files.

She weakly smiled her thanks. With a dozen guilty thoughts bouncing around in her head, she assumed her best professional mien, girded herself for battle, and she placed her hand against the office door scanner. It read her identity and the doors parted.

The admiral was at his desk, head angled slightly away from her, but she clearly saw the eerie glow in his eyes. He was spiked in. Reviewing her report on Serafino? Or spying on—

"Doctor." He leaned back in his chair and motioned to one of the two empty chairs across from his desk, his eyes still luminous but less so.

Eden sat and rested her folded hands properly in her lap, although she really wanted to knot them in worry. The U-Cees had strict regulations about electronic eavesdropping and violating an officer's privacy without due cause. She had to assume the Triad had the same. Therefore, there was no way he could know what was said in her office in sick bay. Or in Tasha's cabin. She straightened her spine. "Admiral, what can I do for you?"

"I gather Serafino is still unconscious." He glanced briefly at what she now recognized—with relief—as her report on the comp screen. "Do you have an explanation for the sudden decline in his condition?"

None that I'm going to give to you at this moment. "Dr. Monterro and I have some theories, but I don't want to get into them until we can present you with something conclusive."

"Such as . . . ?"

Mistrust. She empathically read that, coming

strongly from him. Damn! She fished around for something close enough to appease him.

"It is possible the injuries he sustained in the vortex flare aggravated previous brain trauma." Well, that was somewhat the truth, after all. The implant could be considered a previous injury.

"Or...?"

She tried to remember what little she knew of Serafino—the physical Jace Serafino, rake and scoundrel. She had no intention of telling him about the Nasyry half.

"It could also be the result of trefla use." Potent and dangerous recreational drugs were a well-known pastime for many rim runners and mercenaries. Trefla crystals were one of the more popular. When she performed her volunteer work at the hospital on Kesh Valirr, she saw firsthand just what it could do.

Kel-Paten seemed to accept that. He touched the comp screen. Her report on Serafino vanished; another report appeared in its place, but this one, too, had her medical seal on top. Nothing out of the ordinary, then. Nothing with Psy-Serv's distinctively spooky single-eye emblem.

"TeKrain Namar." He said the name of the Tsarii crewmember and looked back at her.

"Master TeKrain still has difficulty breathing, not to mention speaking, sir. He needs at least another twenty-four hours on the respiratory regenerator."

"I need some answers before the next twenty-four hours, Doctor, and with Serafino unresponsive and Kel-Pern sedated, I don't have a lot to choose from. I'll be in sick bay at sixteen-thirty exactly. I expect to have TeKrain available for questioning."

"That's not possible—"

"Make it possible," he countered coolly.

"Admiral Kel-Paten," she said, equally cool, her tension over this meeting drawing her nerves just a little too taut, "you may run this ship, you may run this Fleet, you may even run the entire Triad for all I know. But I will tell you one thing you do not run, and that is my sick bay. You will talk to Master TeKrain, Master Kel-Pern, and Captain Serafino when, and only when, I give you medical clearance to do so. Rest assured you will have that clearance at the earliest opportunity that I deem to be safe. But know that is my decision and my decision only. Do I make myself clear?"

Kel-Paten blinked at her. She'd give anything to know exactly what was going on behind those faintly glowing eyes of his right now. The little her senses picked up showed confusion, with a small bit of admiration.

"Perhaps I didn't explain myself well," he began.

My oh my! she thought. *Is the unshakable admiral backing down?*

"No one is more aware of your concerns than I am," she offered. "But it was your order that I keep Serafino and his crew alive, at all costs, just so that you could have the pleasure of killing him. I have to assume that 'at all costs' includes even yourself. Sir." She smiled, but it was not a warm smile and she was sure he knew it.

He leaned back and steepled his gloved hands in front of his mouth in what she had come to recognize as a typical Kel-Paten gesture.

"You wouldn't give that answer to Captain

Sebastian," he said after a moment, but there was nothing accusatory in his voice. If anything, he seemed amused.

"Captain Sebastian would know better than to make that request," she told him.

"Captain Sebastian has not had the aggravation of Serafino in her back pocket for the past fifteen years. Nor a veritable flock of Triad department ministers who expect—no, *demand*—the impossible out of me simply because I am Kel-Paten." He raised one eyebrow. "If I can't intimidate you into getting what I want, dare I ask for your sympathy?"

His mouth twisted, and Eden realized the Tin Soldier was trying to smile. It was a small smile and a bit crooked. Barely visible behind his gloved hands, but it was there. She saw it.

He could be almost charming if he ever gave himself half a chance, she noted with surprise.

"You have more than my sympathy, Admiral. You have my complete cooperation, as long as you allow me first to do what I'm here to do."

He nodded. "When do you expect I'll be able to speak to either Kel-Pern or TeKrain?"

"I think within thirty-six hours is reasonable and safe."

"And Serafino?"

"His condition is more fragile until we can identify whatever unknown factors caused the seizure." It was a great non-answer, and she congratulated herself on it. Her good spirits died with Kel-Paten's next remark. This was definitely where she did not want the conversation to go.

"You might ask Captain Sebastian for suggestions. They were acquainted. Years ago, I believe."

Eden dug quickly for another non-answer. She remembered Tasha saying she mentioned Sookie's to Kel-Paten. But she didn't know in what detail, and she suspected the admiral—who could almost have been considered friendly moments ago—had shifted gears and was on a fishing expedition. It made her once again consider what kind of emo-programming he had and who designed it.

"Captain Sebastian's received the same briefings on Serafino that you have, sir. If she knew anything helpful, I'm sure she would have volunteered it."

She regarded Kel-Paten levelly and, at the same time, tried to read him empathically. It was then she realized that the glow in his eyes, which had faded until it was barely noticeable, increased. Not as much as when he was spiked in, but it was there.

He was using his 'cybe power as a block or a filter of some kind as she probed him. She didn't know how she knew that, but it was a guess she would be willing to place money on. That's why her empathic senses had picked up so little before—or with such inconsistency.

He leaned back, the light in his eyes once again a pale mist. She sensed only weariness. "Of course," he said. "But should you—or she—think of anything that might help us all deal with this Serafino situation, I trust you'll bring it to my attention. Immediately."

Trust. Was that what this was all about? Eden pondered that as the lift returned her to sick bay's deck. Was it simply that, even after six months of working together, the Triad wasn't ready to accept the U-Cee officers on board? And these few glimpses she saw of what appeared to be a softening in Kel-Paten's personality, a foray into emotions—was that all just part of the Triad's plan to make U-Cee officers feel they were part of the team when in fact they were not?

Or was the admiral genuinely trying to reach out to them, to Tasha?

Both suppositions made sense. And neither made sense. Being a touch telepath, Eden knew she might find out considerably more by grasping Kel-Paten's hand next time they were together. But she knew that could also result in a lethal charge, ending her life before her body hit the floor.

The fully integrated Jace, being Nasyry, would be able to obtain the truth more easily and safely—if he was willing to put his personal bias against Kel-Paten aside. But in order to get his telepathy consciously functioning, she had to put Tasha Sebastian's career—and maybe even her life—at risk.

She shook her head and exited the lift. Give her a good old bounce-'em-off-the-walls vortex any day. That was something Doc Eden Fynn could understand.

SICK BAY

With a frustrated sigh, Jace Serafino folded his telepathic self back inside his mind. There was so much he needed to share with the *Vaxxar*'s CMO, and he'd let himself get distracted by a too-soft mouth, a blush of pink on pale cheeks, by the very womanly roundness of her body. That wasn't like him. Well, that *was* like the human Captain Jace Serafino, but not the Nasyry Jace Serafino. He was a highly disciplined, well-trained warrior.

All that had gone to hell when he touched minds with Eden Fynn.

He was totally unprepared for her impact on him. It wasn't just her physical beauty; he knew many women who were so exotically beautiful that their very entry into a room caused all conversation to cease.

But then, as his often-so-wise sister would point out, an eight-foot-tall, three-hundred-pound, foul-smelling grenkbeast entering a room would also cause all conversation to cease.

Eden Fynn didn't cause all conversation to cease. She caused his heart to start beating again. She caused him to search his repertoire for the witty phrase just to see her smile. He couldn't seem to get enough of her. His twelve-minute time limit was going to drive him out of his mind.

Literally. Because if the Nasyry element of Jace Serafino felt that way, the human, womanizing, certified rake and scoundrel element of Captain Jace Serafino was going to go completely out of control once he woke up.

The last thing he wanted to do was hurt her, and hurt her he would. There was no room in the human Jace Serafino's life for the kinds of emotion, the kind of commitment, she made him want. Strewn across civilized space were a series of individuals who would not hesitate to strike out at Serafino through his feelings for Eden. Just as they had through Bianca and Jorden.

He couldn't let that happen again.

But, gods, how he wanted to know, just once in his life, what it would be like to be truly loved by a woman like Eden Fynn. He needed her warmth, her compassion, her intelligence. And her innocence. That's what he'd first noticed when their minds touched, and it sent his jaded senses reeling. He felt that he had spent his entire life in a dank and musty room, and suddenly a window had opened and it was spring, with every fruit tree in blossom outside.

Why now, when his life was in such a wretched state? He wanted to offer her the sun, the moon, and the stars—and all he could bring her was pain.

He sighed, physically sighed this time, as the damage from the seizure faded. His other wounds had healed; his Nasyran physiology enhanced his healing rate. Even now his ears picked up the sounds and voices in sick bay. Eden's voice was one of them. A warmth flooded his veins at the sound.

She was discussing with someone named Cal the fact that Captain Serafino's vital signs were rapidly improving.

You want vital, Eden my lovely, come here and I'll show you vital! The thought and accompanying sensation raced through his mind before he could stop it.

A surge of heat flowed from his mind directly into Eden. She stood near the foot of his bed, close enough that he heard her surprised intake of breath as his heat touched her.

Jace felt her question the sensation and respond with a mental bucket of cold water aimed at him, but it didn't work. His physical senses were coming around too quickly, and he was aware of her perfume and the soft sound of her breathing as she moved closer to him.

He groaned softly but audibly.

There was a slight click as Eden placed her medicorder on a nearby table. "Captain Serafino? This is Doctor Fynn. Can you hear me?"

His mouth moved slightly but no sounds came out.

He shifted his focus. On the wall above his bed, the diagnostics panel linked to the sensors in his bed rapidly kicked out data on his improving condition.

Eden leaned across him to key in some adjustments.

"Cal," she called out, her fingers tapping in instructions, her attention on the readout, "I think Captain Serafino is about to return to the land of the living—ohh!"

He yanked her down on top of him, his mouth hard against hers, his tongue taking advantage of her surprised exclamation to probe her warm sweetness. His left hand threaded its way into her hair, his right arm tightening around her waist.

Warm. Soft. Sweet. She was all these things, this woman.

The bald-headed, stocky man near the doorway looked up from the file in his hand. "It appears he has returned," he commented lightly, a definite amused tone in his voice as he stepped quickly toward the bed.

His warm, soft, sweet woman squirmed, extricating herself from his passionate embrace before Cal could intervene. She fell off his bed and landed squarely on her rump on the floor with a very unprofessional exclamation.

She was still sitting there, glaring up at the bed, when Jace rolled over and, propping himself up on his side, extended one hand down to her.

"Come back up here, nurse. I think I need a little more of your special medicine."

"I think you've had quite enough special medicine, Captain Serafino," she snapped at him, ignoring his hand and his chuckles. She accepted Cal's hand instead and pulled herself off the floor.

Jace liked what he saw: womanly curves accented by the well-fitting black and tan jumpsuit uniform that even her shapeless blue lab coat couldn't hide.

"Fynn," he said, reading the nameplate on her coat. "Does Fynn have a first name?"

She squared her shoulders. "Yes, it's Doctor. Please lie back down. I'm going to have Dr. Monterro run some tests on you."

He rested his head against the pillow. "Dr. Monterro, eh? What a coincidence! Two people in the same sick bay with the same first name."

She shot him a withering glance. He grinned broadly in answer. She snatched the medicorder from the table and thrust it toward the other doctor. "I'll advise the captain that Serafino is awake."

Eden . . . sorry. He reached out, softly, haltingly, into her mind just as she exited sick bay. She turned, startled, then shook her head and strode out into the hallway.

He didn't know if she'd heard him or turned for another reason.

He didn't know . . . he couldn't remember what it was he didn't know.

DECK 10

At Eden's request, the ship's computer informed her of Captain Sebastian's location in drive-thruster maintenance on Deck 10, though by the time Eden arrived, Tasha had left maintenance and was walking down Deck 10's main corridor on her way back to the bridge.

"Making your rounds alone?" Eden asked, catching up with her.

Tasha chuckled. "Oddly, yes. The admiral's in the middle of a vidconference with the Kel-Tyras. I'm sure I'll run into him on the bridge later. Anything you need me to relay to him about our house guests?"

"I have some good news and some bad news," Eden said, carefully lowering her voice. "But this is for your ears, not his."

"Want to discuss it in the wardroom?"

Eden nodded and said nothing further on the subject until they were seated at a quiet table next to one of the floor-to-ceiling viewports in the officers' lounge on Deck 8 Forward. The only other occupants were two officers in Triad blacks, obviously off-duty. They were sharing a pitcher of ale at the bar, but they were far enough away, their attention on a sports vid, that Eden didn't worry about being overheard.

"What's up?" Tasha asked.

Eden started with the less complicated of the two issues. "Serafino." Literally, she thought, remembering the telling hardness of his body beneath hers. "He's awake. He was right about his memory. He didn't even know my name."

"Is your link with him broken?"

Eden remembered the soft, sad apology in her mind and shook her head. "Not completely. When his physical body was unconscious, his subconscious or telepathic sense had free rein. Now that he's awake, his conscious mind will dominate. His telepathy, as well as his knowledge of his talents, is blocked. Though after he woke up just now, he was able to very briefly contact me. But I could feel it was a strain."

"Do you know anything more on the implant?" Tasha kept her voice low.

"Not really. But there's something you should know. Serafino has an older sister. And he blames Kel-Paten for what happened to her." Eden gave a concise recounting of what she'd learned from Serafino the night before, ending with his warning that they faced a much larger problem.

"So he's willing to shelve his mission of personal revenge for the greater good?" Tasha shook her head. "I'm not convinced, but he can't lie to you, can he?"

"I'd sense it. He's angry, yes. But he's also scared. And it's not Kel-Paten he's scared of. It's just difficult to find out more while that implant still functions."

"That's priority number one, then. Find out what that damned thing is and get rid of it."

"I sent the sketch I made of the unit as he showed it to me, along with the results of my research, to your in-box. Other than the three possibilities I listed, nothing. I'm sorry to have to give you so little to go on."

"Don't worry about it, Eden. When I access Kel-Paten's files, I'm only going to have time to dump whatever I find and hope like hell you can use it." Tasha sighed. "I wish I'd had more notice about this vidconference—Ralland Kel-Tyra usually keeps the admiral chatting. That would have been an ideal time to get into his quarters and access those files."

"He's interrogating TeKrain tomorrow. Kel-Pern is still out of commission," Eden said. "Maybe then?"

"I have a feeling he'll want us there. You for your empathic readings as to the truth. And me because I'm more fluent in the street-lingo dialect of Tosar that TeKrain speaks than Kel-Paten is."

"TeKrain's Standard is pretty bad," Eden admitted. "Though he does have an impressive command of our swear words."

"Yeah, well, I think that's Serafino's doing. Probably his idea of a joke."

Eden grinned wryly. "Captain Serafino certainly has an interesting sense of humor."

"Around the admiral, that could be fatal," Tasha warned. "You'd better get the message to him to behave himself, or that implant will be the least of his troubles."

Behave? Eden had no idea how she could get Captain Serafino to behave. His inner self didn't seem to be doing a very good job of it, if their recent encounter was any proof.

"I don't think Kel-Paten appreciates being called the Tin Soldier," Tasha was saying, referring to Serafino's brief but notable comments when he was first transported to sick bay.

"I'm sure Serafino knows that. I'm equally sure that's why he uses the term. Whatever's happening in the Alliance is why he's here. But as long as Kel-Paten is too, he's going to use every chance to insult him. Because of Bianca."

Tasha studied her thoughtfully. "I thought 'cybes couldn't experience emotions. I mean, I've seen Kel-Paten act as if he's angry. But our research on him during the war tagged it as a response-simulation program."

"I don't think it's a simulation," Eden said carefully.

"It has to be. He's a 'cybe."

"I'm an empath," Eden countered. "And he's not just a 'cybe. There's still a lot of human biology there."

"You're telling me you sensed genuine anger from him?"

"We need to talk about that." She glanced over her shoulder. The two officers were intent on the vidclips of fumbled plays flashing on the screen. She turned back. "He called me into his office to put pressure on me to release Serafino's crew for interrogations. But he also made this cryptic remark about what you might know about Serafino. Personally."

Tasha's mouth tightened. "I should never have mentioned Sookie's."

"He didn't mention it either. But he was fishing. I read distrust, very strongly."

"Distrust isn't technically an emotion—"

"I've sensed others from him that appear to be, but then, I'll admit, I'm looking now. Trying to read him because..." Eden closed her eyes briefly. "I don't know how to explain this, but there's an emotional resonance that shouldn't be there."

"Are you sure? The U-Cees built their strategies around the fact that between the cybernetics and Psy-Serv's emo-inhibitor programs, Kel-Paten is one six-foot-three deadly emotionless son of a bitch. That was the whole point. No emotions to sway decision-making. Only cold, hard clinical facts."

"You've seen him lose his temper," Eden countered.

"And I've heard your medical diag comps use a compassionate tone of voice when interviewing patients and a firmer tone if a patient starts to babble too much. I even know of bar 'droids in the high-priced Glitterkiln casinos that laugh when customers tell jokes. Those are response simulations. Mimicry, not feelings."

"I know."

Tasha looked quizzically at her. "What are you telling me? Does Kel-Paten need a tune-up, or do we have a Section Forty-Six situation?"

Section 46. Eden had read the regulation so many times the key phrase stuck in her mind: behavior, attitude, and/or reactions clearly in contradiction to the accepted norm. And while emotions were fully acceptable in humans, in biocybes they were not.

"I don't have access to his full medical profile," Eden told her. "All I know is what I sense as an empath. A telepath could tell more."

"You mean Serafino? But you said his telepathy doesn't work as long as that thing's in his head."

"Not consciously. But subconsciously he's very aware. And he is Nasyry. If we put them together . . . he might later be able to tell me what's going on."

"Let me get this straight." Tasha spread her hands on the tabletop. "You want me to put together two longtime enemies: a lethal 'cybe who just might have a screw loose and a rogue Nasyry telepath who has the ability to pick up and use that very flaw to torment him."

"I can try to delay Serafino's interrogation until I have a little more time to check for any changes in Kel-Paten's emo-programming. If the Triad will even let me access that data."

"Try to delay it until we can double the size of your medical staff. And my security staff. And while we're at it, increase the size of the morgue. Because if either one of them loses control," Tasha added, pushing herself to her feet, "we're going to need them all."

ADMIRAL'S OFFICE

The three-way vidconference on the Serafino situation was going as well as could be expected—given Admiral Roderick Kel-Tyra's penchant for perfection. Had it been only Captain Ralland Kel-Tyra, framed by his habitually disheveled office on the deep-space link, Kel-Paten would have freely expressed his frustration over Serafino's appearance and his annoyance over his U-Cee-issue CMO's protectiveness toward the bastard. But the fact that Tasha had, while working for UCID, known that same bastard was something he'd not tell even Ralland. He was still digging into her past. It probably was just a chance meeting and best left unsaid, for now.

But it was imperative that Kel-Paten not let any hint of things being less than perfect in the Serafino matter come to Roderick's attention. He was Kel-Paten, and it was his job to do the impossible.

So he relayed his report, considered hypotheses, outlined strategies—and kept tabs on Tasha while he did so.

She was in engineering, he noted, logging in and out of his 'cybe links while listening to Roderick's laundry list of information the Tri—that is, the Alliance—wanted out of Serafino before the *Vax* made Panperra Station. A few minutes later, he picked up Tasha in Deck 10's main corridor. Waiting for . . . ? He quickly checked nearby comm-link signatures. Ah. Eden Fynn. That could mean nothing or it could mean trouble. He hoped like hell they were talking about Serafino, about their furzels, about anything but him.

"Within thirty-six hours." He answered Roderick's question about his upcoming interrogation of TeKrain Namar. He outlined what he thought the Tsariian might be able to divulge and agreed that—sadly—there were insufficient grounds to hold either crewmember. He confirmed they'd be released to Panperra Medical and noted that Tasha and Fynn were now in the wardroom, Deck 8 Forward. Fynn was probably telling her about his less-than-perfect attempt to gain the CMO's cooperation in his office earlier. Divide and conquer didn't work this time. It reminded him how little he understood about the dynamics of human friendship, especially between women.

Ralland's comment drew him back to the vidconference, and by the time he responded to and settled that, Tasha was moving again. Heading for the bridge. Alone.

Good. He needed to see her. He wrapped up the meeting without further problems, logged off with Roderick, and was nodding good-bye when Ralland's raised hand stopped his move to disconnect the link.

"Something else, Captain?" he asked.

Ralland relaxed back into his chair. "Made any progress with her yet?"

The subject of Ralland's question didn't need identification. Ralland Kel-Tyra was one of the few people Kel-Paten considered a friend. And the only one who knew what Tasha meant to him. Kel-Paten checked to make sure the connection with the elder Kel-Tyra was indeed severed. Then he exhaled, noisily, to let Ralland know this was not something he wanted to discuss.

But knowing Ralland—and he knew him very well—that didn't make any difference.

"No," he said finally, and when the quirking of the younger man's eyebrow let him know that his answer did not suffice, he sighed. "These things take time." *I'm not full human. I don't have your expertise with women,* he could have added but didn't. Ralland had heard those arguments many times. And just as many times he'd heard Ralland's advice—advice he fully expected would be repeated now.

It wasn't.

"You might not have much more time," Ralland said instead. "Now that Tasha has the captaincy, the old man's talking of having you run First from Prime."

Kel-Paten's gut tensed as Ralland's words unfolded in stark images in his mind. He'd be on Prime. Tasha would be on the *Vax*. They'd be separated. "He can't do that."

But even as he said it, he knew the old man could.

"It's your own fault, Branden," Ralland replied easily. "You've done a good job of convincing the High Command she can handle a Triad huntership without a hitch."

She could, but that wasn't the point. "Roderick knows damned well I'm not interested in flying a desk," Kel-Paten countered, anger mounting. Anger was preferable to fear. It was the only emotion that came easily to him, because Psy-Serv didn't bother with any serious inhibitors there. They wanted him angry and they wanted people afraid of his anger. "And what about APIP? It's supposed to reflect a joint Triad–U-Cee command staff."

"Which the *Vax* has with her as captain," Ralland said.

"The *Vaxxar* is my flagship!" And Tasha was his dream for so many years. He couldn't lose this chance with her. Not now.

Ralland held up both hands in mock surrender. "I'm only telling you what I heard. The U-Cees are considering putting one of our people in command. The old man feels we need to make a gesture in kind."

Kel-Paten shot Ralland a narrow-eyed look that relayed exactly what kind of gesture he'd like to offer Roderick Kel-Tyra.

"Unless Tasha formally opposes the change," Ralland said. "As the senior U-Cee officer in the APIP program, she has that authority. It's outlined in the Alliance Personnel Integration Program manual.

Chapter twenty-three, section ten. But I think you might need more than rules and regs here." He paused. "It's not Tygaris, but Panperra does have a few nice quiet pubs. I've told you before: sit her down, buy her a few drinks, talk to her. And not about military theory."

Kel-Paten sat for a few minutes, gloved hands steepled before his mouth, after he signed off.

He was going to lose Tasha. After years of having to be satisfied with glimpses of her as they played furzel-and-mizzet during the war, he finally had her on board his ship and in his life. And now in an absurd twist of fate, he was going to be sent away from her. Unless he could convince her that she needed him—wanted him—on board.

How in hell was he going to do that before the old man made his move? He was trying; Ralland knew he was trying; the godsdamned *gods* knew he was trying to make Tasha see him as something—some*one*— other than a biocybe construct. But he wasn't even to the point where he felt she considered him a friend.

So many things had gone wrong, including an empathic CMO who could read his emotions like a free-running download and who could file a Section 46. Or maybe Tasha would file if he didn't take the time to convince her that underneath the hard cybershell that was Admiral Kel-Paten, there was a man named Branden who was still very much human. Or part human. And who had the same emotions, fears, desires, and joys as any other human male on board this ship.

Ralland was right. He had to stop trying and start doing. He powered down, shunting Psy-Serv's supposedly unmovable emo-filters to the back of his mind. He pushed himself out of his chair with a determination he usually reserved for attacking the enemy and headed for the bridge.

He found her at the bridge's apex, her attention on the starfield flowing by the large forward viewport as the *Vaxxar* traveled at sublight speed toward the nearest Fleet base on Panperra Station. Mouth dry but mind—and heart—refocused, Kel-Paten stepped up beside her. Best to start with something innocuous, something she'd expect him to say.

"What's the latest on Serafino?"

Her face was in profile to him. "Doctors Fynn and Monterro still have tests to perform. It sounds like his condition is still uncertain."

He angled slightly to his right. He needed to see her eyes to read the nuances between her words and thoughts. True, he was trained—he liked that word better than *programmed*—to correctly interpret over one hundred forty human facial expressions and another sixty-seven nonhuman ones. But these classifications were often useless when it came to Tasha Sebastian, and he couldn't risk any margin of error now.

"They don't want him to relapse," she added, tilting her face just slightly as if she was aware of his new, more intense scrutiny.

He looked past her. Casually, he hoped. Bridge officers were bent over their screens or moving with crisp efficiency between stations. Any one of them would know how to turn this conversation into a friendly one. He only prayed he didn't fumble it too badly. "I assure you, Sebastian, I have a great respect for Doctor Fynn's assessment. However, her focus is different from ours." He liked that as soon as he said it. It aligned Tasha with him under the heading of command, breaking her usual allegiance with the CMO.

"As I understand it, we'll have nothing to focus on if Serafino is comatose again. Or dead."

Maybe this was not the topic he should have chosen. Her tone—and her shoulders—were stiff. His attempt at creating a mutual allegiance had failed. He could almost hear Ralland's voice in his mind: *Loosen up!* He glanced down at her again, grasping for some Ralland-like quip. "You have my permission to shoot me should I misbehave during the interrogation."

Her eyes widened—just slightly. The corners of her mouth quirked upward—just a bit. "But we're headed for Panperra. That would leave me alone to deal with Adjutant Kel-Farquin. Cruel and unusual punishment, Admiral."

It was working. He turned the discussion from a professional one to something that bordered on friendly. But he'd been at this juncture many times before. And the rejoinders, the quips, that came so easily to her escaped him.

One-point-four-million credits they'd spent perfecting his flawlessly synchronized cybertronic brain interface, and he came up with nothing.

Tasha cocked her head slightly to one side, as if studying him. Perhaps she knew of the amount and just now realized what a tremendous waste of funds it represented.

"We'll handle Serafino, his crew, and Kel-Farquin without incident," he said finally, because the silence had dragged on too long. And because the lights dancing in her eyes had dimmed. "Doctor Fynn will permit us to talk to TeKrain tomorrow."

Disappointment. He read that in her features. But he didn't know if she was disappointed that they'd handle Serafino together or because she'd lost a chance to shoot him.

"Admiral, sir. Excuse me." Timmar Kel-Faray was on his right. "Captain Sebastian, I have that report, if you have time." He held up a datapad.

"Admiral, if there's nothing else?" Tasha asked.

Yes! He wanted to shout. *Yes, there is definitely something else. My entire life lies at your feet.* But if he said that, she'd Section 46 him for sure.

"Nothing. Carry on." He nodded, then forced his attention away from her to the large viewscreen on the far wall.

Her footsteps and Kel-Faray's moved away from him. He waited until they were almost to the bridge doors before casting his glance their way. Kel-Faray, taller than Tasha, bent his head as they talked animatedly about something. Easily. Naturally.

Why, why, why? The cybernetic enhancements in his body gave him a physical strength three times that of a normal human male. The interfaces and programs in his brain gave him analytical capabilities that matched—and at times exceeded—the computer systems of the best hunterships.

Yet conducting a simple, friendly conversation was beyond his grasp. His face even had trouble smiling.

Why was he so incapable of being human around her? Was he fighting his own fear of rejection...or something else, something he didn't want to think about?

What if—in spite of all the counterfilters and subrouting he'd implemented—everything that had once made him human was finally programmed out of him?

EDEN FYNN'S QUARTERS

Eden woke to her usual prealarm alarm: luminous yellow eyes inches from her nose, relaying one message: *Feed Me*. It was exactly five minutes before her cabin lights would flicker on at 0600 hours. She yawned, stroked Reilly's soft head, then swung her feet out of bed. She was opening the furzel's favorite Seafood Platter Supreme when she realized that she'd slept through the night with no contact with Jace.

That information warranted a mental *damn!* There was so much she still needed to know about him, not the least of which was his physiology. The *Vaxxar*'s med-files contained little information on the Nasyry. And here it was, 0610 hours, and she had no answers.

It was one more thing she'd have to ask Tasha to look for. If anyone had information on the Nasyry, the Tin Soldier did.

The treadmill alcove of the ship's gym was empty, as it usually was at this hour, the simdeck jogging path the preferable routine for most of the officers and crew. Eden arrived to find Tasha already at the barre, stretching.

"What's our ETA at Panperra?" Eden asked, grabbing the barre and arching her back.

"Day after tomorrow, about twenty-thirty hours," Tasha answered.

"I suppose any R and R is out of the question." Panperra had a few good pubs that Eden wouldn't mind spending time in.

"With Kel-Paten, I think that's a given. At least for me. Plus I'll have to meet with Homer Kel-Farquin."

"Hazards of the occupation," Eden quipped, knowing Kel-Farquin's reputation as a pompous bore. "Maybe you can convince Kel-Paten that you need a couple of good rounds of iced gin after. Tell him it's your doctor's orders."

"I doubt he'll let me catch up with you, Cal, and Cisco if any shore leave is approved at all."

"Bring him with you," Eden told her.

Tasha shot her an incredulous look. "Surely you jest."

"I jest not. Bring him with you."

"Don't you think I see enough of him as it is? Or are you looking to file me for a Section Forty-Six?"

"Hardly." Eden grinned. "I have a couple of new theories on our Tin Soldier."

"Like getting him drunk to see if human emotions surface?"

Eden grabbed her towel before it slipped off the barre. "Hadn't thought of that. Not a bad idea."

They both stretched in silence for a few minutes.

"To test for the emotional programming thing, you mean," Tasha said finally.

"Mmm-hmm."

"I think you're misreading him." Tasha paused. "I tried kidding around with him yesterday. Didn't work."

"He might be able to switch it on or off, depending on where he is."

"We were on the bridge."

"Hmm," Eden said again. If Kel-Paten was circumventing his programming, then he'd most likely not do it with such a large and official audience, and she told Tasha so.

"And he's not going to get suspicious if the two of us drag him to some small cozy bar and ply him with drinks? We're U-Cees, Eden. The enemy. Not his perfect, beloved Triad."

"Speaking of his enemies, I'm having some problems with Captain Serafino."

"Such as?"

"There are physiological questions I can't answer."

"Implant?"

Eden shrugged as best she could while deep in a lunge. "Could be."

"Then what?"

"It might be because he's Nasyry." She lowered her tone, even though there was no one near enough to hear. "And the med-files here are damnably incomplete."

Tasha shook her head knowingly. "I guess I'm adding this to my shopping list."

"If you don't mind."

"Your wish, Doctor, is my command," Tasha said, and motioned to the empty treadmills. "Ready?"

They finished their workout without further conversation and then headed to their cabins to shower and change before they had to start their respective shifts at 0800.

Eden's quarters were closer to the lift; the captain's

quarters were farther down the corridor, next to the admiral's and the ready room. They stopped at Eden's door.

"Are we talking to Serafino today?" Tasha asked.

"Not until Cal and I can pin down those unknown readings in his blood. I'm thinking..." She hesitated for a moment, pursing her lips as she attempted to convince herself she was on the right track. "I'm thinking of trying to make some form of telepathic contact with him today, maybe after you and Kel-Paten talk to TeKrain. But I'll need you to run interference."

"Got it. But can you make contact with Serafino while his physical self is still awake?"

"It's not the easiest way," Eden responded. "But he managed to reach out to me yesterday, shortly after he woke up." A very brief apology after a rather startling encounter. "According to him, I'm a touch telepath. If I can strengthen that link through physical contact—"

"Not an altogether objectionable task, Doctor," Tasha teased, her eyebrows raised. "I haven't seen that much of him lately, but what I remember was damned nice to look at."

Eden pulled herself up to her full height and looked haughtily down at the shorter woman. "I am a professional, Captain Sebastian!" she teased.

"Keep a bucket of cold water handy," Tasha retorted, punching her friend good-naturedly on the shoulder before she headed toward her cabin.

"For him or for me?" Eden called out to her.

Tasha stopped at her cabin door. "For both of you! And should you need any help—"

She quickly ducked inside to avoid the balled-up gym towel hurled at her by the professional Dr. Fynn.

TASHA SEBASTIAN'S QUARTERS

Once inside her cabin, Sass was met by another moving projectile. This one was fur-covered.

"No, you cannot have any more food!" Sass told the black and white fidget, who *murrupped* and purred and, plumy tail aloft, wove in and out of her legs on her way to the shower. He flopped down on her bed when she emerged from the sanifac, presenting his belly to be rubbed. She obliged. His loud purr filled the room, softening as he fell asleep.

Sass mulled over the information Eden had given her as she absently raked her fingers through Tank's long, silky fur. She kept coming back to the fact that Jace Serafino was Nasyry. Bunch of overblown snobs. Considered themselves far too good to associate with anyone without mind talents. They called regular humans *ollims* or *odoms* or something. Ah, *oullum*. She could hear her old mentor, Gund'jalar, pronouncing the foreign term. Meant *blank minds* or *dead minds*. They even lumped the Zingara like Eden into that classification, because the Zingara refused to stop trading with the U-Cees.

Snobs. She couldn't mesh that with the Jace " 'Fino" Serafino she'd known. But she could definitely understand now why he was so damned lucky at cards—and at avoiding any traps the Triad or U-Cees set out for him.

And it might explain the Alliance's—and Psy-

Serv's—interest in him. A rogue Nasyry could definitely be a threat to Psy-Serv. But did the Alliance know what he was when they hired him to work undercover? Did Kel-Paten?

He couldn't know. It wasn't mentioned in the briefing. It wasn't in any of the data provided on the mission. If Kel-Paten knew, he wouldn't be pushing so hard to interrogate Serafino—at least, not without a Psy-Serv agent present. So that meant Psy-Serv left out that one, very important fact when they sent Kel-Paten after Serafino.

Why?

Turning that question over in her mind, she grabbed a clean uniform from her closet. Her comm link pinged as she pulled on her boots.

She flicked on the mike. "Sebastian."

"Kel-Paten here. My office, ten minutes."

It wasn't even 0800 yet and still a full hour away from her usual 0900 briefing with the admiral. She knew that an interrogation of one of Serafino's crewmembers was on today's schedule, however. The admiral was obviously anxious to discuss it.

For a moment, she considered spilling what she knew about Serafino. Psy-Serv's omission rankled her. Frankly, it carried the stench of someone playing a very dangerous game. If there was anyone who could counter such a game, it was Kel-Paten. And, in spite of all the suppositions floating through Eden's conversations with Serafino, she trusted Kel-Paten. It was something deeper, something beyond the U-Cees and the Triad. Something beyond the Alliance.

She just . . . trusted him.

But not enough right now to go against her CMO's

wishes and tell him—*warn* him—that Serafino was Nasyry. Yet.

"You promise me coffee and I'll do anything," she responded lightly.

There was a moment of silence, then: "That can be arranged."

"Good," she replied. "On my way. Mahrian blend, black."

A hissing sound stopped her before she reached the door. She spun around. "Tank?"

Another hiss and a low growl.

She headed back to her bedroom. "Tank?"

The long-furred fidget's back was arched, his ears flat to his head. Sass followed his wide-eyed gaze . . . and saw nothing. Nothing but the starfield outside her cabin viewport.

"What's the matter? You just realize you're in the space lanes?" She patted his head, shook her own, and left.

Kel-Paten didn't like to be kept waiting.

Tank trotted around the cabin after MommySass left, sniffing corners, putting his wet nose to the viewports, and then staring nowhere and everywhere. *Be alert,* Friend Reilly had warned him. *Bad Thing watches us with its ugly smelly light.*

Tank knew. He scented another drip of ugliness just now, a fetid ripple in the neverwhen. A small one, yes. But there.

Gone now. He looked again through the neverwhen. Perhaps he'd scared it away. He might be only a fidget, but he was growing stronger. He blinked his eyes, searching for something more pleasant.

Friend? Friend?

He felt Reilly's answering purr.

Play now? Play time?

Play now, came the answer from down the corridor. *Come here. Go Blink.*

Fun! He swished his tail, remembering to do what Reilly taught him. Stretch. Reach. Sense. Go Blink.

He felt the neverwhen ruffle his fur. And then he was in Friend Reilly's cabin, sharing a wet-nosed greeting. *Fun!* he said again, and pounced on his friend's back, wrestling the larger furzel to the floor.

SICK BAY

TeKrain Namar's leathery face brightened as Eden entered his sick-bay cubicle. "Fynn, yes, Doctor. You are. How?" he asked in broken Standard.

It took Eden a moment to rearrange the words. "Fine, thank you, Master TeKrain. And how are you feeling this afternoon?"

"Easier. Pain. Now breathe. Yes. No more." His thin faced nodded rapidly.

Okay, let's decipher this one slowly, Eden told herself. "You are in less pain when you breathe, is that correct?"

The thin face nodded again.

"Good. Stay still for a few moments while I check some of your readings." She held the medicorder near his chest and watched the figures dance across the small screen. Everything appeared as it should for a

Tsariian male of his age who'd been through the injuries he'd sustained. She told him as much, adding, "Then there's no reason Admiral Kel-Paten shouldn't be able to talk to you."

"Kel-Paten!" TeKrain suddenly sat straight up in bed. "Fear! Do cannot! Release sick, now I am!" He coughed profusely and theatrically.

"You're perfectly fine, Master TeKrain," Eden said, with a strong but soothing tone in her voice.

Bony russet hands grasped the sleeve of her lab coat. "Stay! Me with, Fynn Doctor! All we die now! Soldier Tin, all we die!"

She patted his arm reassuringly, her touch bringing with it the strong sense of fear pervading the Tsariian. "The admiral has just a few questions. There's nothing to be worried about."

It was at this point that Cal Monterro stuck his head through the cubicle doorway. "The admiral and Captain Sebastian are here to see TeKrain, if you'll permit it."

A yellowed gaze pinned her. "Now?" A keening sound escaped his lips. "Lost, lost! Is lost all!"

"In spite of the noise, I believe Master TeKrain can withstand a few questions," Eden told Cal, as she tried to dislodge the Tsariian's long fingers from her wrist. She was unsuccessful in that endeavor until she heard the muffled footsteps come up behind her. TeKrain drew back against his pillow as if a battering ram had been shoved against him. He quickly wrenched the bed covers up under his chin.

Kel-Paten assumed his usual military stance on the left side of TeKrain's bed and nodded for Eden to stay in place across from him. Tasha came up and stood more casually on the left, one hand resting on the footboard.

"Master TeKrain, I hope you've found our medical facilities adequate to your needs," Kel-Paten began.

"Sick, sick," TeKrain said weakly.

Eden had no trouble picking up a palpable sense of impending dread. Clearly, the Tsariian was terrified, but whether it was because of who was in the room or because of what he knew, she couldn't tell at the moment.

"I am sure you wish to give the Alliance your full cooperation," Kel-Paten said. "Therefore, you're in no danger."

"Later me know I! Kill you will!"

"The Triad—the Alliance has no real interest in you, Master TeKrain," Kel-Paten said, and Eden noted with a mental grin that she and Tasha weren't the only ones who couldn't keep straight which team they played on.

"You'll be released once we reach Panperra. In the meantime, we need to know what you can tell us about Captain Serafino," Kel-Paten was saying.

Angular shoulders shrugged in a jerky movement. "What you I tell, know? All you, everything, Soldier Tin! Namar, small, stupid!"

"I don't think you're stupid, TeKrain," Kel-Paten said smoothly. "I think you're intelligent enough that someone like Captain Serafino would want you on his ship. Would trust you."

"Trust? Hmmph!" The Tsariian jerked his chin in the air as he spoke. "Orders, no! Question not! This, yes do, question? Not!"

Eden saw Kel-Paten glance at her for confirmation.

She nodded. As far as her empathic senses could tell, TeKrain was telling the truth. Serafino gave him orders and that was all. He wasn't allowed to question.

"What kinds of orders, TeKrain?"

Another nervous shrug. "Here go we!" His voice climbed almost comically at the end of the sentence. "Course this, yes take. Course that, no."

As TeKrain spoke, Eden had her first sense that the Tsariian was, if not lying, then definitely omitting some facts. She shifted position enough to catch Kel-Paten's brief attention and the captain's as well.

Tasha spoke before Kel-Paten could. "TeKrain. *Enk rankrintar narit t'sor enarin.*"

It took Eden a moment to translate the insult—one she knew only because she'd heard Tasha use it before: your tongue and your brain are no longer friends.

Tasha's pronouncement unleashed a flood of Tsariian words from TeKrain, who in his excitement evidently forgot his professed frailty and released his death grip on the coverlet, waving his hands excitedly as he spoke.

Eden caught only a few words: *Money. Betrayal. Hunter. Hunted.* And Serafino's name along with a few others—Admiral Kel-Varen's for one. But it wasn't the words she needed to understand; it was the emotions behind them. She signaled to Tasha what she knew with a system they had devised years before—fingers open, truth. Fingers closed, lies.

The hard tone left Tasha's voice. She moved closer to TeKrain. Kel-Paten stepped back slightly as she inched next to him. Eden knew the admiral's lethal presence was one of the reasons TeKrain was talking at all.

TeKrain laughed at something Tasha said and seemed to relax. Eden's hand remained open. TeKrain was telling the truth, whatever that was at this point.

But his next words were laced with a totally different feeling. Eden closed her hand into a fist and, just as quickly, there was a guttural utterance from Tasha.

TeKrain hissed something back that sounded equally nasty. His right hand swung out to grab the captain.

Kel-Paten intercepted the movement with cybernetically enhanced speed, his black-gloved hand clamping on to the narrow wrist. "Touch her and you die."

The Tsariian paled under his russet skin as he drew in one long, noisy breath of air, no doubt feeling it was his very last. But when after a few moments he was able to take a second breath and then a third, albeit a shaky one, he parted his lips into a taut, stiff smile and puffed out several strained laughs.

"Joke. Yes? Kidding." His gaze went from Kel-Paten to Tasha. Then he let out a long sigh, as if some deep understanding had just dawned. *"Esry'on tura?"* he asked her as Kel-Paten released his wrist.

Tasha frowned. *"Nalk,"* she replied emphatically. *No.*

Two emotional responses hit Eden at the same time. From TeKrain, it was surprise and disbelief.

From Admiral Kel-Paten, it was a similar jolt of surprise but with a distinct twinge of regret that seemed out of context with what was happening in the room. Whatever it was, it was caused by TeKrain's last question, which Kel-Paten obviously understood, along with Tasha's definitive *no.* An interesting combination, Eden noted. Something else to ask Tasha about.

"I think we have all we need to know from Master TeKrain at this time." Tasha looked at Kel-Paten, who nodded.

Eden turned to TeKrain. "We appreciate your cooperation. Thank you."

The thin face nodded rapidly. "Fuck you very much too!"

It was the only Standard phrase he knew in its proper word order, and it was definitely a memorable one.

DR. EDEN FYNN'S OFFICE, SICK BAY

Kel-Paten's first impulse was to upbraid the Tsariian for his insulting parting comment. But Tasha grabbed his arm and propelled him through the doorway before he could do much more than let out an exasperated grunt.

"He doesn't mean it!" She shoved him down into a chair in the CMO's office. "Serafino—or someone—just taught him that to be funny."

She referred to TeKrain's parting words. He knew that, yet it took a moment for her words to sink in and for him to shift his focus from the overly excitable Tsariian to the woman who had him pinned in the office chair. Her hands pushed against his shoulders, her legs were planted between his own, and their combined weight caused the chair to tilt backward slightly, bringing her face inches from his.

Their thighs touched in an undeniably intimate manner, and he suddenly forgot everything—Serafino, TeKrain—everything except how little effort it would take to pull her against him and sear her with the rush of heat that coursed through his body.

"Sebastian." His fingers circled her wrists. His voice was a raspy whisper, and the pause that followed hinted at a deep pain he didn't mean to let surface.

She straightened. "Admiral? You okay?"

He closed his eyes. For a brief moment, his thumbs traced the lifeline of her pulse. Then he nodded, gently removing her hands from his shoulders and holding them together before releasing her, letting her step away.

"I'm fine." He ran his hand over his face, then abruptly pushed himself out of the chair, turning his back to Tasha as he sifted disinterestedly through a small pile of case files on Fynn's desk.

"We need to go over TeKrain's information." His voice sounded strong, angry again. It was always easier to be angry. "Get Dr. Fynn—"

"I'm right here," the CMO said.

He spun around, almost colliding with Tasha, and saw Fynn leaning against the door frame.

"I'm sorry for so rudely commandeering your office," Tasha said, one hand toward Eden, "but I really thought we were about to witness a murder." She grinned.

Kel-Paten waited for Fynn to respond to Tasha's smile. He wasn't the only one to notice that she didn't. And he had a very bad feeling about what Fynn did notice.

Tasha's now-frowning gaze went from Fynn to him, then back to Fynn again. "Just what is going on here?"

"I think," Fynn said, "that we're all waiting to find out what TeKrain told you. You were the only one who understood everything he said." She took her seat and straightened the files on her desk.

Tasha sat also. Kel-Paten remained standing, and Tasha looked up at him. "Sorry. You didn't understand any of it?"

He chanced a glance at Fynn—the empath who had stood in the doorway for the past few moments while he let his thoughts and emotions run rampant. Again.

Fynn knew. The look on her face when he saw her in the doorway told him everything. And if she knew, then Tasha would know, and he didn't want her finding out that way. Not from a medical practitioner who knew what he was, who would advise Tasha that his feelings were most likely nothing more than an aberration, a programming glitch to be rectified. Fynn could order that. That's what med-techs did.

He had to control his emotions when Fynn was around. There was too much at risk and, thanks to Roderick Kel-Tyra, he was running out of time. He stuffed the last remnants of pain back into his emotional strongbox and turned his mind to the matter at hand.

"I had a problem with a few of his responses." He leaned back against the office wall, crossing his arms over his chest. He couldn't sit so close to Tasha in the small confines, because every time he did, her warmth seemed to wash over him and he was caught like a drowning man in a riptide. "His dialect is difficult to translate."

Tasha tilted her chair back and looked up at him. "It's not the dialect. TeKrain speaks an ancient form of Tosar. They often invert the subject and predicate."

"Not to mention twist the truth," Fynn said.

"You caught that well," Tasha told her with a smile. "And damned if he didn't like that one bit."

"Did TeKrain know you were there to read him empathically?" Kel-Paten asked Fynn. Maybe the Zingaran doctor was thinking of the Tsarii. Maybe she wasn't tuned in to his emotions. Maybe. He doubted it.

"I made sure he thought I was there strictly as a medical professional, but he is Tsarii, Admiral. Many of them have a low-level empathic sense."

Gods, no. He had forgotten that fact. The Illithians and the Rebashee were the enemies-of-the-decade and therefore his required focus. Not the ineffectual, quirky Tsarii.

With a deep sense of impending doom, he realized that would explain TeKrain's earlier question: *Esry'on tura?* Is he your lover? Kel-Paten understood the question but thought TeKrain had asked it because he'd reacted when TeKrain struck out at Tasha.

But the Tsarii evidently was reading more than just his physical response. He picked up on the emotional response as well.

While Fynn was scanning TeKrain, TeKrain was scanning him.

And Tasha, with her eclectic linguistic abilities, fully understood the question too. He just prayed she wouldn't understand as well the real reason behind it.

He ran his hand over his face in a weary gesture. "Tell me what happened in there with TeKrain."

TeKrain Namar was a small-time opportunist, arms dealer, and mercenary. He'd worked for Serafino off and on for almost six years. Though he didn't particularly like humans, he'd always admired Serafino's rakehell attitude and allegiance to the only thing that TeKrain himself really cared about: money.

At least, that's all he'd thought Serafino cared about. But the past year, he came to believe that revenge motivated Serafino, and it was a revenge involving a woman.

And, no, the woman wasn't Illithian or associated with the Illithians, though TeKrain admitted Serafino had bragged about a deep contact somewhere in the Dynasty. Yes, he knew someone had hired Serafino to obtain information from the Illithians. But Serafino was definitely evasive when it came to exactly whom he worked for. TeKrain said Serafino told him that "he didn't have a need to know," and TeKrain accepted that, as long as he was paid.

And as for payment, TeKrain was under the impression the two hundred fifty thousand credits were only the beginning. There was more coming—Serafino intimated as much. But Serafino never said from where.

"How did they end up in the vortex?" Kel-Paten ventured as far as the edge of Fynn's desk, where he perched safely several feet from Tasha and directed his question to her.

"Let me state that, before the vortex, his association with Serafino had been strained," Tasha explained. "TeKrain said Serafino's personality drastically changed a few years ago. He'd forget things or people. Became very mistrustful. It got so bad that the past few months, TeKrain was confined to the ship, not even allowed liberty when they hit a raft or station without Serafino giving him permission."

"Trefla," Kel-Paten said. One of the side effects of the illegal drug was a skewed, disjointed personality.

Tasha shrugged. "TeKrain had decided he was going to jump ship, but Serafino wouldn't let him out of his sight. Then, without warning, Serafino broke dockage at Rekerral and headed, as far as TeKrain knew at that point, to nowhere. Except that Serafino fed TeKrain exact coordinates. Exact coordinates that put them right at the epicenter of the vortex."

Rekerral was a small station with a questionable reputation, on the edge of the Zone closest to Illithian space. That was First Fleet's—his—responsibility and the *Nexarion*'s territory, and Kel-Paten had been assured by Captain Kel-Varen that the border was secure, the station not a liability. One more thing now to double-check.

"Why would he head for a vortex?" Fynn asked Tasha.

Kel-Paten answered. "To use its power, Doctor. There are theories that we can use a vortex as a form of intergalactic travel. Faster than the jumpdrives we currently have and without the need for jumpgate technology." It was a hypothesis he'd actively worked on for many years—and, if not for the war, he would've gotten much further. It was one of the reasons he had been so amenable to the peace talks.

But not the only one.

Now, however, he was concerned that the Illithians were ahead of him. Were they using vortices to infiltrate Triad space? Nothing in any intelligence reports he saw suggested the Dynasty was even close to having that kind of technology. But did Serafino know something, and was he helping them?

"According to TeKrain," Tasha continued, "when the *Novalis* reached the coordinates, the vortex was just starting to form. TeKrain has no idea how Serafino knew it would. He was also surprised to see our energy signature, but then the ship began to break up. Serafino took the helm and did what he could to get her within our sensor range, to save the crew. And the rest we know."

Kel-Paten turned slightly on the corner of Fynn's desk and looked down at her. Though the information about Serafino and his use of the vortex interested him most, he was in Fynn's office, and this wasn't the venue for such a discussion. "I'll need a report on your assessment of TeKrain's veracity, Doctor."

"Once the computers translate the vidtranscript of the session, I'll overlay my readings and stat it to your offices." Fynn nodded to Tasha, then to him. "But that probably won't be until tomorrow."

"Tomorrow's acceptable," he told Fynn, pushing himself away from her desk. He stopped behind Tasha's chair and rested his hand lightly on its back. He had to separate her from Fynn before the two had a chance to compare notes. And he wanted to dissect this new information on the vortex with Tasha. He swiveled her chair to face the door before she could object. "Come along, Sebastian. You're with me."

He waited, favoring her with one of his usual glares until she offered a halfhearted wave to the

CMO and fell in step with him as he strode through the doorway.

"Comm me when you're ready for dinner," she called back through Fynn's open doorway. "Give me prelims on TeKrain then."

"Will do." Fynn nodded as her doorway slid closed.

Kel-Paten uncurled his fingers from the fist he'd unconsciously made, and he motioned Tasha toward the corridor as if his world hadn't just taken a nose-dive into a black hole.

Eden Fynn could give Tasha a lot more than pre-lims. He feared that her empathic readings on the Tsariian weren't the only things she would discuss with her captain as soon as they were alone. And he didn't know whether he was more afraid of Tasha's scorn when the Zingaran CMO told her just how hopelessly in love the Tin Soldier was with her or Fynn's resultant order to Section 46 him, removing from his life the only two things he gave a damn about: his service to the Triad through the Fleet and the chance to have Tasha Sebastian by his side.

★ ★ ★
9

SICK BAY

Eden took a half hour to review updates from the medical team on Lightridge Station. There was little chance—with Serafino and all that had happened—the *Vax* would head back there now. But the unexplained deaths plagued her. However, Serafino's medical situation and warnings about a serious threat to the Alliance bothered her equally as much.

Which was why a visit with him soon was on her schedule.

In the meantime, she worked on the Lightridge data, just in case Kel-Paten returned unexpectedly. It wouldn't do to have him find her in Serafino's hospital room so shortly after their interrogation of TeKrain. That would definitely take some creative explanations, but not more creative than what she'd devised as a means to initiate telepathic contact with

Serafino without either harming him—she would set the alarm on her watch for ten minutes—or exposing herself—literally—to the amorous advances of his evil twin. She needed a way to keep the physical Serafino busy while she reached out for the telepathic one.

She caught Cal's eye as she strode toward Serafino's room and nodded slightly. He nodded back. They'd already discussed what she had to do, and he, too, had set his alarm. Neither doctor knew for sure if Serafino would survive another seizure.

The security lock read her palm print and granted her entry. Serafino was scanning a vidmag on the swivel screen that pulled out from the wall by his bed, and he looked up when she entered, a broad smile on his face.

"Well, if it isn't one of the Doctor twins, and my favorite at that! Have I told you how beautiful you look today?"

"You told me this morning." She avoided looking at him and concentrated instead on the data on her handheld medicorder. She wanted to make sure that he was strong enough to withstand her telepathic attempt.

"You can tell me how perfect I am. I don't mind," he teased.

She glanced at him and thought regretfully how true that really was. He was undeniably perfect. Tall. Dark. Handsome. To-die-for blue eyes. Owning a pair of those herself, she'd never before succumbed to their reputed charms. But his were different, a deep azure blue with flecks of green and gold, graced by long dark eyelashes. Oddly sensitive and compassionate eyes, set in a distinctly masculine, chiseled face that tended to an early beard shadow. Which only made him look more handsome and more rakish.

"Actually," she told him, beginning to enjoy the charade, "you're not all that perfect." She sighed and then became quiet. Patients hated that worried-medical-doctor sigh, she knew.

"Hmm," she mused out loud, pretending to concentrate on the readings in her hand.

"Hmm?" he questioned. "Is that a good 'hmm' or a bad 'hmm,' my lovely doctor?"

She shrugged. "Not sure."

"What do you mean, not sure? You're the doctor— the chief medical officer, if I'm correct." He smiled, but it was a tense smile.

"You are. Correct, that is."

"And what else am I, Doc?" he queried. "Look, I got bumped around a bit. But that doesn't warrant being locked up in here."

"That's something you'll have to discuss with Admiral Kel-Paten," she told him.

"I'd love to. Bring him on. Bring on a whole army of Tin Soldiers. When are you going to let me talk to him?" He had made this request before and received the same response.

"When I give you medical clearance, Captain, and you're not there yet."

"Why?"

"Not sure." They were back where they'd started, and that was just where Eden wanted him.

He leaned against the pillows and groaned. "Okay, Doc, what is it? You can tell me. Am I pregnant?"

His query and expression were so comical that

Eden laughed out loud. "No, but I'm glad to see you still have a sense of humor."

"You have a sexy laugh, Doc."

"And you, Captain Serafino," she said, moving in for the kill, "have something that is confounding my best diagnostic equipment. So I'm afraid I have no choice but to resort to drastic measures."

He frowned. "Explain."

"We can't get a definitive reading on your body temperature. There's something in your system—and I've seen it in rare cases—that scrambles the medicorders."

"Something—like what?"

"Electrolyte levels have been known to do that," she lied.

"Which means . . . ?"

She pulled out an antique glass thermometer. "I have to take your temperature. Manually."

"Manually?" He stared at the instrument that bespoke a time long ago of scalpels and sutures and things that actually hurt. "What's that thing?"

"A thermometer. An oral thermometer. Open wide. . . ."

His eyes almost crossed as he stared at it. "You're not putting that thing in my mouth!"

"Are we afraid, Captain Serafino?" she cooed.

"Lubashit, no! It's just that nobody's used those things in centuries, Doc. Where did you get your medical degree, anyway?"

"The same place you got your captain's license. Send away twelve box tops from Starry Loops cereal and you can be anything your heart desires. Now say ahhh."

He clamped his mouth shut. "No," he said through tight lips.

Eden stood back, eyed him in mock anger, and tapped her foot. Then, reaching into her other lab-coat pocket, she pulled out a larger and longer thermometer.

"Fine," she said, holding it out for him to see. "You don't want to say ahhh, we can do it another way. This is a *rectal* thermometer. Roll over."

Serafino actually paled. "You must be out of your friggin' mind."

"Then say ahhh," she told him.

He said "ahhh."

When she was sure the thermometer was securely under his tongue and that he wouldn't bite the thing in half, she surreptitiously tapped at the extra comm link in her pocket, sending a signal to its coded twin on Cal Monterro's desk. Serafino was under control. Now came the hard part.

She took his wrist in her hand as if to take his pulse. Again, an ancient medical practice in an age of scanners and sensors and sonic surgery.

"What now?" he mumbled around the thermometer.

"Shh! Lie back and close your eyes. I need your heart rate to relax so I can take your pulse. The more you fight this, Captain, the longer it's going to take. And if I can't get a good reading out of that oral thermometer, I'll have no choice but to use—"

He fell back abruptly against the pillows, his eyes tightly closed.

She let her hand encircle his wrist and used the blinking red numbers on her watch to let her mind fall into a light trance. His breathing slowed and so did hers, until they were matched in rhythm. She called his name. *Jace?* She had a brief floating sensation and then a comforting warmth.

Eden! What in hell did you stick in my mouth?

She shot him a mental grin. *Had to shut you up somehow. Would you have preferred the other orifice?*

She felt him grin back, a small tickle of warmth in her mind as he sent his words: *A doctor and a comedian.* She felt a question forming. *How did you know this would work?*

There are some Zingaran manuals on telepathic healings. It was an avenue I had to try. Jace, we have problems, not the least of which is a compound in your blood I can't get a reading on. My med-files have so little on Nasyry physiology, I don't know if you have a severe infection or it's just normal. That's the first thing, she told him, and then waited.

I don't have an answer on that. I feel fine, if that's any help.

Not to a doctor. But we have other avenues.

We?

Sass—Captain Sebastian. We think Kel-Paten has accumulated some impressive files on Psy-Serv over the years. Sebastian's going to get them.

You can call her Sass. I know who she is. I know about Gund'jalar, Zanorian, and Lethant. She had quite a reputation on the rim.

That wasn't something she was here to discuss, and she told him so. But it was something she would warn Tasha about. She knew there were parts of

Tasha's past that would put her in serious jeopardy if the wrong person were to learn of those facts.

He caught her concern. *I didn't think her time at Sookie's was a secret.*

That's not. But Lethant...

Got it. What else do you need to know? We're at about six minutes and running.

I have Cal on standby, timing us. Jace, I can't try to remove that implant until I know more about your blood composition. Anything you can remember from past physicals will help me. If not now, then the next chance you get to contact me.

Whatever you can do, love, know that I appreciate it. And I don't blame you for anything that might go wrong. I'm a big unknown here.

Not for long, if Sass can get that data from Kel-Paten's files. In the meantime, I need to know how you bypass the implant. Maybe I can help extend your time.

A flood of information came to her—Nasyry mind-control rituals plus a healthy dose of cybercircuitry tricks. Much of it meant nothing to her, especially the technical data. That would be child's play to Kel-Paten, she knew, but asking his help right now was out of the question. Still, it was an area that Tasha was well versed in.

She felt his agreement. *Tell Lady Sass that 'Fino sends his regards.* It was almost time to break contact.

She wondered whether you'd remember her if she said 'ante up'!

Tell the little card shark I sure as hell do! Tell her I said she ought to play Kel-Paten in a sudden-death round of Starfield Doubles for the control codes to the Vaxxar. *She'd win, no doubt.*

She sent him a smile. *Will do, Captain.*

Then the contact was gone.

She opened her eyes and gently released Serafino's wrist, then tapped at the comm link in her pocket. Her watch told her she had forty-eight seconds to go.

Forty-eight seconds more and she could have killed him.

"Captain Serafino," she called softly.

Bright blue eyes suddenly opened. And looked a bit dazed. There was, she knew, some residual from the telepathy.

She plucked the thermometer from his mouth, glanced at it, and pretended to make a note on the nearby medicorder. When she looked up, he was still watching her.

"You know, Doc, I keep thinking that I know you from somewhere." His voice had momentarily lost its usual arrogance and was closer to the man she knew as Jace. "I keep thinking," and he licked his lips as he thought for a moment, "that we were more than just friends."

She shook out the thermometer and placed it back in her pocket. "In your dreams, Serafino. In your dreams."

She retrieved the medicorder and headed for the door, palming the security lock back on as the door closed behind her. But Jace Serafino was far from safe—not from the damned implant in his head and not from Admiral Kel-Paten's probing. She could no longer deny the admiral the right to do the latter, and she had only vague ideas what to do about the former.

With a sigh, she sent a note to Kel-Paten upgrading Serafino's condition. Providing she was present, she would permit him to be interviewed at the admiral's convenience.

A message waited for her when she returned to her office. The admiral requested her presence at an interview in the ready room at 1845 hours. Dinnertime, to be exact.

And it looked as if Jace Serafino was going to be the main course.

10

READY ROOM

It was a repeat performance. Only this time the players weren't in sick bay but in the ready room—the small but efficient conference room just aft of the bridge. A more fitting place than sick bay to interview the former captain of the *Novalis,* at least in Kel-Paten's mind. Here the admiral felt comfortable, surrounded by the dark oblong table, the repetition of cushioned chairs, the comp screens set at regular intervals into the tabletop. Familiar and functional without the annoying clicking and beeping of sick-bay diagnostics, too reminiscent of a place and time he'd just as soon forget.

No, the *Vax*'s ready room was a place in which he felt in total command, and he didn't want to be anything less when confronting Jace Serafino.

And confront he did. Especially after Serafino responded to questions about his undercover assignment with accusations of corruption in the Triad. The Alliance was a sham; the Triad Houses of Government and Fleet were under the control of a secret, high-powered, and dangerous group. This Faction used murder—not the voting booth—to implement their policies.

The man's lies sickened him.

"You have a reputation for many things in this sector, Captain." Kel-Paten all but spat out the title in disgust. "Veracity is not one of them."

Jace Serafino looked over the tips of his boots, which were propped in a comfortably disrespectful fashion on the edge of the table. "Perhaps," he replied in a tone equally terse, "that's because the quality of truth in this sector depends upon the quantity of money willing to purchase it. Admiral." Serafino smiled, the effect at once disarming yet cunning. "If you'd ever chance to venture out of this sterile little world you've created for yourself, you'd know everything I've told you is true."

He jerked his chin toward the wide viewport where Tasha had leaned for the last half hour. "If you took the time to listen to her, she'd tell you. Unless she doesn't trust you either."

Kel-Paten refused to see what might be an acknowledgment in Tasha's eyes. "I have an excellent rapport with all my officers and crew," he replied firmly.

"Your crew," Serafino put in smoothly, "is terrified of you. Most of your officers are Triad born and bred, and brainless. If you have a chance in hell to survive," he continued, raising his voice over Kel-Paten's angry growl, "you're going to have to listen to me."

Kel-Paten leaned his fists against the tabletop and glared at Serafino. It didn't surprise him that Serafino would shift the focus—and blame—away from his own failure to perform his part of the agreement and instead place the Triad in a negative light. The damned pirate's delusions of grandeur simply wouldn't permit things any other way. And in spite of the fact that he knew Serafino was simply trying to change the course of this interrogation with his allegations, he couldn't let them pass unanswered. Not when Serafino sullied the Triad's reputation with his lies.

"If the U-Cees had proof this so-called Faction exists, don't you think they would have brought out that fact at the peace talks or in council?"

"The U-Cees are as blind as you are, Tin Soldier. Though they have improved after the disastrous scandal Admiral Wembley dumped on their doorstep ten or so years ago. Point is, however, you now have certain people on this ship," Serafino mused out loud, with an appraising glance at Tasha, "who have significant experience in the real universe. Not your A-level military docks on station or your C- and D-level private-money docks, or even your respectable freighter bays on E. But let's go below G, Kel-Paten. Let's take a walk down to where the methane-breathers flirt with the oxys, where trefla is as common as fleas on a furzel. Work the rim worlds like the Doc here has. She knows; they both know."

Serafino turned casually to Tasha. "You've come a long way since Sookie's."

"Up or down, Serafino?" Tasha replied lightly.

"Coming from you, that comment could mean anything."

Serafino laughed heartily. Kel-Paten tamped down his annoyance and used the moment to glance quickly at a series of discreet hand signals from Fynn—the same ones she'd used earlier with TeKrain. Yes. Serafino believed what he said was the truth. Not only the ridiculous accusations about the Triad but about Tasha's knowledge and undercover experience.

"Captain Sebastian," Kel-Paten said, disliking the easy laughter that had flowed between Tasha and Serafino, "is not the one who took two hundred fifty thousand credits. And ran."

Serafino shrugged noncommittally. "That was my insurance policy. Your people wanted to send me on a one-way trip to hell. I had no intention of accommodating them."

"You didn't have to accept the mission," Kel-Paten shot back.

"Death threats have a way of convincing even me."

Kel-Paten regarded him coolly. "The Triad can always use one less traitor." That would leave only Gund'jalar and Dag Zanorian—another damned pirate who enjoyed adding "Captain" in front of his name—to blight the galaxy. A considerable improvement, in Kel-Paten's estimation. Gund'jalar's mercenary operation had lessened since the death of one of his key agents, Lady Sass, seven years ago. And Zanorian had never been half as troublesome as the man before him.

A theatrical sigh escaped Serafino's lips. He leaned back in his chair and glanced over his left shoulder at Eden Fynn. "See what abuse I have to put up with,

Doc? Can't you feed him some be-nice pills or something? Or—I know!" And he snapped his fingers and turned back to Kel-Paten. "We'll just reverse the polarity on your batteries! You know, kind of a biocybe attitude-adjustment hour."

Kel-Paten shouldn't let Serafino's taunt get to him, but Psy-Serv's programming made it so easy to get angry. He slammed the chair against the table with such force that both Tasha and Fynn jumped. Serafino only readjusted his outstretched legs slightly and appeared unconcerned as Kel-Paten rounded the corner of the table and stopped, black-gloved hand pointing threateningly in Serafino's direction.

"I have had," he said, each of his words punctuated with bitter anger, "enough of your insubordinate shit, Serafino." In three long strides he was at Serafino's side and about to grab a handful of rumpled white shirt when a smaller hand clasped on to his wrist. He froze, not by any force of strength leveled against him but because of a look of disapproval in a pair of green eyes.

"Branden," Tasha said softly, "he's playing you. He's no use to us dead. Yet."

She'd stepped between them but still firmly held his wrist, even though she had to see the luminous haze in his eyes. He'd switched over to full cybernetic function right after he slammed the chair into the table.

With the slightest of movements he could toss her across the room. Or sear her with a touch and she'd be dead before she hit the floor.

Yet here she was standing between him and the object of his wrath while holding on to his wrist—with no more concern in her demeanor than if she were about to follow him onto the dance floor.

People didn't like to touch him. Never knew when those power implants in his hands might activate and their last thought would be one of intense searing pain. Yet he could have told them that that could happen only if his cybernetics were powered on—something anyone could tell by the change of hue in his eyes.

Tasha knew that. As an Alliance officer she had access to all the intelligence the U-Cees had on him. So she knew—and yet here she was ignoring the telltale glow. It was as if what he'd wanted to happen for so long was now happening: she was seeing him not as a 'cybe but just as Branden Kel-Paten.

It would have almost been an optimistic thought were it not for the intense disapproval evident in her eyes.

Kel-Paten didn't know if she viewed him as human or 'cybe, but whichever it was, she was extremely disappointed. And more than a tad pissed.

That cut him like no ion lance ever could.

He drew his hand away from hers—not sharply, not in any way to cause alarm—and then, without glancing at either Serafino or Eden, strode quickly for the ready-room doors. He couldn't afford to give the empathic doctor another chance at reading emotions he wasn't supposed to have. He could not—would not—face a Section 46. He'd willingly strand himself in McClellan's Void first. At least there he could lose himself in its hallucinations and he'd never know he'd lost Tasha. The doors clicked closed behind him.

*   *   *

Eden Fynn let out a slow, soft sigh of relief. The sound was not lost on Serafino.

"Is he usually this testy or is it that time of the month?" he drawled.

Tasha Sebastian perched on the edge of the table not far from his boots and crossed her arms over her chest. "You owe me one, Serafino. You are very lucky to be alive right now."

He gave her a confident smile. In spite of her bland black and tan Alliance uniform, her very professional demeanor, and the noticeable lack of glitter he remembered gracing her then much-shorter spiky hair, he could still see the mercenary agent called Lady Sass. It was something in the tilt of her chin or the deceptively loose way she held her body. Ready to move decisively at any moment, this one. He'd seen her in action. Impressive. "You know the Tin Soldier and I go back a long time. He's threatened me before."

"Then you should know better than to push him," Tasha said. "If what you've been telling us is true, then you should be looking to us—to him—for help. Alienating him will get you nowhere."

Serafino considered her words for a moment. Then, with a glance back at Eden, "Ahh, so it's good cop–bad cop here, eh? And what's your role in this little play, Doctor? I hope you're the one they assign to rehabilitate me."

"You know, Captain Serafino," Eden said, stuffing her hands into her lab-coat pockets, "you would have made a great used-starfreighter salesman."

He laughed. "Or politician?"

"Or double agent," Tasha intoned lightly.

He looked back at her, not for a moment fooled by the casualness of her words. She'd been burned, badly, by people she trusted. He remembered hearing whispers of Lady Sass's ignoble death on Lethant. The smile faded from his face. "I'm no saint, Sebastian, but then, neither are you. You've moved in the same circles I have; you know how to check on what I've told you. Your Tin Soldier there, the Triad bought him and built him and owns him. He can't even think in those directions until all that Triadian propaganda is shaken loose.

"But you're right," he continued. "I need his cooperation. Hell, I need this damned ship, if you want to know the truth." A wave of tiredness washed over him. He shook it off. "The Faction suspects I'm on to them. I'm not the only one they're looking to terminate. He's on the list—or will be. Little by little, they will take out anyone who stands in their way, just like they did to Senator Kel-Harrow. The Tin Soldier's too powerful for the likes of them—tell him that."

"And I suppose," Tasha asked, "you're going to tell me I'm on that list too?"

"Why the hell do you think they put you on the *Vax* in the first place?" Serafino replied. "They figured he'd do the job for them. Which is very reassuring, because it proves that they're not infallible; they can make mistakes."

"Serafino, I don't know who this 'they' is that you're talking about."

"The Faction is—" A headache blinded him suddenly. He winced, rubbing his temples for a moment. "Powerful. Deadly." He forced the words out. A hand rested gently on his shoulder—his lovely doctor's. Some of the pain abated. He took a breath and continued. "But in this case, they've misjudged this whole situation, haven't they? With the Tin Soldier. And you."

"I think," Eden said, "it's time for Captain Serafino to return to sick bay." There was a quiet insistence in her voice.

He wanted to laugh at her concern for him—it was just a little headache; he had them all the time.

But Tasha was nodding in agreement. She unfolded her arms and pulled herself away from the table. "Let me wrap this up by saying I don't know what situation you're talking about, unless it's the fact that the admiral and I were adversaries at one point. Keep in mind we're both professionals, career officers. We have our duties and perform them to the best of our abilities. If that means cooperating with someone we once viewed as an enemy, we can do that. And that's something—if you want Kel-Paten's help—I strongly suggest you learn."

She tapped at the comm panel near the door. "Security Team One to the ready room." She looked at Eden. "Cisco will escort Captain Serafino back to sick bay. I'll see you in forty-five minutes in the officers' mess," she added.

Serafino looked at Eden as the doors closed again.

She was frowning. "Captain? How are you feeling?"

"Never been better." He pulled his feet off the table. "Sass has no idea, does she?" he asked as he stepped next to her. "But you do."

"I don't know what you're talking about. I—"

"Kel-Paten," he cut in. "You could file a Section Forty-Six on him. 'Cybes aren't supposed to have those kinds of emotions."

"I didn't feel that his anger at you was out of place," she said mildly, but something that looked like surprise flickered briefly across her face. A face he'd like to explore with his fingers. His mouth.

He forced himself to remember they were talking about the Tin Soldier. "Anger?" he asked. "Oh, there was heat there, but it wasn't from anger. And it wasn't directed at me."

The doors opened, and a muscular man with short brown hair and a laser pistol strapped to each thigh stepped in. "Doctor?" Cisco Garrick nodded to Eden as two burly security officers moved to flank Serafino on either side.

"Ah, yes, table for five, please," Serafino quipped as they headed into the corridor.

He grinned when Eden shook her head in exasperation.

They were in the lift, heading down to sick bay, when he felt something struggle within himself. For a moment he felt like two people, and one of them—how strange!—could reach Eden's mind. With a confused urgency, he mentally interrupted her conversation with a security officer who'd showed considerable interest in the CMO since they'd stepped into the lift.

He only wants in your pants, darling, Jace purred, his telepathic intrusion startling her.

She managed to keep from tripping over her own tongue in answering the officer's question before replying silently. *And you don't?* she shot back with no little irritation.

He chuckled. *Most definitely, but at least I'm enough of a gentleman to let you know first what an unacceptable scoundrel I am.*

Jace—are you telling the truth?

About wanting you? Absolutely. I—

No, damn you! About this Faction killing that senator—

I'm surprised you have to ask that question, Eden. But since you have . . . He flashed a series of images to her, not the least of which was one of Defense Minister Kel-Sennarin standing over the lifeless body of Senator Maura Kel-Harrow.

The contact was abruptly broken by the lift doors opening and Garrick grabbing Serafino's arm to guide him down the corridor to sick bay. He leaned into the officer, feeling light-headed from the effort. And still very much like two people.

It was a risk to attempt the contact, he heard his own voice say in his mind. *I can feel the implant, little by little, destroying everything I've uncovered about the Faction.* Soon, very soon, everything the Nasyry part of himself knew would be gone, and there'd be no one to stop them. Therefore, he hoped—desperately hoped—Eden had caught it all.

They were all dead if she hadn't.

DECK 1 CORRIDOR

Serafino's interrogation had not gone well.

Aggravation, annoyance, and confusion coursed through Sass as the ready-room doors closed behind her. Aggravation at Kel-Paten's mishandling of the last half hour of the interview. Annoyance at Serafino's taunts—and a small bit of fear when he'd mentioned Sookie's. And confusion—Serafino's allegations of corruption in the Triad sometimes matched but at other times were at odds with what Eden learned from him in their sessions. Hopefully Eden would be able to contact Serafino's Nasyry half once they were safely back in sick bay and find out just what in hell the whole story was.

In the meantime, Sass had her own bit of trouble to deal with: Kel-Paten. Something more than emo-programmed anger seethed through the ready room just now. And whatever it was almost jeopardized the interrogation. As his captain, she had to find out what and why that was.

And as his friend—

The thought momentarily startled her. Did she honestly consider herself to be the Tin Soldier's friend? Could a biocybe have one? With a small shake of her head, she realized that it mattered little what a 'cybe was capable of. The extension of friendship was equally her responsibility.

If they weren't friends, they were at least colleagues. So as his . . . colleague, she owed it to him to find out why in hell he acted like such a godsdamned, *trock*-brained idiot.

She laid her palm against the admiral's door scanner and waited while it confirmed her identity and reported it to the occupant of the office. She was granted entry by the almost silent sliding of the double doors into the wall.

The lighting in Kel-Paten's office was unusually dim. She stepped in and saw a tall form silhouetted against the floor-to-ceiling viewport. At sublight speed, the starfield was a black vista dotted with silver-blue points of light. Kel-Paten stood, his back to her, his arms braced on either side of the viewport. He didn't turn when she entered, not even after the doors clicked closed. Yet he had to know she was there; his office doors wouldn't have opened without his verbal authorization.

Something was very wrong.

"What happened back there, Kel-Paten?" she asked.

A tense shrug, more silence, then: "I lost control."

There was an unusual hesitation in his voice, as if the very act of speaking was difficult. "I thought that was obvious."

"That's not like you," she replied. Damn it all, he wasn't even putting up a fight! Everything in his stance, his tone, screamed defeat. This wasn't the Kel-Paten she knew.

"I imagine," he said after a moment, his voice still strained, "that Dr. Fynn is ready to Section Forty-Six me about now."

Was that what this was about?

"Because you lost your temper?" she asked. "That's fairly easy to do with Serafino." Or Namar TeKrain. Or any number of other individuals who came into the scope of Kel-Paten's disapproval over the years. Most rightly so, she realized. She was hard pressed to remember his getting irate without a valid reason. Branden Kel-Paten could be difficult, but he wasn't petty.

"I made it look as if we were playing good cop–bad cop," she continued when he didn't comment. "Serafino thought he was clever picking up on that." At the mention of the name, she saw Kel-Paten's hands, still braced against the viewport, clench.

But no verbal response.

Again.

She thought of the countless times she and the Tin Soldier had traded barbs over their respective ships' vidscreens. He was rarely at a loss for words—if nothing else, there was always their perfunctory name game and its accompanying disapproving tone.

But silent? Withdrawn? And not even turning around to favor her with a typical Kel-Paten scowl?

Maybe a Section 46 wasn't such a bad idea.

"Do you want me to handle Serafino from here on?" she offered. "I can—"

"No!" He swung around to face her, and she noted with surprise the luminous glow in his eyes. He either was still powered up since the session in the ready room or had turned on his 'cybe functions just now.

Maybe Eden was right. Some kind of glitch in his emotional programming had bypassed his safeguards.

He stared at her, that eerie glow in his eyes. "We both can handle Serafino." He stepped away from his desk as he spoke.

In tandem, she took a step back toward the door.

"I think it's *imperative* we handle Serafino together," he continued.

His office comm buzzed, Rissa Kel-Faray's soft voice breaking the tension. "Sir. Admiral Roderick Kel-Tyra's responding to your request on translink four."

"I'm sure that's important," Sass said. "By your command." She nodded formally and was out the door before he could grant or withdraw permission, Serafino's warnings echoing darkly in her mind.

OFFICERS' MESS HALL

Sass watched Eden climb the short flight of steps to their private table in the wardroom, her dinner of stew and cheese bread balanced on a tray in her hand. By comparison, Sass's tray held only a tall glass of iced gin. And the remains of two lime wedges she'd spent the past forty minutes—ever since she'd left Kel-Paten's office—mutilating with her swizzle stick.

Eden noticed. "Drinking our dinner, are we?"

Sass looked up as Eden took the seat across from her. "You have a chance to get anything more from Serafino?"

"Not as much as I'd like, but yes."

"Good. Sit down, Dr. Fynn. I think we have a problem."

To underscore her point, she activated the privacy field around the table as soon as Eden sat, the pale yellow lights in the floor signaling that the two officers didn't want to be disturbed. The sonic buffer itself would prevent them from being overheard.

The smile immediately dropped from Eden's face. "What now?"

Sass gave a short, dry laugh. "I think the correct response is: you tell me. No, I'm sorry. Let me just run some issues by you, and then you tell me what you've learned from Serafino."

Eden nodded and Sass continued: "I'm sure you noticed that the session between Kel-Paten and Serafino was less than a rousing success. Granted, Kel-Paten, being the Triad's biggest fan, wouldn't be expected to be thrilled with Serafino's allegations. But Serafino is telling the truth." She stabbed the lime wedge with her swizzle stick and pointed it at Eden. "Is that right?"

"Well, yes."

"So the logical—and the gods know that's what 'cybes are supposed to be: logical—the logical thing for Kel-Paten to do would be either to discount what Serafino said or investigate the allegations. Right?"

"Well, yes."

"The last thing you'd think he'd be concerned with would be Serafino's nasty little jibes. I mean, he's programmed to be immune to that stuff."

"Yes, but—" Eden started to say.

"Exactly. Yes, *but*. I honestly thought if Serafino called him Tin Soldier one more time, Kel-Paten was going to fry him, right then and there. So I step in. And Kel-Paten walks out of an interrogation." Sass shook her head, the memory still puzzling. "I went to his office to get some answers. If he wanted to play good cop–bad cop, fine, but tell me first, okay? But when I got there, Eden . . . it was strange. He was staring out the viewport, didn't even turn when I came in. And when he finally did, he was still in his 'cybe mode."

"That's not that unusual," Eden offered. "His cyberinterface functions as an emotional discipline—"

"Like he was going to emotionally discipline Serafino? Lubashit." She waggled the mangled lime at Eden again.

"I don't know what you're getting at."

"Then think back about what Serafino told us just before I left. That this Faction intends to take out Kel-Paten, but first they wanted Kel-Paten to take me out. And I don't mean to dinner."

"You're basing your conclusions on one false premise," Eden began, but Sass cut her off.

"You don't know the way he looked at me just now, in his office. It makes too much sense."

"But—"

"Do you think Serafino's telling the truth?"

"I know he's telling the truth," Eden replied

quickly. "Serafino and I had brief contact right after you left. I tried to get more from the, um, other side of him once we got back to sick bay, but I wasn't able to link with him, either telepathically or in Novalis. What I did get, though, was this." Eden described the images that were flashed to her mind of the Triad Defense Minister.

Sass swore out loud and closed her eyes briefly. "Kel-Paten's first posting was on Kel-Sennarin's ship. Now he reports directly to him as head of Triad Strategic Command."

"So?"

"So that's why he's on Serafino's trail. And why I'm on the *Vax*. The two hundred fifty thousand credits Serafino stole is a minor *mullytrock* to the Triad." Sass hesitated and then said the words she had a hard time accepting after six months of working with the admiral. She really believed they'd developed a level of mutual respect. She knew *she* had. Now it seemed that Kel-Paten's interaction with her was all a sham. "First he gets rid of Serafino. Then he gets rid of me. Either directly or by staging it so I'm killed in the line of duty—possibly during Serafino's capture. That's why he was so disturbed by Serafino's ship suddenly appearing, and so suspicious of me at the time. It skewed whatever plans he and Kel-Sennarin made."

"You can't seriously think Kel-Paten would harm you," Eden asked pointedly. "There'd be questions, inquiries—"

"He's Kel-Paten. *The* Kel-Paten—he damned near defines *loyalty to the Triad*. And with Kel-Sennarin behind him—as he's been for years—there'd be no questions."

Eden sat back in her chair, her eyes wide. "But if that was really his intention, I should have sensed . . ."

Sass didn't miss how Eden's comment trailed off. "Remember who—what," she corrected, "you're dealing with here. Out of the ten, twelve 'cybes they created—those others we're not supposed to know about—he's their only success story. They put a lot of time and effort into him. *Psy-Serv* put a lot of time and effort into him. Not to demean your talents, my friend, but you might be a bit out of your league here."

"There was talk about a scrambler being integrated into the biocybernetic programs." Eden's voice was hushed. "Something that could send out false readings. But we could never track down anything definitive. It might just be wild gossip."

"Telepathic scrambler? Or just empathic?"

Eden thought for a long moment. "Empathic. From what I've read, a telepath can detect a scrambler. An empath can't."

There was a moment of studious silence, then: "Serafino," they said together.

"We have to remove that implant before we get to Panperra," Sass continued. "Because, one, I don't know if Kel-Paten will let him live that long. And, two, the only way we're going to know the whole story—not only about this Faction but about what's going on with the admiral—is when Serafino's free of that device. What we have now is a physical body that remembers part of it and a telepathic connection that can't stay online for more than ten minutes." Sass drew a deep breath. "I may not—*we* may not— have that much time."

"When can you get the data from Kel-Paten's files?" Eden asked.

"He's logged for an inspection tour of navigation and stellar cartography at oh-nine-thirty tomorrow. He will probably also ask—no, *demand* that I accompany him. I can't be with him and in his quarters at the same time. And I can't refuse to go with him, because then he might go back to his quarters and find me there."

"We need a way to keep him busy without you."

"We need to make me sick."

"I beg your pardon?"

"What's the herb that raises your body temperature? I want you to give me just enough to simulate a fever. Something that when I weakly collapse in front of him will register to his cybernetic sensors as real. And register on sick bay's diags as real. Then you're going to lock me up in one of your med-rooms and not permit him to see me for at least five hours, during which time I'm going to have to climb up through the ship's interior maintenance tunnels all the way to his quarters, break in, infiltrate his security, download half the universe, and get back to sick bay in time for my miracle cure."

"Sass—"

"You have the hard part of keeping Kel-Paten from going back to his quarters. And if he does, you alert me right quick." Sass leaned over the table. "Got it?"

Eden suddenly smiled and tapped her juice glass against Sass's now empty one. "Feels like old times, girl. Feels like old times."

MAIN LIFT BANK

Sass leaned back against the cool metal walls of the lift and closed her eyes. That foul-smelling herbal compound of Eden's that she downed shortly after her morning coffee had kicked in several minutes ago, first with a feeling of light-headedness that just progressed into a rather unpleasant dizziness.

Admiral Kel-Paten, she noted, was in his usual spit-and-polish military stance as he stood quietly next to her. He made no mention of yesterday's interview—or his loss of control—during their usual morning briefing in his office. The distant, efficient persona she knew as Kel-Paten was firmly back in place. That made it easier to keep her new wariness of him at bay. They were back in a routine so familiar that she could have conducted it with half her brain tied behind her back.

Which was a good thing, because, judging from her body's wobbling, that wasn't far from the truth.

The lift doors opened on nav deck. Kel-Paten turned, evidently expecting her to step in front of him.

By that point, she felt the small beads of sweat trickling down the side of her face.

"Tasha?"

There was an odd hoarseness to his voice, Sass thought, or maybe the herbs affected her hearing as well.

"Tasha, are you all right?"

"Don't think so," she whispered. Her knees gave out and she slid toward the floor.

The next few moments progressed through a hazy,

moving fog. Kel-Paten dropped to his knees and suddenly she moved upward, aware of his arms under her legs and around her back.

For a moment, panic surged through her. Gods, she'd just presented him with the perfect opportunity to kill her. Weak, already obviously ill, helpless. A thought and a touch could finish her off.

If she had the energy, she'd have pounded her head on the lift wall at her stupidity. Instead, a low moan was all she could manage. Then she heard a familiar, discordant trill. He must have activated the emergency comm panel.

"Kel-Paten to bridge. I need an emergency transport to sick bay. Lock on my comm link and Captain Sebastian's. Now!"

And there was the momentary disorientation as her physical form merged with beams of light...and reemerged as physical form in sick bay.

Alive. So he wasn't ready to kill her yet. That thought cheered her.

Eden looked totally surprised. "Admiral! What happened?" Sass had the urge to wink, but her eyes didn't seem to want to cooperate.

"I don't know."

I passed out, she wanted to say, but her mouth didn't seem to be working either.

Caleb Monterro motioned them into the nearest diag room.

"She just passed out," Kel-Paten said.

Do I hear an echo? No, that would be Eden's job, hearing thoughts.

Her back bumped against something hard. An

annoying beeping sound commenced. The diag table, kicking on and downloading her vitals.

Kel-Paten's face hovered over hers. "We had an inspection tour scheduled." He looked at Monterro, then Eden. "She seems to have—"

"A fever. A very high fever." Eden glanced at the readouts on the wall above the bed. "Admiral, I'm going to have to ask you to leave now."

"If it's serious, I'm staying."

Get him out of here, Eden!

As if on cue, Eden shot Kel-Paten a reproving look. "Kel-Paten, you're wasting my time. And hers. I'll send Dr. Monterro out shortly if we know anything."

That seemed to do it. That and a tone Sass recognized in Eden's voice that signaled someone was fraying her last strand of patience. Kel-Paten nodded as if in a trance. "I'll be in your office, Doctor. Thank you."

The doors slid shut. Cal palmed on the security lock. Eden rolled up Sass's sleeve and slapped a transdermal antidote patch on Sass's arm.

"You will," Sass heard Cal say to Eden, "explain all this at a later date."

"Promise, Doc." Eden smiled at him. "The captain said she'd even bring her best gin. Now go out there and keep the admiral occupied. And for the gods' sakes, let me know immediately if he leaves sick bay."

It was a few minutes before the fog dissipated from Sass's vision and her mouth felt connected to her brain again.

"How are we feeling?" Eden crooned teasingly.

"Like lubashit on a lemon." She pushed herself up onto her elbows. The room tilted only slightly. Her head pounded and her stomach felt as if it had gone through a shredder. "Hand me my gear, will you?"

She removed her uniform jacket, stripping down to her dark-gray T-shirt. Into the pockets of her pants and into the small pouches on her utility belt she stuffed the few things she would need, the last of which was a small bag of fidget treats.

"You left Reilly in my cabin, right?" she asked Eden.

"He and Tank were playing 'run around the table' last I saw them."

"They'll both earn their keep this shift." Sass glanced at her watch. "I have about four and a half hours. Don't worry—after this they'll probably name some medical deity after you." She hoisted herself into the large square air duct. "Take a nap, Doc. By the time my day's over, yours will be starting. You still have to operate on Serafino after this."

"Piece o' cake," Eden quipped, echoing Sass's earlier optimism. "Just watch your ass out there."

"Yes, ma'am." Sass flashed her friend a wide grin and shoved herself into the small dark tunnel, ignoring the hundred or so things that could yet go wrong.

Including what one 'cybe admiral—a very deadly 'cybe admiral—would do if he caught her hacking into his private files in his quarters.

$$\overset{*\ ^{*\!\star}}{\underset{}{\boxed{\mathtt{12}}}}$$

TASHA SEBASTIAN'S CABIN

"Okay, Reilly, that's a good furzel," Sass whispered as the larger animal squeezed into the conduit duct too small for any human form. Reilly himself just barely fit, and she knew if it wasn't for the handful of treats she'd thrown through the grating, he wouldn't make the journey at all.

Tank bounded quickly behind him, not one to miss any hint of a meal. She'd clipped two tiny lasers on the furzels' collars, and as they pushed in frustration against the grating that separated them from their snacks, she operated the lasers remotely, punching small holes in the grating's frame.

There was the muffled thud of the grating hitting the floor. The two animals leaped down into the admiral's cabin and devoured the treats.

"Okay, now!" she called hoarsely, having given

them enough time to finish their food. "Out time, furzels! Out time!"

It was a trick Eden had taught Reilly back on the *Regalia* and Sass had subsequently taught to Tank. "Out time" meant the furzels could run loose in the corridors. But to earn that, they had to open the cabin doors.

Which they did by making a mad dash across the room and throwing their small bodies against the manual lock override to the right of every ship's cabin door.

It often took several tries.

Thumpety-thumpety-thumpety-thumpety THWACK! Thud.

A furzel ran, hit the override panel on the wall, and fell to the ground.

Thumpety-thumpety-thumpety-thumpety THWACK! Thud.

In between the *thumpetys* and the *thuds*, Sass made her way back to her quarters and out her own door. She monitored their progress on the small comm link on Tank's collar and prayed no one would see her or hear the bizarre noises coming from the admiral's cabin.

Thumpety-thumpety-thumpety-thumpety THWACK! THUMP!

She should speak to Eden about Reilly's weight problem. That last one almost sounded as if he might crash through the bulkhead.

Thumpety-thumpety-thumpety-thumpety THWACK! Thud.

Swoosh.

The cabin door opened. The furzels raced out. The captain stepped in.

SICK BAY

Eden turned off the bed's diag systems as soon as Tasha left, fluffed the pillow, and leaned against it with a quiet sigh. A short furzel nap would do her good. She'd dozed for about five minutes when she heard the door lock cycle. She opened one eye.

Cal stuck his head in and quietly slipped inside.

"He's looking through the report on the virus," Cal told her.

"Lucky him." Eden stifled a yawn.

"He looks miserable."

"So was I when I read it in med school. Lousiest bit of research I've ever seen," she said.

Cal leaned against the wall, folding his arms across his broad chest. "I didn't mean it that way. I mean the admiral looks extremely upset over Captain Sebastian's supposed condition."

"The admiral," Eden noted, "has several good reasons to be upset, not the least of which is the captain's supposed condition. I just wish I could get a clear reading on whether it's a good upset or a bad upset."

Cal caught her slight frown. "I take it you're having problems placing him in an empathic category. Being 'cybe, he might not react in ways we understand."

"Tell me about it!" She stretched her arms over her head. "His being programmed by Psy-Serv makes it that much more difficult. You've seen his med-files, Cal, and I'm sure you saw the same gaps I did."

"So much for their unequivocal trust of the U-Cees."

"Tasha said the same thing. Looks like we all have a lot to learn."

Cal went back out to keep an eye on Kel-Paten; Eden relaxed into the pillow again.

A little early for bedtime, or are we napping?

The gray mists cleared. Jace had one leg propped up against the stone bench, leaning one hand on his knee. She came and sat down next to him.

Napping. I may have to pull a late-nighter on your account, Captain Serafino.

Jace, he reminded her patiently. *You've used my name before. No need to be so formal now.* He was smiling, and because the telepathic contact was so clear, she saw his smile as well as felt its warmth.

I have a problem, she told him gently, *with such familiarity with a patient.*

We're friends.

I'm not disputing that. She was genuinely fond of the playful, telepathic Jace Serafino. *But even friendship takes time. And the Jace I know here,* she motioned to the gray mists, *is not the Jace Serafino I've been encountering out there.*

Been misbehaving, have I? He sat down next to her, his hands clasped between his legs, and gave her his most innocent look.

She laughed. *That's putting it mildly. You did have a rather nasty run-in with Kel-Paten.*

Ah, the Tin Soldier. He and I never got along,

especially after the Traveler *and I got the best of him at Fendantun.*

Jace, how much are you aware of what your physical self is doing?

Do I remember my conversation with Kel-Paten in the ready room last night? Some. Like speaking now with you, I can't be involved for more than my time limit. So I try to fade in and out, keep myself out of trouble. You can tell, can't you?

Eden nodded. She'd noticed a slight difference in Captain Serafino's reactions from time to time and suspected the internal Jace had a hand in that.

Can you read Kel-Paten? she asked.

He shrugged. *Sometimes better than others. There's a strong cybernetic overlay that Psy-Serv designed to prevent just that.*

Gods, she'd suspected as much. *A scrambler?*

He nodded. *Any telepath worth his salt prevents himself from being read by other telepaths. But since Kel-Paten's not telepathic, he can't do that. Hence the filter or scrambling system, as you put it.*

When I remove the implant, I may ask you to read Kel-Paten.

I don't mean to rush you—I really don't want to make you a widow before I can make you my bride— but do you have a time frame here?

Eden ignored the little fluttermoth that made a brief appearance in her stomach at his words. She had neither the time nor the interest in anything romantic right now. *Within the next twenty-four hours. I know that seems sudden—*

I think it's a necessary risk, he said, a grim tone to his voice. *I'm forgetting important information, more and more. I don't know if I have enough time to explain to you all that needs to be said.*

You mean like what you told me earlier about Kel-Sennarin?

You got that, then? He seemed relieved when she nodded. *I just wish I could tell you more about this damned thing in my head.*

You may not have to. Tasha believes Kel-Paten may have documentation on it in his files. She's chasing down the information right now.

Kel-Paten's permitting this? he asked.

She shook her head and flashed him the mental image of the admiral in sick bay with Tasha in his arms and her subsequent recovery and escape through the ductwork.

Jace raised his eyes in mock horror. *I should have known! Lady Sass was always game for some wild escapade.* He touched her chin, tilting her face up to his. *Well, my Eden, if I'm to die, then let it be in your arms.*

Your optimism overwhelms me.

Eden. He gently stroked her face, his touch causing a trail of heat across her skin. *I don't doubt your medical expertise. I'm just too familiar with Psy-Serv's deviousness.*

I will not risk your life. Unless Tasha brings me exactly what I need to remove the implant, you'll remain a split personality for a while longer. I will not endanger you in any way, she repeated.

You endanger me every day, every hour. His thumb traced the outline of her lower lip, then softly his mouth followed where his thumb was.

For a brief moment, Eden ignored all her mental

warnings about men like Jace and let herself sink into his gentle, wonderful kiss. But when she felt the warmth of his tongue probing her mouth, she turned her face away and grasped his hands, which were getting far too familiar.

Jace, please don't—

Why? Don't you know what you do to me?

This is a wonderful fantasy, but Novalis is not real life. And you're not the same out there.

A sad smile crossed his face and he brought her hands to his lips, grazing her knuckles with a kiss. *I'm a rotten son of a bitch out there.*

And you question why I'm saying no? she asked somewhat wistfully.

And you question why I'm trying? Eden, a woman like you would never love the Jace Serafino out there.

What happens when I remove the implant? Which Jace Serafino will become the real one?

I don't know, he replied honestly. *I was pretty much the same son of a bitch before the implant. What the implant did is force me to look at myself. And it's allowed me to become, with you, someone I might have been if my life was different. But that doesn't mean I know who you're going to get when you've put me back together. I just hope we can still be friends.*

She smiled and started to reply, when he continued, *Because I have this real fear, you know, of rectal thermometers.*

Regretfully, Eden let their link fade. She lay quietly, still feeling his touch on her hand, on her face.

Eden had a fear as well. Tasha might be in trouble, deep trouble. Jace had confirmed her suspicions about Kel-Paten's personal psychic shield. It was very possible the affection she sensed in him when Tasha was around was a deception.

It was very possible, should he find out what she and Tasha were up to, that he'd kill them both.

BRANDEN KEL-PATEN'S CABIN

Sass straddled the swivel chair in front of Kel-Paten's desk and typed a maintenance access code into the small keypad. The recessed comp screen emerged from the desktop, its electronic eye winking on for retinal verification. Quickly, she ran one finger over her mouth and smeared a light film of lip gloss across the small portal.

"Retinal confirmation temporarily off-line," the tinny computer voice intoned softly, after a few moments of frantic beeping through an ineffective—thanks to a few other tweaks Sass had employed—repair program. "Please respond with verbal verification procedures."

She took the wad of chewy candy from her mouth and stuck it directly over the microphone input, then brought up the security program and tapped the check-box to suspend retinal and verbal verifications. The system reversed course and brought up a new series of commands. She ignored those and went through three more screens until she found what she needed: Inoperative Systems Simulations. She chose Sim 374.

It was the Triad-approved version of the program she ran on the *Regalia* to train computers and crew what to do in event of a partial or—gods forbid!— total systems failure. She ran two such sims from her office here on the *Vax* in the first few months she was on board. Just like the manual override on each cabin door, there had to be an alternate way of getting out. Or getting in.

Right now she needed in.

Dutifully, the system responded. She implemented some basic tests just to get further into the program before trying to bamboozle it into letting her into Kel-Paten's coded files.

His cabin lights winked on and off; his cabin temperature raised and lowered. His small galley even produced a nice, hot cup of Mahrian blend, black, which she sipped gratefully while moving the program through its paces. She glanced at her watch— she had a little more than three and a half hours left. A lot of time, yet not. She had no idea what, or how much, she'd find once she got in.

She tabbed down the current page and found the Emergency Data Transfer Simulation Program.

"Please verify through retinal scan," the computer replied audibly. She hadn't dampered its voice, only her own.

She searched parameters and tapped *retinal scan off-line*. Then she rekeyed in her request: *Initiate Emergency Data Transfer Simulation Program*.

"Authorization code required to initiate. Respond with code," the computer said.

She knew that was the next level of security; hell, she'd designed the *Reg*'s programs to respond in a similar manner. But what the *Vax* had that the *Regalia* didn't was Kel-Paten—a biocybe who physically spiked in to the computer systems. She withdrew a small coiled cable and an even smaller—and highly illegal—code-pattern emulator from one of her pockets and quickly disconnected the auxiliary keyboard, inserting a coupler and reconnecting the keyboard through that. She patched the other end of the coupler into the emulator and shoved that into the small port set into the arm of Kel-Paten's custommade chair.

She waited a few tense seconds for the units to synchronize, then directed the program to derive the last known code from its terminal location.

There was a moment of tense silence. Had she tried this from any other terminal, including her own office, Sass knew she wouldn't be able to gain access. But she was banking on the fact that Kel-Paten felt his personal quarters were totally secure. And she was banking on her knowledge that he usually spiked in— a "spike" she hoped the emulator would simulate, as far as the computer was concerned.

"Access granted," the computer intoned softly, and Sass let out a corresponding sigh.

It was all relatively easy pickings from there.

True to form, Kel-Paten's files were disgustingly well organized. She popped a portable datadrive into the download port and initiated copy-file commands. It would have been easier and quicker to tag files and have them sent to her datafiles, but that would have left a trail. Her datadrive was carefully created to leave no input ID.

One of the more interesting things she'd learned to do on Lethant.

There was a lot of data referencing Psy-Serv, an almost equally large amount on Serafino. She copied both directories and, over the next hour, transferred more.

Med-Files–BKP and *BKP–Personal* were snatched. She'd just discovered an encrypted file titled *Tasha* when her badge trilled.

"Sass! Eden here. We lost him!"

"Bloody damn!" She flicked off the comp screen. It slid back into the desktop, but the green light on her drive still flashed, the unit working, pulling data. She heard the smart click of the cabin door lock recycling. Heart pounding, she dove under the desk, fitting her small form into the kneehole and shoving her comm link down the front of her shirt. If it trilled now, she was dead.

Cabin lights flicked on. Heavy footsteps moved across the carpeted floor as the door swooshed closed.

Damn! Shit! Trock! Sass ran through every swear word she knew in five languages as she listened to the sound of liquid being poured. Thank the gods she'd finished her coffee and disposed of the cup in the recyc. She heard a cabinet door *thwump* closed, a short spate of footsteps, and then the *fwoosh* of couch cushions as a body sat.

Just my luck. The Tin Soldier's poured himself a

drink and is now going to sit and watch a season's worth of Zero-G Hockey reruns or something.

He couldn't stay in his quarters. Granted, he had the right to be here. But she was dying in sick bay. Didn't he care about that?

If nothing else, it was a bitch to find command-staff replacements—especially a huntership-qualified captain—on short notice. Surely he had to appreciate that?

Scrunched into the kneehole of the desk, small beads of sweat trickling down her chest, Sass cautiously eyed the small drive. It was still pulling data, and for the life of her she couldn't remember if it beeped when it finished. Or not.

The *or not* would be a relief. Any other option would take a lot of explaining. If she lived long enough.

The tiny green light on its cover panel blinked on–off, on–off. At each "on," she breathed in. At each "off," she held her breath. Why couldn't Kel-Paten listen to music or turn on a vidshow? Anything that made noise! But, no, he sat in a silence far too loud for her liking.

A comm link trilled. For a moment her heart stopped and she clasped her hands over her shirt pocket to muffle any further noise. But it wasn't her link that had activated.

"Kel-Paten here."

"Admiral, this is Dr. Fynn."

Sass squeezed her eyes shut tightly. *Eden! Get me the hell of out here!*

"I would appreciate it if you'd return to sick bay. I

think we may have some good news in a half hour or so."

A half hour or so. That was Eden's way of telling her to *get the hell out and do it now!*

"On my way, Doctor," Kel-Paten replied. Sass heard the clink of a glass against the tabletop.

Thank you, Eden! Sass waited a few seconds after the cabin doors closed before extricating herself from under the desk. The kink in her back complained painfully.

Beep-ta-beep! said her datadrive.

Sass almost jumped out of her skin. "Up yours and the equinnard you rode in on!" She snatched the drive from the port. She tapped at the desk and the vidscreen popped up. She grabbed at the pink candy and quickly wiped her sleeve over the lip gloss smear, then popped the screen back down again.

Sass had replaced the duct grating when she first came in, but she checked it again just be to sure and then did a quick visual to see if there were any other traces of her visit. There were none—it was as if she was never there.

She was out the door and back in her cabin just in time to find Reilly and Tank doing a reprise of "run around the table."

"How did you—?" But, of course, the furzels couldn't answer how they got back in her cabin. Usually they made their way down to hydroponics, where either she or Eden would eventually retrieve them, as they always did on the *Regalia*. "You guys know more secrets than I do," she told them. Then, stuffing the datadrive in her shirt, she climbed into the larger access ducting that opened into her bedroom closet and made her way down the maintenance ladders to the lower deck that housed sick bay.

Caleb Monterro waited for her. "Quick!" He tossed her the silver hospital gown. She stripped off her clothes. He stuffed them and the drive into a small hamper next to the bed as she slid beneath the covers. Just at that moment, Eden stuck her head in the door.

She nodded at Sass. Sass nodded back.

Then Eden turned. "Admiral," she said, "you can see Captain Sebastian for a few moments."

Kel-Paten strode past Eden without so much as a "by your command."

"Tasha." His voice had a noticeable rough edge to it. "How are you feeling?"

"Like hell," she replied, her voice equally breathy. After all, she'd just finished scaling twelve flights of maintenance ladders. Thank the gods it was *down*!

He cleared his throat. "Doctor." Eden looked at him. "I need to speak to Captain Sebastian. Alone."

"I'm sorry, sir, but the captain requires medical monitoring at this time. If my presence disturbs you, then you will have to tolerate Dr. Monterro's."

They needed him to tolerate somebody's as protection until she could find out what Kel-Paten had in his files.

He glanced one more time at Sass. "What time are you releasing her?"

"First shift, most likely, depending upon how she fares during the night."

"I'll be here at oh-nine-hundred to escort her."

"That won't be necessary. One of my nurses can see her to her quarters."

"I'm sure your staff has more-pressing concerns. I'll see her back to her quarters myself." He stared down at her.

"Admiral. Captain Sebastian will be released if and when I say she is released, and if and when she is, she will be released to no one other than one of my medical staff. I'm sure *you* have more pressing concerns."

"I don't. I'll be here at oh-nine-hundred."

Sass didn't think he would murder her in front of witnesses. Obviously, neither did Eden. "I'll advise you at oh-eight-thirty," the CMO said, "if she's ready to be released. Now if you'll excuse me, I have a lot of work to do."

Kel-Paten's icy gaze went from Eden to her, causing a chill to flit up Sass's spine. But no, not a chill. Something else. Something different.

Because his gaze wasn't the least bit icy at all.

SICK BAY

Sass let out a sigh she hadn't realized she was holding in when the door closed behind the Tin Soldier. Then she lunged for her clothes. There was a lot of work yet to be done.

"How much were you able to get?" Eden offered her the small datadrive.

Sass finished pulling on her boots, then accepted it, holding it in her line of sight and squinting. "Won't know 'til I get back into this thing. I don't think it's wise for me to use your office in case you-know-who pops back in. Can I use Cal's in the back?"

Cal's office it was. Eden brought in another cup of coffee and left Sass alone to unravel the data.

She made a backup copy first, in case fail-safes or traps existed. There were over fifty directories, some with names she recognized but most with only numbers. Nothing blatantly labeled *Psy-Serv Secrets*.

A block of files with Triad Med Ministry transit tags caught her eye. They were also security-locked. She unlocked them, bundled them, and shot them over to Eden's personal in-box.

Twenty minutes later a noise caused her to look up. Eden, in her doorway. And not with fresh coffee, damn! But a distinctly pinched look about her eyes.

"Trouble?"

"From the odds and ends you sent me, it looks as if Psy-Serv has experimented with implants for over twenty years, most of which failed and killed the recipient. Serafino's must be one of the more advanced designs."

"Wonderful. For Serafino, that is. At least his won't malfunction—"

"It is. The fact that he's able to bypass the implant means it's breaking down. When it finally does, it'll kill him."

"Not wonderful. How do we fix it?"

"That tidy bit of information isn't in the stuff you sent me. Any more?"

Sass made a quick scan of the files. "Don't see anything here. Maybe it's inside one of these. Can you work with what I've given you?"

Eden sat down with a sigh. "I can increase Serafino's telepathic access time. But I can't remove the implant, no."

"Is it possible Kel-Paten doesn't have that answer?"

"We still have more than we had before, Tasha.

And if Serafino can be more of, well, himself, maybe he can help."

"I'll send you my next download shortly," Sass told her as Eden headed for the door.

"Give me five minutes," Eden said, glancing at her watch. "I need a cup of tea. Desperately."

"Got it." Sass turned back to the comp and resumed scanning the files. The medical terminology meant nothing to her, but she dutifully unencrypted what she could and sent it to Eden.

Four hours later they were no further along except for an added appreciation of the deviousness of Psy-Serv.

This time when Eden appeared in her doorway, she had both tea and coffee.

"I can now understand why Triadian telepaths kill themselves rather than be recruited," Eden said.

Sass blew across the top of her mug. Small steam clouds swirled. "I really thought we'd find the answers here."

"We did," Eden reassured her. "Just not all of them."

"What do we do now?"

Eden thought for a moment. "I can make some adjustments on Serafino with a sonic laser tomorrow, before we hit Panperra. That should increase his access time and slow down the implant's deterioration."

"What about this Faction? And what about the admiral's involvement?"

"Those are command decisions, Tasha," Eden said.

"Command's damned tired and hungry," Sass growled. "I don't like this, Eden. It was so much easier before the Alliance. At least we were relatively sure who our enemies were." She looked at Eden. "How accurately can you read him, being he may have this scrambler installed? You've hinted that he's more human than we all think."

"I can't rule out that he might be programmed to appear more human as a cover."

"So you're telling me you can't read him at all."

"Not reliably."

"Can Serafino?"

"Once I get him fully functional, better than I can. I've asked him the same questions, by the way."

"Because you're concerned you can't read Kel-Paten."

"Because I'm concerned," Eden told her, "that what I'm reading might be wrong. In which case he's masking something serious. But if I'm reading him correctly..."

"If you are?" Sass urged her.

"We've seriously misjudged him. It's not an easy position."

"You're saying there's a chance Serafino's wrong and the admiral may be on our side in this?" Sass asked.

"Yes."

"Don't let me work in the dark. It's too dangerous for all of us."

Eden turned her mug in her hands before speaking. "By tomorrow I should have Serafino's telepathic time increased. We'll have to schedule another meeting. I'll get Serafino to read him and see if he can unravel that inconsistency I sense."

"Just one inconsistency?" As tired as she was, Sass picked up on that.

Eden closed her eyes. "Just one," she said finally. "When he's with you."

"*I'm* the inconsistency?"

"That's when I get the conflicting readings. When he's focused on you."

Sass glanced at the comp screen. "Eden, he has a whole set of files on me. I didn't bother to open them because I thought Serafino was the issue here. But Serafino did say that he thought I was brought on board for Kel-Paten to handle. If what we have here is a list of acceptable fatal accidents with my name on them, then that might be enough for me to contact the U-Cees for assistance when we get to Panperra."

"Do you want to take a break? I can have the galley deliver something."

Sass glanced at her watch. It was almost 1800. "I was hoping to relax with a meal and a beer after we decided there was nothing more with Serafino, but we've just opened up a whole other can of frinkas, and this one's got my name on it. So bring me whatever's quick and easy."

Sass sipped at the mug of hot soup Eden brought and opened up the files, one after another. Most she recognized as her official U-Cee personnel files and even—gods, was he thorough!—an old report on the academy coursework UCID had concocted as hers. Just how long was he keeping tabs on her—and why?

A chill ran up her spine. Did Kel-Paten know not only who she was but who she wasn't? His files on her were only the official ones, the ones designed to create Tasha Sebastian. She found nothing on Lady Sass. That was of little comfort, however. Just because she didn't find them didn't mean they didn't exist. Or that he didn't know about Zanorian, Gund'jalar, and Lethant.

It would bother her if he found out the truth about her unsavory past associations. Oddly—or perhaps not so oddly, Sass being Sass—she realized she could handle his being her assassin far better than she could handle his disdain.

Shaking her head at her own musings, she returned to her work. The next group of files contained transit-tagged downloads from different times and sources. They were coded so that new data automatically appended to the parent file whenever it entered the system. It was a common method.

But why Kel-Paten kept a transit-tag file on her was a mystery. Until she opened and read it.

For one very long moment she sat frozen in disbelief, a series of conflicting emotions churning through her. Then she was on her feet, lunging toward Eden's office, swearing in every language she knew.

SICK BAY, DR. FYNN'S OFFICE

When Eden saw Tasha striding through the main area of sick bay, she knew something was wrong. For one thing, it completely blew Tasha's cover story of being sick. And second, there was always the remote chance that Kel-Paten would come in. Eden's glass-fronted office provided no place to hide.

Tasha didn't try to hide. She plopped down into the chair across from Eden's desk, her eyes wide in amazement. "This is unbelievable. It makes no sense." She waved one hand in the air. "But then again, it makes perfect sense."

"What?" Eden asked.

Tasha picked up Eden's teaspoon and pointed it at her. "I thought at first that this might be part of his cover. That he created all these log entries in the past few weeks. But they go back years, Eden. Since I was on the *Sarna Bogue*!"

"What entries?"

Tasha ignored her question. "He'd have to have a phenomenal memory to do that. Granted, he probably does. But he'd also have to assume that I'd break into his systems and download these files, just to throw me off the track. That would be assuming a lot, even for Kel-Paten. Wouldn't you say?"

"I might if I knew what you were talking about," Eden replied patiently.

Tasha gave her a look as if she couldn't comprehend why Eden wasn't comprehending. "The log entries, of course."

"Oh. *What* log entries?" She was too tired to hide her sarcasm.

"Kel-Paten's. The ones he's been dictating to me. For twelve years."

Eden sat back in her chair. "Oh." Like that should explain everything.

"Yeah. No shit. Oh."

"Tasha—!"

"I'm sorry. Here." She tossed a crystalline disk at Eden. "Here's a small sample. Take a look and let me know what you think."

Perhaps log entries wasn't the most accurate description, Eden noted as she read. Love letters might be more like it. Most written as captain's personal logs, since he was a captain when he first saw Tasha on the *Bogue* twelve years before. They were very personal observations of what he was feeling, dreaming, and hoping for:

Captain's Personal Log . . . encrypt code SBSTN . . . subsequent encrypt code TASHA . . . transit tag this and all subsequent coded logs for delivery to TransGal Marine Depot 31 UPON MY DEMISE . . . Append . . . deliver to United Coalition HQ Varlow attention Lieutenant Tasha Sebastian . . . Append . . . deliver to U-Cee Huntership *Asterion's Star* attention Commander Tasha Sebastian . . . Append . . . deliver to U-Cee Huntership *Regalia* attention Captain Tasha Sebastian . . . Append . . . deliver to Captain Tasha Sebastian, Alliance Huntership *Vaxxar* . . .

Datestamp 351904.2

It's been four days since we first met and I still don't know more than your last name. That I learned from the patch on your jacket: Sebastian. Gods, woman, I need to call you something more than that. My green-eyed vixen? Do you know how you haunt me? Do you know how I've damned myself for not removing you from that U-Cee supply ship four days ago?

You probably thought I was angry over coming away empty-handed. You locked your ship down very well, scrambling its codes with a flair that's more than impressive. Given time, I could have unlocked it—I always can. But standing on that bridge, I realized that your cargo and your ship's military data were not what I wanted at all.

The Triad doesn't take political prisoners—how many times have I heard that? But this wouldn't have been a political action. This would've been purely personal. But in that area my cowardice is rivaled by none. So I walked away. It is an action I will regret for as long as I live.

I cannot accept that I will never see you again. I will find you. If it takes the rest of my life, I will find you.

Captain's Personal Log, Datestamp 350508.6 . . . encrypt code TASHA . . .

You have my hearty approval for your transfer to *Asterion's Star*! Tasha, I'm so proud of you. Your first assignment on a U-Cee huntership. I could tell you they're not half as good as the Triad. But you suffer because of my cowardice. Would you have hated me if I'd pulled you from the *Bogue*? Possibly. In the meantime, you can run circles around the U-Cees. I know you will. Hell, woman, you ran circles around me on that supply ship.

I've read your personnel files, your academy records. Top of your class, all the way. You have no idea how much I respect that. Your family's money could have paved an easy route for you, but you've chosen the harder one. I respect that even more.

I miss you, Tasha. I miss the way you wrinkle your nose. I miss your smile. It's been four months since I've seen you, and the holos my agents bring back to me don't carry your energy.

I may have to engineer an attack on the *Asterion's Star* just to see you again.

Captain's Personal Log, Datestamp 381022.2 . . .
encrypt code TASHA . . .

I'm sitting here in the bowels of Antalkin Station
and I don't know if I'll ever see you again. I'm
recording with an overlay note that should append
to my personal files, all of which will be sent to
you. Very shortly, I think.

The Illithians staged a brilliant ambush. I don't
know if we received bad information or I was just
being more stupid than usual. In any case, they almost took the *Vax*, but my ship maneuvered out of
their reach. Now it's me they're after because—
with station comps down—I stayed behind. I'm the
only thing—person—that can delete our military
data from the station's banks so the Irks can't
get it.

But that's . . . that's not the point. The point is
they managed a couple good shots at me. I'm
not as indestructible as Triad intelligence would
have you believe. Though you and the U-Cees
probably have that figured out by now. Sometimes
I wonder just who we're fooling with all this cyber
shit.

Things don't look optimistic at the moment. I've
found a hiding place, but I'm sure it's only tempo-
rary. They have a couple of teams looking for me.
I'm flattered. Twenty to thirty Irks combing a dead
station for me. I kept moving as long as I could,
but I've run out of energy. And time.

Tasha, gods, I've run out of time with you,
haven't I? All these years I've had dreams of taking
you to Tygaris—we could play the tables. I know
you're hell at Starfield Doubles.

But it's not going to happen now.

Tasha, I'm so tired. I miss you so much.

I have to move again. I hear . . . something.
I love you.

And then, a more recent entry . . .

Admiral's Personal Log, Datestamp 460310.9 . . .
encrypt code TASHA . . .

I don't know where you found that *No, No, Bad
Captain* shirt. Nor do I know where you found those
pink sweatpants. But sweet holy gods, Tasha, you
don't know how close I came to totally losing it and
making more of a fool of myself than I already
have.

It seems all I'm able to do in your presence is
stare at you like some stupid schoolboy. I just
want to talk to you. I've been trying so hard to
reach you, but I'm so afraid, and the gods know if
you found out you'd probably think it hysterically
funny . . . but I'm so afraid of losing you. I don't
know how close I can get. I tell myself all the time
that you're here with me on the *Vax* and I should
be thankful for that! It's more than I ever thought I
deserved. I know where you are, I know you're
safe, I know I can protect you.

And I know to some extent I'm driving you crazy.
You think I'm following you around. You're right. I
am. I just need to be with you, Tasha.

After we handle this Serafino situation, we'll go
to Tygaris. I know I've been saying that for years.
Even Ralland's tired of listening to me. But I mean
it this time.

I've dreamed about this, Tasha. I need to make
it come true. I have to ask you. And I have to figure out another way to keep you from playing racquetlob with that godsdamned lieutenant. Damn

it, Tasha, don't you know what he wants from
you?

I mean . . . that is, I want the same thing, but,
Tasha, I love you, and I don't care what he tells
you, he doesn't. He couldn't. Not as much as I do.
And not for as long as I have.

Eden blanked the screen and looked at Tasha. The
captain distractedly twirled the teaspoon on the desktop. Eden cleared her throat.

"Interesting, eh?" Tasha asked, but the flippancy
in her tone didn't quite match the seriousness in her
eyes. Or the uncomfortable aura Eden strongly
sensed around her. Tasha was more troubled than
Eden remembered in quite some time.

"I'm relieved to know I'm not as bad an empath as
I thought," Eden replied.

"This is what you were talking about a couple of
days ago."

Eden nodded. "Kel-Paten has a hard time controlling his emotions around you. I just wasn't sure why."

"And you are now? What about that scrambler?"

"That doesn't mean he doesn't feel things. It just
means I might not be able to get a true reading." She
tapped her screen. "But these do seem to answer the
question about any recent changes in his emo-
programs. Like you said, I can't see him fabricating
twelve years of log entries on the unlikely chance
you'd stumble over them. Plus, the datestamps—you
did check for forgeries?"

"Genuine." Tasha sounded almost disappointed.

"Then I think I can say his logs accurately state
what he feels—or believes he feels." Eden damned the

fact that Triad Medical had so little information on
biocybes and none at all on Kel-Paten's first sixteen,
full-human years.

Tasha closed her eyes and leaned back in the chair.
"Those logs are tagged to be sent to me only after his
death. I had no right reading them."

"You didn't go looking for them. There were circumstances—"

"The hell with circumstances!" Tasha rasped. "I
feel like a total shit for some of the things I've said to
him."

"He might be relieved to hear that. You could always ask him to go to Tygaris."

Tasha held her hands up in front of her. "Wait. I
just said I feel like a shit. That doesn't mean I'm willing to get involved with him. He's my CO. He's a
pompous, annoying, overbearing—"

"He's a 'cybe," Eden put in.

"That too," Tasha agreed, then added, "It's a
damned shame the Triad wasted such a nice body on
such a shitty personality."

"You could probably earn the eternal gratitude of
the crew by seducing him," Eden suggested.

"Very funny."

"Then let me suggest you carry on as you usually
do but with a little more tact," Eden said. "We still
have a number of problems to deal with, not the least
of which is the removal of Serafino's implant. Just because we know why Kel-Paten follows you around
doesn't mean he's not also following Psy-Serv's
agenda in other areas. Humans can compartmental-
ize. He can too."

"You mean he could still be programmed to kill Serafino?"

"Yes, considering that every time he spikes in to this ship's datalink, he uploads and downloads from Psy-Serv. He might not even realize it."

Tasha nodded slowly, then shoved herself out of her chair. "There are five more directories I need to decode. I may not find out any more on Serafino's implant. But we need to know everything Kel-Paten has on Serafino. Because if this Faction is real and after our hides, Serafino is the only one who knows how to stop them. Kel-Paten kills Serafino, and he's effectively killed us all."

15

SICK BAY

At 0850 Kel-Paten strode in, broadcasting—as far as Eden was concerned—apprehension and anticipation. Apparently he couldn't wait any longer to drag his *green-eyed vixen* out of sick bay, back to where he could keep an eye on her.

At least, she hoped that's what it was. Serafino's warning still echoed in her mind. There were several layers to Kel-Paten's emotions, some of which may have been very expertly manipulated by Psy-Serv.

"The captain will be ready in a few minutes," Eden told him as she retrieved Tasha's file from her desk. "The earliest she's allowed to go back on duty is late this afternoon."

And that went double for herself as well. Neither of them had had more than four hours sleep after decoding Kel-Paten's files and conferencing back and forth. Eden was strongly looking forward to discharging the captain and heading straight for her own quarters.

"I'll make sure no one disturbs her," the admiral told Eden.

Tuck her in and read her a bedtime story, will you?

"Very good," Eden said out loud. "I'll just—"

"Don't be ridiculous. I don't need that thing!" Tasha's forceful complaint flowed out into sick bay as soon as her door opened. Inside, a male med nurse was trying unsuccessfully to talk Tasha into sitting in a hoverchair. SOP for discharging patients, he was telling her.

"Screw SOP. I wrote most of the damned SOPs and—" She looked out the open door, saw Kel-Paten, and immediately clammed up.

Oh, great, Eden thought. *Tasha, this is not acting normally. Keep yelling. Do something. Have another cup of coffee.*

Kel-Paten was already at the doorway. "What seems to be the problem?"

The man looked from the admiral to the captain and back to the admiral again. "Captain Sebastian, sir, isn't cooperating in regard to sick-bay dismissal policy."

"You will learn that Captain Sebastian rarely cooperates in regard to any policies. The day she starts is the day I resign my commission." Kel-Paten looked at Tasha. "Sebastian?"

Pause.

It was, Eden noted, a familiar phrase Tasha needed to hear.

"Kel-Paten." Tasha nodded in return.

"You're off duty until I tell you otherwise."

"I'll be in my office after lunch. Not on the bridge, Admiral. In my office." She breezed past him and headed for the corridor. "Thanks for the hospitality, Doc!"

"My pleasure," Eden replied, but it was automatic. She was still trying to tune in to and sort out the Tin Soldier's emotional resonances.

They were there, oh, yes. She had more faith in her abilities after seeing his personal logs. And if the admiral was full human . . .

But he wasn't. Psy-Serv and Sellarmaris Biocybernetics had seen to that.

Eden chewed absently on her bottom lip and went back to her office to log off duty. She needed some serious downtime. She had to talk to Jace Serafino. And she wasn't sure he was going to like what she had to say.

NOVALIS

Jace reached for Eden's hand and drew her down beside him on the bench. *What's the news?*

There's not enough for me to risk surgery right now. There were references to what I need to know, but the data wasn't there. Eden shook her head. *I'm sorry.*

Don't be. I'm a great believer in all things in their right time. Like you coming into my life. I don't think we met just so you could dig a hole in my head.

She swatted at him playfully. *I wouldn't dare dig*

a hole in your head. All kinds of gremlins would leak out!

Gremlins, eh? Jace responded with a comical growl and drew her against his chest, nuzzling her neck. Eden shrieked, laughing, and finally managed to break free.

She wiped at her eyes. *Jace, stop it! I still have something serious to discuss with you. Just because I couldn't find the data I need to remove the implant doesn't mean I didn't find anything at all.*

I'm listening.

I think I can disable it. In fact, I think I'll have to. She flashed to him all she'd read about the implant's inevitable deterioration.

Damn. He was definitely not pleased with the news. *How much time do I have before I self-destruct?*

You're not going to self-destruct. As for time, you still have several months before any irreversible damage sets in. Now that we'll have Kel-Paten's cooperation—

The Tin Soldier's cooperating with you? What the hell happened?

She hesitated a moment, indecisive about revealing something so personal. Something that, as Tasha said, wasn't supposed to be public knowledge. She wanted to trust Serafino—he had been honest with her so far, even about his own failings. She just hoped his long-standing feud with Kel-Paten didn't override his good sense.

What happened started twelve years ago. She hesitated, needing clarification before she went further. *Jace, I need to know more about this Faction that wants Sass out of the way. You said they put her on the* Vax *to accomplish that. What leads you to believe that?*

From what I've been able to piece together, there are several key people that they want to control or to neutralize. Captain Sebastian's name is one that came up on several occasions.

Why do you think that Kel-Paten's involved?

The Tin Soldier was adamant during the peace negotiations about Sebastian's assignment to the Vax. *He made a few threats and then a few concessions, and here she is. Given that Kel-Sennarin is one of his superiors, I couldn't think of any other reason.*

She could, but if she hadn't read the admiral's private logs, she'd still doubt her own empathic readings of him. *Do you remember what happened in the session in the ready room?*

Mostly. Why?

You said you sensed a heat from the admiral.

He frowned, his blue eyes darkening. *Did I? There are a number of blanks in my mind. I'm sorry.*

So that was Serafino and not Jace's Nasyry side picking up on what was going on between Kel-Paten and Tasha. Evidently he always had a low-level empathic ability, even with the implant. But until she could get Jace talking to Serafino—as she'd started to think of his two existences—the full story on anything wouldn't come out.

Eden?

I could explain what I think is going on with Kel-Paten, but I'd rather have you see it for yourself, she told him, laying her hand reassuringly on his arm. *Because I don't think Kel-Paten understands what's happening. I could use your telepathic guidance, Jace. And your experience with Psy-Serv.*

Right now my telepathic guidance is limited.

That's why I have to disable the implant. That should give you more control and give us some more answers. Believe me, we need answers.

He nodded slowly, but she saw and sensed a tension in his smile. And he felt her question. *I don't know what's going to happen when you put me back together. I don't want to lose your friendship. Your respect. I've come to value that.* He brushed his thumb gently across her cheekbone. *No matter what happens, don't give up on me, Doc. Promise me.*

A lump formed in Eden's throat at the intensity and fear in his words. She knew if she had to answer him out loud at that moment, she wouldn't be able to. But there were advantages to telepathy. *I promise. No matter what happens.*

The gray mists cleared. Reilly's furry presence was warm against her arm. Eden Fynn stared at her cabin's ceiling in the darkness and wondered about her promise. But which Jace Serafino emerged from surgery wasn't even on her mind. As long as one of them did.

Eden's real fear was that in trying to save one, she might kill them both.

CAPTAIN SEBASTIAN'S OFFICE

Sass chewed on a lushberry, the last remnants of lunch at her desk. She found it a necessary action when her instincts demanded she jump down Kel-Paten's throat. It was difficult to chew and yell at the same time, so she chose chewing.

He'd barged into her office less than ten minutes before, angry she was back on duty. And angry that she'd told Kel-Farquin's office that she and Dr. Fynn would, unequivocally, be part of any interrogation on station involving Serafino.

She did not know, however, which action of hers made him more angry.

Not that it mattered. He took up residence in the chair across from her desk and made no motion to leave, despite the fact that she told him she had a lot of formwork to do, none of which would get done while he glared at her.

And glared at her in a very possessive manner, as if he owned her!

Well, he was damned well wrong.

But she couldn't bring herself to tell him so, because behind all the glaring and all the possessiveness, she saw something else. Something lonely and afraid that used the advantage of rank to keep her near him.

She popped another lushberry in her mouth to keep from saying something hurtful. Because she didn't want to hurt him. He was her colleague. Her annoying almost-friend.

"There's been more Illithian activity out by the Mists," she said, wanting to change the subject. "When do you think HQ's going to let us loose on that? We could get Kel-Varen's *Nexarion* to—"

"Sebastian." Pause. "I'm not going to discuss that until we resolve the Serafino situation."

"Kel-Paten," she replied, and paused as well. "I

told you. Doc Eden and I will handle it. Unless you feel I'm not capable," she offered, remembering the old adage about "the best defense."

"Or do you feel I'm not capable?" he asked her quietly. Too quietly.

"I feel," she said, choosing her words carefully, "that Serafino will do all he can to drag you into a pissing contest." Or maybe the newly reintegrated Serafino wouldn't. As they sat there, Eden was tinkering with his implant. Either way, she didn't want Kel-Paten exposed to Serafino until she and Eden were sure which Serafino they were dealing with. "He has no history with me," she pointed out.

"Except at Sookie's."

"That's ancient history."

"I've reason to believe Serafino has a long memory."

"So? You think he's going to challenge me to a game of Starfield Doubles?"

He studied his gloved hands, fisted in his lap. "There are other issues here," he said finally.

She almost said, "So?" a second time, but stopped. She knew what the issue was. It was a who. And she was the who, and that was something she definitely did not want to discuss.

She picked up the last lushberry. "I'll make sure you see everything on Serafino before it goes out, and all that comes in," she conceded, or at least tried to appear as if she was. There were things she could not let him see. His infatuation with her notwithstanding, he was still Kel-Paten. Ol' Loyal to the Triad Kel-Paten. Ol' Rules and Regulations Kel-Paten. Ol'

Programmed by Psy-Serv Kel-Paten. It was the latter that worried her the most.

Almost as much as they way he regarded her now. There was that odd something in his eyes again, and suddenly she was on her feet, nervous and uncomfortable and unsure of what to do. She grabbed her empty plate. She knew what to do with that.

"I need coffee." She didn't offer him any as she made her way past his chair to her office's small galley niche. "I have a lot of work to do," she added, without turning around.

Evidently her lack of manners finally made Kel-Paten realize he was extraneous. He shoved himself to his feet while she waited for the liquid to brew.

"We'll handle Serafino together." His pale gaze pinned her, and his words were not a question.

"By your command, sir," she said blandly. She sagged against the wall as her office door closed behind him. Damn those logs of his. She felt as if she stumbled over herself, when she used to be so confident in his presence. On top of all that, she hated being in a position of having to lie to her CO. It wasn't just the fact that she'd arranged for Eden's and her presence on Panperra without advising him first. There was also the fact that she'd arranged to arrive at Panperra by a shuttle of her choosing, not via direct dock, the latter too risky given her plans. But if the Triad really was in collusion with this Faction, then they'd violated the treaty and there was no Alliance. And if there was no Alliance, Kel-Paten wasn't her CO.

It was convoluted, circuitous logic, but that, and a

hot cup of Mahrian blend, black, made her feel one hell of a lot better, professionally.

Personally—well, she didn't want to even think about personally.

She turned back to her deskscreen and pulled up notes on Panperra's layout and maintenance corridors that Kel-Paten would never see.

16

It wasn't at all procedure, but Eden couldn't leave the recovery room, couldn't leave Jace's side. Not until she knew for sure he'd wake up. When the first twinges of discomfort filtered through her empathic senses, she was elated. When he rose to full consciousness, she thought she'd weep for joy.

"How are you feeling?" she asked, though she already knew the answer. There was a dull, throbbing pain on the side of his head from the sonic scalpel and probe.

Jace grinned at her from his reclining position on the diag bed. "I feel like I hit a brick wall. And I'm hoping you'll tell me the brick wall looks the worse for it."

"No, but you should be the better for it," Eden said, and checked the panel readouts. Everything looked good, due to his accelerated healing rate—thanks to his Nasyry physiology. It was strong enough to counter the sonic surgery. Actual physical removal of the implant, though, would have been significantly more risky. Nasyry physiology or not, he'd still be comatose at this point. As Sass had pointed out, they didn't have time right now for a long recovery.

She touched his shoulder. *Other than that damned thing in your head, you're disgustingly healthy, Serafino.*

His gaze shot up quickly to meet hers. *Well, hello! How did you—oh!*

Relief flooded through Eden. She did it! She'd disconnected the implant. Suddenly, Eden saw and felt a series of images flow through his mind. Memories of Novalis, both the ship and the place; memories of her, of a light kiss placed on her wrist and the accompanying warmth that had flooded both of them. And memories of another woman, dark-haired, and a young boy. Bianca and Jorden. Both parts of Jace Serafino were integrating, merging memories and events of the past four years and, to some extent, ones even older than that. There were age-old memories shared by all the Nasyry. Eden saw and felt only the edges of those. Her fledgling telepathic skills couldn't handle their full impact.

He pulled himself to a sitting position on the bed and reached for her before she realized what he was doing. But he only touched her face, three times, temple, cheek, and chin, in the ritual blessing. He was marking her again, but this time it was for real.

She pulled his hand away, held it lightly in her own for a moment.

"Captain," she said, a slight warning tone in her voice.

"Doctor," he replied, his voice low and enticing.

It almost reminded her of Tasha's "Sebastian—Kel-Paten" routine, and she had to shake her head, chuckling slightly. "You're feeling fine," she said, releasing his hand.

She picked up the chart from the nearby table. He tried to grab it from her and pull her back to him.

"Tell me, Doc, do you kiss as passionately here as when we meet there?" He had no need to explain *here* or *there*. His audible words were accompanied by an equally loud telepathic sensation that woke up those damned flutters in her stomach again.

She looked at him with narrowed eyes. "I was right. There *were* gremlins in there and they escaped. Behave yourself, Serafino. I still have a healthy supply of rectal thermometers."

"Eden—"

"Let's put these silly flirtations aside, okay? We have more serious things to tend to." She glanced out the open door into sick bay and saw only Cal and other personnel she could trust. Still, she lowered her voice. "You're back together, in a sense, but we won't know for how long and to what extent for several hours yet. Captain Sebastian and I need to know everything you know about this Faction that's infiltrated the Alliance. We're only a few hours out from Panperra. We don't know what's going to happen there. Whatever information you have could be crucial."

His expression sobered immediately. "I thank you for your trust. And for believing me."

"You still have to convince the captain."

"And the Tin Soldier?"

Eden sighed. "That job we may relegate to Captain Sebastian."

"Kel-Paten," he told her, "will not credit anything I say. I just want to warn you about that."

"We've already had one experience in that area."

"Ahh." He shook his head, his eyes closing momentarily. "The conference in the ready room the other day. There was something...odd, if I remember."

"Do you? Remember, that is? Specifically, anything to do with the admiral and Captain Sebastian?"

He thought for a moment, then his eyes narrowed. "Yes. There's a chink in the Tin Soldier's armor." He looked up at her. "It's Sebastian."

"You made a vague comment at the time about a heat coming from him and that it wasn't anger."

"Extraordinary. A 'cybe infatuated with a human. Sellarmaris Biocybernetics would not be happy with that."

Something in Serafino's tone unsettled Eden. "I'm not looking to compile evidence for a Section Forty-Six. I need to know if what he feels for Tasha is genuine or something Psy-Serv could have planted to throw off any telepath reading him."

He nodded. Eden waited, but he said nothing.

"I know you have real reasons to distrust him, because of your sister," Eden continued when he didn't answer. "I'm not saying that's not important. It is. But first we really need to know whose side he's on."

"I'm working on that, but I can't get a reading on him right now. Not at this distance, not with that damned thing pounding in my head."

Eden felt immediately guilty for pressing the issue. "Then forget it for the time being. There's some swelling around the implant, but that will subside." She checked the readouts on the diag bed. "You're healing nicely. I'd say another five, six hours and you won't even know I've been poking around in there. In the meantime, Captain Sebastian needs to talk to you as soon as possible. Do you feel up to it?"

Her question elicited an immediate devilish grin. "Well, I don't know, Doc." He made a grab for her hand. "Why don't you feel—"

She slipped from his grasp and groaned loudly. "I'll get the captain," she told him as she exited.

She reached Tasha in her office. Not knowing who might be in there but assuming the worst, she went through their agreed-upon routine: "I'd like to see you now for those final tests I mentioned earlier."

"Of course," came Tasha's voice over the comm. "I'll be there in five."

Jace Serafino watched Eden thread her way through bustling med-techs as she headed for her office. It was a rather pleasant view, the soft curve of her hips apparent even under the shapeless lab coat. Compassion, competence, and a very womanly body, well-padded in all the right places. That was Eden Fynn. She fascinated him. She tempted him.

And she also made it clear that she was off limits. She could flirt, she could smile, and then she could go right back to being the chief medical officer, leaving him hanging on a proverbial limb.

He was definitely not used to that. It was he, Jace Serafino, who would decide upon whom he would bestow his charms. And it was he, Jace Serafino, who would decide when to withdraw them as well and move on to the next interesting little flower.

But Eden was more than an interesting little flower. She was a whole garden of endless delights. He felt as if he were locked outside the gate, unable to gain access but drawn by the sweetness of her scent.

It all came together in the few minutes after he woke up—all the memories of touching her, kissing her in their telepathic meetings. All the memories of speaking to her, flirting with her in sick bay. He put together the warmth with the woman, finally.

And she wasn't to be had. Not by him. He felt that very clearly. He was mystified how she could enjoy his company so much and yet be so willing to let him go.

He knew he was charming. He knew he was good-looking. Scores of women had told him so.

And she was still willing to let him go.

He'd have to correct that notion very shortly. Just as he'd have to monitor the situation between the Tin Soldier and Sass. So Kel-Paten had finally learned the meaning of love. Interesting. Perhaps it was time, then, to teach the 'cybe the meaning of loss.

A flash of movement in the corner of his hospital room caught his eye. He turned, tensing slightly, on the alert. But nothing was there. At least, nothing he could see. But yet...

He reached out telepathically, ignoring the twinges

of pain, the sense of disorientation. *Something* was definitely there. And it was laughing at him.

A noise. He looked around quickly. Nothing. Yet he could feel it, feel the presence...

A large black furzel jumped on his bed, landing gracefully at his feet.

"Murrupf!" said Reilly.

"Murrupf yourself," Jace said, badly imitating the furzel's noise. He reached for its soft head, but the yellow eyes narrowed.

Okay, Jace said. *What's the deal here?*

The answer, as expected, came more in feelings and images than in words. It took a moment for Jace to place them in an order that made sense: *Eden. Warmth. Love. Protect.*

You're the doctor's furzel?

Again, images and feelings: *Eden. Love. Food! Eden. Protect.*

I won't hurt Dr. Eden.

Jace saw his own image, slightly skewed, from the furzel's point of view: *Mistrust. Not know. Strong feelings to Eden. Danger! No bring danger to Eden. Love. Protect. Food!*

I promise. I won't hurt Dr. Eden. She's my friend too.

Reilly cocked his head. *Maybe. Not know. Sense danger. Protect Eden. Love. Go Blink now.*

With a flick of his tail he was gone, dissolving into thin air.

That startled Jace for a moment, then he grinned. No mere alley furzel, that one. A high-level furzel, with telepathic and teleportation talents. He wondered if the lovely doctor knew what she had. Or had the animal—sensing her latent abilities—sought her out?

He tried scanning for the furzel again and flinched when something distant yet uneasy brushed across his senses. Carefully, he reached for it, probing, but his head pounded. The damned implant had him worried, making him a bit cautious.

And the furzel too. *Sense danger,* the furzel told him.

Something was on or near this ship. He couldn't tell. It might be more than just the headache stopping him. He could faintly feel what might be the jagged outlines of a psychic block.

But who or what on this ship could do that? It wasn't another Nasyry. He'd know a Nasyry mind signature immediately. No, this had something else, something familiar yet...

No. Yes. He thought he almost saw it clearly now. Sophisticated yet obscure...

Damn. It almost felt like Psy-Serv. Like the Faction.

SICK BAY, DR. MONTERRO'S OFFICE

Sass leaned back in Cal Monterro's office chair. Serafino lounged in a smaller chair across from her. Eden, on his left, perched on the desk's edge, where she had a clear view, over Serafino's dark head, of anyone coming down sick bay's inner corridor.

They were the only three in Cal's office. Cal was poised outside Eden's office to alert them to any "incoming," which included at this point any Triad officer other than medical staff. Sass and Eden figured the ruse about the medical tests would last about forty-five minutes at most before someone—most likely Kel-Paten—would come hunting.

"Okay, Serafino, we don't have much time," Sass said. "To date you've only been able to give us bits and pieces about a threat you call the Faction. I need answers and I need them without the usual lubashit."

Serafino unlaced his fingers and gestured casually at her. "Why do you think I came looking for you, for the *Vax,* in the first place?"

"I have several theories, but I'd rather hear your version," Sass replied.

"You're U-Cee and a student of Gund'jalar's," Serafino said, naming the Rebashee mystic and mercenary. Gund'jalar was well known—like most of his people—for his dislike of the Triad, even though almost sixty-five years had passed since the Triad had forcibly annexed the Rebashee's Danvaral sector. "Everything I've been able to uncover about the Faction is closely tied in with Psy-Serv and key people in the Triad."

"Psy-Serv?" Eden straightened abruptly.

"They don't want to control just telepaths. They want to control everyone. Whoever they can't, they kill. Kel-Sennarin isn't their only double-agent. Kel-Adro was too. But he's dead. Now."

"Unfortunate shuttle accident." Sass remembered the reports just before the peace talks.

"Timely shuttle accident," Serafino corrected. "He wasn't cooperating."

"And what does Psy-Serv get out of this?" Sass asked.

"My guess is control of every branch of government, every branch of business that relies on its services. Law enforcement, the courts, financial institutions, the medical community. Psy-Serv evaluators determine the guilty and the innocent, the honest and the fraudulent, based on their telepathic probes."

"Which they already do," Eden put in.

"But you see, now the *Faction* decides ahead of time who's guilty and who's innocent based on what suits its needs. And that may have nothing to do with the truth. They'll control businesses, even Fleet, the same way. Evaluators loyal to the Faction will decide where to invest and who gets to helm a huntership." He nodded to Sass. "You didn't undergo a Psy-Serv evaluation before you were assigned here, did you?"

"The U-Cees fought that. We don't use TelTal the way the Triad uses Psy-Serv. So it's not part of the APIP program."

"It will be in two months." Jace's tone was ominous. "Think of the uproar when it's revealed that the *Vaxxar*'s captain has past associations with Dag Zanorian and, more so, Gund'jalar. I'm guessing the Faction already knows or suspects—"

"It's not in my records," Sass cut in, her stomach tense, her breathing constricted as if a black-gloved hand already closed around her throat. If the Faction revealed that information, it could split the Alliance wide apart. And the U-Cees would look like the guilty party for having her in their ranks. That could even spark another war. Gods. "I've seen my APIP records and Kel-Paten's personal file on me. They have my connection with Kesh Valirr and my official stint with UCID. But the time I spent on Lethant is still recorded as official leave and sabbatical, showing me on Varlow and Trillas. And there's nothing on Gund'jalar."

Serafino nodded thoughtfully. "If you weren't a student of his, I wouldn't be here now. That's how widespread the Faction is. I don't know who I can trust anymore."

"So you did come looking for us?" Eden asked.

"I knew from my sources that the *Vax* was in the quadrant, knew the Alliance would send Kel-Paten on my trail. I needed to contact you," Serafino said to Sass, "in a way that the Faction wouldn't deem suspicious—even though at the time, with the implant functioning, I wasn't sure why I had to. *Find Lady Sass* kept echoing in my mind for the past few weeks as the headaches got worse. I guess, subliminally, I thought your UCID connections could do something with this." He tapped his head. "But finding this beautiful Zingaran doctor," and he reached for Eden's hand, "was an incredible surprise. And delight." He brushed a kiss across Eden's fingers.

"Serafino." Sass had to bring his attention back to the problem. "The doc tells me you're a high-level telepath. Is that correct?"

"Except when the damned implant kicks in, yes."

"And part Nasyry?"

"Courtesy of my father."

"Any other talents? Healing? Piloting?" She suspected the latter, given his ability to evade Kel-Paten all these years. Nasyry pilots had the ability to read jumpspace fixes without using gate beacons.

"*Nas garra,*" he corrected her. "Pilot guide. Unofficial, of course. I left Ysanti before I could be ranked by my people. Bianca wasn't happy there."

"And that's how Psy-Serv managed to put that implant in your head."

Some of the haughty confidence left Serafino's features. "You know about my sister."

Sass nodded.

"That was their method to guarantee my cooperation. One I intend to fully thank the Tin Soldier for. But not," and he held up one hand as if anticipating Sass's reaction to the bitterness in his words, "until all else is settled. I guess I should be grateful they didn't kill Bianca or my nephew and settled for this instead."

"And Psy-Serv wanted you to . . ."

"Infiltrate the Triad Ministry of Intelligence by accepting their commissions, including this latest one to track down some possible arms running to the Illithians. This isn't my first mission with the MI. Psy-Serv—the Faction—wants to know everything the MI knows. Only they don't pay with credits, they pay with pain."

"They want to know more than what MI knows," Eden put in. "That implant has a recording function. It's giving them your entire life."

Serafino paled. "It's what?"

"I'm beginning to believe that's why they wanted Kel-Paten to bring you back in—alive," Eden said. "They want that recording in your head of everything you're heard, seen, and thought. This may well go beyond your infiltrating MI."

Serafino sat quietly, one hand fisted against his mouth. Eden's revelation clearly disturbed him. "Bastards," he said after a moment. He rapped his knuckles on the armrest, eyes unfocused. Finally, he nodded. "There's another element to the Faction. Something more than just Psy-Serv, but I don't know quite what or who. But that must be what they're really after. What I know. Who I can expose."

"We need those names," Sass said.

"Names I don't have—yet—other than those I told you about, like Kel-Sennarin. Just images. Some odd snatches of conversation. I must be closer to the truth than I realize. I just wish I knew what I saw or over-heard that's so critical."

"Eden, give him a datalyzer, let him record all he knows. Then get it to me. I'll append it to my file on the implant."

Serafino was still deep in thought. He shifted in his chair, bringing his hands together. "They did the same thing to me that they did to the Tin Soldier. I feel stu-pid for not realizing that sooner. You know when he spikes in, there's a two-way data transfer. He might be looking for a particular report. But from what I've heard, Psy-Serv can just as easily poke around in his programs and alter them as needed."

"That's not reassuring news," Eden said, her lips tight.

Serafino glanced at her and Eden's head tilted slightly, as if she was listening. But Serafino hadn't said anything... *Not that I can hear,* Sass realized. But Eden could.

"Love letters? The Tin Soldier wrote you love let-ters?" Serafino stared at Sass. Damn! She felt her cheeks burn, and she knew exactly what Serafino had learned from Eden's thoughts.

"Log entries," she corrected tersely. "And how did

we suddenly get on this subject?" She slanted a narrow-eyed glance at Eden.

"I . . . we *have* been concerned about the possibility that the admiral's emotions might be part of a program." Eden splayed one hand toward Sass in a somewhat apologetic gesture. "What Jace—Captain Serafino—said just now made me realize that was a possibility we couldn't afford to discount. And he—" She shot a hard look at Serafino. "You should ask first, you know, before you go traipsing around in my thoughts!"

Something between a sigh and a chuckle escaped Serafino's lips. "Sorry, sweetling. But there was this sudden sense of worry emanating from you." He turned back to Sass. "So the Tin Soldier is trying to seduce you through love letters?"

Sass glared at him. Serafino held up both hands quickly, in mock defense. His charming, devil-may-care attitude was back, covering what troubled him, she guessed. It troubled her too. Serafino knew who she was, what she'd done. How much did the Faction know?

"I've seen that right hook of yours, Lady Sass. I surrender!"

"They were logs, Serafino." It wasn't just that she'd read Kel-Paten's logs—almost all of them now. It was that Serafino knew and thought it comical. She could tell by the tone of his voice, the squinty narrowing of his eyes, the twitch of his mouth. She felt embarrassed, not so much for herself but for Branden Kel-Paten, and he wasn't even here. "I wasn't supposed to find them, let alone read them. But they came along in the downloads I filched trying to find data on that damned device in your head."

"That's why I asked you earlier about what happened in the ready room," Eden said. "It's critical to know which side Kel-Paten is on."

"More so because you know who I am," Sass put in quietly. "If the Faction pulled that from your mind, they may have told the admiral."

Serafino's mouth tightened into a thin line, then he shook his head. "I haven't checked in with Psy-Serv in almost three months. I wasn't thinking of contacting you back then, anyway. And nothing I can sense from the Tin Soldier tells me he knows who you are. At least, not consciously. He's very attracted to you and very protective."

Eden let out a soft sigh. "I agree. My readings say he's not a threat—not to you," she added with a nod to Sass.

For some reason she didn't want to explore, that information made Sass feel better.

"But keep in mind," Serafino put in, "the Tin Soldier's complicated, a product of Psy-Serv's and Sellarmaris's best. Which means we can't rule out that the Faction could control him. I wasn't fully myself in the interview. Give me another shot at him."

"The shuttle trip to Panperra will be your next chance," Sass said. "Having Kel-Paten against us will be a definite problem. Having him on our side could be a tremendous plus." Having him also in love with her ... was the most frightening thing of all.

Because the woman he thought he loved didn't exist. And the one that did was someone he hated.

And who would be the one to be hurt when he found out?

She shoved the question away, feeling stupid and uncharacteristically sentimental. "We confirmed with Panperra's outer guidance beacon about twenty minutes ago. I've requisitioned a shuttle for three hours from now, if the doc says you're up to it." At Eden's affirmative, Sass continued, "We're going to have to do some fancy dancing on station. I alerted two of Gund'jalar's people, who will help. I need you back on the *Vax,* Serafino, but without Kel-Farquin or Kel-Paten knowing about it. For all intents and purposes, it's going to look like you're on a long trip to their prison on Riln Marin."

"Do I get to choose whose cabin I hide out in?" he asked, flashing a wicked grin at Eden.

Eden had mentioned to Sass that there was "a slight attraction" between Serafino and herself. Now Sass wondered if the good doctor wasn't underestimating things. Well, if he wanted to be near Eden, so be it. As long as Eden had no problem with it. At least Sass knew that someone would be able to keep the rather rambunctious mercenary in line.

She decided, however, not to reward him with that information yet and instead spent the next fifteen minutes going over just how they were going to engineer his escape from Panperra and his return to the *Vax.* And what roles Gund'jalar and the rest of the assortment of rim runners would play, if what Serafino prophesied came true.

When she was sure Serafino understood, she nodded to Eden. "We'll leave now, just in case there's a certain problem up front." She pulled her extra service pistol from under her jacket and held it out to Serafino. "I hope to hell you don't need this."

He took it and tucked it in the back of his pants. Then he touched her arm lightly as she walked by. "It's good to work with you, Lady Sass. Master Gund'jalar always had high praise for you."

"A lot of what I know, I owe to him," she replied. "Watch your back, 'Fino."

Sass didn't miss Eden's questioning look as they exited Cal's office. She hadn't told her CMO she intended to arm the mercenary captain. Her decision to do so violated at least a half dozen Alliance regs and probably twice as many Triad ones. Eden, being Eden, would no doubt quote a few of those, just to make sure Sass was really certain that what she wanted to do was arm a man labeled—and for good cause—a dangerous and volatile mercenary.

It was. Those were Alliance regs. And she was starting to suspect that the alliance between the U-Cees and the Triad no longer existed.

She just wished she knew where the Tin Soldier stood in the midst of the mess.

CAPTAIN SEBASTIAN'S CABIN

Sniff. Sniff.

Greeting! Friend.

Friend. Greeting!

Food?

Food!

The two furzels touched noses one more time before Reilly followed Tank into Sass's small kitchen. Tank sat and looked up at the countertop. Reilly leaped gracefully, landing next to a shallow bowl of cream.

Tank scrunched his pudgy body against the floor and pushed with all his might, managing only to scramble against the cabinet doors before falling.

Shtift-a! he swore.

Reilly looked down at the pudgy fidget, then indicated with a lift of his nose the other side of the counter and two tall stools. Obediently, Tank trotted around and, paw over paw, grunting audibly, managed to pull himself up to counter level. Reilly graciously left a bit of cream for his friend.

Food!

Food!

Sweet. Cool.

Cool. Sweet.

A noise at the cabin door drew their attention.

Sass. Friend. Love, said Tank. *MommyMommy!*

Friend. Sass, agreed Reilly.

"Well, aren't you two a sight!" Sass pulled off her uniform jacket and threw it carelessly onto the couch. The antics of the furzels were a pleasant diversion after the issues raised in her talk with Serafino. She pushed her worries aside for the moment. "Out of cream, hmmm?"

Two pairs of golden eyes followed her movement to the small fridge. Two noses twitched at the buttery smell as more cream was poured.

Sass patted both heads affectionately as pink tongues flicked small droplets of cream over the countertop. "Have to talk to Eden about how you get in here, Reilly." She peered at the air vents in the wall. They seemed intact. "May have to comm link you both and let the computer track you one of these days," she continued, as she entered her bedroom. She dragged a medium-size duffel bag from the closet, then stuffed the usual items inside: a requisite change of uniform plus enough clothes for a two-night stay on Panperra—which, being primarily a commercial civilian station with the Triad's military presence confined to three small docks, promised to be a bit more fun once they had Serafino safely settled. A Legends Fair was scheduled on Panperra for the next two days.

Conveniently enough, the fair's usual pandemonium and plethora of people in costume would also provide the cover to get Serafino off station and back on the *Vax*.

Almost as an afterthought, she tucked the small datadrive that contained Kel-Paten's decoded files in a hidden pocket of the duffel. There was information she wanted to review; information Gund'jalar would require if all Serafino foresaw came about.

She heard the thud of Tank jumping off the stool and the muted *thumpety-thump* of his overlarge paws as he ran into her bedroom. He pushed his wet nose against her hand and then dug under her clothes in the duffel.

"It's just for a couple of nights," Sass told him, guessing at the meaning behind his burrowing. "Eden and I will be back before you know we're gone."

No Mommy leave! No Mommy leave! Tank go with! Tank go with!

Friend. Reilly sat on his haunches and stared at Tank. The little fidget frantically rooted through the clothes.

Friend!

Tank stopped, ears perked high.

Friend. Safe. Safe. All go. All go with. Plan. Go with. Secret.

"Murrupf?" said Tank.

"Murrupf," said Reilly.

"Good boys." MommySass ruffled Tank's fur. "Now go play! Mommy has work to do before she leaves."

Tumbling over each other, the furzels raced from the room.

CAPTAIN SEBASTIAN'S OFFICE

Sass logged off her office comp as her door chimed. She glanced at the overhead readout.

Kel-Paten.

"Damn," she said softly, standing and touching the mag-seal on her briefcase. Then: "Enter."

The door slid open. "When were we denied permission to dock?" Kel-Paten leaned his gloved hands against the back of one of her two office chairs.

"About an hour ago," she lied.

"Why wasn't I informed?"

She met his gaze levelly. "I left that information on your office comp board."

"You could have reached me in my quarters."

She knew that. That's why she left the message where she did, knowing it would get buried under the usual deluge of information every ship's officer received upon arriving on station.

"It's not a critical issue. I've allocated the *Definator* to transport Serafino in and alerted Kel-Farquin as well." She turned away from him and straightened a stack of data files on her desk, hoping he'd interpret her body language: *I'm busy. Leave.*

She was increasingly uncomfortable around him. Now that Serafino had basically concurred with Eden's analysis, she couldn't stop thinking about his log entries. She couldn't stop thinking that, to him, she was his green-eyed vixen. She wasn't remotely a vixen and had never considered herself more than passably attractive. To be the subject of such undeserved passion...

It almost made her more nervous than when she thought he was the enemy.

"The command shuttle is the *Galaxus*." His voice interrupted her thoughts.

"I thought you might be using her," she offered, but that wasn't the real reason. Given Serafino's warnings, she thought it best not to advertise the status of those on board by using the larger craft.

"I will. We will," he corrected. "I'll accompany you to Panperra."

She'd figured that was unavoidable. Though she had hopes. She picked up her briefcase, declined his offer to carry it for her, and looked squarely at him. "If you do, it'll be on the *Definator*. I've already loaded—"

"I'll order it unloaded." He pulled on her briefcase as she tried to step past him. "I see you've put in for a stay-over on station."

"My schedule's clear—"

"The Triad maintains an excellent officers' club there." He looked down at her. She tried to tug the briefcase out of his grasp. "I'll arrange a dinner meeting with some of Kel-Farquin's key staff."

"Ede—Dr. Fynn and I had plans." She stubbornly

hung on to her briefcase as they moved toward the door.

"After dinner we can take a walk through the fair compound."

We will do nothing of the kind! Sass finally relinquished her efforts to regain her briefcase. All she needed was Kel-Paten traipsing alongside while she and Eden maneuvered Serafino back to the *Vax*. She'd have to think of some kind of diversion for him.

Actually, Eden had thought of one earlier. It would also, she knew, keep him from uncovering their deception. Though it would take her out of the action for a while.

Green-eyed vixen, indeed.

She glanced up at him as they entered the lift and tried to put together the passion in the logs she'd read with this always-in-control Tin Soldier next to her. It didn't make sense.

Until he glanced down at her in return.

People often compared his pale blue eyes to ice, but they were wrong. It wasn't the cold blue-white of ice they resembled but the white-hot blue of the center of a flame.

She'd seen this look from him before, but this time—she wasn't sure why—it seared her, touched her, reached something deep inside her with an unexpected heat.

For a brief nanosecond, something inside her almost melted. *That* scared her and made her realize that there was no way, seeing the intensity reflected there, that she was going to be able to avoid him on Panperra. And his presence would create a big problem in getting Serafino safely off station.

She had no choice. She trusted Eden; they'd worked far more dangerous situations than this, and Serafino was nothing if not a master at getting out of tight spots. She'd just have to let Eden and Serafino hook up with Gund'jalar's people on their own. It was their only chance of success.

"Dinner sounds wonderful." Sass tried to put the right combination of enthusiasm and seductive suggestion in her voice and was surprised to find it wasn't as difficult as she would have thought. A little fun and games, a little flirtation . . . she could handle that. "Actually, Eden has plans to see someone special at the fair. I'd have only been a tagalong." She gave him a small, confidential smile. "Are you sure you wouldn't mind my tagging along with you?"

He almost dropped her briefcase. "I think it would be very nice."

He'd moved closer to her. She turned her face up toward his. In the back of her mind she monitored the muted *ping* as each deck passed by. She waited until the lift was just a few pings from her destination before she deliberately stepped up to him, one hand resting lightly on her briefcase, which he clutched against his chest.

"I think that would be very nice too," she whispered. Parting her lips slightly, she leaned toward him, her eyes half closed.

"Tasha." He breathed her name and brought his head down to close the few inches that separated them. She sucked in a breath, arching, tilting her mouth closer to his. And the lift pinged, twice this time, as the doors slid noisily open.

She snatched her briefcase out of his hands and

sprinted through the doors, pivoting after only a few steps and grinning at him.

"Shuttle Bay Three. Half hour, Kel-Paten," she called, and touched her fingers to her temple in a mock salute.

He stood in the middle of the lift, his mouth half open in surprise, his arms raised as if holding on to a briefcase—or a woman—that was no longer there.

He was still standing that way when the doors closed in front of him.

Sass trotted the short distance down the corridor to sick bay, laughing softly to herself and at herself. Who would have thought it would have been so much fun to tease Branden Kel-Paten?

"You look like the fidget who caught the slither-skimp," Eden said as Sass entered her office. "What now?"

"A slight change of plans once we get on station. You have Serafino's datalyzer for me?"

"Everything he could remember. He said to tell you there are still gaps. I'm telling you as his doctor that until that thing's removed, there always will be."

"Understandable." Sass accepted the handheld and tucked it in her briefcase. Then she pulled out a thin datadisk and handed it to Eden. "Here's Panperra's layout. Serafino shouldn't need more than five minutes to memorize it. Meet us in Shuttle Bay Three in twenty-five minutes."

"Us?" Eden questioned.

Sass sighed. "You were right. I am the issue here,

and the issue's going to have to keep Admiral Kel-Paten busy while you get Serafino back to the ship."

"Busy?"

"Don't look at me like that, Eden. This is duty. Lives are at stake."

Eden's grin was decidedly wicked. "You mean you're going to—"

"Have dinner with him. Engage in some flirtatious conversation. Give you time to find Angel and Suki." Sass hadn't seen Aliya "Angel-Face" Kel-Moro since Angel's pair-bonding ceremony with Suki years before. An Alliance captain couldn't risk being seen with one of Gund'jalar's mercenaries. It was one of the friendships she missed. "They'll make sure Serafino's on the right med-shuttle, purportedly going to Riln Marin. Our shuttle. Coming back here."

"And you'll be?"

"Keeping the Tin Soldier as far away from our shuttle bays as I can until the *Vax* heads out again."

And oddly, that assignment wasn't as unpalatable as she once would have thought.

SHUTTLE BAY 3

Shuttle Bay 3—a cavernous, well-lighted bay in the mid-aft portside section of the *Vax*—housed two of the huntership's five shuttles: the larger *Galaxus* and the smaller *Definator*. Both were elliptical in shape, their silver hull plating emblazoned with the *Vax*'s signature dragon-and-lightning-bolt symbol. When Sass arrived, cargo 'droids were transferring luggage from the smaller shuttle to the larger.

Admiral's orders.

She sighed and found the lanky young ensign in charge of the transfer. "She's fully fueled?" She laid her hand against the shuttle's fuselage.

The ensign saluted smartly. "Yes, ma'am! I double-checked myself. She was last in for maintenance ten days ago. Everything's optimal."

For whom? she wondered briefly. Was there some reason Kel-Paten insisted on using the *Galaxus* other than that she was the traditional command shuttle? *Paranoia,* she chastised herself. She was getting like the Tin Soldier.

She let the ensign get back to his duties with a word of thanks. He turned back to an antigrav flat as it floated the luggage toward the *Galaxus*'s under-belly. A Strata-class shuttle, the *Galaxus* could comfortably seat up to ten people, with a commensurate storage area aft. She was similar in design to a medium-size luxury transport, with a large cockpit area forward of the main cabin. Like a luxury transport, she had a small galley and full sanifac. Unlike a luxury transport, she also had a fully stocked battle-gear locker, a full weapons array, and an enhanced shield-and-scanner system.

Sass was into her preflight check when the sound of the corridor doors opening alerted her to the arrival of Eden, Serafino, and a small security contingent, headed by the muscular Garrick.

"Everything secure as per your orders," Garrick told her as Eden and Serafino climbed the short flight of steps to the shuttle's interior.

"Excellent, Lieutenant." That meant the pistol she gave Serafino was still in his possession and that the sonicuffs that bound his hands in front weren't locked. Garrick knew that when she asked for the unusual, there was always a damned good reason. As her crew on the *Regalia* used to say, there were rules and then there were Captain Sebastian's rules. And the latter usually won out.

Sass had the preflight completed, luggage loaded, her passengers seated comfortably, and herself ensconced in the pilot's seat when Kel-Paten arrived, promptly on time. She heard his heavy footsteps on the stairs and then his muted acknowledgment to Eden. When she heard nothing more, she looked away from the datascreen to find him standing in the cockpit's wide hatchway, a questioning expression on his face.

She could guess at part of it: she was in the pilot's seat, his normal role.

The other part was no doubt their aborted flirtation in the lift. For a moment she felt guilty, remnants of those damned logs surfacing in her mind. But she wasn't, she assured herself, trying to hurt him. She was simply becoming a little more friendly. Nothing wrong with that. Especially since he cared about her. That had to mean he couldn't be part of that Faction Serafino had warned about. It might not make him any less a pain in the ass, but at least he was a pain in the ass who was on their side. She offered him a welcoming smile.

"Ready when you are, Admiral," she said, and turned away to check the latch on her safety straps.

"Sebastian." He slid into the copilot's seat, locked his own straps, and activated the instruments without further comment.

"Bridge, this is Captain Sebastian. Requesting departure clearance, Shuttle Bay Three."

"Clearance granted, Captain." Timmer Kel-Faray's voice sounded through the cockpit's overhead speaker. "Initiate departure sequence."

"Initiating." Her mind clicked into its piloting mode as her fingers tapped the codes. Inside the bay, a small siren wailed. The lights over the corridor doors went from green to cautionary yellow. The ship's computers scanned for life forms and, finding none, the corridor door lights changed to red and the door sealed.

Directly in front of the *Galaxus,* a ring of red lights delineated the outer-bay doors. They flashed and departure systems confirmed their imminent opening.

Sass activated the shuttle's antigrav thrusters just as the air was sucked from the bay.

The wide doors disappeared into the wall, revealing the immense black starfield beyond. Panperra Station wasn't visible; the shuttle would have to clear the huntership first, then drop below her before the multilevel artificial world was visible.

"Main thrusters online," Sass said.

"Confirmed," Kel-Paten replied. "Full power in ten seconds. Nine. Eight. Seven."

She and the admiral worked in synchronization as the shuttle glided through the bay doors, then made a sharp bank to starboard.

"*Galaxus* to bridge. We're clear." She relayed their heading, making adjustments on her console.

"Acknowledged. Turning you over to Panperra Approach Command. Have a nice time at the fair if you get the chance, Captain," said Kel-Faray.

"Thanks, Timm. See you in forty-eight. Don't trash the *Vax* while we're gone."

"The admiral would put a stop to that right away." Kel-Faray's voice clearly held a smile.

Not if the admiral's on Panperra Station, she almost said, but Panperra Approach was requesting her ship ident and clearance codes. She relayed that information and then waited for docking instructions. The momentary lull gave her the chance to question just why Timm Kel-Faray didn't know that Kel-Paten was on the shuttle.

"You didn't tell Kel-Faray—?" The nav comp's chime interrupted her question.

"Theta level security docks," Kel-Paten read out loud as the data scrolled over his screen. "ETA thirty-five minutes, given the current traffic."

The current traffic included at least fifteen freighters waiting for docking clearance and another five commercial transports reporting on an incoming heading through the jumpgate.

"Acknowledged," Sass replied, keying in course adjustments while listening to the pilot-to-pilot chatter on the cockpit speakers. At a thirty-five-minute ETA, she knew the *Galaxus* had been bumped ahead of some of the freighters, the captains of which would be none too pleased. But they all understood, seeing the familiar silhouette of the *Vaxxar* in the distance. Rank had its privileges.

But the *Galaxus* wasn't bumped ahead of the commercial transports, as those spaceliners had tight schedules to keep.

She noted their positions, then turned back to Kel-Paten to find out just why the remaining senior officer on the *Vax* had no idea of the admiral's whereabouts. But she barely got out her first word when an alarm erupted loudly. Five sleek alien fighters—idents scrambled—came screaming through Panperra's jump-gate, weapons signatures hot. They veered suddenly, dropped into a kill-or-suicide formation, and headed straight for the *Galaxus*.

18

ALLIANCE COMMAND
SHUTTLE *GALAXUS*

The *Galaxus* was already more than halfway to the station. That was the first thing Sass checked when the shuttle's alarms wailed, laser fire peppering her shields. As much as she would have loved to respond aggressively to the unknown attackers, her primary concern had to be Eden and Serafino. The *Galaxus* was a shuttle, not a fighter craft.

"Panperra Command, this is Captain Sebastian. I need an emergency landing bay." She adjusted the shuttle's shields. Kel-Paten, she noticed, had the weapons system online. "Get me a comm link to Commander Kel-Farquin. Now!"

She muted the microphone. "Who in hell are they?" she asked Kel-Paten. The data on her screens told her nothing other than they were fully capable of destroying the shuttle.

Kel-Paten's data evidently gave him the same answer. "No idea. Yet," he said tersely. "The *Vaxxar* has them. She's powering up."

But it would take, Sass knew, at least five minutes to launch the first squadron of fighters and ten minutes for the huntership to come to full power. The large huntership had been in stationary orbit around Panperra for over three hours, her main drives off-line per Fleet procedure. This was a Triad civilian station, a "friendly" station. Given the proximity to the station, she couldn't fire torpedoes without endangering the commercial and freighter traffic as well as Panperra's inhabitants.

"What's station's defenses?" Sass asked, then, before Kel-Paten could answer: "Damn! Why the hell hasn't Kel-Far—"

"Vidcomm Link One open," the shuttle's computer intoned.

Sass slapped at the instrument panel before her. Kel-Farquin's fleshy face appeared on the small vidscreen. He looked distinctly troubled.

"Captain, I—"

"Commander, we need emergency access to Theta Bay. We'll be coming in hot, full power." She tabbed the thrusters to sixty percent as she spoke. "The *Vax* is in position to render support. In the meantime, the admiral and I—"

"Kel-Paten?" Kel-Farquin's face jerked toward the dark-haired man seated next to her. "You're supposed to be—"

But Kel-Farquin's comment was lost as the vidlink

dissolved under a burst of laser fire from one of the alien fighters.

"Bogey at five o'clock." Kel-Paten responded by activating the aft lasers and returning fire. "Shields holding at ninety-five percent. No structural damage. What's our ETA?"

"We're still ten minutes out. But I think we can— shit!" The shuttle jerked as another round of laser fire slashed her shields. "Damn it! Who are they?"

Several thoughts clamored for her attention. The mysterious ability of the unknown fighters to infiltrate Triad space. Serafino's warning that the Faction wanted both her and Serafino terminated. His suspicions—which she'd oh-so-recently decided to dismiss—that Kel-Paten might somehow be the agent for that. Kel-Paten's insistence on using the command shuttle to transport Serafino. And both Timm Kel-Faray's and Commander Kel-Farquin's ignorance of Kel-Paten's actions. But more than that, Kel-Farquin's surprise at finding Kel-Paten on board.

Was the admiral here to deliver them to the enemy?

There was no time to puzzle it out. The shuttle dipped harshly as Sass tried to shake the three fighters now on their tail. Kel-Paten seemed to be intent on targeting them. Still . . .

She tapped at the shuttle intercom. "Serafino! Get your ass up front! You too, Fynn."

Serafino burst through the cockpit doorway, Eden in tow. "What the hell's going on? Who'd we pick up?"

The shuttle rocked again from laser impact. "A handful of unfriendlies," Sass said quickly, aware the admiral stared at her, "who seem to be very interested in us."

"What's Serafino—" Kel-Paten began, but she overran his question with a forceful one of her own.

"You tell me, Kel-Paten. You're the one who insisted on transporting Serafino in the *Galaxus*. And you're the one who didn't tell Kel-Faray of your plans. Just whose side are you on?"

"Whose?" He looked from her to Serafino and back to her again. Eden, no doubt knowing someone had to mind the store while these three fought it out, slid into the open station to the right of the admiral and brought the instruments online.

"Why did you change to the *Galaxus*?" Sass asked angrily.

"It's the command shuttle. What are you getting at?" His pale eyes narrowed.

"I'm getting at the fact that you made sure we're transporting a highly controversial prisoner in a highly visible craft, Admiral. We're doing the expected. Or is it the requested?"

"Are you implying—"

"No, sir, I'm *stating*. I'm stating that these changes were made to accommodate those who want both Serafino and myself out of the way." Sass turned to Serafino standing behind her. "Isn't that how you put it?"

Before Serafino could answer, Kel-Paten grabbed her armrest and swiveled her chair in his direction. "Do you really think I would—"

"Incoming, three o'clock," Eden said loudly. "Shields eighty percent and holding. Tasha—"

"Taking evasive action, Doc, and thank you!" She

returned her attention momentarily to the shuttle's instruments. Why the hell hadn't Panperra sent assistance?

"I don't know, Kel-Paten." She replied to his question through clenched teeth. "But if you've set me up and I live through this, I promise you I will dismantle you, piece by piece, and sell you as scrap."

Something painful flashed across Kel-Paten's face. She knew the vehemence of her words had cut him. She might have threatened to kill a man, but only to a 'cybe would she threaten dismantling. Like an unusable KS3 unit or a malfunctioning bar 'droid.

He released his hold on her chair and sat back abruptly. "You're wrong." His voice was strained.

"Am I?" She glanced at Serafino, who'd strapped himself in at the small-weapons station next to her and worked with the data Eden fed to him. "Scan him, 'Fino. I need to know everything, and I need to know now!"

"Scan?" Kel-Paten focused on Serafino, then suddenly jerked back as if he'd been hit. "Mindsucker!" He spat out the word and whipped his face to the right as if by so doing he could break the probe.

"Nasyry mindsucker," Serafino said quietly and in a voice filled with pride.

Kel-Paten turned back to him, unlatched his straps, started to rise.

"Sit down, Admiral." Sass's tone brooked no argument. Neither did the Ryfer in her hand. She pointed it not at his head or his chest—both areas cybernetically protected through layers of microfine but impenetrable plasteel—but at a small vulnerable area at his throat. U-Cee Intelligence was thorough.

He took his seat again, slowly.

"Tasha, I need you." Eden's voice had a singsong but firm quality designed to get her friend's attention.

It did. Sass reholstered the Ryfer, glanced at her instruments, and made the necessary corrections. The *Vax,* she noted, was already on the move, the first squadron wheeling away from her bays. At least someone was on their side!

She felt Kel-Paten staring at her. When she turned slightly, she caught the undisguised pleading in his eyes. He could, she knew, have moved with such speed when she drew her Ryfer that he could have killed her and Eden before Serafino would even have had time to react. Or he simply could have grabbed her arm and, with just a thought, ended her life.

But he hadn't, nor had he even tried. And that very fact—coupled with the pain she now saw on his face—made her temper her words and offer him a halfhearted apology.

"If I'm wrong about you," she told him quietly as the shuttle jerked again in response to another incoming barrage of laser fire, "then I'm sorry. But circumstances right now are a bit strange."

"Tasha, I'd never hurt you." His voice rasped.

"He's clean," Serafino said. "I can find no trace of loyalty to the Faction."

"Eden?" Sass looked past Kel-Paten to where her friend sat at the nav station.

Eden nodded. "I'm not sensing any duplicity."

"But he's also," Serafino pointed out, bringing Sass's laser pistol from the back of his pants and clicking off the safety, "one of Psy-Serv's prized projects. He might've set this up, he might have set us all up, and not even been consciously aware of it. I can't—there's no time to do a deeper probe. Have any tune-ups lately, Admiral?"

She heard Kel-Paten's sharp, angry intake of breath at Serafino's words.

But any comment—or threat—he might have made was lost as the shuttle jolted violently to starboard. Lights flickered. The horrifying squeal of metal straining under impact filled the cockpit. Kel-Paten reached for the instrument panel before him, tried to throw more power to the shields and at the same time locate the problem. Serafino was back at weapons, returning fire, swearing loudly.

Sass worked to coax more power out of the shuttle's engines. Panperra Station was so close! If they could just make it to—

But they couldn't, as two fighters peppered the portside of the shuttle with laser fire, forcing her to turn off course.

"Feeder-valve failure in the port thruster," she told her shipmates over the wailing of the sirens.

"Working on it," Kel-Paten said.

A quick glance confirmed he was. She hated having to double-check him. But so many things didn't make sense. And Kel-Paten—in spite of his denial and Eden's assurances—was the biggest unknown and most likely possibility. She shoved away her fears. " 'Fino! I need some room!"

The fighters forced them out into open space, away from the station.

"Can't seem to break through their shielding," Serafino replied, a note of frustration in his voice.

Sass saw the shuttle's lasers doing only minimal damage.

"Try a reverse phase modulation!" The shouted suggestion came from Kel-Paten.

"Bloody damn!" replied Sass as the shuttle jerked and cockpit lights dimmed again. Suddenly everything went green as the emergency-override power supply kicked on.

She did another double-check. As far as she could tell, the power failure wasn't Kel-Paten's doing. He was working as hard as she was to keep the ship functioning. "On backups!" Sass quickly tapped in the adjustments on her instrument panel. "Switching to manual on five. Four. Three. Two. On manual."

Around her, Kel-Paten, Eden, and Serafino mirrored her movements.

"Navigation online," Eden said.

"Shields at seventy percent but dropping. We have a rupture, coolant feed section four," Kel-Paten added.

"Weapons off-line," Serafino said angrily.

"Shit!" Sass looked quickly from Serafino to Kel-Paten.

"Seal the cockpit and divert power to the shields," Kel-Paten said, already making the changes.

"Rerouting life support takes five minutes. We don't have that." Sass turned to Serafino. "Well?"

He hesitated only a second. "Throw all power to the engines. Head for the jumpgate. The section-four thruster will blow. We'll just have to deal with that."

"Agreed." Sass nodded and moved to implement his idea.

"We're not locked on to the gate beacons," Kel-Paten shouted. "A blind jump—"

"It's not blind. He's Nasyry," Sass answered back. She unlatched her straps and reached across to tap instructions into the instrument panel. "Go, 'Fino, go! You have the con."

She stepped swiftly away from her seat and Serafino slid in, his hands moving rapidly over the panel. The shuttle lurched forward, pounded by laser fire.

"I'll drop aft shields last as we cross the gate," Serafino said.

"Then we can kiss our asses good-bye," Sass said ominously as she grabbed the back of Kel-Paten's chair to keep from falling over. She monitored the admiral's movements—still not sure she trusted him—and felt more helpless than she had in years. Fighters on their tail, spitting death. No help from Panperra. The *Vax* unable to respond in time. Their only chance at escape didn't guarantee survival. The ship could be torn apart by the fierce currents of a blind entry into the gate.

As if he could read her thoughts, Kel-Paten glanced over his shoulder at her, his gaze as desolate as she felt.

Then she heard Serafino chuckle. It was an odd, almost cruel sound.

"Be careful if you do." Serafino looked at Kel-Paten. "Lady's got a mean right hook."

Kel-Paten took his attention from the instruments just long enough to send a look full of hatred at Serafino. "Go to hell."

Mind reading. Serafino read something in Kel-Paten's mind and responded out loud. His answer clearly angered Kel-Paten, but what Serafino sensed, and who it involved, suddenly held little interest to Sass.

The ship burst violently through the perimeter of the jumpgate, raked by energy currents. The *Galaxus* shuddered wildly as Serafino and Kel-Paten fought to keep it under control.

" 'Fino, grab the closest fix!" Sass shouted. They needed a secure energy trail with an active guidance beacon at both ends. Right now the data on the console showed that Serafino had managed to input only one—at Panperra, behind them. They needed that second beacon.

The Nasyry's forehead was creased in concentration.

Kel-Paten had spiked in. "Scanning," he said, evidently not willing to trust Serafino's ability any more than Sass trusted his.

Between the two of them, they had to find something, anything, somewhere—

The ship dropped suddenly as if into an endless cavern, throwing Sass almost over Kel-Paten's seat. Eden pitched sideways, her strap's clasps springing free. Sass made a clumsy grab for her, but Eden ended up on the floor, just as an overhead nav panel exploded in a shower of sparks.

Serafino yanked off his straps and lunged for Eden, pulling her away from the falling debris. Sass saw him grasp her wrist as the ship was thrown to starboard this time, rolling up on one end as if slammed from below. Eden slid rapidly into him, and he locked his legs around hers to keep her from careening into the bottom of the weapons station.

Strong arms grabbed Sass's waist just as the shuttle jerked again. She abruptly found herself in Kel-Paten's lap. Her hands sought his shoulders for balance as a spray of sparks filled the air. Another panel blown. He turned quickly, shielding her. She let out an "oomph" against his chest, then she pushed. She had to get control of the shuttle, had to find a fix, had to get away from the Tin Soldier, who could yet end her life with only a thought. . . .

But he was pulling her back, fumbling with the chair's safety straps, trying to wrap them around her.

Then something yanked her and the admiral out of the chair. Sass swore as they slammed against the wall.

Or the floor.

Or the ceiling. She couldn't tell.

The emergency lights failed. The cockpit plunged into darkness.

The last thing Sass saw from over Kel-Paten's shoulder was the green glow from the instrument panels winking out. . . .

Serafino unlocked his legs just long enough to pull Eden beneath him, his hands securely on her shoulders, his mouth hard against hers.

We're not going to make it. I'm sorry . . . regret, frustration, and passion all washed over her.

Eden kissed him back fiercely, letting her mind flow into his, no longer caring about protocol or patients. She felt his desire, physically and telepathically, felt the tension and the tenderness, felt him fill her mind with his fervor as he wanted to fill her body with his physical being. The latter would never happen, but the first granted her a few moments of something so pleasurable that she gasped out loud. She arched against him in an eternal, primal response, her hands threading tightly through his long, dark hair.

He whispered her name in her mind just as the shuttle rolled over one last time. He was torn away from her and thrown against the weapons-station wall. It responded by buckling, the stack of power units jarred loose from their couplings and raining onto his body like large metal boulders.

"Jace!" Eden screamed, reaching for him. Another wave of energy whipped the ship around. Her head connected with the metal cylinder under the pilot's chair. Pain crested just as Eden heard the sound of bodies thudding against the forward viewport, accompanied by Tasha's very familiar "Bloody damn!"

Then her world went black.

So she didn't see the other bodies that tumbled just as the *Galaxus* began a violent ass-over-teakettle spin.

Friend!
Friend!

19

It was a familiar dream and one that always left him with an empty ache upon awakening. He fought the rise in consciousness and held more tightly on to his fantasy, taking in the sandalwood scent of her hair, so soft against his face. And the warmth of her body, so neatly fitted against his. In his dream she sighed, arching her back, and her round bottom pressing against him caused an immediate reaction of heat and hardness. He groaned her name, drawing her closer, his hand finding the swell of her breasts as he did so. His thumb found a gap in the fabric of her uniform and his fingers slipped inside. . . .

She stirred, let out a ragged breath as one finger traced that taut peak, and he didn't know if it was the sound of her pleasure or the ever-present yellow data readout across his mind that alerted him to the chance that this might not be a dream:

Tactile Data Input—Subject female humanoid—

approximate age: mid 30s—body. temperature 98.6—
respiration fast—metabolic rate normal—

Sweet holy gods. Kel-Paten's eyes flew open. In his field of vision was a tangle of short, pale hair and an immense black starfield. And not another ship in sight. Their mysterious attackers hadn't followed them through the gate, though he'd double-check that once he got ship's systems back online.

"Tasha." He said her name softly, remembering the bastard pirate's comment about Tasha's "mean right hook." A telepath. A Nasyry telepath—something that should have been in Serafino's file and wasn't, he realized with a start. An error or a deliberate omission? He'd ponder that later. Right now he was more bothered by the fact that Serafino had easily pulled the fantasy of making love to Tasha from his mind, along with his fear that—with death imminent—he'd never get the chance.

Yet he didn't feel dead. But he knew if Tasha woke up now and found his hands placed where they were, there'd definitely be that mean right hook to worry about. Still, the intimacy of their position was an opportunity to assure himself of her well-being—since he doubted any of the med-panels functioned right now. He opened his hand slowly, let it rest against her chest, and dropped quickly into full 'cybe function, running a cursory med-diagnostic on her with the sensors linked through his gloves. No internal injuries and only a slight bruising on her shoulders and back, probably from impacting the viewport. She'd be sore for a while, but nothing more.

He simultaneously ran his own diagnostics, expecting no damage and finding none. His brief lapse into unconsciousness, and hers, was due no doubt to a sudden drop in air pressure as life support shut off and recycled back on.

He withdrew his hand, letting it come lightly to rest on her hip as she let out a small, "Oh!" and rolled over to face him.

Her eyes fluttered opened. Her face wore a slightly lost expression. "Hey."

"You okay?"

She seemed to study him. "Yeah. Must have been a helluva bar fight. Who won?"

"I think we did." He had the distinct feeling she had no idea who "we" were.

"Hmpf!" She gave a short, low laugh. "Then the other guys must feel like shit." She sighed, snuggling against his chest.

She *definitely* had no idea who he was.

The feel of her pressing so intimately against him destroyed what little restraint he had left. He clasped her to him and was drawing her face up to meet his own when he felt her tensing, her arms stiffening. He knew that she'd just realized who—and what—he was.

"Bloody damn!" she said.

"Are you all right?" He tried to make his voice sound as normal as possible, hiding the hard edge of passion in it much better than he was able to hide the hard physical response of his body to hers. He shifted position away from her, let his hand fall from her face to the slick surface of the viewport on which they lay.

She followed the movement. It looked as if they were lying suspended in deep space.

"Gods!" Tasha sat up abruptly.

He pushed himself up, reaching for her as she wavered slightly.

"Those ships—"

"I think we lost them. But I won't know more until I get things working." He motioned to the darkened console. The cockpit was bathed in a green glow, casting eerie shadows on the total disarray of cables and floor tiles—floor tiles?—and seat cushions and panel covers and Doctor Fynn's boots—

"Eden!" Tasha clambered around him onto the instrument panel before sliding to the floor. The CMO was curled peacefully around the base of the pilot's chair.

Kel-Paten pushed himself off the viewport and saw a suspiciously damp section of Fynn's shoulder-length hair. He grabbed a med-kit from a nearby panel.

"Let me take a look," he told Tasha as she searched for the medicorder. He laid his hand flat against Fynn's face and chest, then relayed to Tasha what his diagnostics found.

"Concussion. No major internal injuries. No broken bones."

Tasha flicked the scanner on, confirming his words with the unit's data.

"We briefly lost life support," he told her, seeing the worry and concern on her face even in the dim lighting. "She'll come to shortly."

Tasha's eyes were a little wild. "Okay." She drew a deep breath and nodded in what he understood were her thanks. "Let's get this ship stabilized, make sure we're not in danger. I'll secure her."

The *Galaxus* was only slightly skewed. A minor

adjustment to her internal gravs—thank the gods that still worked!—fixed the problem, though there were a few strange clanks and thuds.

Together they moved Fynn from under the chair and arranged the loose chair cushions around her. She stirred slightly. Kel-Paten left her in Sass's care and checked the pilot's console, still worried about their unknown attackers. But scanners were off-line. And the viewport showed no other approaching ships.

"Serafino? Where's—oh, shit!" Tasha grabbed Kel-Paten's arm and dragged him to the back of the cockpit, where Serafino lay under a pile of rubble. "Wait 'til I scan before you move anything."

He crouched next to her, glanced at the data on the medicorder and then back at the man called Jace Serafino. A Nasyry telepath. A mindsucker with who-knew-what capabilities. He would like to believe Serafino was dead, but his brief glance at the scanner plus his years in combat told him he wasn't going to be that lucky. Serafino was alive. Injured but alive. The man had the proverbial furzel thirteen lives.

"Only a broken arm, so I think we can move this stuff," Tasha was telling him. She turned unexpectedly, caught the expression on his face before he could mask it.

"Don't look so damned disappointed that he's alive, Kel-Paten. He just saved your unworthy ass back there."

She was defending Serafino—not only defending him, he thought as he carefully moved the debris, but she'd obviously been on Serafino's side even before they boarded the *Galaxus*. The laser pistol Serafino had pulled was Alliance command issue, and Kel-Paten doubted the doctor owned such a weapon. Tasha had ordered Serafino to telepathically scan him, and he had, without hesitation. Tasha knew Serafino was Nasyry.

He had a thousand questions, including whether Tasha and the U-Cees had known what Serafino was before the mission. But he was equally if not more concerned that Serafino or Fynn had told Tasha about his feelings for her.

He couldn't forget her comment about selling him as scrap. That, in many ways, told him what he really wanted to know.

They supported Serafino's body in much the same way they'd secured Eden's. Tasha collapsed awkwardly into the pilot's chair. It squeaked in complaint. She looked up at him, pain and weariness evident on her face.

Even though he doubted she believed him, even though he knew she trusted Serafino more than she trusted him, he had to try. "I had nothing to do with those fighters."

She was quiet for a long moment. "Any idea of their origin?"

"If our databanks are intact, I'll replay all images we have of them. But right now, no."

"Were they after us or Serafino?"

"I don't know." He saw skepticism in the slight narrowing of her eyes. "I'm not lying, Tasha."

"We need to have a serious, honest talk, Kel-Paten," she said after a moment's silence—during which, try as he might, he could read neither her face nor her eyes. "But we have more-pressing issues, starting with ship's status." She ran one hand through her hair, then turned to the damaged instrument panel at her station.

She was right, they did. He leaned against the back of her chair, studied the data as she did. It told him virtually nothing that he couldn't discern with his own eyes. They were alive and in deep space. Somewhere. Life support functioned but minimally so, and only in the cockpit. The ship's structural damage was unknown, as was fuel reserve, engine status, their supplies.

The only good news, as one scanner suddenly flickered to life, was that the mysterious attack squadron had disappeared.

Tasha turned her face toward him. "Can you spike in, or are the systems too far gone for that?"

He eased himself down in the copilot's chair, faced her, and rested his elbows on his knees. "I can try. No promises."

"Could it damage your systems?"

"No." He turned abruptly away. Not *could it damage you*. Your *systems*. He heard the words and hated them. "There are safeguards. But I need to sit there," he added, nodding to the pilot's chair she occupied.

She changed seats with him. He tried to forget that she watched as he tugged down his right glove, sliding the small plasteel flap that covered his dataports to one side of his wrist. The arm of the pilot's chair housed an extendable pronged input that fit neatly into his wrist, and he pushed it in place with his thumb, his eyes momentarily closed as he put his 'cybe functions fully online.

When he opened them again, he was in the pilot's chair, but he was also in the ship—in the cabin, the engine compartment, the small storage bays. And outside where the vidmonitors that still worked continuously scanned the ship's exterior. He let the data flow into him, scanning and sorting as need be and, at the same time, watching Tasha from all different angles, imprinting her into his cyber memory, into subdirectories of subdirectories he created that no one—not even Psy-Serv—could find and erase.

The image this time was a Tasha he'd never seen before. Disheveled, tired, and in pain. Worried. About Fynn, he surmised, as she kept glancing toward her friend on the floor. Once or twice she looked at him, but he was in profile to her, seeing her not through his physical eyes but through the various monitor lenses in the cockpit.

Finally she unfolded herself from the chair and sat on the floor next to Eden, taking her friend's hand in her own and patting it absently.

He went back to work, very aware that the damaged, malfunctioning shuttlecraft he was linked to was the only thing keeping them all alive.

NOVALIS

The gray mists seemed thicker this time. Eden telepathically felt him before she saw him. And when she did, her relief was so great that she ran across the short expanse and threw herself into his arms.

Jace! What's happened?

He held her tightly. *We got through, though I'll be damned if I know how.*

Eden looked up at him, brushed a stray tear from her cheek. *Are you okay?*

Broken arm, that's all.

She stepped back. *You look fine . . .* She touched both his arms and he laughed.

This isn't my physical self, sweetling, though we can still have fun.

She blushed. Of course. She still had a difficult time adjusting to two worlds. And two existences. *Can I start the healing process from here?* She laid one hand on his chest. *Which arm?*

He held his left arm out to her. *We can join our energies in a healing.*

She ran her hand up his arm, wincing when she sensed the location of the break. *I can feel the break. How odd.* Then she closed her eyes and sent healing energy to that area.

Jace lay his hand over hers, adding his energy to her own. A warmth flooded her. She'd never shared a healing before.

Then his hand traveled up to the back of her neck. *You have a bit of a lump there.* He applied a light pressure. She was aware of the pain and then not. It was as if he drew it out of her.

The Tin Soldier's working on the ship, he continued. *He's spiked in, making himself useful, though he's most uncomfortable doing it around her.*

Around Tasha? Eden questioned. *I've noticed that too.*

Jace drew Eden back against him, lightly kissing the top of her head.

I thought I'd lost you, he said suddenly, his voice rough. She felt an ache in him, a frisson of fear, an anger at being caught so helpless.

She held him tightly, then sighed as his mouth left a hot, wet trail down her neck. He was breathing heavily—odd how even an incorporeal body could exhibit those sensations!

He pulled her against him with such force that she let out a small, startled cry. He held her that way for a long time, his face in her hair, and it was only when she finally began to pull away that she realized he, too, was trembling.

Jace—she started, but he hushed her and kissed her fully, in control again, the pressure of his mouth on hers insistent, demanding.

She nibbled on his lower lip and he groaned. *Oh, Eden. There's work to be done, and all I want to do is play with you.* He looked in the distance again. *Your friend's worried. The Tin Soldier ... well, he's wished me dead a hundred times already. But Sass is upset. So go wake up and tell her we'll make it.* He touched her face three times, temple, cheek, and chin.

And ended by brushing his mouth lightly across hers.

It was getting to be a rather nice ritual.

GALAXUS COCKPIT

Sass saw Eden's eyes flutter open.

"Hey," Eden said weakly.

"Hey, yourself, Doc." Sass grinned, trying to hide her relief. Eden was a Healer. Sass shouldn't have been overly worried about her, but she was. "How's the head? You had some tomato juice leaking out there."

"Throbbing, but it's getting better. I . . . we worked on that."

Sass glanced back at Serafino's quiet form. The Nasyry had healing powers too. "Wondered what took you so long. He has—"

"A broken left arm." Eden struggled to sit up. "We're working on that too. And you?" She accepted Sass's hand in assistance. Sass knew it was for more than just support. Her CMO often did quick med-scans with a touch. Her next words confirmed that was part of her reason. "Last time you felt like that was in that bar fight in Port Braddock. The one where the Cryloc hit you with the bar stool."

"While my back was to him, the coward!" Sass said, and then sighed. "Wondered why this felt so familiar. Odd how the mile markers in my life are a collection of bar fights."

She pulled Eden up with her. "He's checking on the damage," she said with a nod to where Kel-Paten sat behind them. "Should we wake up Serafino? Maybe he can give us a hand, even if he only has one usable one."

Eden accepted the med-kit from Sass and turned her attention to Serafino. Sass returned to the co-pilot's chair and sat, her legs crossed underneath her. Kel-Paten watched her, his eyes luminous.

"Doctor Fynn is fine." His voice when he was

spiked in was always a bit softer than normal and oddly monotone. And he was more prone to make statements than questions, even when those statements *were* questions.

Sass nodded. "Bit of a headache from the concussion, but she can deal with that, as well as with Serafino's arm." She ran her hand over the lifeless instrument panel. "What's the situation? Do we need to send out a distress signal?"

It took a moment before he answered. "We've sustained major damage to engine section four. I'd estimate at least four to six hours to repair it. Life support is functional, the main power grid is stabilized, and the scanner array is functioning at seventy-eight percent capacity. In essence, we have enough food, water, and power to last us approximately two weeks, should we require it.

"That's the good news," he added.

She turned back to him. She didn't like the way he said that last sentence at all.

"The good news? Meaning?"

"Meaning there is bad news, Sebastian."

"Which is?"

"I have no idea of where we are or how to get back to Triad space. Or even U-Cee space, for that matter. Nothing in our nav files matches what I find out there." He thrust his chin toward the viewport.

Sass leaned back in the chair and regarded him in disbelief. "You're kidding."

"I do not kid."

No shit, she thought. "There's nothing familiar out there?" She pointed to the starfield. "Not a star? Not a constellation? No guidance beacon to get a fix on?"

He was kidding. He had to be kidding. But the finality in his voice when he answered made her stomach clench.

"Nothing."

Lubashit on a lemon. They were lost.

GALAXUS

Lost. In a damaged shuttle.

Not a sturdy, functional Raider-class transport but a bloody, godsdamned luxury command shuttle! If it wasn't such a frightening realization, Sass would've laughed.

"That can't be!"

"Why not?" Kel-Paten's demeanor was annoyingly calm. "We've not charted our entire galaxy."

"Yeah, but, we've charted—and by 'we' I mean, you, me, the Irks, the Rebashee, the Tsarii, and a handful of others," she ticked off the names on her fingers as she spoke. "We've charted a really big chunk of it. You'd have to go damned far to get to a point where nothing correlated with even the edge of one of the charts."

"I believe we have."

"*You* believe?" she repeated, her voice rising.

"Sebastian..."

"Don't 'Sebastian' me, Kel-Paten. You *could* be wrong."

"I could. But the *Galaxus*'s nav comps are intact. And correct."

"That's impossible." She glanced to the back of the cockpit. "Maybe Serafino can help. The Nasyry have been around a lot longer, and a lot farther, than any of us."

The bright glow in his eyes flared briefly. "How long have you known he's Nasyry?"

"Two, three days," she replied after a moment, knowing he wouldn't be satisfied with that answer and knowing they were opening a can of frinkas here. But if they were going to find a way to get home, maybe it was time that particular can was opened. "Eden told me."

"Dr. Fynn—"

"Is a telepath too. Yes." Might as well cut to the chase.

"Her personnel records—"

"She didn't know. Working with Serafino uncovered it. She confirmed he's Nasyry, or half Nasyry. And if Eden says so, then it's so." She tried to look sternly at him but failed. She was too damned tired.

Evidently so was he. With something that was a cross between a sigh and a groan, he slid his wrist from the contact cradle embedded into the arm of his chair. Then he closed his eyes briefly, letting his head rest against the high back of the seat.

"You okay?" she asked softly after a few minutes.

He turned his head toward her, his eyes once again

their familiar pale hue. "It's something I've gotten used to."

She ran her hands over her face, his soft, apologetic tone tugging at her. That, and the realization that he more than likely wasn't behind the attack by the mysterious fighters. Kel-Paten was a perfectionist. Had Kel-Paten orchestrated the attack, they would have succeeded. "I'm sorry. I know you're just doing what you have to do." She hesitated. "Are we really lost?"

"Technically, no. I know exactly where we are. It just doesn't relate to anything in our nav comps."

"Let's look on the bright side, then. That means there's a whole galaxy of pubs out there that haven't banned me. Yet."

"If Serafino can't help us, finding those pubs may become your full-time job," he said. "We're going to need supplies, eventually."

True. "Did your scans pick up any habitable worlds?" It would be nice to know there were a few places they could bunk in with breathable air and potable water. "Or how about a station, a miners' raft?"

"No rafts or stations yet, but I've only scanned based on our known frequencies. I'll recode a second scan shortly. But as for habitable worlds, a few possibilities. I'll know more once we get the engines back online and full power restored."

Sass looked out at the silvery points dotting the blackness, hoping that a planet would suddenly send up some sort of welcome flag, something like *Beer Here! One-Credit Shots 1900 Hours to Closing!*

Kel-Paten's voice cut into her wishful thinking.

"Go check on Serafino. Sounds like he's functional now. I won't be able to make the proper appreciative noises at his survival."

"Aye, sir. By your command." She gave him a wry smile and vacated her seat, surprised at his candor. Evidently there were times he could act almost a little bit human.

Friend? Sleep. Sleep. Tank hurt.

Friend. No sleep. Sleep bad. Alert! Alert! Help Friend. Help Sass. Help Mommy.

Friend ... hurt ...

Reilly hurt too. Friend. Alert! Help. Soon food. Soon.

Food?

Food. Soon.

Sass sat cross-legged on the floor next to Jace while Eden activated the small bone-regeneration device on his left arm. In six to eight hours he'd have little more than some tenderness at the area of the break. "Though the admiral may never tell you so, we're both appreciative of what you've done."

"What I've done," Jace said, from his position propped against the bulkhead wall, "is get us into a blind jump. I already explained to Eden that I did not get us out. I thought," he continued, with a nod to Kel-Paten in the pilot's seat, "he might have spiked in and taken control. But evidently not, from what you tell me."

"Then who pulled us out? Someone had to initiate

the deceleration sequence. The computers were off-line; we were on manual," Sass said, remembering their wild ride.

"Could you or the admiral have done that by mistake?" Eden briefly glanced up from the medicorder. "Hit something when the ship inverted and you ended up on the viewport?"

"Unlikely," Sass replied. "The only other possibility is the emergency shutoff, and that's not even up front. It's back..." and she turned toward the rear of the cockpit, toward a long access panel whose door was skewed on its hinges. There was a broken air vent directly above it. And a yellow furzel collar torn in half, snagged on a jagged edge of the vent.

Sass's stomach clenched and her heart stopped at the same time.

She sprang to her feet. "Kel-Paten!" She didn't know quite why she called for him. Except she was afraid that if she found what her sinking heart told her she was going to find, she was going to need something large and immovable to pound on in her grief. He was the largest and most immovable thing she knew.

She yanked on the access-panel door as he strode up beside her.

"The door's stuck!" she cried. "I need in there. Now!"

Deities be praised, he didn't question but tore the panel off its hinges.

And there, balancing on the metal emergency shutdown bar, were two furzels—one rather large black one with a white tuxedo blaze, and a smaller, more furry black and white one. A fidget, really, with his collar tangled in the equipment.

"How in hell—?" Kel-Paten's question ended abruptly as he was roughly shoved aside by two laughing and crying women.

"Tank!"

"Reilly!"

Kel-Paten watched from the pilot's seat as Tasha, her face still damp from tears, gently rubbed the shoulders of the pudgy creature that fit nicely in her lap as she sat cross-legged on the floor. He had never heard of furzel massage. But that evidently was what was being performed at Fynn's medical direction.

The larger furzel in Fynn's lap didn't fit as well but received the same loving attention.

When I die, Kel-Paten considered thoughtfully, noting the adoring look Tasha bestowed on the small furzel as she and Fynn discussed what had happened, *I think I know exactly what I want to be reincarnated as.*

Serafino, in the copilot's seat, leaned toward him, his voice low. "They're traditionally neutered at six months. You might not find that as rewarding. Or maybe you might not even notice."

Kel-Paten started slightly, the comment making no sense. Then he realized what had happened. Serafino had picked a thought out of his mind—again. Biting back a response, he automatically activated an additional set of mind filters. He shot Serafino a look of pure venom. Serafino shrugged, unconcerned.

But no rejoinder. Good.

Then he caught the narrowing of Fynn's eyes.

She'd evidently heard Serafino. Had she been reading his thoughts all along as well? He should never have dropped his mental filters. But they were confining, like wearing three overcoats, and he knew they made him act stiffly around Tasha. So he made a habit of disabling them when she was around. Unfortunately, most times when she was around, so was Eden Fynn. And now Serafino. Empaths. Telepaths.

He'd have to be on his guard and try, somehow, to circumvent the programming when he dealt privately with Tasha.

He glanced over as Serafino, with a wince of pain, adjusted his position. Kel-Paten would have gladly added to that, but the show—and that's what he felt Serafino's actions were—wasn't for his benefit but for the doctor's and Tasha's.

"Domesticated furzels form a bond with their human counterparts," Serafino said. Kel-Paten only half-listened to the words, the furzels were of slight concern to him. He was more interested in studying the mercenary, now that the man was revealed to be Nasyry. He was, he realized grimly, stuck with the bastard until the shuttle was fixed and they could return to Triad space.

"Telepathic furzels—they're fairly rare, you know—can also form a psychic bond." Serafino smiled at Fynn, and Kel-Paten didn't miss the slight pink tinge on the CMO's cheeks. Sad. He respected the woman, thought she was smarter than to succumb to the bastard pirate's oily charms.

"You can scan Reilly and know for yourself," Serafino said to Fynn. "But since Tasha and the Tin—Kel-Paten can't, I'll explain."

Tin Soldier. Kel-Paten didn't miss the way Serafino constantly slipped it in and then corrected himself. Another bit of playacting.

Now, Tasha...Kel-Paten had no delusions about his ability to second-guess her, but he did believe she had no idea Serafino was Nasyry until Fynn told her. She also didn't appear totally comfortable with that fact. Neither was he—or with the fact that Serafino's heritage was not part of the data either the Triad or the U-Cees had on him. He hadn't known. Tasha hadn't known. He was sure that rankled her as much as it did him. Perhaps that would be one more thing he could use to keep her allied with him.

He was having a hard time forgetting her remark to sell him as scrap. Or that she'd armed Serafino. But when she needed someone to rescue her beloved fidget, she called for him, not Serafino. Did that mean something? He hoped so. They did need to have that talk—but not with either Serafino or Fynn around. How he was going to manage that in a small shuttle...He turned his attention back to Serafino.

Serafino nodded to the large black furzel now purring loudly in Fynn's lap. "Reilly came to me when I was in sick bay with a warning. With all else that was going on, I didn't take it as seriously as I should have. I accept blame there."

"A warning?" Tasha asked before Kel-Paten could voice the same question. "They knew those ships were going to attack us at Panperra?"

"It's more like something felt very wrong. Because of their bond to Eden and you, they decided to take things into their own hands. Uh, paws." Serafino grinned.

Kel-Paten almost put a stop to the ridiculous conversation then and there but decided it was better to let Serafino make a total fool of himself. He leaned back, resting his fist against his mouth.

"Because they'd accompanied Captain Sebastian and Doc Eden on emergency drills before, Tank and Reilly knew that they'd have to shut down the engine to drop us out of the jump," Serafino continued. "They don't have the knowledge to initiate a shutdown via the command panel. But Reilly remembered seeing the emergency shut off. And, of course, it's labeled."

"You want us to believe they can read?" Kel-Paten had had enough. It was time someone injected some rationality into this insane recounting.

"Of course not." Serafino looked pleased that his comment had finally elicited a response from Kel-Paten. "But it's documented that furzels can recognize symbols or patterns. They don't actually understand the word *fish,* but when they see those shapes on a can of furzel food, they know it's something they like."

Reilly's head shot up and Tank wriggled in Tasha's lap.

"I believe our stowaways are hungry," Serafino said.

Fynn stood and handed Reilly to Serafino. "I'll check the galley."

"Until Captain Sebastian and I can complete our assessment and repairs," Kel-Paten said as Fynn turned away, "we need to keep tight control on all supplies."

"Understood, Admiral."

"And we need," Kel-Paten continued, focusing back on Serafino, "to keep our discussions to useful, factual topics. Not flights of fancy."

A slow smile crossed Serafino's lips. "Guess there's no room in your narrow-minded programming for—ow!" And he stopped mid-sentence as the tip of Fynn's boot caught him in the ankle. The smile was replaced by a sheepish look on his face and a stern one on the CMO's. They were conversing telepathically; Kel-Paten had no doubt now as he watched Fynn lower a bowl of what looked—and smelled—like a meat stew onto the floor. Reilly squirmed in Serafino's lap.

"You might want to release him," Fynn said to Serafino, "before he breaks your other arm."

Kel-Paten heard the warning tone in her voice and felt it had little to do with the hungry beasts and more to do with Serafino's being back in the insult business. He wanted to tell her not to worry on his account, but Tasha's soft chuckle drew his attention. Whether she was laughing at the furzels, now head to head in the bowl and slurping loudly, or at the interaction between Fynn and Serafino, he couldn't tell.

"Time to get to work," she said, pulling herself off the floor. "Out of my chair, 'Fino."

"Where do you want us to start?" Fynn put in.

"Captain Sebastian and I have to get the engines, life support, and computers back to optimum—or as close to optimum as we can manage," Kel-Paten told her. "We can't stay in this ship much past two weeks. I'm running searches now for stations or rafts. But our chances might be greater for finding a habitable planet."

Fynn was frowning. "Can't we just return to Panperra?"

"Not easily." Tasha sighed as she sat in the copilot's chair. "Nothing out there," she said with a flick of her hand toward the main viewport, "tells us how far away we are."

Fynn shot a look at Serafino. Again, Kel-Paten was sure something passed between them. The man sighed loudly as he plopped down at the nav station. "Let me take a look at the nav data."

"If you can find something the admiral and I couldn't, I'd love to hear it," Tasha said.

As much as Kel-Paten was loath to cast Serafino in the role of savior, he grudgingly hoped Serafino could provide them with some kind of fix. He was, after all, the one who'd brought them here—albeit accidentally.

Or perhaps not so accidentally? No, if Serafino had planned a double-cross, there'd already be at least a pair of Strafers, bristling with weaponry, on the *Galaxus*'s screens. Still, it was something he wasn't ready to completely discount. And it was one more thing he wanted to discuss with Tasha.

When—*if*— he ever got her alone.

"If you could make the main cabin one of your first priorities," Fynn said to Kel-Paten, "I think we all might benefit from a little more room. None of us—and that includes you, Admiral—is in perfect condition after what we've just been through."

"Understood, Doctor," Kel-Paten said. "We should have life support back in the cabin within three hours."

He glanced at Tasha. She was working data on the

copilot's screens, and when she glanced up at him, there were shadows under her eyes. Fynn was accurate in her assessment that they all needed some downtime.

He shoved his wrist against the chair's contact cradle, spiked in, and briefly wondered if he'd ever stop feeling uncomfortable doing so in front of Tasha.

No, probably not.

Life support's base programs cascaded in front of him. He saw the truncated code lines, damaged when the system had overloaded.

"I'll handle those," he told Tasha without looking at her. "You check for transfer-point integrity."

"On it," she said, and for the next ten minutes they worked in compatible, if tired, silence. Fynn moved from peering over Serafino's shoulders to tending to the furzels, her footsteps soft. Then a rough grunt broke the silence.

Kel-Paten looked toward the nav station just as Tasha did.

"Damn." Serafino swiveled around. "Sorry," he said. "Nothing in my memory, collective or otherwise, ties in to what I see here."

Fynn's shoulders sagged. "So we could be two quadrants or an entire galaxy away from Alliance space and we wouldn't know."

"Not two quadrants." Serafino turned his chair toward Fynn. "There'd still be something recognizable. A distant star cluster we could hone in on. That's not the case."

Wide-eyed, Fynn switched a look from Serafino to Tasha. "How do we get home? To the *Vaxxar* or even the *Regalia*?"

"First, we get this shuttle operative so that we can find supplies and fuel," Tasha said gently to her friend. "Then we can concentrate on getting back." She paused. "We've been in tighter spots than this, Eden."

"Yes. That's true." Fynn knotted her fingers together, then, with a loud sigh, released them. "Well." She looked around the cockpit. "Well," she said again, more firmly this time.

"I've picked up three possible worlds in stable habitable zones of F- to K-class stars," Kel-Paten said. The doctor was uncharacteristically rattled. She needed something to occupy her mind. And he could use her medical opinion on planetary habitability determination. "I need you to review the data, Doctor, and give us biocompatibilities or hazards. Use the nav station."

"Here, sweetling." Serafino rose and made a sweeping gesture with his right hand.

Kel-Paten caught Tasha's bemused shake of her head out of the corner of his eye. He swiveled the pilot's chair to face the console. Tasha mirrored his movement and looked questioningly at him.

"Let's finish getting life support back on in the cabin and maintenance deck. I'm almost done with the preliminaries." He transferred to her comp screen the data he'd worked on while spiked in, then leaned on the arm of her chair, about to close the distance between them in order to bring her attention to the results of a diagnostic scan, when a small, furry body thrust itself under his arm.

Tank positioned himself on the edge of Tasha's chair and looked up at Kel-Paten with a noticeably determined and possessive expression.

Tasha wrapped one arm around the fidget and

snuggled him closer against her. "Does it bother you he's here?"

"No," he lied. He angled back toward his console and tried to concentrate on the problems at hand. They were lost in a malfunctioning shuttle, out of range of help from any sort of civilization as they knew it. That should be the problem he needed to address. Not that he was on that same shuttle with a woman who'd never see him as anything other than a 'cybe and two telepaths who knew exactly how he, and that woman, felt.

Even her damned fidget wouldn't let him get close.

All he'd need to find out now was that there was something wrong with the shuttle's engines. Then Fynn wouldn't need to file a Section 46 on him. He'd do it himself.

21

"Jace . . ." Eden said his name softly, but not without an underlying tone of warning.

It wasn't that she was angry, though the gods knew she would be if it were anyone other than Jace Serafino whose fingers now oh-so-innocently traced a trail along the side of her breast, sending small shivers of excitement—and distraction—up her spine.

"Jace!" She said his name a bit more emphatically this time. Maybe she *should* be angry with him. They'd been attacked, they were lost, and even though life support was now back on and functioning, they could well die in this damned shuttle. But those were also the very reasons—coupled with the fact that she'd never experienced another telepath before—that Eden couldn't muster her anger. She wasn't ready to die, but if she had to, she very sincerely wanted to do so with a smile on her face.

With a snort of self-awareness, she realized she

likened the mercenary captain to a condemned man's sumptuous last meal.

She turned her face away from the scanner and tried to look at him. But his chin rested on her shoulder—which was how his arm had snaked around her waist and, eventually, his fingers had explored upward. All she could see in this almost nose-to-nose position was an out-of-focus Serafino. But even in such a position she could see he was smiling his usual devilish smile.

"Hmm?" he questioned.

"You're distracting me." Even a last meal had a proper time and place.

"Mmm." This time the deep voice dropped an octave to respond in a low growl.

"How am I supposed to analyze a habitable world with—oh!" Eden gave a little ticklish squirm. "You're making this . . . difficult."

"The Tin Soldier's not here."

After spending almost three hours working on life support, Kel-Paten and Sass had headed belowdecks to the shuttle's engine compartment. Their return, Eden knew, would be preceded first by a series of loud noises as that hatchway groaned back into place and then by the sound of their footsteps through the main cabin.

"You're incorrigible," Eden told him.

"I've never denied it." He suddenly swiveled her chair around and dragged her to her feet, his mouth on hers, demanding yet at the same time teasing.

"You get," he told her when they both gasped for air, "too serious, sweetling. Yes, we have to find someplace to put this bucket down to finish repairs. But there's something else," he said, as she moved her arms up to encircle his neck. "You're worrying, and I know why you're worrying." His voice became softer now, his smile more faint. "I've been apart from people I love too. For a long time now. It doesn't help keeping that worry in the front of your mind all the time."

She leaned against his chest, grateful for his warmth and his words. She *was* worrying. About her cousins back on Glitterkiln, who were unwavering in their support of her when her ex-husband had decided he wanted a "wife with a smaller dress size." About Cal, back on the *Vax,* who never voiced the prejudice some did about working with an empath. And about others on the *Regalia,* who were almost like family. They would believe she was dead, and their useless grief pained her.

"How do you deal with it?" she asked quietly into the soft fabric of his shirt.

"One minute, one day at a time." He kissed the top of her head. "I've been doing better since I met you. I don't feel as lost anymore."

She looked up into deep blue eyes. She understood the feeling. "Thank you."

He smiled. "No, I—" The back of the shuttle resounded with a *thunk* and a *clank*. "The troops return," he announced, and let her regain her seat.

There was a smudge of something grayish on Tasha's right cheek. She looked distinctly annoyed as she stepped into the cockpit and took her seat in the pilot's chair. Kel-Paten followed moments later, looking equally rumpled and annoyed.

Eden looked from the admiral to Tasha. "Bad news?"

Bad news, Jace confirmed to her telepathically, but she didn't know whose mind he'd plucked that information from.

Tasha wiped her sleeve over her face, smearing the gray streak. "We've got a break in the main fuel line."

"Okay, not good news," Eden said, tamping down her initial alarm. "But workable, if..."

But it was more than a line break. It was a *major* line break, Kel-Paten explained, which had resulted in a contamination of the fuel supply. Their estimate of being able to survive in the shuttle for two to three weeks was now drastically shortened. They had maybe three to four days before the *Galaxus* would cease being a shuttle and become a coffin.

"How much usable fuel do we have left?" Eden asked.

"About thirty hours." Kel-Paten's voice showed no emotion, but Eden sensed Tasha's frustration loud and clear.

The admiral's words chilled her. She swallowed hard before giving her own report.

"I've reviewed the habitability factors of the three worlds you indicated. HV-Two appears to be the best choice, as it has a large landmass inside its temperate zone, good biodiversity, and orbits an F-Nine star. HV-Three also orbits an F-class star and has good biodiversity, but it has a smaller temperate zone that's adversely affected by the planet's axial tilt. Either world meets all parameters for supporting human life. However," and Eden sucked in a deep breath, "the closer of the two is more than four days from our present location. At top speed. Which we don't have. So with thirty hours of fuel, the only world in range is HV-One."

She caught a slight knitting of Kel-Paten's brows. Clearly, HV-1 wasn't his favorite either. "Its biggest positive is that, like HV-Two, it has a large landmass inside its temperate zone. Plus it orbits a G-class star. But it's on the outer edge of that star's habitable zone and has a slower rotation rate, which would leave us with very uncomfortable temperatures during its long nighttime. I'm also picking up some compounds that don't make sense in relation to planetary density." Kel-Paten was nodding, and she guessed his analysis was the same. *Guessed* because any of her empathic probings in the past few hours seemed to be meeting a mental brick wall, ever since Jace had—quite wrongly, in her opinion—intruded on the admiral's thoughts.

"But that could be due," she continued, "not only to our relative distance but whatever damage our sensors took coming out of the jump. I'm running tests on that." Tests that Jace's teasing had interrupted.

Tasha leaned over and lifted the chubby fidget into her lap. "HV-One it is, then. Tell us about our new home."

Eden brought the data up on her screen, simultaneously transferring it to the other workstations. HV-1—"Haven-1" as she nicknamed it—had three significant landmasses: one large one in a decent temperate zone and two smaller ones that were polar and less habitable. She ran through the other pertinent data: water regions, mountain regions, the small desert area in the southermost tip. And two moons orbiting the planet, which contributed to frequent coastal flooding.

"Life forms?" Tasha asked.

"Unknown at this point, Captain. We're too far for the damaged sensors to provide that data. In another twelve hours, I should have more information. I'm not, however," Eden continued, "picking up any evidence of technology."

Eden felt Jace's concentration shift. She could feel him reaching out across the blackness of space. Yet she couldn't see what he saw. He'd temporarily shut her out, putting all his energies into finding out what he could about Haven-1, picking up on the life threads that all physical things emitted, sensing its oceans, its mountains, its small and hot desert region. And . . . something else.

But they were too far for Jace to be able to define exactly what that something else was.

Jace pulled back, gave his head a light shake, much as Tasha had minutes earlier.

What is it? Eden asked.

Not sure. It might be just a gravitational flux. Those moons.

Show me.

Difficult to do that right now, he said gently through the curtain that had tumbled down between them. Gauzy, opalescent, but a curtain all the same.

Why not? Is it the implant?

There was a pressure. She could feel a headache starting, but she didn't know if it was his or hers or both.

Let me work with it when we get closer. I can't scan and maintain a connection to you at the same time.

Tasha swiveled abruptly in her chair, jerking Eden out of her connection with Jace. "Talk to me, 'Fino."

He glanced up, amusement replacing the frown on his face. "Do you have telepathic abilities I don't know about?"

"Hardly. But I've known her," Tasha said with a nod to Eden, "long enough. That little dip of her mouth, that twitch of her foot—that's not good. And she was looking at you."

"Jace sensed something in or on Haven-One," Eden explained quietly, unsure of what was happening and not willing to push Jace. Yet. "It could be the moons creating a gravitational flux."

"Or?" Tasha prompted.

"Or it could be a form of energy there," Jace explained. "And, yes, it could be a residual from a flux. But it feels slightly different. And not," he glanced at Eden, "overly happy."

"You can't be serious—" Kel-Paten's words halted as Tasha raised her hand.

"It doesn't like that we're here?" Tasha asked.

Jace shook his head. "We're too far away for me to get anything consistent."

Eden clearly saw the admiral's disbelief as he turned back to the data on his console. Tasha's face showed thoughtful interest. Unlike Kel-Paten, she wasn't going to discount anything, especially not in an unknown, uncharted quadrant.

Jace, please show me the problem. Maybe—

No.

The word sounded harsh in her mind this time, and she started, surprised.

No, sweetling, he repeated, more gently. *It's probably nothing.*

And if it isn't? she asked, realizing that other than

hearing his voice, she was getting nothing from him now. That puzzled her.

We'll handle whatever it is when the time comes, Jace told her.

His *we* reassured her. Though that time, Eden knew, would come more rapidly than she'd originally thought. Thirty hours of fuel was all they had left. Half that time to get this shuttle stable and functional enough to make a dirtside landing.

The unknown energy pulsation seemed the least of their problems.

Exhaustion was taking its toll, and when Kel-Paten saw Tasha waver in her seat, he ordered her and Fynn—whose stability was equally tenuous—off duty for at least three hours.

"Main cabin. Now."

"Kel-Paten—"

"Sebastian." He paused and, in the midst of all their troubles, found the ritual comforting. "Before you fall over. Main cabin. Doctor, you too."

That left him alone with Serafino, but the bastard had been quiet since his ridiculous proclamation about some evil alien energy source inhabiting HV-1. Yes, there were a couple of contradictory readings, including the one relative to density. He knew that before Fynn mentioned them. And there was a gravitational flux pattern he didn't like and couldn't explain. Yet.

But Serafino was ever the showman, and his current show, Kel-Paten surmised, was that of Mystical Nasyry. No doubt very shortly the chanting and burning of incense would commence. Something to scare away the evil energy source haunting the planet.

Something to make him appear the hero to Tasha and Fynn, his current audience.

"Looking to murder me without witnesses?" Serafino asked as the cockpit door closed behind Fynn's retreating figure. The smirk in his voice was unmistakable. He tapped at the dark band barely visible under the edge of his rolled-up shirtsleeve: the bone-regen device. "I'm still wounded. Easy prey, you know."

Kel-Paten turned away and bit back an equally snide reply. He would *not* let the bastard bait him again. He was encouraged by the fact that his fleeting—pleasurable—thought of venting Serafino's lifeless body out the shuttle's garbage chute did not elicit a rejoinder. Keeping his mental filters at maximum was cumbersome but worthwhile. "I think Dr. Fynn would be pleased by an improved functionality of our sensors." He spiked back in and shunted the sensor-recalibration data to the nav station. It would keep Serafino busy and keep him away from his audience.

"Is that an admission you need me alive?"

"It should take you about an hour and a half to get them back to full range. Unfortunately, our current location doesn't provide us with any workable correlatives." Because there were no predamage sensor scan reports to use as comparisons on wherever they were. It was an annoying problem but, considering all else, a minor one, in Kel-Paten's opinion. "We're going to have to assume a margin of error."

"Ah! Not only do you admit to needing me, but

you trust me too." He paused. "Does that mean I'm forgiven for Fendantun?"

Kel-Paten couldn't help himself. He shot a warning glance at Serafino in time to see the bastard theatrically clutching one hand over his heart. "Get to work."

Serafino only snorted in reply and turned back to his screens.

Kel-Paten did the same. The fuel leak and subsequent contamination wouldn't be a crucial issue—if they were headed for a space station or miners' raft. But they weren't. That altered a serious problem into a potentially fatal one. HV-1 was a planet, and that meant an entry—hot—through that planet's atmosphere. And it also meant a landing with a craft that had, at best, rudimentary heavy-air capabilities.

Those capabilities would have to be augmented. He checked the *Galaxus*'s service logs. The ship—only a few months old—had never made a dirtside landing. So here, again, he had no comparative data. Nothing but untested specs to tell him what the shuttle might do as it hurtled through the atmosphere.

He shook his head. Twenty-two hours, eighteen minutes, and twenty-two seconds until they'd reach a workable orbit of HV-1. A month ago, if someone had promised him twenty-two hours with Tasha Sebastian in the small confines of a shuttle, he'd have been delighted at the prospect. Now he felt only desperation.

While part of his mind redacted the information on the shuttle's shortcomings, the other found the main-cabin video links. The ten high-backed seats in the main cabin reclined fully into cotlike beds, but

Tasha's seat back was angled only halfway down, as if in defiance of his order to rest. He watched her sleep, her arms loosely folded at her waist, her head turned to one side. She looked more vulnerable than he'd ever remembered seeing her.

The desire to pull her into his arms was almost overwhelming. He wanted nothing more than to press his body against hers and kiss her until neither of them could think straight.

But that wouldn't work. If nothing else, his own mind ceased to think straight whenever he got within a few feet of her. Plus he believed that her reaction would be to think him straight to hell.

"Fantasizing again, are we?"

Serafino's words shattered Tasha's image in his mind. He spun toward the Nasyry. "Stay out of—"

"That prosti didn't want you." Serafino's voice was soft but had an oily, menacing tone. "Found out what you were. You couldn't pay her enough to touch you."

Kel-Paten was out of his chair in one swift move. He lunged for Serafino, who was standing, arms folded across his chest, laughing. He shoved him hard against the workstation's upper panel, pinning his arms at his sides. Kel-Paten could feel the man's muscles bunch and tense under his fingers. Narrowed eyes met narrowed eyes only inches from each other. But one set of narrowed eyes had a distinct and dangerous luminescence.

A muted noise sounded behind him. He ignored it until she spoke.

"*What* is going on?" Tasha's question was a definite command for information. She stood rigidly in the cockpit's open hatchway.

Kel-Paten couldn't answer her. And he'd kill Serafino if the bastard said one word right now.

It was Eden—following Tasha toward the nav station—who spoke up. Her words were measured, clipped. "Gentlemen. Now is not the time. We have work to do."

Kel-Paten spun on his heels and marched through the cockpit hatchway, his only audible response a fist slamming against the hatchway's frame.

GALAXUS, AFT CABIN

Kel-Paten leaned over the small galley sink aft of the main cabin and splashed cold water onto his face, surprised to find that his hands trembled.

He could've killed Serafino.

He wanted to kill Serafino.

But for Tasha and Eden Fynn, he would have.

How Serafino had circumvented Psy-Serv's best filters and found that deep memory of the prosti, he didn't know. But Serafino had dredged it up from the darkest corners of Kel-Paten's mind as if he knew just where to look. Shore leave on Mining Raft 309. He was a lieutenant and alone, as usual. The rest of the *Pride of Kel*'s crew was off to find what amusements they could in that godsforsaken locale that held a scattering of dirty pubs, two eating establishments that promised a healthy dose of intestinal parasites with the food, and one nighthouse, its crude flashing sign advertising both male and female prostis.

He would never have considered going inside had it not been for a conversation he'd overheard at the dingy bar where he'd sat, bored and restless. There was no casino license on the raft, but there were games. Or, to be more specific, a game. One illegal poker room in the nighthouse.

What he—in his twenty-three-year-old innocence— didn't realize was that the nighthouse, in order to ensure its profits, routinely spiked the gamblers' drinks with any cheap and handy pharmaceutical concoction.

When he started winning, the bar manager started slipping drinks laced with Heartsong into his black-gloved hands.

He should have run an antidote program the minute he was aware of his body's reaction to the drug. But then a sloe-eyed, skimpily clad prosti draped herself in a chair next to him, and the sensation was so pleasurable, he overrode his safeguards, forgot about the stack of chips at his place on the table, and followed the woman down a back corridor and into a musty room that smelled of cheap perfume.

He didn't care about the cloying smell, didn't care about anything except removing his uniform and that thin bit of lace sloppily wrapped around her. . . .

Then she saw the scars on his chest and arms. And as his hands moved to cup her heavily powdered face, she saw powermesh on his palms and the two small ports at the base of his wrists.

She jerked back, her mouth pursed as if she'd just tasted something sour.

"Yer that *thing*, that 'cybe, ain't you? Whassyer name?" she drawled.

"Kel-Paten," he answered automatically, swaying slightly toward her.

"Yeah, thass right." She looked him up and down. "You may look like real people all right, but they ain't payin' me enough to do the likes of you." Then she snatched her lace robe from the bed and bolted out the door.

He stood there shaking, pained. Shamed.

Killing Serafino wouldn't have erased the pain or the shame. But it would have helped.

GALAXUS COCKPIT

Eden sat cross-legged on the floor of the cockpit next to the nav station and sipped at her cup of hot tea. Serafino swiveled his chair around, his back to the nav station, Reilly sprawled across his lap. Tasha— very much in the role of captain—had just spent a good ten minutes laying down the law to Serafino and then, with a sigh, ordered him off duty. Everyone was tired, everyone was worried. Tempers were short. Take ten, she'd told him, and let Eden check your broken arm.

So they took ten, during which time Eden removed the regen band and certified him fit for light duty—at least, his left arm was. She wasn't making any prognosis about his head. Oh, he was still talking to her telepathically. Teasing her. But he shut her out from anything beyond that. She took another sip of her Orange Garden. At least the galley stocked that. She needed some good news.

She glanced at Tasha in the captain's chair, hunched

in concentration over the command console, her aura pulsing tiredness, frustration. Kel-Paten was nowhere to be seen.

Bringing the admiral's image to mind—and the hard, frightening edge of anger that rolled over her empathic senses earlier, jolting her awake—she reached out in thought for Jace, nudging his foot with hers at the same time. *Did you need to hurt him that badly?*

Jace gave a mental sigh.

It's not cruel, sweetling. Remember, he's a protégé of Psy-Serv and no doubt the annual winner of the Most Devoted Triadian Officer award. Until I peel away those impenetrable layers he's concocted, I won't truly know whose side he's on. Whatever happened to him because of Sass opened a hole in his defenses. That's my only way into his mind and his only way out of whatever programming Psy-Serv embedded in there. Do you understand now?

She did. But it was a frightening and dangerous route he'd chosen. All the more so because he was blocking her view of his path—a path he seemed to enjoy a bit more than she was comfortable with.

It had been almost an hour since the admiral stormed off to the main cabin. On a small ship like the *Galaxus,* there was no room for histrionics. But Sass gave Kel-Paten some space because what precipitated his departure had wrenched Eden out of a deep sleep, made her grab Sass and propel her to the cockpit with no explanation other than a frantic "Make them stop it now!"

Sass had stopped what looked to be a spillover from the admiral's botched interrogation of Serafino. He'd walked out of that too. So she knew he needed time to power down. But when he didn't return after a reasonable time, she decided to go after him—not out of concern for whatever sparked the tiff, she told herself. What sparked the tiff was Kel-Paten and Serafino in a small ship. And not because she was worried about him. She wasn't worried about him. He was a 'cybe, and his anger—his love letters to her notwithstanding—was programmed. The fact was, they had to make some important decisions to get the shuttle dirtside. Decisions she knew the admiral wasn't going to like. Best to get that over with. They were about twenty hours out from a max GEO orbit, at which time additional critical decisions would come into play.

Serafino was placing both his and Eden's empty mugs into the recyc panel when Sass stood. The two had been suspiciously quiet during their break. She had a feeling—no, she *knew*—Eden knew what had set Kel-Paten at Serafino's throat. She trusted her friend would tell her when Serafino wasn't around. "You have the 'con, 'Fino. I'm going to brief Kel-Paten on our schedule."

Jace started to head for the captain's chair. Sass laughed and pointed to the copilot's chair. "Over there. I'm still in charge here, big boy."

"Just wanted to see if you'd notice," he drawled with a wink.

"My ass," she quipped back, and hit the hatchway release. His laughter followed her as she stepped through.

Kel-Paten was seated in the last row, staring out a small viewport. He didn't turn when the hatchway opened, or at the sound of Serafino's deep laughter, or when the hatch thunked closed. He didn't turn when her footsteps came down the aisle toward him. And he didn't turn when she sat next to him. It was as if he'd crawled in somewhere deep and dark and locked the door after him. Locking everyone else out.

However, with less than twenty hours of fuel on board and stuck in some gods-forgotten corner of the gods-knew-what galaxy, Sass had no time to mollycoddle him.

"Serafino and I will take the shuttle in," she announced without any preliminaries. "We have considerable heavy air time, and he has more freighter experience than any of us. And this thing, once we hit heavy air, is going to fly like an overloaded ten-bay freighter."

That got his attention. His face jerked toward her, and she was surprised by the bleakness in his eyes. She expected anger after what had happened in the cockpit. Or perhaps even righteous indignation.

The surrender she saw made no sense. Though his question did shed some light on the subject.

"You think I'm losing my mind, don't you?"

"Serafino excels at fraying your last nerve," she said. "And you, no doubt, also fray his. We're all stuck in a rather small shuttle with very little fuel left. Whether or not you're losing your mind is the least of my worries."

"Then why did you decide to have Serafino assist without consulting me?"

She shrugged. "I knew you wouldn't agree. And we don't have time to argue."

"Am I arguing now?"

His tone was too calm. It worried her. But she didn't have time to worry.

"No," she said.

"Do you think I don't trust you?" he asked quietly.

She'd thought that for quite some time. Until she read those damned personal logs of his. Logs she tried hard to forget every time she caught him looking at her with that almost pleading look in his eyes.

Like now.

She picked at some nonexistent lint on her sleeve. "I think there have been misunderstandings on both our parts. You and I operate from different command methodologies." She looked back at him. "I didn't ask Serafino to fly right seat to undermine you, Kel-Paten. He *has* the heavy air experience. It's not like we're going to get a second chance at putting this bucket down."

"You made a wise decision," he told her softly.

She tried unsuccessfully to keep the look of surprise from her face. "Thank you."

"If the engines do start to blow, I can do a lot more good hands on than I could in the cockpit," he continued.

Being in the engine compartment would also put the necessary space between himself and Serafino. "You don't sound overly optimistic."

"I'm not. You saw the damage. The *Galaxus* has only rudimentary heavy-air capabilities. When we hit the planet's atmosphere, we could encounter additional problems."

Sass understood now what was so odd about Kel-Paten. It was as if he'd deleted the part of him that was human. His phrasing was automatic, mechanical. And, save for the humanly strained look in his pale eyes, he was all 'cybe. Unemotional. Reporting the facts.

"Are we talking total engine failure here?" she asked.

"Do you want probabilities?"

She had to keep herself from raising her eyes to the mythical Five Heavens. He was definitely in a mechanical mode now. "Why not?" she replied grimly.

"There's a seventy-six-point-five percent chance of total engine failure. A forty-three-point-two percent chance we'll experience more than a fifty percent loss of power upon atmospheric entry. A—"

"Miracle, Kel-Paten," she cut in. "What's the percent probability for a miracle?"

He regarded her plainly. "I don't believe in miracles."

"I base my life on them."

He seemed shaken by her statement, a small spark of human emotion flashing briefly in his eyes. "Do you?"

"Bet your ass I do." She stood, braced one hand on the back of his seat, and looked down at him. "Any landing you can walk away from is a good one. We're all going to walk away from this one. I'll give you a one hundred percent probability on that, flyboy."

She hadn't called him that in a long time. He closed his eyes, but not before Sass saw the undisguised heat in them.

She straightened, stepping back. She was so used

to interacting on a personal level with her crew, sometimes she forgot and did the same thing with Kel-Paten. Only things weren't the same. He was a 'cybe. And he wanted her in a way a 'cybe shouldn't.

She tossed a light parting comment over her shoulder as she headed back to the hatchway. "When we land, you get to buy me a beer, Kel-Paten. And if we don't make it," she stopped at the hatchway and turned, "you still get to buy me a beer. In the hell of your choice."

She returned to the cockpit, tried to forget the bleakness in Kel-Paten's pale eyes. And the exactness of his probabilities: seventy-six-point-five percent chance of a total engine failure.

Seventy-six-point-five percent chance that twenty hours from now, they'd all be dead.

And she'd be sipping hot beer in hell.

22

"Let's take her in, 'Fino."

Sass tapped a command into the console before her. The *Galaxus* responded, her sublight engines cycling off. And, with a slight jolt, the emergency heavy-air engines kicked on. All systems were—if not at optimum—at least showing green. And, equally important, Tank and Reilly were securely stowed in a makeshift survival kennel just outside the cockpit hatchway. Eden came up with the design, and the admiral somehow created it—from what, Sass had no idea—while Serafino took his required three-hour nap in the main cabin. She and Eden had done what they could to keep the two apart in the hours following the confrontation. The kennel was simply an idea that served double-duty.

Sass glanced at the furzels' life signs, knowing Eden monitored them as well.

They were annoyed, perhaps, at being cooped up, but fine.

She turned back to the ship's readouts and coordinated landing data with Serafino. Eden had designated a southern area of the largest landmass as the most amenable area for them to put down. The CMO's scans showed a sizable freshwater supply, lush vegetation, and, more important, an adjacent mountain range that contained a possible fuel source if they could mine and convert the natural ore. But that was a distant problem. Getting this bucket down was the immediate one.

"Firing thrusters," Serafino told her. She watched their attitude, speed, and temperature carefully. Coming through the planet's atmosphere, they could encounter any number of problems, not the least of which would be in response to the damage the vessel had already incurred.

She tapped open the mike on her headset. "Status, Kel-Paten."

"Holding our own," came back the reply from the engine compartment belowdeck.

"I'm keeping this line open," she told him. "First sign of any trouble, you talk to me, got it?"

"Affirmative."

The shuttle shimmied slightly. Sass glanced over at Serafino. "We're getting some vibrational feedback from the deep-space shields."

"Hmm." He keyed in a few adjustments. "I don't want to reduce them more than that. Not yet. We need the drag."

She noted his changes. "Agreed."

Serafino put the shuttle through the first of a series

of S-curves, bleeding off extra speed. His flamboyance, his arrogance, was noticeably absent, and his focus as he handled the bulky craft was almost Kel-Paten-like.

"ETA thirty-two minutes thirty-four seconds," Eden said from her post at navigation.

"Thirty-two thirty-four," Sass repeated. "You hear that, Kel-Paten?"

"Affirmative."

"Talk to me about the drop in coolant level," she continued. "What's our rate?"

"Moderate," came back the reply.

"Moderate, my ass. I need numbers!" Next to her, Serafino adjusted the craft's attitude as the shimmying started again.

"Your job is to bring this thing in, Sebastian. I'll keep the mechanicals online."

"You can be very annoying sometimes, Kel-Paten, you know that?"

"Thank you."

Serafino raised one eyebrow. "Sometimes?" he said loudly enough for her headset mike to pick up.

"Fuck you, Serafino," Kel-Paten's deep voice growled over the speaker.

"You're not my type, Tin Soldier," Serafino shot back.

"Enough, boys!" Eden voiced her displeasure before Sass could.

The black starfield outside the forward viewport was replaced by a deeper blue, then a lighter blue as the shuttle hurtled through Haven-1's atmosphere. Hull temperature increased, not critically but worth watching. Serafino worked the shields, but Sass could tell by the frown on his face that they weren't responding as he would have liked.

"Thing flies like a rock," he muttered when, for the third time in less than five minutes, the shuttle shimmied almost out of control, her thrusters straining audibly.

"Worse than a ten-bay freighter," Sass agreed. She needed to be able to buffer their descent with the thrusters. But given the damage they'd received, she didn't dare bring them online until she absolutely had to.

Gravity exerted a more potent pull on the shuttle, warning messages flaring correspondingly.

"We have to reduce those shields," Sass told Serafino.

"I don't like this, but..." He made the adjustments.

"I know. Eden?"

"Twenty-two minutes, fifteen," Eden replied, and wiped her hand over her brow. The interior temperature of the shuttle had increased dramatically in the past few minutes and would get worse as the deep-space shields came off-line.

But it had to be. The *Galaxus* wasn't a heavy-air craft. The only way the ship would be able to negotiate in that foreign environment would be to reduce power to the shields and siphon it to the engines and thrusters.

Minutes later, the grating whine of the engines crested, then sputtered. The shuttle veered sharply to port.

Sass grabbed the armrest with one hand and frantically keyed in adjustments with the other.

"Kel-Paten! Talk to me!"

The response that came back was strained. "Thruster failure . . . feed lines one and two out . . . doing what . . . I can."

"Shit!" she said. " 'Fino?"

He was already rerouting the remaining power feeds. "We've just encountered a storm cell. It may not be the smoothest of entries," he said through gritted teeth.

"Seventeen minutes, ten," Eden told them over the ship's rattling and groaning.

They broke through into the cloud layer, the brightness of a flash of lightning almost blinding.

"We're coming in way too hot!" Sass tried to alter the angle of their descent, with no success.

"Braking vanes will shear off at this speed," Serafino noted tensely.

As if in response, the shuttle shuddered violently again, prompting a flurry of activity in the cockpit. Sass watched the readouts with a critical eye. She had no doubt they were pushing the shuttle to its design limits. She was surprised there weren't more systems shutdowns than the ones already . . .

Then she knew. She knew what was keeping them together at this point. Her breath caught.

"Fifteen minutes even," Eden said.

"Damn him! Bloody fool's spiked himself in!" Sass unsnapped her harness and thrust herself to her feet, ripping the headset off. " 'Fino, you have the con. Just do what you can!" She bolted through the cockpit hatchway, past the kennel, and ran toward the rear of the craft.

Sass scrambled down the ladderway into the engine compartment, one look confirming her guess.

Kel-Paten sat on the floor next to the dismantled main power panel, datalinks snaking from the panel to the small ports in his left hand. His head was bowed, his breathing ragged.

She hunkered next to him and grabbed his forearm. "What in hell do you think you're doing? Spike out now!"

His face was covered with a sheen of sweat, his eyes a bright luminous blue. "Desperate...times." His voice was thin, raspy.

"Spike out, Kel-Paten, or I'll rip those things right out of you," she said harshly.

"Too risky. Systems are...unstable."

"Damn it, this'll kill you!"

"No..."

"I don't have time to argue." She reached for the datalines. His right hand clasped her wrist.

"No. Tasha..." His voice was barely above a whisper, and the hand that held her wrist trembled.

She stared at him. He'd kill himself. She knew that, knew the energy requirements of slowing and landing the shuttle would take every bit of life from him. Suddenly she realized how very wrong everyone's appraisals were of the man called Branden Kel-Paten. He was willing to lose his life to save hers. To save even Serafino's.

He was choosing to die. She had to make him choose to live.

She kissed him with a passion born of desperation, fear, and anger, taking advantage of his gasp of surprise to let her tongue probe his mouth. He leaned into her, wanting more, and she willingly gave it. Because behind her desperation and fear and anger was something else. Something that recognized how empty her life would be without his damnably annoying steadfast presence. His devotion to her—so misplaced, but so very much needed.

Damn him for making her feel this way!

He released her wrist. She broke their kiss, placed her hands on either side of his face. His luminous eyes blazed like a white-hot flame.

"Spike out," she told him softly, her thumb against his lips, stilling his attempt to claim her mouth again. "Please."

He closed his eyes briefly, cycled into a shutdown. He pulled out the datalinks before she could. She wrenched him to his feet, and for a moment they stood in an awkward half embrace as the shuttle jerked and trembled around them. Her heart pounded, the solid feel of him reassuring in a strange and bittersweet way.

"Tasha—" he started.

The ship bucked, hard. His arms tightened around her as an alarm wailed briefly, then was silenced. She pulled abruptly away, lunging for the ladderway. He followed, swearing, his voice still raspy.

She clambered back into her seat, raking the safety straps across her chest as Serafino fought to control the bucking shuttle, which seemed to want to do nothing more than drop like a rock out of the skies.

Kel-Paten, at the station behind her, manually adjusted the failing engines.

Sharing a beer in hell was beginning to look more and more like a realistic possibility.

"Thirty-three hundred feet...Twenty-five hundred. Two thousand..." Serafino read out their descent as he manipulated the controls. Another flash of lightning arced through the dense cloud cover blanking the viewport.

"Eighteen hundred. We're still coming in hot," he said.

"Got to chance the braking vanes," Sass told him.

"Try one more steep bank first." This from Kel-Paten.

"Hard to port," Sass said, and the shuttle's frame groaned under the pull of gravity.

"Eleven hundred," Serafino said. "Starting landing sequence."

"Extending vanes," Sass noted, a lot more calmly than she felt. A lot more calmly than the shuttle reacted.

"Heading corrected," Eden said for the third time as the craft slipped out of control.

"Hope you found us someplace soft!" Sass managed a tense grin.

"Like a baby's bottom," Eden replied.

Suddenly the dark clouds parted. Rain spattered the forward viewport, which was filled with deep greens and browns of a forest and, beyond that, a long wet expanse of meadow below.

The meadow. They had to make the meadow. The shuttle's power—

—died.

Screens blinked off. Lights blinked out. The rush of air through the ventilation grids ceased.

"Brace for impact!" Sass grabbed her armrests just as the shuttle carved a deep furrow into the soft, green-carpeted ground.

✦✦✦ 23

HAVEN-1

The sound woke her. A thin, high-pitched keening cry, grating in her ears. Painful and only slightly less so than the throbbing discomfort now blossoming like some crazed, viciously spreading weed running rampant over her back, her arms, her left side.

Something restricted her breathing, her movement. She pushed against it, pain flaring. A click sounded. Then it was gone.

"Tasha?"

Warmth on her face, her neck, her left side. Someone prodded her, but that wasn't uncomfortable. Even her name sounded nice, though a tad insistent.

"Tasha."

If only the damned wailing would shut up.

"Hmm," she said, finding her mouth dry, her eyelids sticky. She fluttered them. Light and dark. The light was hazy. The dark . . .

A man blocking the light. Her brain recognized the square-jawed face, the luminous eyes. The steadfast, unshakable presence. "Kel-Paten?"

Mommy? MommyMommyMommy!

Kel-Paten's lips quirked slightly, trembling—trembling?—into a small, crooked smile. "Tasha."

MommyMommy!

"I'm not your mother," she told him over the shrill wail she now recognized as a ship's emergency siren.

Kel-Paten frowned. "What?"

She leaned forward, grasping his arm. She—they were on the floor of the cockpit. Her chest ached, exactly where the safety straps would have been. Kel-Paten was on one knee, his arm around her back holding her upright, the empty copilot's chair behind him.

Gods' feathered asses! The shuttle. Haven-1. Kel-Paten's death link to the failing power panel. The landing, had they, were they—

"Status!" She leaned against his shoulder, trying to stand. Her legs failed to cooperate.

"Easy," he said, his arm tightening around her. "Take it slowly."

Good idea. She steadied herself against him and remembered the last time their faces were so close together, remembered what he had attempted to do. For them. For her. "You . . . you okay?" She touched his jaw briefly, concerned about him yet feeling oddly awkward about this new closeness. If that's what it was.

He nodded as she withdrew her fingers. "It's you I'm worried about."

She was worried about herself too, but not for any reasons he'd guess.

"And Eden?" It was easier to focus on Eden. She tried to turn her face toward the nav station and received a shooting pain in her neck for the effort.

"Coming around. Serafino survived." He glanced past her, eyes narrowing. Serafino must be there. "He's with her. Emergency shutdown completed. Shuttle has some structural damage but no fatalities." He repeated the last words more firmly.

No fatalities. Everyone was alive. It sunk in.

And the voice began again. *MommyMommy!*

But Kel-Paten's lips weren't moving. And the sweet-sounding, almost childlike tone wasn't remotely the admiral's deep voice.

MommyMommy!

"Who's—" She turned slightly, trying again to stand. Her legs worked this time. Kel-Paten drew her to her feet. "Who's saying, 'Mommy, Mommy'?"

"That's the emergency siren. It's stuck. I can—"

"No, it's not." She limped toward the cockpit hatchway, half pulling Kel-Paten, half leaning on him. "Someone's crying. It sounds like—Tank?"

The kennel was tilted sideways but intact. Through the grated opening, a furry paw reached frantically toward her.

Mommy!

"Tank?"

"I checked their vitals. They're fine." Kel-Paten guided her—hands on her waist and arm—as she dropped into a crouch. "I don't think it's safe to let them out yet."

Sass clasped the frantic paw, then pushed her fingers through the kennel's small opening. A soft ear rubbed, hard, against her.

Mommy! Tank scared. Reilly scared! Bad here! Bad Thing!

"It's all right," she crooned, tickling the fidget's chin. "I know it's bad being stuck in the kennel. But you have to stay there until we're sure it's safe to let you out."

Safe soon?

"Soon," she promised.

Food soon?

"Soon."

O-kay.

Okay. Okay? Oh, gods. Sass's knees gave out and she sat down, hard, on the decking. She was having a telepathic conversation with a furzel!

Kel-Paten's concerned face swam before her. "You shouldn't be moving around yet. Sit still." His fingers gently probed her neck. "Let me—"

"You didn't hear him, did you?"

"Serafino? No, I—"

"Not Serafino. Tank. The fidget. He's calling me Mommy, and then he told me he was scared. And hungry. And that Reilly was scared."

Kel-Paten cupped her face with his right hand. "Take a few deep breaths. You've been bumped around a bit."

"I've been bumped around a lot." Damn but her shoulder throbbed. Probably tore her rotator cuff. Again. "And I've been bumped around a lot worse.

But I've never had my fidget talk to me before, and he's talking to me now."

Kel-Paten frowned, but it was one of those half-condescending, half-sympathetic frowns. Her fist itched to clock him one. "Of course. Just take a few deep breaths. It'll pass."

"Branden." She paused. Deliberately. She glared up at him.

One dark eyebrow quirked up slightly. "Tasha."

"I can hear Tank. In my mind."

"Reilly's talking to Eden." Serafino's voice came from behind them, over the siren's wail.

The dark eyebrow that had gone up now slanted downward.

"How? Why?" Sass asked. If anyone knew anything about telepathic talking furzels, it would be a Nasyry.

"Fynn's a telepath," Kel-Paten said in a low voice.

"But I'm not," she countered. "And I can hear Tank. And he understands me. This is ... strange." She shook her head slowly. She raised her voice. "You didn't answer me, 'Fino. Why?" She turned slightly, trying to see past Kel-Paten's wide shoulder and back into the cockpit.

"Don't know yet," came the answer.

"Yes, Reilly. Food soon," Eden called out.

Food? Soon? Food? Tank asked.

Sass pinched the bridge of her nose with her fingers. "This," she said, "is going to be an experience."

It was. For the next hour, disjointed sounds, half words, and odd images bombarded Sass as they worked through the required postlanding checklist, reconfirmed the planet's habitability factors, and

Eden poked, prodded, or patched their various infirmities. Furzel ears were far more sensitive and furzel eyes considerably closer to the ground. Sass became intimately acquainted with Kel-Paten's and Eden's boots—through Tank's eyes. His small, singsong voice floated in and out of her thoughts. Some things—*most* things—made no sense.

"It takes a while to unravel what they're saying," Serafino advised from his seat at the copilot's chair, where he was keying in a basic repair program, coordinating with Kel-Paten belowdeck in the engine compartment. The engine and power grids had fared the worst. Luckily, they had no hull breeches or major structural issues.

Sass felt talking to TeKrain Namar would have been easier.

"What's this 'protect, protect'?" she asked, plopping down into the pilot's seat. Her back ached. Her knees ached. She'd spent the past twenty minutes hunkered down in the corner of the main cabin, trying to reroute a starboard power line so the exterior rampway stairs would function.

"A result of the bonding process, I think." Eden was at the small science station, running the final tests on outside air samples. "Something in their nature makes them feel it's their duty to guard their 'person.' I'm getting it from Reilly too, off and on."

"Because something's bad here or they just fear anything that's not MommySass or MommyEden?"

Eden shook her head slowly. "I'm not sure. *Jace* isn't sure." She glanced at Serafino, who leaned back in his seat and nodded.

"We were just discussing that," he said. "Reilly

was in that protect mode on the *Vax* too. I thought . . .
I sensed something then. But there are so many vari-
ables, including . . ." and he tapped his head, indicat-
ing the disconnected Psy-Serv implant. An implant
Sass knew she'd have to discuss with Kel-Paten at
some point. Now, however, did not seem like a good
time.

"Jace may have some residual effects from the surgery we have to deal with," Eden continued. "The
med-panel on board doesn't have any equipment to
accurately test that. And I'm sure getting bumped
around during landing hasn't helped."

"But it could be this place, this planet?" Sass
asked.

"They've been confined on a ship pretty much
their whole lives," Jace said. "Any kind of dirtside environment with things like wind or natural sunlight
or rain will feel very strange to them. It could be as
simple as that."

It could be, Sass thought, bundling Tank once again
into her arms as *Protect Mommy! Love Mommy! Protect Mommy!* sang through her mind. She stroked his
ears, his audible purring replacing his mental pleas.

He relaxed against her as Eden pronounced a deci-
sive "all clear." Kel-Paten's agreement came moments
later from belowdeck. The shuttle was secure. The
planet was safe. They weren't going to fry from
the radiation in its atmosphere or take a breath of the
outside air and die.

Perhaps that's all it was. A new place with new
sounds and new smells.

But what if it wasn't? She swiveled around in the
pilot's chair and gazed out the viewport at the greens

and browns of trees and grass and earth. Dirtside. Tank's nervousness notwithstanding, she hated being dirtside.

It reminded her of Lethant.

It was a hazy morning, or perhaps early afternoon. Light—broken by the irregular line of tall trees—flickered over the expanse of green in dappled patches, reflecting now and then off small, irregular pools of water. The storm that had accompanied their arrival was nowhere to be seen. The smell of raw, wet earth was pungent. The smell of hot metal and burning plastic, acrid. Coolant, steam, and other fluids hissed and whistled through the various exhaust ports of the leviathan called *Galaxus* that had dropped from the sky and partially embedded itself into the soft ground.

Tasha marched around the shuttle, datalyzer in one hand, her plump fidget trotting alongside. Every few steps she uttered a soft but insistent "Damn it!"

Kel-Paten trailed through the damp grass behind them both, bemused. He should be as upset as she was. The shuttle had damage. Nothing a good spaceport repair dock couldn't fix, but they had no reason to believe HV-1 offered such facilities.

So the captain's frustration was understandable.

However, they were alive, and—other than the odd fact that Tasha and Fynn could purportedly communicate with their furzels—they were recovering as well as could be expected from their assortment of bumps, breaks, and bruises.

But their physical condition only contributed to

the source of Kel-Paten's good humor and bemusement. It wasn't the cause of it.

The cause of it was that Tasha had kissed him. And let him kiss her back. And didn't flinch at his touch.

Gods' blessed rumps, she kissed him! Even called him Branden. And ever since then, something changed in the way she looked at him or spoke to him. It wasn't just his ability to expertly analyze human facial configurations that told him this either. It was . . . something else. Something warmer and real and . . . human.

Even Serafino's presence failed to completely disturb that.

Tasha stopped at the shuttle's rampway and ran a hand through her hair, wincing as she moved her shoulder. He could tell she was exhausted. So were Serafino and Fynn. Even *he* was tired, and his artificially enhanced endurance level was far beyond theirs. They all had been awake and in crisis mode— save for a few hasty furzel-naps before landing—for almost forty-eight hours. His last-ditch efforts to subroute the shuttle's power through his systems had taxed him, temporarily compromising a few functions, but there was no permanent damage. Once they determined the shuttle's status and secured their perimeter, he was going to order them all off-duty for six hours, and himself for two. That would make Fynn happy. Or at least stop her from scowling at her medicorder so often.

Tasha was tapping the datalyzer's screen, transmitting her scans to the main computers inside. "Got that, 'Fino?"

"Yeah, got it," Serafino's voice replied through the unit's small speaker.

"Wish it was better news." She sighed and handed the unit to Kel-Paten.

He dropped out of *Tasha kissed me* mode and scrolled quickly through the data. The appraisal was more thorough and slightly worse than his initial scans conducted from inside the shuttle, but—given the condition of the shuttle's equipment—he'd expected as much.

However, key components and mechanicals— engines, thrusters, power grid—were surprisingly intact. The news was bad but not devastating, and he told her so.

She rocked back on her heels and looked up at him, a slow grin spreading across her mouth for the first time in almost two hours. "Then I guess you owe me a beer, eh?"

Whatever rejoinder he could offer was interrupted by the sound of footsteps from inside the shuttle and the appearance, seconds later, of Eden Fynn at the top of the rampway, bioscanner in hand. Which was just as well, because he really didn't have a rejoinder. His limited social skills went into stasis whenever Tasha smiled at him. Kisses notwithstanding, this was all too new—and he had no data by which to judge it. He had no experience flirting with women; he had no experience with women at all. He'd never even—

"No known toxins or poisons," Fynn announced, turning the scanner in a slow half circle. "A few molds and mosses. Pollen spores all register as benign."

"Any edibles?" Tasha asked.

"Don't stick anything into your mouth until I run a lab test on it." The CMO trudged down the short flight of stairs, her furzel at her heels. She'd donned her blue lab coat over her rumpled uniform, and her hair—usually so neatly tucked behind her ears—was mussed. A small med-broche, affixed to her neck just under her right ear, peeked over the edge of her uniform collar, mitigating the effects of her concussion. "I'm also picking up evidence of fresh water. A spring, most likely." She glanced to her left, squinting, then raised her free hand to shade her eyes. "That mountain range is probably the source."

It was the same mountain range where earlier scans had showed deposits of sharvonite. Essential if they were to refuel, though refining the compound would prove to be a challenge. Kel-Paten segued back into work mode, though not completely. Tasha was inches from him. He felt her presence like a sun's heat against the cold metal hull of a ship.

"Fortuitous choice of locations," he told Fynn, and briefly calculated the odds that they should find, exactly within their limited fuel range upon coming out of a near fatal jump, a habitable planet with breathable air, edible vegetation, and potable water. The odds weren't staggering, but they were sizable.

When he added to that the fact that Tasha had kissed him—and what were the odds that *that* would ever happen?—it occurred to him that he might be dead and this was the gods' Lost Paradise. After all, he never had this kind of luck when he was alive.

"Enough room out here to set up a workable repair bay," said a voice behind him.

Serafino. So much for his theory about paradise.

"We need to set up the security field first," Kel-Paten said. He strode several paces away from the shuttle—and Serafino—and analyzed the optimal field layout, then paced off a few more. "Here," he said, digging his heel into the ground, making a long gash. Six more long paces toward the bow. "Second sensor here."

Tasha came up alongside him, plucked the datalyzer from his hand. She entered the coordinates as he delineated them, transmitting them back to the shuttle's computers.

Serafino stared at him for a moment, then, with a shrug, turned back to Fynn.

"What's out here we should be afraid of?" Tasha asked as they rounded the ship's bow, putting Fynn and Serafino out of sight.

"According to what ship's sensors show us, nothing." No animals, no insects, not even a slitherskimp. Nothing remotely inconvenient, let alone threatening.

"Do you find that odd?"

"I'd not welcome any further problems, but yes. It's illogical."

"The furzels agree with you, if that's any consolation." She stopped and squinted at the forest on her right.

"I think ship's sensors are better diagnostic tools."

"Are they?" She was still staring at the trees, then gave herself a small shake and turned back to him. "If we were in the wilds of Fendantun or one of the worlds in the Far Reaches, I might agree with you. But here . . ." And she glanced at him with a challenge in her eyes that was very familiar.

It was admiral and captain again, hashing out

issues in his office. Except now his office was a large green meadow and neither of them had their usual cup of coffee in hand. "Parameters may be different," he admitted. Then, as he always asked during their meetings: "Your hypothesis?"

A small smile touched her lips. "Coffee would definitely help with this discussion, but since you've not offered any, Branden, we'll just have to proceed without it."

Branden. Perhaps not the gods' Lost Paradise but definitely a small slice of heaven. "An oversight. My hospitality skills are lacking."

She chuckled softly, then her mirth faded. She drew a short breath. "Are you sure we're actually here? That we're not stuck in jumpspace? You know, lost in McClellan's Void and hallucinating? I thought maybe that's why Tank's so upset."

McClellan's Void. Dreehalla. The entertainment industry loved to use that as a setting for its horror vids. Drunken spacers—claiming to have uncovered the secret of the mythical Captain McClellan—loved to use it as a means to cadge another drink. He knew of three planetary cultures that used it as a term synonymous with hell. The Rebashee refused to utter its name, only making an odd protection symbol with their fingers to prevent its noticing them. He knew of no one—no sane person—who had ever experienced it. But that hadn't diminished the legend of a Captain McClellan, who escaped from an alternate dimension where friends and enemies—some long dead—tortured him through bizarre recreations of his life. Friends he'd trusted betrayed him; women he'd loved spurned him; ships he'd captained imploded under his boots. He was a broken man—shivering and babbling incoherently—when the crew of a passing ore freighter found him and his ship, a hundred years ago. Or so the legend went.

Kel-Paten preferred to think of paradise. Though no paradise of his making would ever contain Serafino. McClellan's Void, on the other hand, would be just that paradoxical. If it existed. But it didn't.

"To exist in a layer of nonexistence is scientifically impossible," he told her.

She stepped closer to him. "I've heard of mathematical theories—"

"I wrote three of them." Because he couldn't help himself and because he saw the slight glimmer of trepidation in her eyes, he touched her cheek gently, brushing some short wisps of her hair back from her face. "And have disproved those and ten more," he added.

Her lashes lowered to pinkened cheeks, but she didn't pull away from his touch.

Dear gods, he'd made her blush! And they were talking about hypothetical equations.

"Well, then," she said, once again looking up at him. The small smile was back. She tapped him in the middle of his chest with the datalyzer. "Best finish up before Serafino comes looking for us."

He stepped away from her reluctantly and paced to the next sensor point, just aft of the shuttle's midsection. She followed, making notations, the fidget never far from her heels.

"And your hypothesis, Admiral?"

"Still in process. We're working with possibly erroneous data until we get ship's sensors recalibrated.

Certainly," and he glanced overhead at the now pale blue sky lightly streaked with cottony clouds, "this doesn't match what I'd expect from this planet's location in the hab zone or its slower rotation. Other than that storm we came in on, temperatures and vegetation don't reflect the extremes we should be seeing."

"You mean it shouldn't be so perfectly conducive to our needs."

"Exactly." He cupped her arm, guiding her along as he paced toward the shuttle's aft end. She didn't pull away. Amazing.

"So why is it?"

"We don't know that it is. We only know this small region has attributes in contradiction to our scientific expectations. We haven't scanned this entire planet— we may be in an environmental pocket, like an oasis in a desert. We've also only been here," he added, "three hours and forty-two minutes. Ask me again in a week. I'll know more."

"Aye, sir. Logged and noted," she said, then: "What's your estimate on repair time?"

He'd thought about that. The preliminary damage-assessment list was long. The more thorough, detailed one that would emerge over the next twenty-four to thirty-six hours would no doubt be worse. "A month, easily. Six weeks wouldn't be out of the question."

"The *Vax* is probably looking for us, along with the *Prospector,* the *Dalkerris,* the *Nexarion,* the *Pride*—hell. The whole fleet's probably on alert."

There was a tone of hope in her voice. But they were far off any chart either the Triad or the U-Cees had. Even the damned Nasyry pirate couldn't find a fix to work with.

"Tasha—"

"I know, I know. Don't give me probability percentages, Kel-Paten. I'm too tired to take any more bad news right now."

He gave her the coordinates for the final sensor, then: "There are always miracles, you know."

She glanced up at him, lips parted in surprise. "You said you didn't believe in miracles."

"I didn't, but..." A dozen things he'd always wanted to say to her, about what she meant to him, ran through his mind. None came out, because Serafino suddenly appeared around the side of the shuttle, datalyzer in hand. His long hair was haphazardly tied back, strands dangling around his face. His high-collared shirt was open at the neck, its sleeves rolled up unevenly on forearms that showed purplish bruises acquired during landing. A U-Cee weapon still graced his hip. Kel-Paten increased his mental filters automatically, even though he suspected the Nasyry could get through if he wanted to. And even though those same filters made him feel detached from Tasha. He hated that.

"I'm picking up a signal! Very clear readings. It's an outpost or small spaceport. Damn it all, I get nothing from the sensors inside the shuttle. We got nothing coming in on entry, but," and he shoved the unit's screen between Kel-Paten and Tasha, "here it is."

There it was. Structures. Power fields. Life-form readings—those were the faintest, but they were there, where nothing had been a half hour before, according to their sensors. Sensors that were—with a broken main power coupling and two bent antennae grids—admittedly not functioning optimally.

Kel-Paten didn't like it, even though a spaceport could—ostensibly—be very good news.

"You said there were erratic energy pulses while we were still in orbit." Tasha motioned to Serafino. "Could it be this?"

"Doesn't feel quite the same, but I'm not going to discount anything. Not until we get a closer look." There was a tone of excitement in Serafino's voice. Clearly he'd found a mission where he could cast himself in the role of hero.

"*We,*" Kel-Paten said, stressing the word, "need to first finish securing this ship and the perimeters. Then we all need some downtime. That will also give us more time to analyze—"

"It gives *them* time to make the first move. And we have no idea who they are or what they're capable of. I'm guessing the reason that they haven't already come calling is that storm that covered our approach. Their power grid," and Serafino tilted the screen so both Kel-Paten and Tasha could see it, "shows some cold spots. Looks like they're just getting things back online. I've put our systems on yellow alert, just in case."

Kel-Paten studied the screen in Serafino's hand, the hint of technology that could solve many of their problems. "I'm not going to put us all through a forty-five-mile forced march when we have injuries and exhaustion to deal with." And a forced march it would be. The shuttle had no transbeam unit.

"I'm not talking about 'us all.' You and me." Serafino waved the datalyzer back and forth. "I only took a few bruises on landing, and I logged my downtime in orbit. Sass—Tasha and Eden can finish calibrating the security sensors, then nap in shifts until we get back."

Yes, they could. And as much as it grated on Kel-Paten to admit it, Serafino was right. This outpost did need to be investigated, because it was Kel-Paten's sworn duty as a Triad officer to return to the Fleet as soon as possible. If this outpost contained the technology and the charts to assist in that endeavor, he had to make every effort to acquire them. He and Serafino were best suited to make the trek, even if Serafino did have more than his admitted "few bruises." But Kel-Paten didn't like it, and not because Serafino was more injured than he said or because Kel-Paten had no desire to be in Serafino's company more than he had to. "I can cover the distance faster than you. *If,*" and he stressed the word, "the locals do send a probe 'droid or scout team, I'd prefer the three of you be here to handle the situation."

"Negative, Tin Soldier. You need me. Unless the natives have some kind of telepathic shielding that I can't circumvent, I'll find out far more about them far more quickly than you can with your charming personality."

" 'Fino," Tasha said, a clear warning tone in her voice.

That heartened Kel-Paten but shamed him too. He didn't need her to defend him. "Don't interrupt him. He's teaching me how to be charming."

Tasha sputtered out a laugh.

Serafino cocked his head slightly. "Very good," he said after a moment. "When do we leave?"

There was no way he was going to change Serafino's mind. He knew that. And the bastard did have a point about the usefulness of his talent. But he hated leaving Tasha alone with Fynn to guard the shuttle. Fynn was a doctor, not a soldier. He doubted she'd picked up a weapon since basic training.

Plus, he simply hated leaving Tasha right now. Something was happening between them, something he needed to understand. He had so many questions, not just about what he hoped were her feelings for him but about her knowledge of Serafino and her suspicions about himself. About the mysterious ambush and Fynn's newly found telepathy. About where they were going from here—and he didn't mean their eventual destination via shuttle. There was so much they had to clear up, and there hadn't been a chance since they left the *Vax*. More questions kept coming. And he knew of no answers.

A forty-five-mile trek with her would have been an ideal time to obtain those answers. But that was not to be. It felt almost as if his old luck—or lack thereof—had returned.

"How strong is your telepathic link to Eden?" Tasha was asking Serafino.

"In case our comm links don't work?" he asked. "She's primarily a touch telepath. But there are ways I can reach her. She just can't initiate contact with me as easily."

"How about Tank and Reilly?"

This time Serafino laughed. "I'm not taking your fat fidget on a recon mission."

"Tank says," Tasha replied, her eyes closed and a wry smile on her lips, "that you're rude." She opened her eyes. "But I was thinking about Reilly. Eden told me your link to him is stronger."

"No," said Serafino.

"No," said Kel-Paten at the same time. "Since our preliminary scans of this ecosystem are obviously in error, we don't know what natural predators are out there. I can't be watching after him," and he jerked his chin toward Serafino, "and a furzel as well."

Tasha shrugged. "Just a thought."

Somehow Kel-Paten knew she was talking to the fidget, even though he was having a hard time accepting that she could.

"No," he repeated, giving her a stern look, which honestly had never had much effect in the past.

"Aye, sir. If there's nothing else," she stepped back, turning the datalyzer over in her hands, "I need to initialize the program, do a test run before we set the sensors in place."

The warmth he'd sensed from her before was gone. Because of Serafino most likely. Or maybe because she didn't want him to leave? Maybe it was time... and the excuse of checking on her test data would be perfect.

He nodded. "I'll look it over before we go."

"Good." She ducked her head briefly in acknowledgment, then turned.

"We need to verify coordinates, put together two backpacks with water and emergency provisions," Serafino said as Tasha headed back toward the rampway, Tank bounding after her. "That shouldn't take more than twenty minutes."

"Half an hour," Kel-Paten told him. "I want to replace an external power coupling on the main sensor dish before we leave. Have Dr. Fynn pack a small med-kit." He fixed Serafino with his "that's an order" glare. It was bad enough he had to spend the next several hours with the bastard. He needed his next thirty minutes free of him. Because he had something important to do after he fixed the sensor dish.

Calibrating the security-sensor field with a fidget tail twitching across the cockpit's console screens was no easy task. Calibrating the security-sensor field with a twitching fidget tail on the console, an unhappy CMO in the main cabin, and a furzel-to-fidget mental commentary was getting damned near impossible.

Sass set the security program into a diagnostic loop, plucked Tank from the console, and marched through the hatchway into the main cabin. Eden had converted one of the cabin's fold-down seats to a makeshift staging table. She was on one side, arms across her chest. Serafino was at the other, hands on hips. Reilly was hunkered between them, tail thrashing much as Tank's had. Only his tail thwacked first one half-loaded backpack and then the other.

Sass didn't need to ask what was going on. She'd been getting an abbreviated furzel's-eye view for the past fifteen minutes.

"I know it's risky," she told Eden when her friend turned to her with a pleading expression in her eyes. Tank flowed from her arms onto the makeshift table with a muted *thump*. The two furzels touched noses, and a chorus of *Friend! Protect!* echoed in Sass's mind. She ignored it as she was learning to ignore a lot of their chatter. "The admiral knows it's risky. Serafino's never struck me as suicidal. They're not planning to attack the outpost, Eden. Just gather information and return."

"As chief medical officer, I'm responsible for the health and well-being of the officers and crew."

"I'm responsible for their lives too."

"None of us," Eden went on, as if Sass hadn't commented, "should be doing more at this point than what's minimally required. Damn it, Sass, if we were back on the *Regalia*, I'd have you in sick bay. I'd be in sick bay!" She rubbed her forehead, wincing. "I'm concussed. You have rotator-cuff damage, a collateral ligament tear in your left knee. Jace—"

Serafino held up one hand. "I'm Nasyry. I heal faster."

"I don't care!" Eden stamped her foot, which signaled to Sass that she cared very much indeed. Eden was not by nature a foot-stamper, resorting to that tactic only when she was down to her last sliver of patience. "Shall I detail your two cracked ribs? Or how about the lumbar sprain? Or—and you!" Eden whirled, pointing at the admiral, who—judging from the footsteps Sass just heard—had entered the main cabin only moments before. "If you've run a diagnostic, you haven't shown me the results. You were damned near half this ship's power supply for, what, an hour or more? That was a mere four hours ago—"

"Four hours, eighteen minutes, twenty-seven seconds," Kel-Paten corrected, his voice flat. It sounded as if he was in 'cybe function, but Sass wasn't about to turn around to find out. Things *happened* when he looked at her. Things she wasn't sure she was ready to feel. She vacillated between regretting kissing him and wanting to tear his uniform off and have wild, insane, sweaty sex, just to get him out of her system.

That had always worked in the past.

"I agree with your assessment, Doctor," Kel-Paten was saying as the two furzels bounded off the table and raced past Sass's legs, heading for the cockpit, "but these are not ordinary circumstances."

"Another four hours," Eden challenged. "We rest, eat a decent meal, spend some time on the shuttle's regen table."

"No. Our duty to return to the Triad takes precedence over any personal concerns."

"Three hours."

"Captain Sebastian is staying behind. By the time we return, you'll have her well-fed and completely healed."

"Two and a half."

Serafino shoved a small med-kit and a rations pack into one backpack and sealed it. "Ready when you are, Tin Soldier." He yanked it up to his shoulder.

Sass saw the momentary thinning of his lips. So did Eden or, given their telepathic bond, maybe she felt it.

"See? See?" Eden glared at him. "Those ribs are *not* healed yet."

"You worry too much, sweetling," Serafino answered with a smile.

Eden turned back to Kel-Paten. "Okay, one hour. With him," she pointed to Serafino, "on the regen table the whole time."

When Kel-Paten didn't answer, Sass glanced over her shoulder and saw a slight hesitancy in his expression, his brows angled down. Was he considering it or just annoyed at the whole situation?

"The sooner we leave, the sooner we'll return," Serafino quipped, edging for the rampway door.

"Twenty minutes," Kel-Paten said to Eden. "I have to review the security sensors with Captain Sebastian. That gives you twenty minutes to work on your patient." He jerked his chin toward Serafino. "Everything else will wait until we get back. Sebastian?" He looked down at Sass.

She couldn't read his expression, so she went with routine: "Kel-Paten." And paused.

The slightest of nods. "Your presence at the command console, please."

Well, now *that* was a tone she hadn't heard in . . . days. If Timm Kel-Faray suddenly appeared behind the admiral with his usual "By your leave, sir!" she wouldn't be the least bit surprised.

She returned his nod and followed him to the front of the ship, wondering what in hell was going on now?

GALAXUS COCKPIT

Tank watched from his perch on the console as Reilly, nose to the floor, stalked the perimeter of the cockpit. *Safe? Safe?*

No smelly light, Reilly told him. With a sigh, the older furzel sat on his haunches and took a moment to wash his left whiskers. *Outside not safe. Mommy's not listening,* he said finally.

I try! Tank pleaded. *Mommy says all is safe. All is not safe. I try again. Furzel talk. Human talk. Too different. And JaceFriend is quiet now. And Mommy does not listen to furzel words.*

Tank wrinkled his nose. *JaceFriend makes Mommy-Eden sad.*

JaceFriend thinks he hunts Bad Thing. Silly. Bad Thing here. Outside. Waiting. Flows ugly in, ugly out.

I know. Tank sneezed. *Bad smell.*

Time to fix again. Time to Blink. Reilly arched his back, standing.

Tank help?

Friend stay with MommySass. Protect.

O-kay, Tank said, but he was disappointed. He wanted to be the one to hunt Bad Thing. If only he was a big furzel like Reilly and not just a fat fidget.

Protect is important, Reilly told him from the cockpit hatchway. *Part of Bad Thing touches this ship. Still smelly. Needs more Blink. One furzel hunts. One furzel protects.*

Reilly had called him a furzel! Tank preened in satisfaction. *O-kay. Tank protects.* He narrowed his eyes and peered through the neverwhen as Reilly trotted away. Bad Thing touched this ship. Bigger Bad Thing waits outside but won't get in. Because Tank the furzel is here, on guard. Tank protects.

Jace let the backpack sag slightly off his shoulder as Kel-Paten and Tasha disappeared through the cockpit hatchway. "I'm sorry, but I can't go into it any more than I already have. I repeat: if and when I have something valid, I'll tell you and Sebastian. Until then, you're just going to have to trust me."

Eden folded her arms over her chest again and fought the urge to start tapping her foot. Jace was wearing one of the best chastised-little-boy looks she'd ever seen on a grown man. It made her want to forget the real issue here and tug off his clothing. She had to ignore that impulse. "How can I trust you when you're blocking me, blocking Reilly?"

"It's for your own protection."

Her protection! Gods' feathered rumps, how she hated that phrase.

Something was very wrong about the appearance of this outpost. Something was very wrong with this whole planet. Jace had sensed it when they were still hours out, and she'd picked up on that—immediately. So did Reilly and Tank. Ever since landing on Haven-1, Reilly had wanted to protect her from something bad, but she couldn't figure out what the threat was. She wasn't sure Reilly knew, and until she had facts, she didn't want to bother Tasha—the captain clearly had enough problems. And trying to talk to Kel-Paten about it wasn't even a consideration. She didn't think he gave much credence to furzel intuition.

Jace could help in translating Reilly's thoughts, but Jace wasn't talking. He'd shut her and Reilly out of his mind ever since they neared Haven-1—limiting his mind contact with her to basic, required conversation and, of course, his habitual flirtations. She even took a quick nap, hoping he'd draw her into Novalis. He didn't, even though she could feel him just on the edges of her mind's shadows. He was there, reading her, watching her. But he refused to come to her, because she'd start asking questions.

Nor would he tell her why he was so intent on traveling alone with the admiral. That worried her too. Because she knew his sister was always on his mind. Even if she could no longer read it.

She waved one hand toward the back of the main cabin and the small sick-bay diagnostic panel glowing from the wall. "I've fifteen minutes to work on your ribs. Strip off your shirt." She strode to the panel and then initialized the regen program. The multipurpose table slid from the wall as his footsteps came up behind her.

She turned.

"Long as I can keep my pants on," he said with a grin as he climbed on. "I still have a fear of those rectal thermometers of yours."

She tapped at the unit's screen with more force than necessary. "Don't tempt me, Captain Serafino. Don't tempt me."

GALAXUS COCKPIT

Tank sprawled on the command console, his tail and one hind foot obscuring the screen. *Protect Mommy!* he chirped as Tasha stepped past Kel-Paten. The cockpit door grated closed behind her.

Food? Tank's large eyes watched her approach.

She swiveled the pilot's chair around and sat, taking a moment to chuck him under the chin. "Sweet baby. I have work to do." She pushed his foot, encouraging him to relocate. He rolled onto his back and splayed four furry feet in the air, his tail still across the screen. She lifted it and peered at the data. Good. The program was finished. "I had the computer run a level-three diagnostic on the security field, just to be sure we hadn't overlooked anything," she told Kel-Paten as the copilot's chair squeaked. She glanced over. "There's always—"

The words she wanted to say died on her lips, because every trace of 'cybe she'd seen in his face and in the set of his shoulders was gone. He was *looking* at her again. And looking at her with that something that made her stomach flutter, coated her cheeks with a flush of heat, and made her suck in a slow, careful breath. This was a "come hither" look if she'd ever seen one. He leaned forward, reducing the already small distance between them to mere inches. His pale eyes were half hooded, his lips slightly parted. Even under his dark lashes, his gaze heated and probed her. She felt it as if it were a physical thing. Tingles ran down her spine and pooled between her legs.

Loooove Mommy... Tank purred.

Yes, there was that too. His logs. His love letters to the woman he thought was Tasha Sebastian. Who wasn't.

She could handle "come hither." Hell, she was actually looking forward to "come hither" if they could ever get around to it. Hot sex was such a great stress-reliever. But love...she couldn't risk that. Especially not with Branden Kel-Paten. She liked him too much.

"Tasha, I—"

"Security perimeter's functional," she cut in quickly, damning the unexpected breathiness in her voice.

"—don't want to talk about the perimeter. We need...I need to tell you—"

"About repairs. I've worked out a schedule." *Please don't say you love me! Kiss me, tear my clothes off. But do not tell me you love me.* "Want to see it?"

"Tasha, please. I've waited a long time to tell you this."

Oh, damn. Here it comes. She needed to do something, fast. Something to keep him from saying what she didn't want to hear and had no idea how to respond to.

"And I have only fifteen minutes," he was saying.

The solution hit her. Something he would like. Something she could handle. "Good point. Let's not waste it." In two heartbeats she closed the short distance between them by grabbing a fistful of his shirt. Her kiss landed a bit off center—she'd surprised him, she realized—but she angled her face, correcting that slight miscalculation. She flicked her tongue over his lips as his hands found her shoulders, pulling her against him.

She released her hold on his shirt and pushed her fingers through the short thickness of hair at his neck. She nudged his mouth open again and kissed him, her tongue teasing his.

For a moment he trembled under her touch. Then he grabbed her waist, pulling her awkwardly onto his thighs.

Subtle he wasn't, which was good. Neither was she. She disentangled her right leg from his left, let go of him long enough to push both armrests back, and straddled him. When he groaned in her mouth, she deepened her kiss, clutching his shoulders.

His arms crossed her back, then one hand cupped her rear, squeezing, kneading. She turned her face slightly, her mouth pulling back as she changed the angle of the kiss and the kneading stilled. There was a hesitancy in the way he held her, as if he was unsure she wanted to be touched.

Silly man. Of course she wanted to be touched. To prove her point, she brushed her lips against his and sucked his lower lip.

His breath stuttered. He arched against her, his hands tightening on her waist and hip as he pulled her toward him.

When she kissed him again, his mouth was already opening. His tongue met hers boldly. He stroked her spine, his hand splaying to push her against his chest. She rocked against him, tasting, savoring. The comm panel chimed. Then chimed again.

He broke their kiss with a barely audible "damn!" and, holding her face against his shoulder with one hand, reached out and slapped at the panel with the other. The chair jiggled. "Kel-Paten."

His voice—raspy, deep, and definitely annoyed—rumbled against her body.

"Ready when you are, Tin Soldier."

"Outside at the rampway. Five minutes." He cut the link with a tap.

She moved her hands to his shoulders, wanting to straighten, but he held her firmly. "Wait," he said, his mouth brushing against her ear, his fingers massaging slow circles on her back. "Wait." He was breathing hard. So was she. Suddenly his breathing stilled, and the next breath was slow and controlled. She did push herself upright this time. His hand slid slowly down her back. His eyes were closed.

When he opened them, they glowed. He was under full 'cybe power. Because of Serafino, she guessed. But perhaps more so because of whatever waited for them at the outpost.

Loooove Mommy, Tank cooed. *Protect*.

"Well, that was fun while it lasted," she said lightly. "I'll activate the security perimeter after you leave." He let her go but not without some reluctance, gloved hands trailing down her thighs as she slid from his lap.

He watched as she regained her seat. "Don't be afraid of me. Ever."

The remark wasn't what she expected. Did he

think that was why she'd left his embrace? She gave him a wry smile. "I'm more afraid *for* you."

"I can handle what's out there." He folded the armrests down and stood.

Silence descended, suddenly awkward. The quick repartee she'd always shared with Dag Zanorian or any one of her other occasional lovers after a playful, heavy-petting session was noticeably absent. And that's all this was, right? Stress relief. Fun while it lasted.

"Kel-Paten," she said finally, when he reached the hatchway. "Check in every half hour or risk a demerit."

The cockpit door opened at his touch. He glanced through it, then back at her, looking at her in that searching, wanting way. Even the glow in his eyes did nothing to lessen that look's intensity. He turned without answering her comment, stepped over the hatch tread, then turned back.

"I love you, Tasha."

He held her startled gaze for a long moment, then was gone.

Damn him.

IN THE FOREST

The gnarled trees towering above them seemed ancient, their moss-crusted trunks thick with centuries of age. Roots twisted and turned through dense underbrush. Detritus on either side of the path was more than ankle deep. The trail itself was inexplicably clear.

Like the appearance of Haven-1 and its almost perfectly matched habitability.

"I don't want to stay on this route much longer," Kel-Paten told Serafino, who was scanning ahead of them, listening for anyone or anything. It was almost as if they were being led to the outpost.

"We go too far off course and they'll know we suspect something. Or they'll tag us as attackers, intruders. Another hour." Serafino glanced at the datalyzer in his hand. "We're not even at the halfway mark."

They'd been moving at a hard, steady jog for almost an hour already and were due to check in with the *Galaxus*. Kel-Paten could have easily doubled his speed, but there was no way the Nasyry could keep up. And as much as he loathed admitting it, Serafino's telepathic skills would be an asset coming in to this situation as blindly as they were. If Serafino was honest about what he sensed.

Kel-Paten wasn't sure about the Nasyry's honesty. But he had no choice. He needed to know what they were getting into up ahead at the outpost.

He had no idea what had just happened back at the shuttle.

Not just. It was forty-eight minutes, thirty-two seconds...thirty-three seconds...And the forced, solitary pace of their journey—solitary because, after an initial, perfunctory discussion of tactics, he felt disinclined to make idle chatter with Serafino—left him far too much time to mull over "fun while it lasted."

He had been so very sure that this was the time to tell her how he felt. She'd kissed him, no longer stepped away when he touched her arm, and blushed when he engaged in his—admittedly clumsy—flirtations with her.

So he allocated five minutes to fix the sensor dish. Then he'd get her into the privacy of the cockpit, close the door, and tell her how he'd felt for so many years. And she'd answer that she loved him too. He played that scene over and over in his mind as he marched up the shuttle rampway and finally—with Serafino suitably occupied with Doc Fynn—was able to usher her into the cockpit.

Then someone rewrote the scene.

He fully imagined kissing her again. But he imagined their kiss ending with a declaration of love. Not a pronouncement that it was "fun while it lasted."

He could almost hear Ralland in his head: *After a session like that you're complaining?*

No. The feel of her on him, the taste of her was incredible. For him. For her it was fun.

"Hey!"

Serafino's shout behind him made him slow down. Deep in thought, he'd outpaced the Nasyry again. *Running from my troubles?*

"If you need to rest..." he offered, part of him hoping the man would say, *Go on ahead without me, I'll catch up.*

"I'm not even winded." Sweat beaded on Serafino's face. He was panting. "But I don't have rockets in my pockets like you, Tin Soldier."

Kel-Paten stopped, let Serafino close the distance between them, then moved into a hard jog again. Probably would be best to keep Serafino with him. He didn't trust him at his back.

The dirt trail took them over the crest of a small

hill. The trees thinned but still offered cover and shade. HV-1's sun was no longer overhead but on their left. Kel-Paten judged it to be early to mid afternoon, but the planet's day might well be longer.

The forest grew denser at the base of the hill. He slowed slightly. Time for their second check-in. He pulled out the small comm link, now discreetly clipped on the inside of his shirt. He had a scrambler running on the shuttle's communications equipment but no way to verify its efficacy, so his report was brief. "Rover One to base." He relayed time, coordinates, and status in a truncated, prearranged code.

"Base to Rover One. Copy," said Tasha's voice, muffled and soft. "Acknowledged. Base out."

And that was it for another thirty minutes. No long conversations, nothing for the outpost to intercept. And no way for him to ask her about "fun while it lasted."

GALAXUS COCKPIT

There had to be a way to get the shuttle's sensors to pick up data on that outpost. Sass swiveled in the pilot's chair and watched the third test program she'd tweaked into the ship's computers run through its latest batch of queries. It made absolutely no sense why the handhelds were the only pieces of equipment able to get a fix—and just the basics at that. The powerful sensors on the shuttle could provide so many more answers.

She stopped swiveling for a moment and, leaning back, peered into the dim main cabin. Eden was still asleep. Sass had ordered the CMO off duty right after Serafino and Kel-Paten left, but Eden had insisted on hooking up a small regen unit to Sass's shoulder first. Her friend had a bruised look under her eyes from stress, lack of sleep, and—Sass suspected—Serafino. Sass's slight prodding into what might be the issue was met with an exasperated sigh and a terse "Testosterone."

Well, yes, the flamboyant Captain Jace Serafino had never lacked in that area.

So while Eden slept, Sass monitored the scouting party's check-ins (two so far, right on time) and tweaked the damned sensors, because she didn't want to think about Kel-Paten's kisses. Or his parting words.

I love you, Tasha.

It was bad enough to read it in his logs. It was worse hearing it in person, because she could no longer pretend it didn't exist. His speaking those words gave them life, made them real.

She was cursed and she knew it.

The test program finished its loop and beeped. She studied the screen. Nothing. All sensors still showed as operating within normal parameters, when she knew damned well they weren't. They couldn't be— they'd pick up the outpost if they were.

Mommy tired? Naptime. Tank, sprawled in the copilot's chair, rolled over onto his back and presented his belly to be rubbed. *Love Mommy. Protect!*

At least, that's what she thought he said. The rub-my-belly pose was unmistakable. She'd figured that out long before his voice—and often disjointed images—ever appeared in her mind. The images were the easiest to understand. His "verbal" conversations tended to be fraught with miscommunications.

Love Mommy, he said just now. But when Kel-Paten had been in the cockpit with her, it was *Loooove Mommy.* She didn't know if it meant anything; if she didn't have such a natural ear for linguistics, she wouldn't have noticed the difference in tones. It was probably nothing. Tank also had at least four different-sounding purrs.

Other words were simply indecipherable: squeals and chirps and coos that sometimes found their way inside usually decipherable words. *Blank-cooo-ket,* Tank had said just before pouncing on Eden's make-shift bed in the main cabin. Sass had scooped him up so that Reilly could take his rightful place. Reilly...

Sass hesitated. He had been with Eden when she'd ordered her CMO off duty. But the last few times Sass glanced back in the cabin, she hadn't seen the black furzel.

"Tank, where's Reilly?"

Friend? Friend hunt-ing. Run run jump. He stretched one hind leg. *Tank protect.*

Hunting? Tank's images in her mind were tinged in browns and greens. Did Eden awaken to let Reilly go outside at some point when Sass was occupied with a sensor program? She couldn't have. A double chime sounded whenever the main hatch opened.

She checked the security logs just to be sure. The last time the main hatch was accessed was when she'd gone out for an exterior inspection of the perimeter sensors, just after Serafino and the admiral left.

If Eden had opened the main hatch—or even an emergency hatch—it would be on the log.

It wasn't.

"Where's Reilly hunting?" she asked Tank, and pointed out the viewport. "Outside the ship?" She hadn't seen as much as a slitherskimp. She couldn't image what the furzel would hunt out there.

Run run jump! Tank answered. *Friend hunt ugly smelly light. Here. Not here. Bad smelly. Safe here. Tank protect.*

Ugly smelly light? Sass tried to decipher the phrase she'd heard so often in the past few hours. Was there something in this planet's light spectrum that furzels could see and humans couldn't? Something dangerous, a form of radiation their sensors couldn't detect? Eden had checked for all known parameters, but so much about Haven-1 seemed to border on the unknown.

"Where is the ugly smelly light, Tank?" She picked him up and held him up to the viewport. "Out there? In the sky?"

There. Not there. Here. Not here.

"Where, Tank? Don't talk. *Show* me. Think a picture, if you can."

Think picture?

"When you look at the ugly light, what do you see?"

Bright blue with green swirls flowed through her mind. Just color. It could be a blue ball or a blue box or a blue huntership from close up. Nothing recognizable. Damn.

"So it's blue. Can you take me to where you saw it?"

No ask, please? Reilly not like. Danger to Mommy. Tank protect!

"I understand, but this is important. Tell Reilly that. You have to show me the ugly light."

Danger to Mommy!

"But you and Reilly protect me and Eden. You're big furzels."

Tank rubbed his head thoughtfully against her arm. *O-kay. Maybe. Tank protect.* He wriggled in her grasp. She let him go. He jumped to the deck and gave himself a shake, then trotted toward the main cabin. She stripped the restricting regen unit off her shoulder and followed, tiptoeing past a sleeping Eden Fynn. Tank stopped at the engine-compartment hatchway and pawed it.

Sass hit the release to open it. "Ugly light down there?" she whispered.

There. Long time. Not there.

Not direct radiation from the planet's sun, then. She tucked the fidget under one arm and climbed awkwardly down the ladderway, her damaged shoulder protesting. "Where in here?" She put him on the floor.

Plumy tail aloft, he trotted to the far-port bulkhead and a smaller maintenance accessway. *There. Long time. On Big Ship first. Leave Big Ship. On here. Now small here. Big out there.*

A sick, cold feeling formed in the pit of Sass's stomach. Big ship. That had to be the *Vax*. Something that was on the *Vax* had moved to the *Galaxus*. Something ugly and smelly and bad. Something the furzels hunted. Something the furzels protected them from.

This was definitely not a problem with an unknown level of radiation.

She pulled the datalyzer from her utility belt, then flicked on its hand-beam function and, squatting down, tabbed open the accessway cover. She played the light up and down the narrow duct and watched readings on the screen, looking for any kind of mechanical device. Something with a blue screen or light on it. Did this Faction that Serafino so feared have an agent on board the Kel's prize huntership? Did that agent plant a tracking device, a bomb?

No box, Mommy.

Box? Mechanical device. Tank had seen the images in her mind.

"Okay. No box. What am I looking for?"

Yellow eyes glared at her. *Ugly. Smelly. Light!* If the fidget had added "you stupid human!" to his comment, Sass wouldn't have been surprised.

Okay. Ugly smelly light. She sniffed. Nothing smelled out of the ordinary, but then, furzels had a wider range of senses than she did. She took a deeper breath. Nothing.

Ugly smelly light! Tank shoved past her and, before she could grab him, jumped through the small opening, directly into the narrow ducts that ran behind the bulkheading.

"Tank, no!" Gods' blessed rumps, it was going to be hell getting him out of there. When she did, he'd be filthy. And if there was something dangerous in there . . . "Tank, get back here now!" She angled the hand beam in his direction, caught a swish of his—now filthy—tail.

He stretched his short, pudgy body up on his hind legs as if reaching for something. She brought the beam up as well.

Then she saw it.

She had no idea what it was, but she could see something vaguely oval, faintly glowing, pulsing blue-purple-black. It was about the size of Eden's medicorder or smaller. It didn't look like a device, but she didn't discount that it could be. It registered as a complete unknown on her small datalyzer.

Tank poked one paw toward it.

"Tank, get away from that thing now!" She didn't even try to disguise the note of fear in her voice. Her heart pounded.

Tank protect. Safe.

"You're not safe. Get away!"

Safe. Small Bad Thing. Fidg—furzel bigger. Blink stronger. Watch! He slapped at the light with his paw. The light skittered sideways, undulating, purple fading to black.

Holy lubashit on a lemon. The damned thing was alive. Sass yanked her pistol from its holster, the datalyzer now in her left hand.

Bad Thing not like Tank, not like Blink. There was a distinct note of pride in his voice.

Blink? Another word she was probably misunderstanding. "Get back here now. Or no more cream. Ever."

Cream? Food, sweet!

"Jump back up now!"

Jump? No jump. Go Blink!

Go blink?

Tank disappeared. One second he was there, the next he wasn't. Frantically, she played the hand beam back and forth in the duct but could find no trace of her fidget. The ... thing on the outer bulkhead pulsed darkly but didn't move. Then something butted her thigh.

She glanced down and saw golden eyes and a smudgy, dusty, furry face.

"Tank!" She hugged him hard against her.

He made a soft *ooof* noise, then: *Tank protect. One furzel hunts. One furzel protects.*

"This," and she motioned with her pistol to the interior of the duct, "this blue-purple thing. This is ugly smelly light?"

Very small Bad Thing. Ugly. Smelly.

"And Reilly...hunts this? He's down here?" She glanced around. In her surprise at finding the thing in the accessway and her fear for Tank's safety, she'd forgotten about the older furzel. "Where's Reilly?"

Run run jump!

Greens, browns assailed her. The smell of wet soil, the sound of leaves and branches cracking.

Friend hunt Big Bad Thing. Very big. Very bad. Bad Thing hunts, kills. Furzels protect.

It took only a moment this time for the scenario and sensations to come together in her mind. And when they did, she didn't like what she'd figured out at all.

She shoved herself to her feet and lunged for the nearest comm panel. "Eden! Get your ass out of bed. Reilly's taken off after Kel-Paten and Serafino. And there's some kind of nasty creature hunting them all."

Eden Fynn, CMO and Zingaran Healer, shelved her worries about her furzel and—per the captain's orders—focused on analyzing the small glowing oval stuck to the outer bulkhead. Ugly smelly light. Bad Thing. She couldn't judge if it was ugly or not, and it didn't have an odor she or her bioscanner could detect. But it did emit light.

As for bad—she was working on that right now. Empathically. Telepathically she couldn't pick up anything without touching it, and there was no way Tasha would permit her to touch it, even if she could somehow manage to squeeze into the narrow duct. Just as well. Something she couldn't define told her that touching Bad Thing—which is what she and Tasha agreed was the most useful name for it— wouldn't be pleasant.

But whether it would be lethal—fatal—she wasn't sure. Yet.

It was almost dead. That much she did sense, *if* her comprehension of life essence was valid for its species. That was also in agreement with what Sass could decipher from Tank. Reilly had hunted this smaller piece of Bad Thing and somehow neutralized it.

And now Reilly was gone, run off into the forest on this strange planet.

No, don't think about that. Find out what this creature is. That's the danger. Not this place. Besides, Sass was back in the cockpit contacting Kel-Paten and Serafino right now. They'd find Reilly. He'd be fine.

She relaxed her mind once again and probed.

Sensations trickled through her. Weakly, but there. It felt as if she watched a vid from a distance. But, no, wait. Not a vid. She recognized the man. Her ex-husband, his face, lips twisted in a sneer. He was younger, *she* was younger, a holo-catalog suspended before her. She remembered the dress she wanted to buy, a soft swirl of blues and golds. Beautiful.

"Doubt they make it in a size big enough for *you*."

Her ex-husband's voice. His harsh laugh.

Her shame. His cruelty. She wanted to curl up in a ball and die. . . .

"Eden!"

Sass, shaking her shoulders. Tank frantically pawing her leg.

"Eden, snap out of it."

"Huh?"

"That thing just got bigger."

It took a moment for her to shake off the feeling of unworthiness, of ugliness, the horrid memory . . .

The purple oval glowed more brightly now. And it was slightly larger, plumper. If light could be said to be plump.

"Gods." Eden exhaled the word. She understood suddenly. "It was reading me. Feeding off my memory, my emotions." No, not her memory exactly. But a much more intense version of a minor memory. Her ex-husband's comment had only irritated her at the time; she'd grown used to them by then. But linked to Bad Thing, the memory was crushing. Horrible.

And Bad Thing loved it.

"It's like a parasite, feeding on hatred. Fear," she told Sass, letting her friend draw her to her feet. "If you can link to it, it grabs something you remember, makes it worse, until you want to die." She stopped, the import of her words coming to the fore. "That means every empath, every telepath that it comes in contact with is at risk."

"Maybe not just empaths," Sass offered. "What if that's what happened on *Degun's Luck* or those other ships before that? Officers and crew on a ship that shows no sign of attack or intruders, all dead from fear."

Eden stared at her, comprehension coming with crystal clarity. "We stopped at Lightridge. *Degun's Luck* was berthed there. Maybe this thing killed the crew and then, still hungry, came on board the *Vax*. Tank told you it was on the *Vax*, right?" When Sass nodded, Eden continued: "And from there, for some reason, it went to our shuttle."

"We were headed for Panperra. Big station. Lots of people," Sass suggested.

"And it can split itself. Or there's more than one." Eden grabbed Sass's arm. "Part could still be on Lightridge, on the *Vax*. People will die, and no one will know the reason!"

"The furzels know. They hunt it. They trap it using something they call a Blink."

"Blink?"

Sass nodded. "I pressed Tank for an explanation while you were down here running an analysis on it. He sent me thought pictures of a telepathic energy shield, like a force field. Furzels create it from this Blink space. Tank and Reilly encased that thing. That's why it didn't affect me when I was close to it. But you probed it. Tank felt that, dragged me down here to stop you."

Eden looked down at Tank, rubbing against her leg. "And Reilly?"

Sass nodded. "He went after the admiral and Serafino because the rest of that thing," she motioned to the glowing oval in the duct, "is out there, after them. Given what those two feel about each other, and given that Jace is a telepath, there's a lot of hatred for it to feed on. And who knows what else if it gets to that outpost."

"You warned them—"

"I tried. Pinged them twice." Sass tugged at the strap of the rifle slung over her shoulder. It finally registered with Eden that the captain had donned her jacket and was dressed in full battle gear. "They're not answering. Is your telepathy strong enough to reach Jace?"

An icy hand closed around Eden's heart. *Jace? Jace!*

Silence.

Eden shook her head. "No," she said. *Damn him.*

"Get your gear, Fynn." Sass's words were clipped, her expression grim. "Tank's going to fix that Blink shield. Then we've got a long, hard jog ahead of us."

25

Go Blink!

Sass watched in amazement and disbelief as her fidget disappeared and reappeared before her eyes. It was as if he'd jumped in and out of a hole in the engine-compartment bulkhead—except there wasn't one. Now she knew how he'd gotten out of her cabin and into Eden's to visit Reilly when the door was locked.

Go Blink!

With those few movements he repaired the small rip in the shield around Bad Thing, once again a darker shade of purple when Sass cautiously peered into the accessway. Dying. Eden had confirmed that much.

She picked up the purring fidget, holding him close against her shoulder, then climbed up the ladderway to the main cabin and Eden, her thoughts on what might even now be threatening Lightridge and the *Vaxxar*. Threatening Kel-Paten.

I can handle what's out there, he'd told her.

She had no doubt the Tin Soldier could. With his cybernetics and Psy-Serv's emo-inhibitors, he was one six-foot-three emotionless son of a bitch. But he was more than the Tin Soldier. He was Branden. He had bypassed all those emo-inhibitor programs and loved her.

If Bad Thing caught up with him when his emo-inhibitors were off-line, his loving her—or hating Serafino—could well get him killed.

She pushed the fidget through the hatchway and then pulled herself up into the main cabin. Eden was sealing her backpack on top of the tangle of blankets that was her makeshift bed.

"Ready?" she asked the CMO.

"When we find him," Eden said through thinned lips, "I don't know what I'm going to do first: kiss him or kick his ass."

Sass didn't know if Eden was referring to Serafino or Reilly. It didn't matter. She understood the feeling only too well.

She made one final check of the gear and spare power packs on her utility belt, then hoisted her own backpack over one shoulder. "Let's go."

Run! Jump! Run!

THE FOREST

"Shit." Jace Serafino stared through the binoculars at the ship sitting on the tarmac on the edge of the small outpost. An outpost that—based on all previous data—should still be a good hour's hike from here. And a ship that—based on his personal experience—had no possible way of being there. He knew exactly how and when he'd lost the *Mystic Traveler* to that slimy son of bitch Rej Andgarran. Almost eight years ago. Being ambushed and then trussed up like a kurii hen was far from the high point of his career. Having his ship stolen by Andgarran was even worse. And he'd never had a chance to steal it back, because Andgarran disappeared a few months later and hadn't reappeared in U-Cee or Triad space since.

But how in hell had it gotten here? The same way the *Galaxus* had?

He lowered the binocs and studied the readout on his handheld again. "It's real. Whatever it is."

"Having trouble recognizing your own ship?" Kel-Paten asked, his voice low. They were on the edge of a hillside, crouched down among thick bushes and haphazard stacks of felled trees. Trees that, Jace guessed, at one time populated the field now occupied by this unexpected landing site. At the moment, with the deepening shadows of late afternoon, they also provided excellent cover.

"She's not mine. I sold her years ago," he lied.

Kel-Paten's silence irritated him. He wondered if the 'cybe knew the truth.

"And it's still not the *Traveler*." Or was it?

"Logically, I agree, it shouldn't be the *Mystic Traveler*. But even if I didn't recognize her configuration, there's her name emblazoned on her port side."

"Dream about her nightly, do you?" Jace had held back from needling Kel-Paten to this point, but this was something he could no longer resist. It was one of the reasons he missed the *Traveler* so much. She was the one ship to take the infamous Tin Soldier down a peg. "Is she part of your sexual fantasies too?"

Kel-Paten shot him a hard look. Jace answered with a raised eyebrow but let it stop there. They had larger problems than his desire to see Kel-Paten squirm. Problems like nonworking comm links that required Kel-Paten to order him to check in telepathically with Eden.

Jace had no intention of taking orders from Kel-Paten and wasn't about to open any kind of telepathic link to Eden Fynn. There was too much at risk. More so now that he stared at a ship that was but wasn't his.

So he lied to Kel-Paten about checking in—though he could sense that Eden was alive and well, which was all that mattered.

Kel-Paten returned to studying the sleek ship. Without binocs. He didn't need them. "So, Nasyry, what are we looking at?"

"A ship someone wants me to think is the *Traveler.*"

"And that someone is?"

"I won't know until we get closer," Jace admitted. "I can't read specific thoughts at this distance. I *can* sense overall emotional levels. I'm not picking up anything unusual." If anything, things seemed too calm. His experience with spaceports and dock hands was that someone, somewhere, always had his ass puckering over something.

"To have someone provide you with a ship would not be unusual. *If* they expected you to arrive." There was a flat, hard tone to Kel-Paten's voice, and Jace didn't like it.

"What are you getting at?"

"You brought us here. You were at the controls when the shuttle entered the jumpgate. I found it very unusual that we should just happen to end up, blindly, near a habitable planet. But now we have not only a habitable planet but one with your former ship. Something to warrant a further investigation, bringing us, bringing *me*, closer to whoever waits on that ship. Or in the hangar." Kel-Paten shifted his weight slightly, rebalancing. "Perhaps that blind jump wasn't so blind. Who owns you, Nasyry? The Illithians? The Cryloc Syndicate?"

"No one owns me." Jace's voice was equally hard.

"Your contract with the Triad was a sham. Who put you up to it?"

"Since when is 'cooperate or we'll kill you' considered a contract?"

"The Triad doesn't—"

"Don't they?" Jace tensed. If the Tin Soldier made a move, he was ready. More than ready. This confrontation was overdue and they both knew it. "Or does Psy-Serv conveniently delete that fact during your weekly tune-ups?"

"*You* must have forgotten you received two hundred fifty thousand credits. That's hardly fatal. So someone is paying you more. Is it me they want, or is kidnapping two Alliance officers part of the plan as well?"

"If someone wanted your head on a platter, they wouldn't have to pay me. I'd do it for free."

"Wise on your part. You're not going to live long enough to spend a reward, anyway."

There was no way Jace could see Kel-Paten move. The 'cybe was too fast. But he sensed it, sensed the surge of power through his aura, and rolled to his left, Kel-Paten's hand just grazing his shoulder.

He sprang to his feet, breathing hard, laser pistol in hand. But the 'cybe was already there, unarmed, not needing a weapon. The eerie glow in his eyes confirmed he was one. Jace fired into a blur of movement, not knowing he missed until two black-gloved hands slammed against his shoulders, pinning him to the hard earth. The pistol skittered away in the grass.

"Who owns you?" Kel-Paten ground out.

A bizarre sensation of fear surged through him. He tried to push it away as he wrestled against Kel-Paten's grip. He was too damned busy fighting for his life to be afraid. He blocked the suffocating sensation and dropped again into Nasyry warrior mode. He tensed his body, then bucked against the 'cybe in a move that would have tossed an ordinary man into the bushes. It only managed to dislodge Kel-Paten a few inches, but that was enough. Jace twisted again, ignoring the flare of pain from his cracked ribs. He sprang up into a crouch, catching only a glimpse of a surprised look on the 'cybe's face over the fact that Jace was still standing and fighting.

But it was a brief, fleeting reward.

The fear—a cold, cutting terror—returned, hitting him with such force that he gasped for breath. Before Jace could take a second, the 'cybe was on him, flattening him to the ground, knee in Jace's chest, hand on his throat . . .

Something dropped down from above. Darkness descended, Kel-Paten's chest smothering his face. A muffled shout. Fear swirled maddeningly through his mind, death beckoning as the only respite.

Then there was light. He could breathe again. The overwhelming sensation of fear faded...no, vanished, like a popped soap bubble.

Jace opened his eyes and struggled to sit up, leaning against—Eden?

"Eden!"

She brushed his hair out of his eyes.

He blinked, looked over her shoulder. Kel-Paten, a few feet away, was flat on his back. Sebastian was sitting on his chest, arms folded, lips pursed.

Lady Sass did not look happy.

Neither did Eden. "Sweetling," he croaked. His ribs ached like hell.

"You godsdamned son of a bitch." Eden Fynn balled her fist and smacked him hard across the jaw.

Sebastian snickered. "I thought you were going to kick him in the ass. It's on the other end, Doc."

"Don't worry. I'll get there."

JaceFriend! MommyEden not happy.

A strong sense of disapproval on his right. Wincing, he looked down. Reilly. And beyond him, Tank. The fat fidget looked positively gleeful, even with twigs stuck to his tail.

JaceFriend, Reilly continued. *Bad to not talk to Reilly. Bad. Bad.*

Oh, hell, the mental block he'd erected to keep Eden and Reilly out of his thoughts was gone. He didn't remember letting down his guard, but that's probably how Eden located him—and then came right up behind him without either him or the 'cybe noticing. Of course, they were a bit occupied. He rubbed his jaw and put his telepathic senses on full scan.

The fear slammed into him full force. Biting, cold, gnawing. It knocked the breath out of his lungs, blinded his eyes with its intensity.

He heard a scream—a high-pitched furzel-like yowl—and then a woman shouting his name, hands clinging to his shoulders.

His brain spun in dizzying rotations, and the last thing he remembered before falling into darkness was a small voice giving a very odd command.

Go Blink!

"Eden!" Tasha's anguished cry tore through Kel-Paten. She bolted upright off his chest, her boot catching his side as she tried to stand. She stumbled forward, arms out toward...

Nothing. Eden and her furzel were gone. The bastard Serafino was gone.

Kel-Paten was already on his feet. He grasped her shoulders, holding her steady. He didn't know where the two—no, three of them—went, but he suspected a transporter beam. Not from the *Traveler* but a smaller ship overhead, probably a security skimmer. He fine-tuned his hearing, listening for the low thrum of an engine. If that was the case, the ship could be searching for other biosignatures to lock on to. He didn't intend for them to find his or Tasha's.

"Come on!" He dragged her backward a few steps, a flash of black and white at her feet. The fidget. "We have to get out of here before they realize they missed us."

"But—"

"*Move,* Captain." He snatched his backpack and Serafino's from the ground. "That's an order!" Or by the gods' blessed rumps, he'd throw her over his shoulder and carry her.

She moved, or, rather, let him drag her back into the forest, the fidget darting this way and that in front of them.

They needed cover, something thicker than the tree canopy shadowing them on the hillside. Something with other biosignatures to muddy the scan would be ideal, but he opted not to head for the outpost. Whoever hunted them probably had his biosignature, or thought they did. His real one wasn't in any file Serafino or his ilk could have accessed. He had six others his system could emulate. He triggered that program now as they charged through the brush.

He didn't think they'd have Tasha's. He doubted they even cared they'd kidnapped her to this unusually convenient planet. But just in case, he kept her as close as possible to him as they ran away from the unusually convenient path. That, too, should muddy their sensors.

"Wait! Tank says...it's not..." She tried to wrench her arm from his grasp.

He held on. "A small ravine. There, at the base of the hills." The uneven topography promised some outcroppings and overhangs. Good visual cover, if nothing else.

He heard no following whine of an engine overhead. Of course, he hadn't heard one just before

Serafino disappeared, but then, with Tasha perched on his chest, he admittedly wasn't paying close attention.

He was now. He could not, would not lose her.

"It's not following us!" she said.

So she didn't hear an engine either. Good. But he would feel better when they were tucked out of sight. They could regroup, analyze, come up with a plan to get Fynn back.

He ducked under a group of low-hanging branches, his mind working on who was behind this and the attack near Panperra. The problem was twofold. First, who wanted him incapacitated or dead? That list was lengthy. Second, who had the knowledge and resources to enact such a plan of ambush and obfuscation? That list wasn't quite as lengthy, but it did include the Illithian Dynasty. Those alien fighters that forced them into the jumpgate prematurely could have been an Illithian ploy so Serafino could "pretend" to find this planet by happenstance.

Yet no matter how much he hated the man, he had a hard time seeing him in any kind of relationship with the Irks. But he could see him allying with that Rebashee mercenary, Gund'jalar. Zanorian had. And there'd long been rumors the Rebashee had charts to the far edges of the galaxy, if that was indeed where they were.

"Here." They reached a narrow section of the ravine. The forest was thick, filled with twisting vines and the jagged outcropping of rocks overhead. "We should be safe here for a little while." He yanked the backpacks' straps from his shoulder and dropped them at his feet.

Tasha was breathing hard. She bent over at the waist, resting her hands on her thighs. Tank plopped down on one of the backpacks. "Damn." Her voice was raspy. "Damn."

"We'll find Fynn. I don't think he'd hurt her. He has her either on that ship or somewhere in that outpost. More likely, they'll want to trade her for me." He pulled his handheld out of his utility belt and adjusted the screen's light as he activated the datalyzer, checking for pursuers. It was late afternoon, judging from the sun's position. But the foliage shadowed everything. He tilted the screen, better to see the data. Nothing. Right now.

"He doesn't have her." Tasha straightened. "*It* has *them*."

He dragged his gaze from the datalyzer and looked at her. Her hair was ruffled, a few green leaves sticking to it. There was a smudge of dirt on her cheek. But her eyes were clear, steady, and troubled.

He wanted to pluck out the leaves, smooth the dirt from her face, but held back, unsure now of what response he'd get. He helped her untangle her backpack's strap instead. "It? What are you talking about?"

"It. The furzels call it *Bad Thing*. It's here with us and is some kind of psi-based creature. Telepathic. Teleportation too, evidently." She drew in a breath. "I think it killed the crew on *Degun's Luck* and came on board when we made Lightridge Station. Then it hitched a ride on the shuttle, maybe because it wanted to get to Panperra. Or maybe it was after one of us. I'm not sure. But it almost killed Eden after you left. That's why we came after you. Now it has her and Serafino and Reilly. Tank says they're alive. He can sense them. But he's not sure he knows how to get them back without Reilly's help."

If it were anyone other than Tasha Sebastian telling him this, he'd discount every word. But that troubled gaze didn't waver, and her mouth was a thin, grim line. Something threatening had been found on the shuttle—had been on the *Vax,* if he understood her correctly. And he'd left her and Fynn to face it alone.

"Sit down," he said, because she looked like she was ready to fall down. He pointed to a mossy boulder. "Catch your breath, then start from the beginning. Tell me everything."

She sat and rummaged in her backpack. "You do know," she said, extracting her canteen and flipping open the top, "that I cannot run as fast as you do." She took a mouthful of water, closing her eyes as she swallowed.

Damn. He hadn't run at full speed, but he hadn't run at her speed either. And he'd hung on to her arm the whole way. "I did think about throwing you over my shoulder. We'll try that next time."

She wiped at her mouth with the back of her hand, and for a brief moment something sparkled in her eyes. Then it was gone. "I'm not sure where to start. So much of what I'm learning about this Bad Thing creature is a jumble of information from Tank. The furzels talk in a combination of images, sounds, scents, and words. Some of this may be wrong. And I might be missing what's really important."

He eased down on a fallen tree trunk across from her. "Tell me whatever you know."

She did, starting with the way Tank's *protect, protect* always sang in her mind, to finding Reilly missing, to Tank's revelation of something trapped in the shuttle's engine compartment. She described the dark glowing oval and what Eden said it felt like to have the thing sending images, sending desolation into her mind, making her want to die.

He thought of the way Serafino pulled the shameful memory of the prosti from his mind. But the shame didn't make him want to die. It only made him want to kill Serafino.

Tasha glanced at Tank from time to time as she talked, touching his head, stroking one ear. She was listening to the fidget, he guessed. Knew she was when she said, "Tank's trying to get a clearer fix on them through the Blink."

"A blink?"

She explained the Blink, how the furzels used it not only as transportation and communication but as a shield. "They manipulate its energy. Eden said the Nasyry have something similar, a place called Novalis."

"I've heard of the legend."

"It's not legend. Eden's been there. Serafino knows far more about it, but he stopped talking to her telepathically once we found this planet."

"Why?" This psi-creature notwithstanding, he was still mistrustful of Serafino.

Tasha shrugged. "To protect her, he said. We think he knew about Bad Thing. Telepaths and empaths seem particularly susceptible. Which brings me to something else I think you need to know." She drew a short breath. "Serafino has an implant in his head, courtesy of Psy-Serv."

"An implant?"

"A telepathic inhibitor. And, we suspect, some kind of data recorder. It was starting to break down and we—she—thought it might kill him. Eden couldn't remove it, but she did manage to disable it."

He thought of Fynn's insistence to get Serafino on the med diag table right before they left the shuttle. "She operated on him two hours ago?"

"Um, no." Tasha looked down at her boots and toed at a clump of grass. "Couple of days ago. Maybe three. I've lost track of time, a bit."

"Why wasn't I informed—"

"I'm sorry." She raised her face. "But we weren't sure whose side you were on. When Serafino started talking about Psy-Serv corrupting the Triad—"

"You thought I'd be part of that?" His allegiance to the Triad was not only unshakable but irrefutable. But she did arm Serafino. And she did believe he'd sent the alien fighters after them at Panperra. She'd threatened to sell him as scrap.

"Kel-Sennarin is."

"Impossible." Her allegations shocked him, and for a moment he was almost angry that she could even suggest such a thing. But then, she was U-Cee. She couldn't be expected to understand. "He's a Triad Defense Minister. I've known him for years. His reputation is impeccable."

"Serafino says he has proof."

"Says," he countered strongly, but she was still talking.

"That thing in his head is also a recorder. Eden and

I suspect that's why Psy-Serv wanted him brought back in. It's not the two hundred fifty thousand. It's his memories. But they didn't know Eden's a telepath or they never would have assigned his capture to the *Vax*."

Kel-Paten tamped down his annoyance at her allegations about Kel-Sennarin and focused on the information about Psy-Serv. He refused to accept the Triad was behind the ambush. But Psy-Serv had no honor. "Then the fighters that intercepted us by Panperra were after him. And willing to kill the rest of us in the process."

"Eden is the only innocent. Serafino said I've been on the Faction's hit list for some time. You weren't until recently. Psy-Serv feels they can no longer control you."

"Psy-Serv never controlled me!"

"Can they access you when you're spiked in?"

He closed his eyes briefly, watched the yellow numbers dance in the lower corner of his vision. He was a 'cybe again to her. And though part of him had started to believe that didn't matter to her, the rest of him still felt alien. So much less than human. "They can," he said, watching her for any of the one hundred forty expressions he knew, "upload and download certain information, yes. But they cannot reprogram me." He hated the word, but it had to be said. He knew that's what she was really asking.

She nodded. He read acceptance in her features. It was preferable to disgust. "That's all rather moot, isn't it? Because they're on the other side of that jump we made. And we're now dealing with some kind of psi-energy alien that wants to play mind games with us until we die." The fidget butted his head against her hand. "Tank's still searching."

Kel-Paten leaned his elbows on his knees and steepled his fingers over his mouth, not really hearing her last comment. Something bothered him about the information she'd outlined. He felt as if he were missing something. Granted, it all had happened so fast— it was only eight days since they'd stopped at Lightridge to let Fynn investigate the deaths on *Degun's Luck*. Then there was the vortex, Serafino, Panperra, the fighters, the blind jump. The illogical world they were on. And a mindsucking psi-creature... that could create a duplicate of a bastard pirate's ship?

"Ask Tank," he said, feeling slightly foolish even making the request, "if this Bad Thing can manipulate matter." At Tasha's slight frown, he continued. "Could it create the copy of Serafino's *Mystic Traveler*?"

"The *Traveler*'s here?"

"What appears to be the *Traveler* is at the outpost. Could it create an outpost, a ship," and gods, that was a staggering thought, "this world? Ask Tank if he knows where Bad Thing's home world is."

She pulled the fat fidget into her lap. "Do you understand what the admiral asked you, sweet baby?" She stroked his whiskers. "Okay," she said after a moment. "Let's take this one thing at a time. Bad thing. Furzels know Bad Thing for a long time, right?"

Silence from the fidget. A narrowing of eyes from Tasha. "Where are there lots of Bad Things? Big Bad Things, baby Bad Things, all together. If Bad Thing goes home, where is that? A ship? A cloud world? A green world?"

More silence. More narrowing of eyes. Then Tasha's eyes closed. "Holy lubashit on a lemon," she said softly. She looked at him. "Tank says they come from the void. McClellan's Void. He calls it Big Crazy Silly Space."

"That doesn't mean—"

"He showed me," she continued, as if he hadn't spoken, "an image. A Rebashee gesture." She touched her thumb to her little finger, arching the other three, then made a small slicing movement in the air. "Dreehalla. It appears, Admiral, all your mathematical theories are wrong."

SOMEWHERE IN THE OUTPOST

The fear was no longer nameless, faceless. It was real. And, as expected, it wore the austere purple and black robe of a Nasyry warrior priestess.

He knew they'd find him eventually.

Jace felt Eden's fingers digging into his arm. So much for trying to protect her from this. One moment they were blinded, clinging to each other as their world shifted from outside in the forest to here, this stark, high-ceilinged room about the size of an average freighter cargo bay. Then his vision cleared and he saw *her*. Immediately, he stepped in front of Eden—or tried to. It was an instinctive move, which she deftly blocked.

Eden evidently would have none of that. *Where in hell are we?*

"Hush," he said softly. "Not now."

The robed woman standing at the far end didn't

turn or give any indication she knew they were there. There was a long, narrow window or viewport in front of her, shadowy figures shifting in the distance. Window, he decided. Though the room reminded him of a cargo bay, with wide joists curving out from the walls or bulkheads at regular intervals, nothing told his senses he was on a ship.

At least, not one in space.

"Let me handle this," he told Eden. Then chanced it: *If I tell you to run, you run. Don't look back.* He tried to block her from his mind then. He couldn't raise a block, not even the smallest mental filter. Something was stopping him, something—

Psy-Serv. He recognized that taint of arrogance immediately.

Psy-Serv, here? With a Nasyry Great Lady?

Something was wrong. He took a quick scan. There were others in the room. He saw only edges of shadows in the irregular overhead lighting but felt much more. Six, no seven. Eight, with the Great Lady. Eight against two. No, three. They had Reilly....

Reilly was gone.

Eight against two.

"Who is she?" Eden whispered.

My past come back to haunt me, probably kill me, he wanted to say, but didn't. The presence of Psy-Serv puzzled him. But Eden had a right to know the basics. "They," he whispered back. "Eight. All around us." And he'd lost his weapon in the scuffle with the 'cybe.

"Oh, Jace! I'm so frightened!" Eden's voice warbled theatrically. "What do they want?" She clutched the front of his jacket, wailed loudly in his ear.

Tucked something into his hand as he moved to dislodge her.

A laser pistol. He hoped she'd retrieved his from the ground and wasn't giving him hers. He slipped it into an inside pocket. "Ahh, Eden. I really do love you," he whispered in her ear, unable to keep a slight chuckle out of his voice in spite of the circumstances. Gods, she was a terrible actress.

He wanted to believe she was also armed. Or at least had several useful items clamped to her utility belt. He felt them as she bumped against him.

But if he knew, chances were the other eight knew. Psy-Serv missed little. A Nasyry warrior priestess missed nothing.

Sniffling, Eden let him draw her to his side. He patted her lightly on the rump, then took a half step forward. He was already dead. It would matter little if he violated sacred protocol.

"Great Lady," he began, his voice carrying clearly. "I acknowledge this unspeakable transgression in addressing you without permission. But I am a lowly *saj-oullum*, and my crude audacity knows no bounds."

A rustle from the shadows in the room but no response.

Then the woman raised her right arm slowly, stopping when it was about even with her shoulders. Her robe fanned out. A glowing blue orb emerged and floated by her side, expanding until it was about three feet across.

It took a moment for him to access collective memory and identify it. Bloody holy damn. His stomach clenched. A Ved'eskhar. A legendary monster. Impossible. But this one was real. Now he knew where his psychic block and paralyzing sense of fear had originated. And he knew what had snatched them from the forest to this room. But what was one of his people doing with a Ved? The Ved were parasites, psi-vampires. A telepath's worst nightmare. And banished by the Nasyry centuries ago to some unnamed dimension where they would feed upon each other and die. But they hadn't, and suddenly with a sickening jolt he knew where he was.

Eden sucked in a sharp breath.

"Ved'eskhar," he told her quietly.

Eden shook her head. "That's Bad Thing. Reilly—" She glanced quickly down, looking left and right. *Reilly?* This time the panic in her voice was real.

Don't know. He tried to send her reassurances. Reilly was smart. He was probably hiding in here somewhere.

Reilly and Tank killed one of those things on the shuttle.

Killed a Ved? On the shuttle? He didn't know they could be killed by a furzel. And he sure as hell didn't know one had been on the shuttle.

One was on the Vax *too. And Lightridge.* Degun's Luck. *At least, that's what Reilly told me.*

The disturbing undercurrent he'd felt on the *Vax.* A Ved'eskhar.

Things slowly started to make sense. And then the Great Lady turned and spoke. And nothing made sense at all.

"I will speak now, Jacinto. You will listen. Then, when I'm ready, both of you will die."

Even if he didn't recognize the face, the voice, the use of his name was unmistakable. Only one person in his life had ever called him Jacinto. It was her loving, special nickname for him.

But there was nothing loving in her face or tone at all, and her aura seethed with poisonous colors. The brief elation he'd felt upon seeing her evaporated like a drop of water falling on the Riln Marin Desert as he quickly tallied the scene before him: a Nasyry holy robe, a Ved, and the stink of Psy-Serv. All on a world created by the Ved out of the thoughts of humans dragged into the neverwhen.

This time he did manage to push Eden behind him. He faced his sister squarely, pain slicing his heart as a thousand questions whirled through his mind. He voiced only one: "What kind of game are you playing here, Bianca?"

She stepped closer to him, the Ved following, and held out her other hand. He'd always thought his sister had the most beautiful smile. This one carried the chill of the grave.

A small form walked stiffly from the shadows. A boy, almost a young man. Gods, no! Young Jorden. The nephew who had his uncle Jace's talents. Talents his mother didn't have. Or did she? Another puzzle.

Jorden took his mother's hand, and she turned him so the shaved area in the back of his head clearly showed. A long thin stripe to allow easy entry for an implant. With a sickening feeling, Jace remembered his fingers finding his own missing thatch of hair after Psy-Serv did the same thing to him.

"What kind of game?" She stroked Jorden's dark hair away, just in case Jace hadn't seen it. "One of control, Jacinto. A game of ultimate control."

26

Eden paced the small windowless office, looking for anything she could use, any way out. Two male human guards in nondescript gray freighter jumpsuits had escorted her here—at gunpoint—after removing her utility belt and pistol. Then they frisked her for any other weapons.

Three other guards—all human, one a woman— did the same thing to Jace, finding the pistol she'd passed to him.

But he wasn't in this makeshift holding cell with guards outside the door. Through his telepathic link with her, he flashed her images every few minutes: a long gray corridor, then wide double doors. More guards. Then an examining room that contained an array of medical equipment that, under other circumstances, she'd drool over.

Now it terrified her.

Don't be scared, sweetling. Use what I'm showing

you. He sent her the image of the corridor and its various doors again. *Find a way out.*

How could she when she was surrounded by Psy-Serv telepaths who were seeing and hearing everything Jace sent her?

They're not all telepaths. Eden; watch their aura. Those that are have implants like I do.

She stopped pacing. Damn! She reached empathically for the guards on the other side of her door. Only one was a telepath. But wait...yes. There was something in his aura. An odd wiggly red line, very faint.

That's what the implant looks like?

She felt Jace's affirmative.

But Bianca—

She's oullum, he told her. *And...* he hesitated, and Eden could feel the hurt radiating through him. He loved his sister. But his sister was no longer someone to love. *She's emotionally unstable, and not just from her relationship with the Ved. She hates telepaths, hates the Nasyry for making her feel inferior—*

She's wearing a priestess's robe.

She fancies herself the high priestess of the Oullums. Jace sounded disheartened but angry too. Frustrated. Eden felt that, felt how difficult it was for him to deal with this.

And that's why she kidnapped you?

We haven't quite gotten to that part yet. I have to go. I'll check back in a few minutes.

And the warmth she knew as Jace vanished.

Damn. Back to the problem of getting out of here. Eden examined the sole desk in the room, large and metal with three drawers on either end. It had also held a data terminal at one point, but that slot was empty. She rifled the drawers. Not even a lightpen so she could stab a guard in the neck. If she could get out of here. Or get them to come in.

Now, that was a thought. Maybe if she started screaming, pounding on the walls, the guards would have to investigate. But what could she hit them with? No chairs. Only the desk, and she couldn't lift that. She'd tried.

She looked up. A recessed light panel. A plastiglass insert surrounded by a metal frame. Her mind worked quickly. Drag the desk under the light panel, stand on it, and yank down the covering—if she could reach it. The insert would be too lightweight, but maybe the metal frame could be fashioned into something sword-like. Of course, she'd have to break it apart first, but maybe that would provide her with some nice sharp edges.

She went back to the desk, grabbed a corner, and tugged, her hands slipping on its rounded surface. It budged an inch or two. This wasn't working. Perhaps if she pushed?

She sidled around to the other side of the desk. Pushing gained her another two inches, an ache between her shoulder blades, and a scrape on her palm when her hand slipped again. Her head pounded.

Damn. Maybe if she took the drawers out. She pulled out the one on the top left, but it stopped. A safety-latch mechanism, she realized. She knelt and reached into the open space, feeling blindly with her fingers. Swearing. Finally, she found it, and the heavy drawer slid completely out.

The door to the office opened, startling her. Three

guards, including the woman who had taken Jace away. Jace...gods, how long was it since he contacted her? She reached, sensing him on the edges of her mind. But he wasn't talking.

The guards stepped in. The woman was the telepath, her aura tinged with red squiggles.

Eden pushed herself to her feet, bringing the long desk drawer with her. It was bulky, unwieldy, but if she could slam one of them in the head with it...

Three pistols appeared as she lifted the drawer.

"Don't be stupid, Dr. Fynn," the taller of the two men said. He had reddish hair, cropped very short, and a nose that looked too small for his broad face.

She lowered the drawer. "Where's Jace?"

"This way." Small Nose waggled his pistol.

She recognized the gray corridor. Three doors, a cross corridor, another two doors. All closed. No signs that said *Escape This Way*. She listened again for Jace or Reilly but heard only silence.

They came to the double doors, and when they opened, she recognized the medical facility. No Jace. "Where's Jace?" She put a firmness in her voice she didn't feel.

The two male guards assumed position by the door. The woman kept walking, disappearing behind a single door on the right. It closed behind her.

No one answered her question.

The single door opened again. Bianca strode through, the blue orb floating sinuously off her left shoulder. Bianca the Beautiful Bitch, and her Bad Thing. If Eden wasn't so damned mad and so damned scared, she might have found the moniker she'd bestowed on Jace's sister amusing.

"I want to see Jace," she told Bianca.

"What did you do to his harness?" The woman fairly spat out the words.

Harness? "He doesn't have a harness."

"Of course he has a harness. He's a telepath. They all must have harnesses!" Bianca almost shouted the last few words. The blue orb's glow increased, pulsing. "They must be controlled. But you . . . you!" She pointed at Eden. "What did you do to his harness? It's changed. It's not responding to commands. Dr. Kel-Novaco will not be pleased."

The implant. Oh, gods. Were they trying to access Jace's implant? She'd altered it the only way she could: by changing the codes by which it accessed each function. It was still functionally active. It just couldn't talk to the programs that told it what to do.

"It was malfunctioning. I had to deactivate it or it would have killed him." Surely Bianca cared if her brother lived or died?

"Of course it would have killed him! It's an older prototype. But now it's not responding to basic commands. We'll learn nothing from it when we extract it."

Extract it? "Extracting it could cause severe brain damage. Or kill him!"

Bianca frowned. "He's served his purpose."

Gods. Jace was nothing more than an experiment to her? "He's your brother!"

"He's a filthy mindsucker," Bianca shot back. "The data in the harness is more important."

"And your son? Your husband?"

She smiled. "Galen's harnessed. And Jorden listens to me. To us. We," and she gestured to the blue orb at her side, "know best when their mind habits can be used. Like in bringing my brother to us, so he could be harnessed. We had to play a little game, pretend I was in danger. I knew Jacinto would respond to that. He always has. Dr. Kel-Novaco put an excellent unit into him—at the time. Then it developed problems. Problems we think we can avoid in future harnesses. But we need to extract it and its data for that."

Bianca tilted her face slightly. "You're a doctor. Surely you know the importance of medical research." Her expression hardened. "How did you deactivate his harness?"

Eden's mind raced. Bianca would kill Jace. Her only concern was the unit, not her brother's life. But Eden had watched Sass in the casinos enough times to know that sometimes you had to bluff and bet it all, even when you held only one good card. This, she felt, was one of those times. "I changed the access codes."

"I want the new ones."

"No."

"No?"

Eden crossed her arms over her chest. "No." The only chance Jace had would be for Eden to be the one to remove the implant. Unlike Bianca, she would do everything to keep him alive. She had to convince Bianca to let her be the doctor in charge.

Bianca motioned to the blue orb.

Fear slammed into Eden. Cold, oily, invasive. Bad Thing crawled into her mind. She was in the cockpit of a shuttle, alone, as it hurtled out of control toward a sun. Then she was a child again. No, older, perhaps fifteen. Yes, fifteen. It was Maridee's birthday party at the lake. A horrible day. The memory was actually worse than the out-of-control shuttle, because the party was real.

Eden didn't have the lithe, slender body the other girls did. Feeling plump and uncomfortable with her curves, she wore a shapeless bathing suit. The boys laughed at her. "Drown the fat girl, drown the fat girl!"

No, no. They never said that. They just laughed. But it didn't matter. They were saying it now. And it felt real. Water in her face. Water in her nose and mouth. Hands, feet pushing her down, kicking her. Water in her lungs. Pressure. Horrible pressure. She wanted to scream but couldn't. Fear smothered her. Dying . . .

Let me die. Let me die. Death is good . . .

No, sweetling! Don't listen to it. Hold on to me . . .

"Bring her back!"

Bianca's voice jolted her.

Eden found herself on her knees, trembling, bile rising in her throat. But she'd heard Jace. Warmth flooded her.

"She has the codes," Bianca was saying. "We need those codes."

Yes, they did. They needed her alive. She struggled to her feet, swaying. "I will be the one to extract it." Her voice was raw, raspy. She could still taste the murky lake water. "Or you will not get the codes."

Bianca stared at her, eyes narrowed. "If you were a telepath, I'd order a harness implanted in you. You'd obey me then."

Bianca didn't know she was a telepath! To her, Eden Fynn was just a CMO. Ship's doctor on the

Vaxxar. An *oullum*. But surely the Bad Thing knew? Or was it reading her only as an empath because it had no solid form and couldn't touch her?

"I perform the surgery or no codes," Eden repeated.

It took several minutes. Finally Bianca nodded and thrust one hand toward the single door. "Your patient's in there. I want the implant and the codes by sunrise or . . ." and she let her voice trail off.

"You'll kill me?" Eden supplied sarcastically.

"No, Dr. Fynn. But you'll wish I had."

THE FOREST

Kel-Paten knew Tasha no longer trusted the data on the handhelds. To be honest, neither did he. But those units and his own cybernetically augmented senses were all they had to go on as night closed in on the forest at the edge of the outpost.

He refused to believe they were in McClellan's Void or any kind of hallucinatory anomaly. Too many other indicators told him this world and everything on it were real. He even had an explanation as to how Tasha and Fynn traversed the same distance he and Serafino did—in less than half the time. He and Serafino ran at a faster clip. They must have missed a shadowed shortcut, an alternate but more direct trail.

As to why the outpost was not where it was supposed to be, he blamed mechanical error. Something—perhaps the planet's magnetic field—was skewing their scanners and sensors. They did have the correct direction but the distance was off.

"Then tell me why talking furzels are normal," Sass countered, her face hidden not only by the twilight but by the binoculars she held over her eyes. They were conducting surveillance on a hillside overlooking the outpost—not the same one from which Serafino and Fynn were snatched or transported or blinked away, but the one closest to the side of the outpost where Tasha said Tank sensed emanations from Reilly.

Kel-Paten took more care in scouting out a better hiding place this time, one less likely to lend itself to a sneak attack or ambush. Although if whatever had kidnapped Serafino and Fynn came back for them—especially if it wasn't a skimmer with a transbeam but some kind of psi-creature—thick bushes, a solitary narrow access path, and Kel-Paten's biosignature jamming program would be little hindrance. The fact that nothing had kidnapped them in the past hour, though, seemed an encouraging sign.

"Stress," he said, in answer to her question about talking furzels. He angled up on his elbows. They were side by side, both flat on their stomachs, watching the lights flickering on below while the fidget alternately paced or pounced around them. Kel-Paten had often dreamed of lying close to Tasha in a verdant grove, stars and a moon or three glistening overhead. He just didn't picture doing it in full battle gear. "Under stressful conditions, the body's senses are heightened and the physical frame is capable of unusual feats—a crewmember lifting a huge section of bulkhead single-handedly to free a trapped friend, for instance."

Tasha lowered the binocs and eyed him skeptically.

"Tank isn't lifting me up. He's talking to me in my head."

"Telepathy is a sensory ability. Did it ever occur to you that you might be a latent telepath? The stress of the blind jump in the dirtside landing might have triggered it. Do you have an aunt or uncle who was telepathic or even empathic?"

She raised the binocs to her face again. "I have no idea." Her tone was flat.

He thought for a moment she was withdrawing from him, then he realized it had nothing to do with him at all but with another friend.

"Tasha. We'll find her." He took a chance and brushed her short bangs back from her face, trying to put into his clumsy caress what he didn't know how to put into his words. Especially since he'd been running on full 'cybe function for several hours now. It made him feel as if he were encased in that metal that comprised his infamous nickname. "I promise you."

For a moment she tensed, then with a soft sigh she leaned her face into his hand. Even with his emo-inhibitors in place, it was all he could do not to pull her against him, cover her body, her mouth, with his own.

He touched her lips with his thumb. She shook her head slightly. "We have work to do," she said, and turned her face and attention back to the outpost. "Tank says they're alive and unharmed. So far. Figured out a way in yet?"

He shouldn't have touched her. His timing, once again, was so wrong. "Tasha, I'm—"

"Branden. Please." Her voice was suddenly raspy.

"I'm about thirty seconds from tearing your clothes off. Believe me, I'd like nothing better—but under the circumstances, that's not an option. And it's definitely not going to help us find Serafino and Eden." She huffed out a short, exasperated breath and stared out into the fading light.

He found himself shocked into silence. A dozen familiar fantasies sprang into his mind. She wanted to be with him. More than that, she *wanted* him. He cleared his throat nervously. "May I take you up on that offer at a later date?"

She glanced over at him, her lips twitching slightly as she fought a smile. Then the binocs came up again. "Sooner's always better than later."

Sweet holy gods. "Then I guess we better get this rescue operation under way."

"So how are we going to get inside that building?"

"We're not." He pointed to the *Mystic Traveler*. "We're going to get inside that ship instead."

THE OUTPOST

"Ah, my favorite doctor twin," a familiar voice drawled as Eden followed Bianca through the single door into the smaller room. "But my manners are appalling. You two haven't been formally introduced. Bianca," Jace said as his sister stepped toward the diagnostic panel on the near wall, "may I present my bride-to-be, the lovely Dr. Eden Fynn?"

Eden stopped in her tracks, and not only because of his jesting or the hard tone of anger she heard under his words. Jace Serafino—grinning in spite of the

deep sense of hurt she felt emanating from him because of his sister's betrayal—was strapped into a
diag bed, shirtless and . . . hairless. Not just the stripe
that Jorden had. Jace's head was shaved completely
bald.

Bald as a Morrassian Elo Orb, he told her, and she
sensed that the lightness in his tone was forced.
Bianca got a bit carried away.

*Your sister was going to remove the implant and
let you die.*

Sibling rivalry stinks, doesn't it? He winked at her
and continued. "Eden, the bitch over there with the
blue glowing pet is Bianca Serafino Kel-Rea, my once-
beloved older sister. A Faction favorite. Human symbiont to a Ved'eskhar that—although she won't
acknowledge it—is draining her, killing her inch by
inch." His smile faded abruptly, and a wave of weariness washed over Eden. When he spoke again, his
voice rasped with emotion. "Damn it, I wish you'd
listen to me just this once, Bee."

"You bore me, Jacinto." Bianca turned to Eden.
"Nando and Mara will assist you." She motioned to
a man and woman standing on the other side of the
diag bed. The woman was the telepathic guard who
had accompanied her earlier. "Both are experienced
med-techs, and they will know if you try to damage
the harness.

"Give Dr. Fynn," Bianca told the pair, "what she
needs to perform the surgery. I want the harness
safely removed by sunrise. Max and Dr. Kel-Novaco
are waiting for it."

Her long robe swirled as she turned then exited

back to the main room, the door sliding silently closed behind her.

"What do you need, Doctor?" Mara stood rigidly, almost as if at attention. So did the taller Nando.

Sleep, Eden admitted ruefully to herself. About a week's worth. And a decent hot meal would help.

Sex? Jace volunteered.

Gods, how could he be so teasing at a time like this? But even as she questioned his demeanor, she knew the answer: he was as frightened as she was, but he was not going to give his sister the satisfaction of knowing it. And he was not going to let his fears drag Eden down. She had a feeling the hurt and weariness she felt from him were just a small part slipping past his usual tight controls. Unlike herself, Jace Serafino was an excellent actor.

"Would you happen to have any Orange Garden tea?" Eden asked. "Then I need all the specs, the schematics on his implant—harness."

For two, three heartbeats the pair didn't move, then: "I will find some tea," Mara said. "Nando will send you the required data to this station." She pointed to a small console and chair in the corner.

They turned almost in unison. Mara stopped at the doorway. "The door will lock behind me. It's bio-coded. You can't get out. Don't waste valuable time trying."

"Lovely to see you again too," Jace called out as the door closed. He looked up at Eden. "Such a charming couple."

The tears she'd been holding back filled her eyes. "Damn you, Jace Serafino!"

"Ah, sweetling. I love when you talk dirty. Here, unhook these straps, will you? I think I need some of Dr. Fynn's special medicine."

She hit the release button. He sat up swiftly, pulling her into his arms. She kissed him through her tears, her hands stroking his shoulders, his back, as if reassuring herself he was whole and real.

He murmured soft, sweet words into her mouth, her ear, then trailed kisses down her neck.

"Jace, I'm so sorry," she whispered, "about your sister—"

His arms tightened around her, and for a brief moment, a deep, wrenching sense of loss trickled through. Then it was gone.

The door opened. "Your tea, Doctor," she heard Mara say. Eden didn't turn around but buried her face into Jace's shoulder.

"Leave it on the table," Jace told her.

There was the slight clink of ceramic on metal. "You're wasting time," Mara said.

"Doubled up on our bitchy pills today, have we?" Jace shot back.

Mara said nothing. Her footsteps faded.

Eden raised her face, then ran her hand over Jace's shaved head. "You're incorrigible." She smiled through her tears. And he was still one handsome devil.

"That's my evil twin, not me. I'm the nice one, remember?" He kissed her nose. "Share your tea with both of us?"

She stepped reluctantly out of his embrace, then returned with the tea. He angled the head of the diag bed up to ninety degrees. She nestled by his side, took a sip, and let her eyes drift closed for a moment. She was mentally, emotionally, and physically exhausted. "What are we going to do?" she whispered.

Not share our concerns or plans where others can hear them, for starters, he told her.

It's safe this way? But all the telepaths—

They have implants.

And that Ved thing?

They're emotional parasites, not telepaths. They've not acted on anything I've done telepathically.

What have you tried?

Besides flirting with you? I've had a few conversations with Reilly.

Reilly? Joy fluttered in Eden's heart. *Reilly's okay?*

He's one very tired furzel, but he's okay. And you were right. Furzels can neutralize the Ved. He's hunting them, one by one. When he passes through overhead ducts, he talks to me in small snatches. He doesn't have the bond with me that he has with you; our range is limited. If he comes back this way, you'll hear him. In the meantime, you'd best start going through that data on the implant.

I will not operate on you unless it's completely safe.

You may not have that luxury, sweetling. Bianca has some powerful friends.

You'll need recovery time after surgery. How can we make a run for it if you're unconscious?

There was a long, hard silence.

Jace, if Reilly gives us a chance to escape, I'm not leaving without you.

If Reilly gives you a chance, take it. Go find Sass and Kel-Paten.

Are they alive? Can you reach them?

Another silence. *Reilly has seen them through his contact with Tank. It looks like they're going to make a move on the perimeter guards. But I don't want to start a psi-trace for them here. The Ved can't sense the furzels. And they don't read normal telepathic conversation. They do pick up strong emotional vibrations or psi-energy surges, like a psi-trace. I was in trace mode*—and in an emotional upheaval, he remembered—*when it grabbed us. I can't take a chance that one of them might be able to follow a trace to Sass or Kel-Paten. I have to trust Tank will tell Reilly when there's something we should know.*

The Ved don't just attack telepaths?

They're parasites, Eden. They feed on anything with the capability for strong emotions. The difference is, with telepaths and empaths, they come into your mind to feed. With oullums—*nontelepathic humans*—*they can't create as strong a sensation, so they physically bring you into this dimension and play with you, torture you. Like a furzel with a mizzet, you know?*

Where is this dimension?

If there's any truth to the legends I've heard, it's not to be spoken of, Jace said, and sent her an image: thumb and little finger touching, with the other three fingers curved.

McClellan's Void.

*   *   *

Reilly Blinked into a section of overhead ductwork and sneezed. His mouth was dry. His eyes watered. His whiskers were filthy. His paws hurt. But there was still a lot of work to do.

Bad Thing was so very many here. He lay his head down on his paws for a moment, panting. He had to protect MommyEden. He had to protect JaceFriend. But to stay by their side meant he couldn't hunt Bad Thing.

He almost went to MommyEden when Bad Thing pushed her in the lake. Then Bad Thing pulled back. And Reilly returned to weaving his Blink shields.

Eight so far. Three big. Five small. Eight Bad Things now glowing blue to purple.

But there were so many more.

He didn't know if he could Blink them all in time.

Tank can help! the small voice said.

Tank protect MommySass. Tank protect Branden-Friend, Reilly admonished. But even as he said it, he knew he couldn't do this alone. Tank was only a fidget, his shields not as tight and strong as a furzel's. But there were just too many Bad Things.

He hated—hated!—leaving MommySass and BrandenFriend unprotected. They weren't mind talkers like MommyEden or JaceFriend. They couldn't sense the neverwhen like JaceFriend. They were like newborn fidgets! Helpless.

A blue glow spun through the corner of his sight and disappeared.

Another one. *Shtift-a!*

Reilly had no choice. *Friend?*

Friend? Tank ready! Tank help!

Yes. Go Blink now. Help FriendReilly.

The neverwhen glistened, and with a thud, Tank arrived. *Hunt Bad Thing! Kill Bad Thing!* The fidget danced from paw to paw, sending puffs of dust flying.

Reilly groaned low in his throat, then sneezed again. Fidgets!

27

THE FOREST

Tank go hunt! Love Mommy! Go Blink!

The small voice sounded in Sass's mind just as she and Kel-Paten neared the base of the hill outside the compound. She stumbled slightly, quickly glancing behind her and under nearby bushes for a flash of white. The furry fidget that dogged her heels had disappeared.

"Tank?" Her voice was soft but urgent. "Tank!"

Kel-Paten turned, eyes narrowed. Calling out for a fidget didn't engender an aura of stealth. But Sass knew underneath that stern look was also a concern for her safety and her fidget's.

"He's gone." She kept her voice low. They were too far for anyone at the outpost or on the tarmac to hear them but close enough that they might intercept a foot patrol—though they didn't see signs of any on their trek back toward the outpost.

He put his hand on her shoulder, guiding them both down into a crouch. They were well off the trail, moving as quietly as they could through the thick underbrush. Darkness had fallen and so, correspondingly, had the temperature. Sass had pulled down the sleeves of her black jacket and sealed its front. A black cap covered her pale hair.

Kel-Paten's luminous eyes were muted, on night vision. Which meant he could see far better in the dark than she could, even with her binocs on ambient. They were generic binocs, not field-spec, because the *Galaxus* wasn't stocked as a field-combat craft. On ambient they tinged everything green. Kel-Paten's enhanced full-spectrum optics didn't have that problem.

He glanced around carefully, intently, then shook his head. He couldn't spot the fidget. He leaned toward her ear. "He can't run that fast."

"He didn't run. He Blinked. He said, *Tank go hunt.*"

"Not after a slitherskimp, I trust." His voice was a deep rumble.

"He must be with Reilly."

Kel-Paten's grip on her shoulder tightened, turned into a small massage. "He'll be back."

She pursed her lips, pushed away the worry. "Yeah."

He stared at her a long moment. "Let's go." He pulled her to her feet but kept his hand lightly on her shoulder for the next few minutes.

Reassuring her, she knew. She was very aware of him. Far too aware. And she really had been very close to tearing his clothes off earlier. Their little bit of fun in the cockpit had not lasted long enough. Godsdamned stress.

They slowed, cutting to their left when the forest thinned unexpectedly, moonlight breaking through the canopy of trees. Without Tank's constant singsong patter filling her mind, she needed something else to think about other than the fidget's absence.

She watched Kel-Paten move with an almost sensuous grace through the shadows and let her mind play with what it would be like to be lovers. She could usually peg most men's styles after being with them for ten minutes. But Kel-Paten was a mystery and she'd known him more than ten years. He could be forceful and demanding as an officer, but his touch was invariably gentle. Almost . . . hesitant. Not at all what she expected. Especially not after reading his personal logs.

Of course, that might be exactly why he acted that way—as a means to tease her, intrigue her. He was, she reminded herself, close with Captain Ralland Kel-Tyra. Rowdy Rall. The good captain had a reputation as an accomplished lover. Did he and Kel-Paten cruise the pubs together on shore leave? Probably not. She'd been with Kel-Paten on liberty. Around his crew, his officers, he was strictly by the regs.

Somehow she suspected that once he was out of uniform and off duty, he'd be anything but. He couldn't have accompanied Rowdy Rall all these years and not be.

So if they became lovers, would she measure up? Did he like his sex fun and flirty or more elegant and seductive? She wasn't sure. She could see him in an expensive suite with silk sheets. But she also had a feeling he was equally prone to stop a lift between floors and pin her against the wall, his body hard with passion.

Um, *No, No, Bad Captain!* for sure.

But when she thought of her pink T-shirt, she thought of the *Regalia*. And when she thought of the *Regalia*, she thought of Tank. Where *was* he? More than that, was he safe?

She followed Kel-Paten around a pile of fallen trees. She'd learned to move quickly and carefully at night on Lethant. But Kel-Paten could quite literally see in the dark. His guidance was infallible.

He slowed and, with a hand on her shoulder once more, pushed her into a crouch, coming down close alongside her. Their thighs touched, and she could feel his breath on her temple when he spoke.

"One guard on the tarmac. Male humanoid. Armed."

She brought up her binocs. At this distance, she could see the greenish outline of the *Mystic Traveler* and, beyond that and off to the right, the green glow of floodlights marking corners of the outpost's larger buildings. The guard, however, was little more than a dark cipher. But then, she wasn't Kel-Paten.

"Just one?" She panned, found nothing else, and let the binocs fall on their strap. "Sloppy. Or a trap."

"Agreed." He was still scanning the ship and its surroundings. Suddenly, he tensed, his body going rigid beside her.

She tensed too, not knowing what he'd seen. It didn't matter. If he didn't like it, she'd like it less. She put her hand on the pistol on her utility belt but didn't pull it.

Kel-Paten nodded so slightly she felt it more than saw it.

"Good news, Sebastian," he whispered in her ear. "We're not in Dreehalla. And we're not lost."

She leaned into him, a small bubble of hope in her heart. "We're not?"

"There's also bad news. The guard by the ship is carrying a Zonn-X Seven."

A Zonn-X? "That's a Triad weapon!"

"Not Triad," he corrected her firmly. "Psy-Serv. Disrupts brain-wave functions."

Triad. Psy-Serv. Same thing, to her. But not to him, she remembered.

"This is a Psy-Serv facility?"

"I think that's a possibility."

"But what would they be doing with the *Traveler*?" She'd heard a couple of versions of how Rej Andgarran stole the ship from Serafino years ago and then disappeared. Was he so afraid of Serafino's ire that he went as far off the charts as he could? She almost asked Kel-Paten but then realized that would be admitting to knowledge she wasn't supposed to have. "And why not confront us directly at the shuttle? They had to know we landed."

A slight nod again. "I would very much like answers to those questions."

She recognized something in his tone, something that said he'd already formed an opinion. She had heard it often enough in their discussions in his office. She dropped forward on her knees and swiveled to face him. "You're still thinking Serafino's in on this?"

"Prove to me he isn't."

"We're alive. He knows we're out here. If he wanted us dead we'd already be dead. Plus, Eden would have sensed something from him if he was setting a trap." But Eden did say Jace was blocking her ever since they found the planet. Gods, she didn't like this at all. She wished she could see what Kel-Paten saw. Just because the guard had a Zonn—"Is the guard in uniform?"

"Freighter grays," Kel-Paten said.

"Could be anybody, then. Possession of a Zonn doesn't mean you're a Psy-Serv agent. I could name you five sources right now where you could pick one up if you were willing to pay the asking price."

"A merc stronghold. We could be dealing with Gund'jalar or Zanorian. All the more reason I'd suspect Serafino had a hand in this."

Sass held herself very still. Two people she did not want to discuss with Kel-Paten were Gund'jalar and Zanorian. But she couldn't prove this wasn't one of Gund'jalar's cells without admitting she had been in touch with the Rebashee merc as recently as yesterday. He knew she was on the *Vax*. Had this been one of Gund'jalar's cells, then a rescue team would have been outside the *Galaxus* before she'd even pulled herself off the cockpit floor. "Cryloc Syndicate?" she countered, hoping to distract him from his options. The Syndicate was on the lunatic fringe. They hated the Triad over some centuries-old incident that no one could even remember.

They bounced hypotheses back and forth— quietly—for the next ten minutes, Kel-Paten intently watching the guard and the ship. The admiral would not make a move until he was relatively sure who they were up against. Pulling a raid on a Psy-Serv facility required different tactics than taking on a Rebashee mercenary cell.

She knew that. She knew exactly how Gund'jalar ran his cells. And this was not any kind of operation Gund'jalar would run. But she couldn't tell him that without telling him how she knew.

Yet the more he focused on Gund'jalar as the answer, the greater the risk they'd be caught off guard by whoever was really running the outpost.

She sucked in a breath. "Gund'jalar's people would never leave a ship so lightly guarded." A ship was an asset. A valuable, expensive one to a mercenary operation. *You don't squander your assets,* she could almost hear Gund'jalar telling her. "Psy-Serv is different. They're not military. They have an open-ended budget."

"All the more reason I think this is a Rebashee merc outfit," Kel-Paten argued, shifting forward in his crouch. "Psy-Serv doesn't have their own ships, let alone an attack squadron. Their evaluators travel on fleet pinnaces."

Damn him. He was wrong. "Kel-Paten."

He looked down at her, the glow in his eyes barely visible. "Sebastian."

"This is not a Rebashee operation. You go in there expecting merc responses and you're going to get killed. And then not only we will not get to *sooner,* we'll never get to *later* either." She pinned him with a hard knowing stare, as much as she could in the darkness. She needed him distracted from the Gund'jalar topic, and if it took a hint of sex to do it, so be it. The fact that her words had to be low, almost whispered, only added to the effect. "We go with the Psy-Serv model. We rescue Eden, Serafino, and the furzels, commandeer the ship. We do that, and *sooner* could well be on that ship. I'll bet it has one hell of a well-equipped captain's cabin. Silk sheets and all."

"Tasha—" Kel-Paten's voice rasped.

"You want to hear my ideas for later? A suite, at one of the casino hotels on Glitterkiln. Three, four days. We might even have time for a hand or two of Starfield. On the last day. Maybe."

Sometime during her whispered recitation, Kel-Paten's hand had come to rest on her shoulder. After a teasing offer like that, Dag Zanorian would have had her flat on her back, mouth hard on hers, one hand either up her shirt or finding its way down her pants, while the other would still be on the trigger of his laser rifle, in case the enemy rudely interrupted.

Kel-Paten just gently traced the line of her jaw with his thumb.

Damned emo-inhibitors! He probably had them at full power.

"Tasha," he repeated. "I've been to Glitterkiln. The suites in Tygaris are better."

She grinned in the darkness. Gotcha. "And that wouldn't happen to be because they're Triad owned and operated?"

"Of course." He was back to watching the ship and the guard. But there was a hint of a smile on Kel-Paten's lips.

"We'll go with the modified diversion plan," he said. "Draw the guard past the perimeter, take him out just after his next check-in. That's in twenty minutes, from what I've seen. That will give us fifteen to secure the ship, bring weapons online. Then we prime the engines, engage the transbeam. The furzels will be easy to find and retrieve. But pinning down Fynn and Serafino's biosignatures among all the other humanoids will take some work."

Actually, it wouldn't. She had them in the data she'd copied from Kel-Paten's personal files. Eden's records were appended to her own. And she'd snagged Serafino's file while looking for implant data. It all resided in the small datadrive now secured in her backpack.

One more thing she couldn't tell him. She had to find a way to sneak them into the ship's database or transfer the data to her handheld. It would take only a few seconds.

"If the ship has sufficient fuel," he was saying, "we should be back in orbit in under two hours, depending on their pursuit capabilities. From there we use the charts on board, which we have to assume would be current to this sector, to get back. If the ship's low on fuel, we stay in heavy air but make a workable landing this time and go into full defensive mode."

"Aye, sir. Got it."

He turned to her, his mouth suddenly a thin line. "Fair warning: if Serafino is allied with the enemy, I will kill him."

"But—"

He held up one hand. "It will be my call. It has to be." He hesitated. His tone softened. "You mean the world to me, Tasha. I respect your opinion more than you know. But Serafino is a known problem in the Triad—an immoral mercenary, possibly with ties to

Gund'jalar, who still challenges our ownership of the Danvaral sector. The fact that Serafino may have uncovered some suspicious activities doesn't absolve him of his crimes or his past associations. He is the enemy until he proves himself otherwise."

Or his past associations. And what about hers? She would no longer mean the world to him if he found out.

She nodded in the darkness, her voice strained. "Aye, sir. Got it."

He was silent. She didn't dare look at him but shrugged off her backpack and knelt stiffly, hands on her thighs, trying not to succumb to exhaustion. She couldn't remember the last time she'd slept or ate, but their push through the forest and their discussions—flirtatious and otherwise—kept those issues at bay. Now, with plans decided, her adrenaline dropped and her energy flagged.

His arm slipped lightly over her shoulder. She let out a sigh she didn't know she was holding in, and he pulled her more closely against him. He was warm. She was chilled from the cold night air and her knees hurt.

"I will try very hard not to kill him," he said softly.

"I know, Branden."

"Come here." He scooted backward on the ground a few feet, then leaned against the wide trunk of a tree, drawing her with him, nestling her between his legs. Her back was against his chest. He wrapped his left arm around her waist, holding her more tightly. She angled her head against his shoulder, skewing her cap. His warmth seeped into her.

"This is against regulations while on field surveillance," she whispered.

"Screw regulations."

"If someone sneaks up—"

"I will hear them or see them. Take a ten-minute nap. You need it."

Funny, she thought as her eyes closed. If there was a spare ten minutes with Zanorian, he'd undo his pants and demand a quickie. Kel-Paten gave her warmth and comfort and asked for nothing.

Branden Kel-Paten felt the tension ebb from her body, felt her muscles loosen. Her breathing slowed.

In contrast, every inch of him crackled with awareness. He didn't lie to her: he would know of anyone coming before they could be considered a threat. He had his 'cybe senses at max, listening, scanning, sensing.

But not just his surroundings. He was scanning, sensing, recording Tasha Sebastian. Memorizing the feel of her in his arms, the warmth of her on his chest. The fine tickle of wisps of her hair against his neck as they escaped from under her dark cap.

The scent of her.

The guard resumed his plodding path around the tarmac. One part of Kel-Paten's mind worked out angles of attack, noted escape routes, blind corners. The other knew she draped her arm over his, curling her fingers around his hand. It was such a small thing, but it made his heart stutter.

Because it was deliberate. She wanted to touch him. He knew she wasn't asleep—not really. She'd learned, as most Fleet officers did in boot camp and then later in field training, to snatch a furzel-nap to recharge. You couldn't survive long missions without it.

Being 'cybe, he didn't need to do that. He always stood guard, like now. Except guard duty was never so pleasant before.

He'd wake her simply by saying her name, in four minutes. She'd come fully alert, ready to conquer the galaxy, he thought with a smile.

Why not? She'd already captured his heart.

Tasha woke at the eight-minute mark. She had an uncanny ability to sense the progression of time when she was forced to nap on the run. Kel-Paten said to take ten. She'd set her internal clock for eight because she honestly wasn't one hundred percent sure what they were going to come up against at the outpost.

And she'd be damned if she was going to die without kissing him one more time.

It could only be a short kiss, she knew that. But she'd make sure he knew it held the promise of much more. Because she had come to the most amazing, incredible realization during her eight-minute nap.

She loved that annoying, pompous, overbearing, biocybernetic bastard.

She opened her eyes. "Hey, flyboy," she whispered.

He glanced quickly down at her, slightly startled. Good.

"Kiss me. That's an order." She wrapped her arm around his neck as she tilted her face up to meet his and put everything she felt into the kiss.

He responded with a groan, clasping her tightly against him, his mouth hot on hers.

This was dangerous, she knew it was dangerous. But it was only two minutes—and it felt so damned good.

She laid her palm against his jaw as she slowly, reluctantly broke the kiss, pulling back. He leaned forward, his breath still mingling with hers. He whispered her name, his voice thick with emotion.

The ground beneath them dropped away. She clung to him, panic cresting. They were free-falling, speeding into a black abyss, searing cold raking her skin, sucking the air out of her lungs. She couldn't scream. She couldn't even think.

Then...nothing. Quiet. No searing cold. She stumbled, realized she was standing, and locked her knees. Closed environment. Warehouse. No, hangar. People. Two ships. Skimmers—short-haulers used to run between stations or rafts and a world. Her mind tallied the scene quickly, impersonally. No overt threat. Still, her heart pounded. She drew in a large gulp of air. She could feel Kel-Paten behind her, saw his arm in the edge of her vision.

She wanted to turn and look at him, but a tall figure—blond male humanoid—moved away from the closest skimmer's rampway. Others—two— walked toward her from a servocart on the far left. Her vision was clearing. Details sharpened.

"Tasha..." Kel-Paten's voice was low.

"I'm okay. You?"

"No damage."

"Behind us?"

"Bulkhead. Three feet four inches."

No threat from behind then, but not much room to run.

"Any idea where we—" She didn't finish the sentence. She didn't have to. She knew where they were. Raft 84. What worried her more was the man walking toward her.

Dag Zanorian hooked his hand through the strap of the laser rifle crossing his back as he strode up to her. His legs were encased in his usual dark leather pants, his gray shirt nondescript but—as usual—form-fitting. His blond hair was about as long as Serafino's, but he wore it loose to his shoulders. He came closer and his mouth quirked in a smile she remembered well. "Sass. Took you long enough."

Zanorian? Shit. What was going on?

"And you got him. Damn, bitch, but you *are* good." The rifle flipped forward and didn't point at her but higher over her shoulder, at Kel-Paten.

Her hand reached for her laser pistol. It wasn't there. Damn! She must have lost it in the forest or . . . in transit. Whatever that was.

It didn't matter. She knew trouble when she saw it. "Back off, Dag."

"Possessive are we, little girl?" Zanorian chuckled. "I know it's your mission. Just having some fun with the Tin Soldier."

"Zanorian." Kel-Paten's tone was flat, but that didn't bother her as much as the fact that something was wrong here. Very wrong. She wasn't on any mission with Dag. She hadn't seen him in over five years.

Two others approached. Humans. She recognized them immediately: the taller, dusky-skinned woman—black-haired, muscular—was her friend Angel Kel-

Moro. The shorter, slim man, also carrying a laser rifle, was Jonn Drund. And then she knew what was wrong. Angel was on Panperra, waiting for Serafino. And Jonn Drund had died on Lethant the first month she was there.

Gund'jalar—keeping an eye on her because Ace had asked him to—had killed him.

She looked back at Dag. He had only one scar on his cheek, not two. And Angel's left wrist was bare of her lover's commitment tattoo.

Gods. What in hell was going on?

"Never thought you'd see this day, eh, Tin Soldier? Captured by a rim runner." Zanorian still trained his rifle on Kel-Paten. Drund raised his weapon as well. "Though my Lady Sass was always more than a mere rim runner."

"Lady Sass." It wasn't a question. And it wasn't Zanorian's voice that said her name. It was Kel-Paten's. And she didn't like the way he said it, not at all.

"Good catch, Sass!" Angel stepped over, tugged on her arm, pulling her forward.

Sass tugged back. "Wait. Damn it, Dag, put the rifle away. Angel—"

"Time for a beer." Angel grabbed her wrist this time. "Hey, c'mon. You earned it. We'll go back to the *Windblade* and let Dag do the dirty work for once."

"Let *go!*" She wrenched free of Angel, not missing the confused, hurt look on her friend's face. And promptly stumbled sideways into Dag.

He grabbed her, spun her around, and planted a kiss on her mouth. "You are such a fine little bitch."

She jerked back. He slapped her on the rump. "Go with Angel. I'll meet you on the *Blade* after Jonn and I secure the Tin Soldier here for Gund'jalar."

She didn't think; she just grabbed his rifle with one hand, lunged forward, and planted a knee to his groin. She thrust the weapon up as he arched toward her. It slammed into his face. Blood spurted as Angel grabbed her from behind.

"You crazy, Sass?" the woman shouted.

A fist slammed against Sass's face. Zanorian or Drund, she couldn't tell. She didn't care. She had to get a rifle and she had to get Kel-Paten, and they had to get out of here.

If he'd even go with her.

Lady Sass. He knew now. Her past associations.

She fought back, kicking, then landed an elbow to Angel's midsection. She held on to Dag's rifle with one hand. He yanked it—and her—back to him, his face smeared with blood, his eyes blazing. She dropped to a half crouch, kicked his knee. He bellowed in pain, falling.

And let go of the rifle.

She hit the floor with it, rolled, aware of Angel lunging for her, aware of Drund just now putting her in his sights. . . .

I'm going to die. And I never told Branden I love him.

Fear, hopelessness washed over her like a thick, oily tide. Panic choked her.

She struggled to her feet, swinging her rifle up, but Drund was squinting, finger on the trigger. Then he was gone, jettisoned sideways by a black-clad blur.

Someone grabbed her shoulders. She swung

around, slamming the butt of the rifle into a face. Angel screamed, flailing backward.

Gods, Angel, I'm sorry. But this is wrong. Crazy.

Bootsteps on her right. She spun back, rifle coming up.

Kel-Paten. With Drund's rifle in one black-gloved hand. He stared at her, his expression hard, his eyes glowing with luminescent power. With hatred.

She saw that clearly. So very clearly.

And the heart that she'd so carefully guarded for all those years—never giving it away to any man—shattered. Into a thousand tiny sharp-edged pieces.

A hatchway groaned open. The hangar filled with shouts, boots pounding on the floor. Kel-Paten jerked around, but she grabbed his arm. "This way!"

He yanked his arm back. "Another trap, Lady Sass?"

"No. I swear." She'd never felt so helpless. And she'd just taken down two of the best-trained mercs in the business.

Kel-Paten hesitated long enough to make sure she knew he didn't trust her. But he also had no choice. Laser fire spit overhead.

He ducked. She grabbed his arm again and ran.

THE RAFT

They reached the maintenance accessway just as laser fire sizzled on the decking around them. Sass tapped in the override security code she knew by heart. Kel-Paten, at her back, laid down cover fire. He could have as easily turned and killed her.

Part of her wished he would. The pain in her heart was almost unbearable.

The hatch slid open. "Go!" She swiveled, swung her rifle up, and strafed the hangar, then ducked in after him, slapping the hatch closed and locking it. "No time to scramble the security codes. They—"

He pushed her roughly aside, lay his hand flat against the back of the locking mechanism. It sizzled, sparked, and went dead. Only then did she realize his gloves were off, tucked into his utility belt. He'd fried the lock shut.

In spite of her pain—or perhaps because of it—she quirked an eyebrow at him. "Damn. Works for me. This way."

She sidled past him, heading for a ladderway she knew would lead to a central maintenance tunnel. There'd be a half dozen ways they could go from there. And Dag—when he stopped rolling on the floor in pain and cursing her—would spend a lot of time trying to figure out which.

If he could still walk. She thought she'd broken his knee.

They reached the ladderway. She grabbed the gritty metal rung and stopped. "One deck down is the small-skimmer bay. They probably expect us to go there, hot-wire a skimmer or transport, head dirt-side."

"The outpost is dirtside." His tone was flat, his expression telling her nothing.

"We're on a miner's raft off Kesh Valirr." It sounded crazy even as she said it. "Please. Just listen. We don't have much time. Three decks up is the main maintenance tunnel. Breaks out to six smaller tunnels. Gives us a lot more choices and a lot better chance to lose them. But the call is yours, Admiral. I know you don't trust me. So you decide. You want to hot-wire a skimmer, we hot-wire a skimmer. You want to gain a bit more breathing room, a few more options, we go up." She jerked her face toward the ladder.

"Up," he said tersely. And that was the only thing he said for the next ten minutes as they climbed, ran down narrow tunnels lined with encased conduit and red-striped piping, and climbed some more.

Three times they had to double back. Someone was coming—legitimate maintenance crew in orange overalls each time. It gave Sass a chance to catch her breath but not to speak, to offer Kel-Paten an explanation. Hell, she didn't have an explanation.

She didn't know if one would matter.

She just wanted to live long enough to get this nightmare over with. She wasn't even sure if they were physically here or if this was some kind of hallucination and their bodies were back in the forest on HV-1. But her jaw ached where Dag or Jonn hit her. She rubbed it. Felt very much as if she was really here.

She thought of the crew of *Degun's Luck* and the lifeless bodies strewn about the ship. Were their minds taken elsewhere and tortured while their bodies stayed on board? Or was the entire ship taken, drained of life, and then dumped back in the space lanes?

Emotional parasite, Eden had said about Bad Thing. The dying one had tortured Eden's mind on the *Galaxus*. But in the forest, something physically took Jace and Eden away. Bad Thing, Tank told her. A Bad Thing that wasn't weakened or shielded.

Something to consider . . .

The maintenance workers' voices became fainter.

"Clear. Let's go," she said, after the exit hatch clanked shut.

Kel-Paten nodded. She trotted past him. They were in an older part of the raft now, built on top of a section of the original cavernous ore-processing plant. Though they couldn't see them, Sass knew suspended gridways and automated conveyor belts crisscrossed in a dozen layers under their feet, moving the raw ore to the appropriate grinding stations. But this tunnel was inactive, with conduit cobbled together, power panels heavily patched. A lot of overheads had burned out, but that was okay. She knew where she was headed. There should be a row of abandoned offices coming up at Maintenance Access 7714. The whole corridor needed a complete rewire job. Until then, with no accessible power for equipment, the small offices lit only by emergency lighting were useless.

But they could use them. Maybe she could get him talking. Maybe they could figure out where they really were, how they'd gotten here, just what in hell was going on. If not, she knew of one office that had a working sanifac. She no longer had her backpack or canteen, and she was desperately thirsty.

Too bad she couldn't take Angel up on that offer of beer. Getting *trocked* up seemed like a nice idea right about now.

She watched for Access 7714. If she couldn't pick the lock on an office door, Kel-Paten could probably fry it. But she'd never met a lock she couldn't pick, given enough time. Only . . .

It was a large coil of black conduit that blocked their path instead, spooled like a bloated snake, blocking more than half the tunnel. Damned thing had to be five feet high. Access 7714 was just beyond it. Sass flipped her rifle around to her front and, putting her back against the metal-paneled wall, pushed against the pile and squeezed sideways by it.

The wall gave way and Sass fell backward, down into darkness and the grinding, chugging machinery below.

A scream caught in her throat. Her arms flailed, smacking something, tangling. It hit her in the face, knocking her cap off, and she grabbed for it instinctively.

It was the conduit. She clawed madly at it, but it slid through her grasp as it tumbled, unspooling as she fell.

She closed her hands tighter and jerked to a stop, almost losing her hold on the slick tubing. Gasping, she clung to it, feet dangling. She didn't dare look down. Not yet. She was still sucking in huge gulps of air and trying very hard not to throw up.

She should try to climb back up, but what if her movements started the conduit falling again?

She chanced a glance down. She was suspended at least twenty feet above the top level of gridways. It was a long way to the bottom.

Kel-Paten. Gods, did he fall too? Had one of the things that hit her in the darkness been him? He was so close behind her. *Please. Don't let him be down there.* Sweat trickled down her cheeks. It had to be sweat. She wouldn't cry.

"Tasha!"

"Kel-Paten?"

"Hang on!"

Like she had a choice? The conduit jerked again and she slipped another few inches. "Shit!"

"Wrap your legs around it," he called, but she was already doing that, her Fleet training kicking in. Wrap one leg, lock the other foot on top of it. Lock your hands. Pray.

The conduit jerked, jiggled. The rifle—miraculously still slung over her chest—cut into her breastbone. But up she went. It seemed like hours, but when she reached the gaping hole that used to be a wall, her tears hadn't dried.

Kel-Paten grabbed her collar first, then one hand came under her armpit. He lifted her easily, her boots catching on the tangle of conduit that still remained. His arms went around her back and, holding her tightly, he dragged her back into the tunnel.

It felt so incredibly good to have something solid under her feet. Someone solid to lean on. For a moment she thought she felt his face against her hair, his breath in her ear as if he were going to whisper something. But she must have imagined that, because his arms loosened, his hands coming to rest on her shoulders when she swayed toward him. "You can let go now," he said, and she realized she still held a section of the conduit between them in a death grip.

Slowly, painfully, she unfolded her fingers. "Oh, gods." She bit down on her lip. How could she feel so numb and be in so much pain at the same time?

"Wait." He unhooked her rifle's strap, tossed the weapon on the pile of conduit next to her, and then lowered her to the floor. Kneeling in front of her, he took her hands in his, stroking, kneading. He hadn't put his gloves back on, and in the uneven lighting she could see the scars striping his fingers, glimpses of the silvery powermesh implants on his palms. Yet his touch was so gentle. Her hands stopped spasming. The length of conduit—her lifeline—landed with a muted thud.

She stared at it for a moment, then looked up at him. "Thank you," she said softly. "I'm sorry." *For causing you so much trouble. For having past associations. For loving you when all I can do is bring you pain.*

His eyes were luminous in the patchy lighting. His face was a shadowed mask. "Can you walk? It's not wise to stay here."

She nodded, snatched her rifle, and struggled to her feet. His hand on her arm guided her. "There," she said, pointing to the hatchway with 7714 stenciled on it. She winced. Her shoulder ached like hell. So much for Eden's best efforts with her rotator cuff. "There are some abandoned offices. I think ... I need to sit down for a while."

The office with the sanifac was exactly where she remembered it. It took Kel-Paten only a few seconds to trip the lock. She stumbled in, her body shuddering every few minutes as fear spiked and receded, spiked and receded. A green strip of emergency lighting glowed in the ceiling; a smaller one was in the sanifac. Both rooms were empty.

Kel-Paten locked the door behind them as she crossed the room. She propped her rifle against the wall by the sanifac. It had an old-fashioned lever-operated sink, but it worked. She splashed water on her face, then, cupping her shaking hands, took several long drinks. And felt abysmally selfish. "Water's clean and cold, if you want some."

"No."

She left the sanifac, walked over to the corner farthest away from where Kel-Paten stood in the dimness, and folded herself down onto the floor. She hugged her knees against her chest and stared at the dark outline of her boots.

Please, someone wake me up. Get me out of this nightmare.

Another pair of boots walked across the room and stopped in front of hers. "Tell me again how this isn't Serafino's doing."

Logical conclusion: Serafino and Zanorian were both mercs. Both hated Kel-Paten and were hated by Kel-Paten. But Kel-Paten didn't know what she did. She raised her face. "A Nasyry can do a lot of things, but I don't think he can resurrect the dead."

"Explain."

"The short guy with Dag Zanorian? That's Jonn Drund. Know the name?"

"Vaguely."

"He died seven years ago on Lethant."

"You know this for a fact?"

"I was there."

"On Lethant?"

She nodded.

"Then you *are* Lady Sass."

"I *was,* off and on until seven years ago. But Lady Sass is dead now too." She gave a short, mirthless laugh. "Damned inconvenient when the dead don't have the good graces to stay dead, isn't it?"

"What kind of game are you and Serafino playing here?"

"Didn't you hear what I said?" She sat up straighter. "Drund is dead. Yet he's here, alive. And Zanorian's here, but he has only one scar. Last time I saw him—about five years ago—he had two. Damned proud of them and not about to have his face vanity-patched. Angel doesn't have the commitment tattoo on her left wrist from when she and Suki pair-bonded. It has to be at least nine years for them."

She sucked in a breath, damning the fact that he could see her expressions far better than she could see his. "Zanorian and Angel would never call me Lady Sass, blow my cover in front of you." They'd worked with her for too many years, whenever UCID needed to resurrect Lady Sass for a mission. "And Serafino would have to raise the dead to pull off this kind of shit. He's simply not that good. He's not even a full-blooded Nasyry.

"Moreover," she continued, anger forcing her brain to work again, "everything that you saw back in that freighter bay, everything that happened, is wrong and you know it. Gund'jalar doesn't put contracts out on people, doesn't abduct them. But if for some bizarre reason he did, he sure as hell wouldn't put a wild-ass freelancer like Zanorian in charge."

"He'd put Lady Sass in charge," Kel-Paten intoned.

"Damned straight he would. But we didn't do abductions. You know that. Hell, you've tracked his cells for years. But you only know him because he funds the Danvaral liberation movement by hitting up Triad freighters. What you don't see is that he's also the law—sometimes the only law—out in the Far Reaches. People listen to him because he's intelligent and fair. He's not a wanton murderer and he's not a kidnapper."

He was silent for two, three heartbeats. "I almost kidnapped you once."

Sass caught a slight change in the tone of his voice, or thought she did. A degree or two of the intense chill around him thawing. She was probably wrong. Then she thought again about what he said: he'd almost kidnapped her. *Sarna Bogue* and the entry in his logs.

She looked away for a moment, then back up at him, her face hiding nothing. "I wish you would have," she said quietly.

He turned abruptly and headed for the sanifac. She heard the water come on and in the muted green glow watched his silhouette cup his hands and drink as she had earlier.

He shut the water off but didn't return to the room. He stayed with his hands planted against the edge of the sink, back bowed, looking down, saying nothing. She didn't know if he was working up the courage to tell her he loved her or to kill her.

Either seemed a valid possibility right now.

THE OUTPOST

Go Blink! Tank panted, tired and thirsty. And hungry. His stomach growled. Hunting Bad Things was hard work. He wanted to nap but knew he couldn't. FriendReilly was tired too.

There were just so many Bad Things here.

Friend? Here! He heard Reilly's call and heaved a sigh.

Tank here! Go Blink! He appeared next to Reilly, who was facing down a large ugly smelly light. Tank wrinkled his nose in disgust. It must be a really old one. The stench was terrible.

A Blink shield encased much of its glowing body,

but the Bad Thing pushed against it, straining the lines of energy.

Reilly wavered on his paws, one hind leg almost buckling. The sight of his friend stumbling shot fear through Tank. *Friend hurt?*

Friend tired. Help. Finish here. Go Blink for Friend.

Tank help! he said, but he wasn't sure. He was just a fidget; he didn't completely understand how to weave a perfect shield.

And the Bad Things weren't dying fast enough.

This one strained against Reilly's shield lines. Three snapped.

Shtift-a! Tank narrowed his eyes and ignored the rumbling in his stomach. *Love MommySass. Love FriendReilly . . .* He paused, sensing something that had been in the back of his mind for a while but he'd been too busy to notice.

Mommy? Silence. No, not silence. Pain.

No! Tank stood frozen, trembling. His stomach heaved. Mommy was gone. Bad Thing took Mommy. *Tank go! Tank help Mommy!*

Friend, please! Reilly's voice was strained.

Another shield line snapped.

Shtift-a! Shtift-a! Tank's ears lay flat to his head. His tail thrashed. His heart cried out in pain.

Reilly's left hind leg collapsed completely this time. And he was too close to Bad Thing.

Misery closed in on Tank. If he left now, Reilly might die.

He bared his teeth, growling, and focused on old, stinky Bad Thing. *Go Blink!*

*   *   *

Eden studied the data on the implant, Jace coming over now and then to ruffle her hair or stroke her neck. What she would have given to have this information on the *Vax*! She could have removed the implant. And he would have had time to recover.

Now, although the medical equipment here was excellent, recovery would be a problem. That Bianca intended to kill both of them she had no doubt. She just didn't know how long after the surgery they'd be allowed to live.

Which led her back to the only logical option, one she and Jace had fretted over as she paged through the data—they had to get out of here soon.

We not only have to get past the guards, we have to get past the Ved, Jace told her. *The furzels have neutralized a number of them. But from what I can sense, there are still far too many alive. We'd never make it to the ship.*

Not the *Galaxus*. The *Traveler*.

We have at least eight hours before sunrise, she told him. The planet's slower rotation worked in their favor. *Reilly and Tank are working hard. And Tasha and Kel-Paten know where we are, because of Tank. Another two hours, and we'll be able to—*

Something large and dark suddenly appeared out of the corner of her eye. She spun the chair toward the diag bed. Jace was already moving toward it.

Tank, fur matted, ears flat to his head, stood unsteadily in the middle of the bed, a large black furry form by his front paws. A low, keening cry was coming from the fidget's throat, and his tail lashed frantically back and forth.

"Reilly!" Eden gasped out the name, lunging for the furzels.

Jace had one hand on Tank's head, another on Reilly's back. Eden grabbed Reilly's front paw.

FriendReilly sick. Tank's small voice whispered in her mind. *Help FriendReilly, MommyEden. JaceFriend. Help...*

And Tank collapsed.

THE MINING RAFT

"Hypothesis, Sebastian."

Sass raised her forehead from where she'd rested it on her hands and looked at Kel-Paten. Arms crossed over his chest, he leaned against the sanifac's door-jamb. That was the first thing she noticed. The second was that his eyes weren't luminous. He had powered down. That had to mean he no longer regarded her as a threat.

But most important, he called her "Sebastian" and demanded her hypothesis.

She chanced it. "You still owe me coffee from the last one."

"Noted."

His tone told her nothing. She opted for the premise that he recognized they were, if not friends, at least on the same side. "I posit Big Crazy Silly Space, as Tank calls it. Bad Thing took Jace and Eden to the outpost. Then came back and brought us to a place where it could set up scenarios and feed from our reactions." She touched her thumb and little finger. "McClellan's Void."

He mimicked the Rebashee gesture. His gloves were back on. "Gund'jalar taught you that?"

She shook her head. "Worked on a Rebashee freighter when I was a kid. Not that that has anything to do with my hypothesis."

"It has everything to do with your hypothesis. Unless what we see here is not part of your life."

"What you see here," and she made a broad sweep with one hand, "are people I know, but their roles or relationships are wrong."

"But the United Coalition knew you were Lady Sass when they permitted your transfer to my ship."

"The United Coalition killed Lady Sass seven years ago. Up until that point, I was either Lieutenant Sebastian or Lady Sass, depending if Fleet or UCID needed me. But after Lethant, I was just Sebastian, happily cruising the space lanes on the *Regalia,* assigned to Fleet, not UCID. Then *you* asked for my transfer. Demanded it, from what I heard. Surprised the hell out of Ace—Admiral Edmonds—and shocked the shit out of me. You even brought me on board before the official start of the APIP. I'm here on your orders, not because I'm a spy or a traitor." She drew in a breath. "I did not set you up."

She waited for his next question but he stared past her. She wanted him to keep questioning. In spite of her hypothesis, she wasn't sure if she was on HV-1 and hallucinating or physically in the void. She suspected the latter. Kel-Paten, with his 'cybe senses, should be able to tell for sure.

"You withheld information about Serafino from me."

"Initial evidence suggested you were part of the

problem. I had to put aside my personal feelings and focus on protecting the Alliance. And since Serafino was the repository of that evidence, I had to protect him as well." She leaned her head back against the wall and regarded him evenly. "You never gave me any reason to think you trusted me. How was I supposed to trust you?"

"Fynn knew my reasons. Knew," he hesitated, "how I felt. She told you."

"She only said that she got conflicting readings from you. We didn't know how to interpret that."

He walked over to her, then hunkered down, hands loose against his knees. His eyes narrowed. "So 'fun while it lasted' was a game you played to find out?"

Fun while it lasted. Kissing him in the *Galaxus*'s cockpit because she didn't want to hear that he loved her. Gods, the depth of her own stupidity never failed to astound her. But to explain that meant to ex-plain—*admit*—that she had broken into his cabin and downloaded his files, including his personal logs. She wondered how much more he could possibly hate her.

She could obfuscate her way around it, but then this damned void would no doubt plop them in a sce-nario in his cabin just so he could watch her be ex-actly who she denied being: Lady Sass, hired by the U-Cees to steal the *Vax*'s secrets.

And maybe, she realized with startling clarity, con-sidering how damned exhausted and turned inside out she was, that was their ticket out of here: don't give Bad Thing anything to work with. No more se-crets, no more lies. No more games.

She looked at him squarely. "I knew how you felt about me before we left the *Vax*. By mistake, I ended up with copies of your personal logs—"

He dropped down on one knee, his back straightening, hands fisting. "You what?"

She held up her hand. "Let me finish. You can kick my ass all over this damned void if you want to after that, but let me finish."

His mouth thinned, but he nodded.

"I found them. I read them. They scared the hell out of me—"

"Because I'm a 'cybe," he cut in tersely.

"No, you *trock*-brained idiot! Because *I'm* not the top-of-her-academy-class well-bred Tasha Sebastian you fell in love with. I'm not anyone you *could* fall in love with. I'm a merc, a rim runner from Kesh Valirr. An undercover operative that Ace Edmonds and UCID deliberately recruited after the Admiral Wembley scandal—you remember: prostis, trefla, double agents." She ticked the items off on her fingers. "He got off with a hand slap. UCID couldn't risk that again. I was their off-the-books project, just like Gund'jalar's been for years. The enemy of my enemy is my friend, you know?"

His only response was a slight narrowing of his eyes. But the fact that he didn't like what he was hearing didn't stop her. "They dangled something I couldn't resist: the chance to legitimately be somebody, to be part of Fleet. I was nineteen years old, a raft rat 'jacking Triad haulers. So I took it, gladly, went deep cover with Gund'jalar, worked with arms runners, other mercs wanting to stop the Triad, stop you from doing to the U-Cees what you did to Danvaral.

"But they also put me on their own ships and stations as Tasha Sebastian, looking for double agents like Wembley, for security leaks, for abuses of power.

"But when I killed a senator's son they cut me loose." She thrust her hand through her hair as if she could shove the memories away. "He was selling children for sex. His father's position made him untouchable. UCID unofficially gave me and Gund'jalar the go-ahead to set up a compromising accident. That's all it was supposed to be—just something to put him in the hospital long enough that we could dismantle his organization. We spent five months tracking him, making sure we had the facts right. Then things went very wrong." She sucked in a deep breath, shuddering. She'd forgotten how much pain was involved.

"He had two little boys with him, on his estate," she continued, watching his face for a reaction, seeing none. It didn't matter. He had to know the truth. "If I didn't take him down, he was going to kill them. I had no choice. But Internal Affairs didn't see it that way. I was tagged for death or a mind wipe. Then Ace intervened and made deals I can't even begin to comprehend."

"Lethant," he said.

She nodded. "Lady Sass had to go to prison and die. But Commander Sebastian had turned out to be one damned decent officer and could still be useful. But *not*," and she stressed that, "as a UCID agent anymore. My posting to the *Vax* was a total surprise. Ace and I figured that if you—if the Triad—knew who I was, I'd be the last person ever assigned there.

Then Serafino shows up and says he has proof of Triad corruption and that my posting was part of that. Something like 'killed in the line of duty, courtesy of Kel-Paten.' So I thought the Triad knew."

"That's insane—"

She held up her hand again, silencing him. "The implant in his head left big gaps in his knowledge. We needed the whole truth. My only option was to go to the one source that might have details on a highly classified Psy-Serv-ordered implant that was blocking his memory, details Eden couldn't find anywhere else. Your personal logs just happened to be in the same directory as those files."

He stared at her for a very long minute. "The only access to those files is in my quarters."

"Yup."

"You broke into my quarters?"

"The furzels did." Gods, she missed Tank. "They unlocked the door from the inside."

"The furzels." He glanced away, shaking his head slightly, then turned back to her. "And did the furzels also bypass all my security to get the files?"

"No, I did that. If we ever get back to the *Vax* I'll show you how, and then you can court-martial me for it."

Another very long stare. Probably hand-picking the jury. Then he relaxed back into a half crouch again. "I've been thinking about that."

"Court-martialing me? UCID will deny any knowledge of who I am, of course. But since Lady Sass wasn't supposed to resurface again, they'll roll over." She huffed a short laugh and stretched out her legs. "Tell me Riln Marin at least has a decent bar in the prison compound. I really need a drink." She knew she was being flippant. It was a defensive mechanism that had always worked in the past. Her impromptu confession left her feeling drained and uncomfortably vulnerable—she had no idea where she stood with him. And he wasn't offering any clues.

"Sebastian." He paused.

Her heart—idiotic optimist that it was—did a tiny flip-flop.

"Kel-Paten."

"I think I know a way out of the void."

Well, next to "I love you," those were undoubtedly the words she most wanted to hear. "What do you need me to do?"

"Help me hijack a ship."

"Any particular one in mind?"

He nodded, a small crooked smile curving his lips. "Zanorian's."

"The *Windblade*?" A Strafer-class cruiser maxed out to any respectable pirate's specs.

"This is a semblance of your life we're stuck in. I assume you know where she's docked. Zanorian's likely in sick bay on board." His mouth quirked again. "And won't put up much resistance."

"He's more likely at Ranza's," she told him, naming a nighthouse. "One of the prostis there is also a Healer. He'd have Angel or Drund—is Drund still alive?" She didn't remember seeing him get off the floor after Kel-Paten hit him. Annoying if he had to die twice.

"Should be."

"Then he had Angel or Drund seal the ship. He thinks his codes and his security are impregnable."

"I know the feeling."

Complaining or commenting? She couldn't tell. "And where are we taking the *Blade* once we get her?"

"Remember those mathematical theories I used to prove that McClellan's Void couldn't exist? I reworked them based on the hypothesis that it could. I've narrowed them down to two. One of those, and the *Blade*'s hyperdrive, should get us home."

"HV-One first," she corrected him. "That's here in the void too, isn't it?"

"We'd be in a stronger position to rescue them if we leave the void and come back with a team from the *Vax*."

"We would. But I don't think Eden and Serafino have that kind of time."

THE OUTPOST

The Ved will pick up on it as soon we start using the energies of Novalis, Jace told Eden. He was sitting on the diag bed, an unconscious furzel cradled in the crook of each arm. Lights were dimmed as low as possible. They had informed Mara they needed at least an hour's rest before starting the surgery or else Eden's skills would be impaired by exhaustion.

What they were actually doing was just as risky as the surgery, given the number of Ved in the outpost. But he knew they had no other choice. *You'll have to be ready.*

Eden, next to him, nodded. Her eyes were shadowed. He knew her heart was breaking. Reilly was fading, would have died if Tank hadn't transferred some of his life essence to the older furzel. That, in turn, almost killed Tank.

But on the Galaxus *we used the energy, and there was a Ved on board.*

The furzels weakened it. They must have done the same thing on the Vax. *But there are a lot more of them here. Dozens. So I don't know if we'll have time for a strong healing. Plus, I've never taken a telepathic furzel into Novalis. I'm not sure how they'll react to its concentrated energy. But whatever kind of healing we can achieve should at least keep them alive until their bodies' energies kick back in.*

Sad to say, he didn't know if he and Eden had that much time left. There wasn't anything more they could do against the remaining Ved. They knew their only chance of escape now had to come from outside—from Kel-Paten and Sebastian, who might not know anything about the Ved but could definitely handle Bianca's human guards.

Bianca. He didn't know what bothered him more: that he had been so blind as to what was really going on with her, or that he'd been so easily manipulated. Psy-Serv plucked his petty hatreds out of his thoughts and twisted them, making him believe the very people who could help him were his enemies. Like Kel-Paten, the infamous Tin Soldier.

He'd justified his taunting of the Triad admiral as a means to break down whatever programming Psy-Serv had put in the 'cybe—when in truth he was the one who'd been programmed.

Jace. Eden's hand rested on his arm, her fingers touching the furzels' soft fur. Her warmth, her love washed over him. He was so unworthy, but he clung to it, absorbing all he could.

As soon as you're there, start working on Tank.

Jace, being stronger, would start the healing process with Reilly. *Don't let anything distract you. No matter what you see, what you hear, ignore it. Focus on Tank. Furzels are a Ved's only natural enemy. He'll know if there's a problem.* He drew a deep breath. *Ready?*

Ready. Jace?

I know, Eden. I love you more than life itself too. Never doubt that. Never forget that. Now come, sweetling. Close your eyes. He reached out mentally for her, laying a light trance over her mind. Her breathing slowed, steadied, and he matched his to hers.

Heart of my heart, breath of my breath, life of my life...

Gray mists swirled and parted, sparkling. She was a few feet in front of him. He waited, holding the sleeping furzels as she hurried to his side. He passed Tank to her. She held the limp form as if it were the most precious thing in the universe.

Jace sought one end of the stone bench as Eden found the other. He sat, positioning Reilly against his heart. *Friend,* he called. *Friend. Follow me. Follow my voice. Follow my energy.*

The Ved erupted around him like howling demons. He flinched in pain as lasers slashed and split his skin. Fire raced up his spine. He was on the bridge of the *Novalis*—his ship, not this dream place—as the ship imploded around him, his crew's lifeless bodies sucked out the hull breach into the dark, cold vacuum of space.

He felt it all. He saw it all. He spoke to Reilly.

Friend. JaceFriend is here to help. MommyEden is here to help. Reach for us. Reach for our energy.

A small answering glow. A slight twitch of a black tail.

Beside him, Eden swayed. He scooted over, let her lean against him. The Ved were wearing her down. He could feel it. But she was fighting, sending energy to Tank. He could feel that too.

A ship's corridor. A lift bank. He pushed the vision away, but it slammed back on him. A ship's corridor. A lift bank. He was waiting for the lift, Triad crew in black moving around him. The *Vaxxar*. He was on Kel-Paten's ship. The lift doors parted and he started to step in.

Eden stopped him. Eden in the lift with a Triad officer, clinging to the man in an intimate embrace. The man kissed her, caressed her roughly as Eden demanded more. Then she looked at Jace and laughed. . . .

No, no. It never happened. He'd been in that lift. So was the man, a security officer. And Eden was there, but nothing had happened. She hadn't laughed at him; she still loved him. . . .

Reilly. Where was Reilly? Jace forced himself to step away from the hallucination, concentrated on the feel of fur beneath his fingers, the small rise and fall of the narrow chest, the tail now curling over his arm.

Jace . . . Friend?

Reilly's voice was weak but it was Reilly. An indescribable joy surged through Jace. *JaceFriend is here, Reilly. Right here. You're safe. Grow strong. Use my energy.*

Tired. So many Bad Things.

You killed a lot of them. You did very well. Use my energy. Grow strong.

Tank?

Tank's here too. With MommyEden.

Bad Things . . . JaceFriend.

Don't worry for now. Grow strong.

No, JaceFriend. Bad Things. Reilly's tail twitched harder. *Bad Things took MommySass. BrandenFriend. Gone. Gone.*

And from the fidget in Eden's arms came a low, keening cry. *Mommy gone!*

Jace? Eden's voice in his mind wavered. Their hope of assistance from the inimitable Tin Soldier had just vanished.

I'll think of something, sweetling, he told her as another Ved poured boiling oil over his face. *I'll think of something.*

THE MINING RAFT

It was too risky to use the main corridors on their way to the *Blade.* McClellan's Void or not, an officer in Triad blacks wouldn't be welcome on a U-Cee raft off the rim world of Kesh Valirr, home to many Danvaral refugees and the target of raids by the Triad over the decades.

In the main corridors, Zanorian's mercs would be the least of their problems. The tunnels, while not remotely safe, were less risky. And only the mercs would be looking for them in there.

Kel-Paten watched the way Sass stopped and listened at each tunnel junction, tested the security of each ladderway before climbing. Watched the way she held her body with a deceptive looseness, as if she could be caught unprepared. He doubted she could. She was moving, thinking, and reacting less like Tasha Sebastian and more like Lady Sass now. It was one of the reasons he hesitated completely trusting her, hesitated sharing his thought processes. Hesitated telling her how his entire world had ended when she disappeared through that hole in the wall and fell into the blackness.

He'd lunged for the cascading conduit on instinct, logic telling him that the chances she might actually be holding on to the other end were slim. A heartbeat later he hung over the edge himself, every 'cybe sense at max as he desperately searched for her.

When the conduit tugged back, his heart caught in his throat. It wasn't until he had her back in his arms that he remembered to breathe again.

He almost told her, then and there, *I don't care who you were in the past, what you've done.*

But he couldn't. He didn't yet know if she was even real and not just a psi-induced hallucination.

She seemed to believe it was her personal hell they were playing out, but it was also his. She was once again unattainable. At least with Tasha Sebastian he had the common basis of the Fleet and the Alliance. But the Tin Soldier and Lady Sass were on opposite ends of the spectrum.

And Lady Sass was Dag Zanorian's lover. He didn't need to see their interaction in the bay earlier to know that—nor was he dissuaded from that notion by the fact she'd decked him soundly. Her

relationship with Zanorian was part of the profile the
Triad had on her, a profile that included the very few,
rare images of Gund'jalar's top student. He wondered
why he'd never noticed the resemblance in the years
since he first saw her on the *Sarna Bogue.*

Or maybe he had and just chose to ignore it.

He was already hopelessly in love with her by that
point.

She slowed, one hand splaying out. "Can you spike
into any system or just Triad?"

A rectangular data-systems panel jutted out from
the wall a few feet in front of them, its cover tar-
nished and dented. He reminded himself that there
were very serious issues at stake here—hallucinations
that could kill. The crew of *Degun's Luck* had
learned that. Who she was and whether she viewed
him only as a 'cybe had to be tabled for now. He
peeled off his gloves and answered without looking at
her. "Do you really think I wouldn't know how to get
into U-Cee hardware? But if you remember the primary security codes, I can work more quickly. Are we
looking for Zanorian's dock assignment?"

"We're looking to create a diversion. RaftTraff
gets mighty testy when a ship breaks dock. And I'm
not willing to wait for clearance."

RaftTraff. Mining Raft Traffic Control. Definitely
not Fleet terminology.

He flipped the cover open, studied the interfaces
and crystal boards while she rattled off the codes. A
patched mess but not unworkable. One stroke of
luck: a compatible dataport. "What kind of diversion? I need location, start time, and duration."

"I'd love to launch a raftwide *mullytrock,* but then

we'd have every other damned jockey in straps burning bulkheads. 'Course, that would work too. Raft-Traff wouldn't know which one of us to send the sec tugs after first."

Mullytrock. Definitely Lady Sass. He remembered Ralland at fourteen getting his mouth washed out with soap for saying that.

"You want a *mullytrock*, Sass, I can give you that." Roving, sporadic power outages, ventilation failures, lift malfunctions. For starters. "But I still need start time." He took his attention from the panel and looked at her. "How far are we from the *Blade*?"

"She's right there." She pointed to her left. "But we have to go down two access panels and up one level. That'll bring us out about six docks up from her airlock. Figure fifteen minutes to get to that point. Five to ten to get on board the *Blade,* depending on who's around."

"I'll start with lift lockdowns at the fifteen-minute mark." He absently studied the panel as he thumbed back the covering on his left wrist port, wishing she wasn't watching him become part of the raft's datagrid. So her hand clasping his arm startled him.

She had her datalyzer out. "Let's make sure you're not going to get your ass fried when you spike in."

"I doubt maintenance—"

"We're overdue, flyboy." She glanced up from the handheld's screen and shot him a look that labeled him *trock*-brained idiot more than flyboy. "It's been almost forty-five minutes without a major calamity. No collapsing walls or resurrected dead men. No intense emotions for this thing to feed on."

He hated explaining this. "I have...fail-safes to prevent permanent damage from a backwash surge."

"And for the five minutes you're in a reboot-and-recover mode, who'll be restarting *my* heart?" She shook her head as if in annoyance and looked down at the datalyzer again. "Everything looks normal. But be careful, okay?" She released his arm.

She was worried about him. But of course she was. He had the formulas to get them out of the void. He pulled his own datalyzer from his utility belt, retrieved the files, then linked the datalyzers, transmitting the information. "If something happens to me, there's the data you'd need."

Another glance down at her datalyzer and up again. "Thanks. But unless it's really inconvenient, would you mind making sure you stay alive?"

A trickle of warmth grew inside him, in spite of his uncertainties. "I'll make it a priority."

"You do that." She shoved the datalyzer back on her belt. "Now let's see how much trouble we can cause."

He caused considerable, starting with the lift lockdowns just as they exited into the corridor leading to the *Blade*. Sass took off her jacket and tied it around her waist, then unsealed the collar of her tan and black uniform, trying, she explained, to make it look less like a uniform. He left his jacket on but shoved up the sleeves and opened his collar too. His gloves were off, his admiral's insignia and comm link in his pocket. They had to survive for only five, maybe ten minutes in the public corridor and hope no one realized they were Triad Fleet officers.

Two maintenance workers hurried past them, a

third trailing behind, guiding a loaded antigrav pallet. They threaded into an oncoming group—males and females—in a variety of coveralls and shipsuits in grays, dark blue, and green. Six, no seven, he counted, noting the position of hands and weapons. Noting where eyes looked. But the group was busy chatting and barely glanced at him or Sass as they passed.

"Thirty-Seven Blue, next one after this." Sass kept her voice low as they neared a yellow-and-white-striped docking port, its airlock set back three feet from the corridor by a short accessway. "It'll say *Devan's Duty* on the ID plate. Shit!"

He saw them at the same moment she did. Four U-Cee Fleet officers in regulation tans coming toward them. Williamson would recognize him immediately—she was a smart, tough captain but no match for the *Vaxxar* when he'd pushed through the Zone in her sector at the beginning of the war. Kuhn was UCID and could easily tag himself and Sass. The other two—both males—he didn't know.

Overheads flickered and popped, but the damned lights didn't dim enough for cover and wouldn't go out for another ten minutes. He grabbed Sass's arm and veered sharply into 36 Blue's accessway as if that was their destination. They needed cover, they needed to look like they belonged, he needed to look like anyone but the Tin Soldier.

He kissed her, pinning her against the bulkhead because there was no time to explain his impromptu maneuver—and he didn't want to give her enough room to take a swing at him. *Mean right hook,* Serafino had warned. She tensed for half a second, then her lips parted and her arms moved quickly up around his neck. His ploy be damned, the taste and feel of her was electrifying, and it was all he could do to keep focused on the approaching footsteps. She deepened their kiss and leaned up into him, her body a contrast of soft places and hard utility belt.

"It's our job to keep their lives interesting." A woman's voice came from behind him. Williamson, he thought, listening to the answering laughter.

"No arguments about that, Captain," another female voice said. "In the meantime..."

The voices and the footsteps trailed off.

He kept kissing Sass. He didn't want to pull away from the hands caressing his neck or the tongue teasing his or the warm soft body arching against him, starting a riot of sensations that left him aching for more.

But he had to. The Tin Soldier and Lady Sass had a ship to hijack.

He released her mouth, stepping back, but her hands locked around his neck, stopped him. Her eyes fluttered open and the look there sent a flare of heat through his body.

"We have to go." His voice was rough.

"Shhh." One hand slid forward to cup his cheek. Rising up on her toes, she very gently brushed her mouth over his.

Her feather-light touch seared him. He bit back a groan. "We don't—"

"I know." Her voice was as raspy as his. She shook her head. "Never mind. Let's go."

She turned away, adjusting the strap of her rifle. He wondered what she was about to say. He wondered why she kissed him with that gentle kiss. But there was no time to wonder.

He swept the corridor left and right with a quick but expert glance. No more U-Cee officers, no limping pirate captain coming to reclaim his ship. Only a maintenance worker in orange coveralls heading away on the left.

He put his hand against the middle of Sass's back and guided her out.

"An hour," she said, as they ducked into 37 Blue's accessway, where the ID plate read *Devan's Duty*. She tapped at the lock's keypad. "An hour and no major calamities."

"Only because Williamson or Kuhn didn't see me." He paused, checking the corridor, covering her back. "Three . . . two . . . one."

An alarm blared discordantly through the corridor. Right on time.

"Tell me that's your doing."

"It is. The light system will fail on alternate decks in eight minutes. Ventilation fans will be on half power three minutes after that. All will restore at the fifteen-minute mark, then the sequence, starting with lift lockdowns, will repeat, starting at the twenty-five."

She grinned. "A master of the *mullytrock*. No wonder I fell in love with you."

A hydraulic hiss signaled the hatchway opening, halting his verbal reply, but it didn't stop his chest from tightening at her words. Was this just another teasing quip? He didn't ask—couldn't ask. He pulled out his datalyzer and scanned for biosignatures or any anomaly that might indicate the presence of one of those psi-creatures on board.

She cradled her rifle against her, a look of determination on her face.

"Clear," he said.

They stepped through the airlock, rifles at the ready.

"I don't like this," she murmured, locking the hatchway behind them. "It's too godsdamned easy."

They moved with deliberate caution down the narrow corridor. A Strafer-class cruiser wasn't a large ship: three small cabins, two cargo holds, a galley—ready room combination, and a large cockpit that was too small to be called a bridge.

But its equipment and security were not average cruiser fare. They were customized—and ingeniously too. The *Blade*'s systems were set to come online once the ship read Zanorian's biosignature and palm print. Unfortunately, they could provide neither.

Zanorian had much to be proud of, Kel-Paten mused, disabling security lock after security lock on the ship's drives while Sass decoded the navigation system. He worked manually; there was no compatible dataport at the command station and too much else to do for him to leave the cockpit and search for one belowdeck in the drive room. It was almost as if Zanorian knew that one day the Tin Soldier would sit in the captain's chair of the *Blade* and had intended to deny him access to spike in.

Which brought him back again to the woman he'd kissed and who'd gently kissed him. He had some very hard questions that needed asking. But they had to wait until they broke dock and avoided any pursuit. However, they'd have at least two hours in jump before they reached Panperra's coordinates, which, by his calculations, should correspond to the location of HV-1 here in the void. Two hours where they'd be little more than passengers, the ship's computers fully in charge. Two hours for him to ask those questions.

Lights flashed green before him. "Drives online," he announced. "Priming sublights."

"Almost there," she told him. "Okay. Nav's online, weapons are online."

"Life support at optimum."

"Scanner, shields . . . we have a go." She slid out of the chair at the nav station and strapped herself into the copilot's chair next to him.

"Looks good. Still not happy, Sass?"

"Me? Nervous as a long-tailed fidget in a room full of rocking chairs." Her grin lacked its usual confidence. "It's still too godsdamned easy."

He initiated two diametric systems checks, not only because he wanted full data on Zanorian's ship but because he didn't discount her concern. "Maybe it's finished playing with us."

"The void doesn't start or finish playing. That's what it is—continuous emotional upheaval for its own pleasure."

"The void is an anomaly and as such obtains no enjoyment." He studied the first systems check. Nothing unusual. "What feeds off our experiences is the psi-creature you said the furzels found."

"Bad Thing."

"So maybe we've bored Bad Thing. It's moved on to someone more interesting."

"Is that your hypothesis?"

He glanced at her. "It's one I'm working on."

"Gathering evidence can get fatal. Remember that."

"Noted." Data scrolled on his console screen. The second check came back clean as well. "Sublights ready, thrusters primed," he told her. "Do we at least give traffic control a courtesy warning?"

She shot him a narrow-eyed look, her mouth pursed. "Of course not."

"Humor me," he said, and disconnected the air-lock, then began retracting the ship's tether cables.

She sighed, keyed open the comm on her armrest. "RaftTraff, *Devan's Duty* looking to flash out in two minutes."

"*Devan's Duty,* this is Raft Traffic Control," a man's voice replied from the speaker, sounding very annoyed. Kel-Paten checked the local scanners. Two freighters and a bulky transport skimmer streamed away from the raft at speeds that explained the con-troller's testy tone. Four other ships were in various stages of undocking. The exodus from his *mullytrock* had started.

"You are *not* cleared for departure at this time. Follow procedure and upload your flight plan. A slot will be assigned—"

"RaftTraff, *Devan's Duty* is flashing out, one minute fifteen. Unlock your clamps or I'll sheer the suckers."

"You still owe for the damage from the last time!"

"Then unlock your clamps, darling," Sass's voice dropped to a throaty purr, "or we will be burning bulkheads. *Devan's Duty,* out."

A series of muted thumps ensued. Kel-Paten keyed the thrusters, then eased the sublights to fifteen percent as the ship dropped away. The *Blade* handled well, feeling like a heavier ship than she was and without a Strafer's usual tendency to yaw at undocking.

Sass tapped in a heading as he increased power, guiding the ship closer to the four departing freighters. Two more broke dock behind them and were on a similar path. He altered thrusters and sublight output.

More ships joined the exiting pack, and for the next ten minutes Sass wove their way toward a large ore freighter. Kel-Paten worked smoothly with her but didn't know why she chose that particular ship. Then he recognized what she was doing. The mirroring maneuver was called "riding the shadow," and it was dangerous and illegal in both the U-Cee and Triad Fleets.

"Hit her with a comm wash, will you?" she asked, sending a short stream of data to his console. "I want her ins and outs."

He keyed in the wide-band invasive scan designed to obtain a ship's unique communications codes: one for incoming transmits and one for outgoing. Codes within those codes could be used to emulate a ship's energy signature. That little trick she might have learned from UCID, but he doubted it.

Now the *Blade* would not only look like part of the freighter on another ship's sensors—most specifically the automated, unmanned sec tugs—it would sound like it too. But they had to keep her on a very precise, very narrow course.

"The sec tugs shouldn't bother us," he said, locking in the pattern. They weren't one of the ships "burning bulkhead," as she put it.

"It's not the sec tugs that worry me. I'd like to be as invisible for as long as possible. There's a lot of traffic between the rafts. I don't know friendlies from unfriendlies."

"You don't have to. Logic," he told her. He'd given this psi-creature problem a good deal of thought. "None of the emotion-inducing experiences to date were fatal."

"Falling through that wall sure as hell could have been!"

"But it wasn't. I've analyzed everything that's happened since we made HV-One. Your fall wasn't fatal because if it was, you'd no longer contribute an emotional response."

"And sending a skimmer on a collision course with the *Blade* wouldn't create an emotion?" She snorted softly.

"A hull breach in space is instantaneous death. We'd be useless to it. That's why we had to get off the raft, where it could continue to throw problems at us, and into a smaller environment, where it needs to keep us alive."

"The *Galaxus* going cold into the jumpgate, the fuel-line break?"

"All within range of a habitable world," he reminded her.

"So your hypothesis is, the safest place we could be is in a small ship in the middle of nowhere?"

"It won't try anything until we get back dirtside on HV-One."

She took her gaze off her console for a few seconds and stared at him. Then, with a shake of her head, she went back to keeping the *Blade* on her very tight course. "Humor me," she said after a moment, mimicking his request minutes before.

"I need some time to program in my calculations. Unless that freighter makes a big course change, you can keep us shadowed to her for another ten minutes."

"She's going for the jumpgate. So are we," she argued, without taking her gaze from her console. "It would be a lot safer if we stayed shadowed to her the whole way."

"It's not necessary, and it ties you up. You're too tired to hand-fly this ship for any length of time."

"Get me some coffee and I'll be fine. And let me know if you see any blue glowing blobs in the galley while you're there."

He linked his handheld to the ship's computer and, when his calculations were downloading smoothly, unsnapped his safety straps. 'Cybe senses at max, he performed a quick visual check in the cabins and corridor for any blue glowing blobs his datalyzer might have missed. He returned to the cockpit with two cups of coffee, knowing it would please her.

She inhaled the aroma, a small smile returning. "Mahrian blend, black. Thank you." She tapped at the console, then looked at him. "I'm not trying to be a bitch. But there's a lot to be said for trust no one, suspect everything, and never take your hand off your weapon. I know you don't understand that. It's instinct for me. I wouldn't be alive if it wasn't." She went back to the console, taking a sip of her coffee.

He watched the data flow from the handheld to his console's screen, then he looked at her. "Does trusting no one include me?"

"You thought I sold you out to Zanorian back on that raft," she said without glancing at him. "Yet I let you walk at my back with a loaded rifle. You tell me."

He thought for a minute, wanting to make sure he said exactly what he wanted to say. He knew his timing was terrible—he probably should wait until they were safely in jumpspace. But she had asked him. "When I saw you with Zanorian, when I realized who you were, I thought nothing in my life could be worse than that. I was wrong. When that wall collapsed and you disappeared with it, that was far and away the most horrible moment I've ever had. And believe me, I've had some bad ones. But nothing could be as bad as losing you."

She turned to him, her cheeks flushed, her lips parted as if she wanted to speak.

He leaned forward, elbows on his knees. "You read my logs. Then you know I've been in love with you for a long time."

"You've been in love with Tasha Sebastian," she said softly before going back to her screen. "She doesn't exist."

"Didn't you read the very first letter I ever wrote you?"

She looked up from the console. "When I was on the *Bogue*? Yes."

"I had no U-Cee profile on you. I didn't even know your first name. I fell in love with you anyway."

She was looking at him with that odd mixture of

confusion and elation, but elation seemed to be winning this time.

He took a chance—a huge one considering the uncertainties, considering he was a 'cybe officer and she was Lady Sass. But when she fell through the corridor wall, something inside him had changed. "Will you please quit shadowing that damned freighter so we can finish what we started in the airlock accessway?"

A blush colored her cheeks. Elation? Gods, he hoped he hadn't lost his ability to read human facial expressions. "I have to set a course for that jumpgate—"

"Already done."

"Show-off." She made the final changes on her console, turning the ship over to the navigational systems. Then, with a swift move, she unhooked her safety straps and flowed across the short distance into his lap.

He didn't give her a chance to change her mind. He pulled her hard against him, their mouths fusing. He wrapped his arms around her, not wanting to think about who she was or where they were headed. They had a half hour to the jumpgate, and he didn't want to waste a second until the ship needed his attention again.

He had twelve years of emptiness to fill, twelve years of touching her only in his dreams, twelve years of imagining the softness of her body, which suddenly was real and his to explore.

He caressed the curve of her hip as she did things to his mouth—her teeth gently pulling on his lower lip—that made his breath hitch. He thrust his fingers into the hair at the nape of her neck and mimicked her movement, nibbling on her mouth, tracing her lips with the tip of his tongue. He was learning—though, gods, he knew he'd never had a teacher like this.

She arched back, guiding his mouth down her throat. He lost his grip on her hair and his hands fell to her waist as she—sweet holy gods!—rocked her hips against him, stroking him. He gasped against her skin, the unexpected pleasure of it almost blinding as he throbbed beneath her.

He licked her throat, trailed kisses over her collarbone as she arched again. The front of her uniform was open almost to her waist. He didn't know how or when, but her hand on the back of his head told him that was where he needed to go, and he wasn't going to argue. Not when the soft swell of her breast under his mouth felt so incredibly good. Then the tight bud of one nipple brushed against his lips, surprising him. He circled it experimentally with his tongue before taking the tip of her breast into his mouth.

Her low moan set hot, tingling sensations roaring through him. Something primal in him responded, his groin pulsing, his desire to bury himself inside her blanking out all thought, all reason. There was only Tasha, his Lady Sass, and the feel and taste of her as he found her mouth again, his hands on her waist grinding her against him.

He hated uniforms, he hated the restriction of clothing, he hated the damned confines of the captain's chair. And he hated that incessant pinging noise . . .

Shit! The jumpgate.

She seemed to realize it as he did. She jerked back,

reaching blindly for the console. But he was quicker and closer. He swiveled the chair around, bringing her back against his chest as he keyed in the gate codes and activated the preprogrammed course to Panperra.

"Branden—"

"Shhh." He took a moment to steal a kiss from her lips. "Under control." At least, the ship was, as the nav comp locked on a fix. He was another matter. He was well out of control. If Psy-Serv traced his emo-patterns right now, he knew he'd melt their damned systems.

He could feel her breathing hard against him as the ship flowed smoothly past the edge of the gate, all systems optimal. Two more taps on the console and the computers were in charge.

They had two hours.

He swiveled back around.

She leaned up, palms on his shoulders. Her face was flushed, her lips slightly parted and swollen. He thought she'd never looked more beautiful.

He ran his hands up the curve of her breasts until they came to rest on her shoulders, then drew her to him, kissing her softly, gently. She kissed him back with small teasing kisses that made his heart race. Someday he'd ask her how she did that, how she knew just the right amount of seduction and playfulness. It mystified him. *She* mystified him.

She pulled her face away, one side of her mouth quirked in a small grin. "Pick a number between one and three." Her voice was breathy.

"One and three?" He shook his head quizzically. "The only possible number is two."

"Ah, good choice." She pulled out of his lap, one hand locked in the fabric of his shirt, bringing him with her.

He stood, tried to draw her back in his arms, but she was laughing softly. "This way," she said, tugging him toward the corridor.

"This way?"

"You chose cabin number two." She stepped over the hatch tread.

He followed. *Cabin number two?*

She tapped in a code at the second doorway. "Remember sooner or later, flyboy? Well, it's sooner."

The door opened. He saw a dimly lit cabin and a wide pillow-strewn bed.

His body heated.

Sweet holy gods.

Two things warred within Branden Kel-Paten as he stepped—almost stumbling—into the small cabin after Sass. The first was his overwhelming desire to make love to her. The second was his growing fear that in doing so, he'd lose her through ineptitude.

She knew exactly the right amount of playfulness and seduction. He had no idea. Over the years, he'd read books on human sexuality and various articles on lovemaking. And he had one brief failed encounter with a prosti on Raft 309. He should probably call up at least a few of those articles from his memory banks, but, gods, she was unsealing his shirt, tugging it out of the waistband of his pants as they stood only a few feet from the edge of the bed. He wasn't even sure he could find his memory banks right now.

"Sass." He stilled her hands, bringing her fingers to his lips. If she removed his shirt she'd see the scars crisscrossing his body. Ugly things that had made the prosti recoil. 'Cybes didn't get vanity-patched, because their bodies were made for war, not love.

And his hands...his black gloves were a stark contrast to her soft skin. Touching her perfect body with them seemed unnatural. Touching her perfect body without them was worse. His hands were synthderm and powermesh, with powernodes in his fingertips and palms. An abomination. He was an abomination. He had no right to—

"Branden?"

Her face tilted up to his, as if begging to be kissed. That he could do, because she'd taught him how. He brushed his mouth over hers, still gentle, then came back for a deeper kiss. But not too much. He had to control this, had to control his body's reactions or he'd end up embarrassing himself. While her tongue toyed with his, he tripped the code in his mind, segueing into full 'cybe mode. Emo-inhibitors activated, hitting him like a cool draft of air. Her eyes were closed, but he put his vision on night function, just in case. No sickly glow as one more reminder of what he was.

He released her hands, enfolding her tightly against him, and rested his face on her hair. He caressed her back, the rise and fall of her breath steadying him.

He had to be in control. He couldn't let her find out how shamefully inexperienced he was. He couldn't let her see the ugliness that was a biocybe.

Her hands splayed against his chest. For as wonderful as she felt against his skin, he wished he could close his shirt. They should sit on a couch—there had to be a couch in here somewhere. Sit on the couch and talk. Kiss, touch, but not too much. He wouldn't be able to react beyond a certain point, anyway. His emo-inhibitors—

She lightly dragged her nails over his chest, raking a nipple he had no idea was so sensitive. Heat spiraled through him. He sucked in a sharp breath as her fingers moved across his chest again.

"Hey," he said, letting the breath out, but that was all he could say, because her mouth locked over his. And she wasn't being gentle.

He broke the heated kiss carefully. "Tasha."

"Mmm, Branden." Her hands slid down his chest and tugged the rest of his shirt out of his pants before he gathered his wits to stop her. When he finally did grab her hands, she'd shrugged out of her shirt and stood half naked before him—even more enticingly beautiful than his dreams, her skin soft and creamy in the cabin's dim light. Without thinking he stepped forward, reaching to touch one perfect breast.

Her hands curled into his waistband and unsnapped his pants.

Oh, sweet holy gods! He took a half step back and realized that would only undo his pants faster. He moved toward her instead, before those clever fingers went further and tested the already strained limits of his emo-inhibitors. He grabbed her arms, trying for another kiss, but she was pulling him with her. He caught her against him just as the back of her legs hit the edge of the bed. Her knees buckled, and suddenly she was on her back and he was on top of her, his bare chest against hers. Warmth flowed where they touched. He levered up quickly on one arm, but she'd already locked her hands around his neck. Her impish smile pleaded for a kiss.

He fought the impulse for all of 3.25 seconds, according to the readouts in the lower left corner of his vision. Kissing was good. It was something he was getting better at. It kept her from seeing the patterns of his surgeries. It kept her hands—wrapped around his neck—away from his pants.

He rolled onto his side, taking her with him in the kiss, one hand against the small of her back. He could do this for two hours, holding her, kissing her. Letting this warm trickle of pleasure drift through him. It was just a small trickle, it was just . . .

Her hand slid down his abdomen into his half-open pants and cupped him, making his breath stutter in his throat as her clever fingers stroked his erection. Molten waves of passion crashed through his emo-inhibitors. Instinctively he arched into her hand, his mouth hard on hers, drawing pleasure from everywhere he could. He ached with the desire to love her—finally—after all these years. It was wrong. He knew it was wrong. He was a 'cybe, the Tin Soldier, an unholy creation, but gods help him, he loved her. And just once he wanted to be someone she could love—scars, synthderm, wrist ports, and all.

"We need to get rid of these," she whispered, stilling her delicious torture to push his pants down his hips.

Briefly he thought of the scars encircling his thighs, but she kicked off her boots and, kneeling next to him, was shimmying out of her pants. He stopped and stared in unabashed admiration, his shame over his body's imperfections usurped by his desire to feel, taste, and explore every inch of hers.

Heart pounding, he stripped off his gloves and the

rest of his clothes and then pulled her down on top of him. Close like this was good. The cabin's dim light was good. She couldn't easily see what he looked like. He kissed her hard, heat and passion spiking and swirling through him, causing reactions in his body far beyond what he thought possible. His inhibitors were off-line, quite possibly decimated as she moved sensuously against him, their skin now slick from excitement. Her lips brushed his jaw, his neck, and when her tongue found the hard ropy scar on his left shoulder, he tensed involuntarily.

"Don't," he rasped, wincing when he realized he'd said it aloud.

She raised her face. "Does that hurt?"

Sweet gods, she was so beautiful it made his throat tight. "Not anymore," he managed, brushing her hair back from the side of her face.

She lightly ran her fingers over the scar that circled the point of his shoulder, then found the wide one that went straight down his upper arm to the inside of his elbow. "Bet it hurt like hell at one time, though." Her voice was soft, almost understanding.

"Yes." He watched her face, saw the slight dip of her eyebrows into a frown. He was breathing hard, the warmth of her fingers on his skin mesmerizing.

She glanced at him. "Kisses make it better." She brushed her lips over his, then kissed his left shoulder again, then the wide scar on his arm. His right shoulder and arm were next. He was amazed, humbled, and very aroused by her gentle touch, by her loving his ugliness. He twined his fingers in her hair, wanting her mouth on his—the only activity in which he felt confident—but she shook her head and angled back.

"Tell me what you like," she said, her voice throaty.

"What I like? Just you. With me." He touched her cheek.

"Nothing...special?"

He closed his eyes. He knew what she asked, but the descriptions of positions he'd read failed to surface in his mind. "I wouldn't know," he said finally, honestly. Because even if he could lie, his body couldn't. "I never..." and he let the sentence trail off.

Her eyes, half hooded with desire moments before, widened slightly. Her lips parted. "You mean—"

"You're the only one." His voice was rough from desire and shame. "My whole life, you're all I've wanted."

She closed her eyes briefly, that impish smile returning when she looked at him, something twinkling in her eyes. "Don't worry, love. I won't be gentle."

"Sass—"

But she'd already dipped her head, her tongue trailing down his stomach. She lightly nipped his abdomen, then took him fully into her mouth.

"Oh, sweet gods!" he gasped. Pleasure beyond description flowed through him, swirling, as she licked then stroked him. He was at the very edge of what little control he had, his body heating, his breath stuttering at her touch. Finally, at his limit, he reached blindly for her, found her hair, urged her up his body. A soft, wicked giggle rumbled against his chest, then his throat. Damn her, what she did to him! He loved her so much.

He found her mouth, kissed her as if she was the sole thing keeping him alive—because she was. Trembling now, he ran his synthderm and powermesh hands over her, wanting to give her the pleasure she gave him. But he didn't know how, didn't know where to start or what she wanted, so he caressed, kneaded, the feel of her body moving against his intoxicating and dangerous. Too dangerous. If they didn't slow down, he was going to—

She mounted him, taking him into her body, a heated wetness enveloping him. He sucked in a harsh breath of surprise and astonishment and then he was thrusting greedily into her, hands clasping her hips, matching her rhythm. All rational thought ceased. There was just overwhelming pleasure, cresting ecstasy; there was her low moan of desire and his own rasped utterance of her name, over and over. Then Admiral Branden Kel-Paten's orderly cybernetic world exploded into a cascade of heat, pleasure, and passion.

Gods' blessed rumps, he's a virgin! Well, not anymore, Sass corrected herself sagely, her wry grin hidden by the fact that her face was snuggled against Branden's neck. It made sense. His hesitancy in touching her, his shyness—and that was the only word for it—in dealing with her. His sudden almost about-face when she'd brought him to Angel's cabin. Somehow she thought her friend wouldn't mind.

But Kel-Paten did mind once she'd started removing his clothes. When she saw the scars, she understood. They weren't like Zanorian's thin affectations. These were knotty, full of pain and bad memories. Unpleasant. Best kept hidden.

She understood that too. She had scars. But hers

were inside, while his were on the outside. Her experience on the raft had forced her to reveal hers to him, though far less pleasantly.

His arms tightened around her and he rolled over onto his side, taking her with him. She brought her hands to his shoulders, her face up to his, sensing a kiss coming. He needed a lot of kisses. That was okay. She did too. Kisses were reassuring. They both needed reassurance.

His mouth found hers, gently. He always started gently. Still cautious. Still unsure—but of her or himself or both, she didn't know. She wasn't yet ready to ask. Odd how she could lay here naked with him and yet not be able to ask a simple question such as "do you trust me?" But she couldn't. So she kissed him back instead.

He broke the kiss with the same gentleness with which he started it.

"You okay?" she asked, because that was the kind of stupid thing first-time lovers always said. More so because their first time was really his first time.

"Beyond wonderful." His deep voice rumbled between them. They were almost nose to nose. "But I don't think I was—*it* was—that wonderful for you." He stumbled over the last few words.

Her heart ached for him. Mister Perfection. Ol' No Excuses Kel-Paten. "It was incredible for me," she said, brushing her fingers over his jaw. "And not just because I finally know more about something than you do."

"Gloating is unprofessional."

She laughed softly. He did have a wry sense of humor.

"But thank you," he continued. "I hope—I'd like to do better."

"I'm available for private lessons."

He reached for the blanket. "You should get some sleep first," he said, drawing it up over both of them. "We have an hour fifteen before we need to be at the controls."

An hour's nap sounded like luxury, and she said so.

He kissed her forehead. "I'll wake you."

No. She'd wake herself in forty-five minutes. And teach him just how much fun they could have in thirty.

THE OUTPOST

Jace wove his mind tightly into Reilly's until he wasn't sure where the furzel started and he ended. It seemed the best way to utilize the healing energies of Novalis that were so much a part of him and so foreign to the furzel. The Ved continued to thrash at his memories. He ached at his father's rejection, cried at his mother's disdain. Through it all he held on to Reilly, now rapidly growing stronger. The furzel seemed to blossom in Novalis.

So did Jace's knowledge. The collective memory of his people resided in this dream state. Linked to the furzels, amplified by the power in Novalis, Jace learned exactly how the Ved had infiltrated the Triad.

A Psy-Serv experiment? Eden, bonded to Reilly, was stunned by the revelations.

A dangerous one. Exiled to the malleable dimension of the void centuries before by their creators, the

Ved had found an escape route when a dangerous Psy-Serv mind experiment opened the first pathway into Dreehalla. And the Faction was born—a parasitic symbiosis between human and Ved in the Triad. The human—the host—eventually died. But until that point, the Ved provided the human with a feeling of invincibility, power, omnipotence—whatever the human craved. And the human *would* crave, because the Ved needed more emotions to feed on.

The humans in Psy-Serv learned to offer the Ved sacrifices to keep them from destroying the host human: sacrifices such as ships' crew, like *Degun's Luck* and the others before it.

They answered the hail of a Psy-Serv pinnace with engine trouble. Jace relived the scene with the information the furzels had pulled from the Ved they'd neutralized. The Ved fed off the kidnapped crew's terror but also off the resulting fear as it spread through Lightridge. Mass hysteria was a tasty tidbit. Even stronger than the pleasure they were created to amplify for the Nasyry.

The Nasyry? Eden's shock was palpable.

One of my people's shameful secrets, Jace admitted. *So long ago that the Ved'eskhar became legend, not fact: an energy being bred for the purpose of pleasure enhancement. A link to a Ved could make a simple kiss feel like an adventure into ecstasy. Then that memory could be augmented and you could experience it over and over, in greater intensity each time.*

Like trefla, Eden said. *Only a thousand times worse.*

It drove people to the brink of insanity. To suicide. And then a Ved, released from its human host, would be frantic to find a new one. Its quest for pleasure changed to a quest for fear and pain, one where they no longer simply merged with a host's mind but drew the host into this dimension with them, thereby opening a greater range of emotional experiences. Though our scientists said they couldn't, the Ved learned, evolved. Thousands of Nasyry died in our attempt to banish them into the dimension you call the void—an empty place where, feeding on one another, they'd die. But they didn't. Because of Psy-Serv, they're able to move in and out of the void. And control my sister.

He knew from her aura that Bianca was beyond his help. The Ved liked *oullums.* Though their lack of telepathic talents made them more difficult to bond with initially, *oullums* made stronger hosts because they had no ability to detect and possibly defend against a Ved. That's why the Ved encouraged the Intergalactic Psychic Concordance and Protection Statutes and the harnessing of telepaths. No one to warn the *oullums* they were coming. They'd learned from their mistakes with the Nasyry.

Reilly stirred, stretching his back legs. His tail twitched. *Friend? JaceFriend?*

Tank, sitting in Eden's lap, shook himself, then licked a spot of fur on his side. *Friend? Food?*

Jace felt Eden smile, even through her fear and heartache. *Time,* he told her. *Mara, our keeper, grows restless as we rest.*

But I'm not ready! The operation is too risky. Eden's panic flowed into Jace.

He sent back warmth, a mental embrace. And a plan. *There's no way we can neutralize every Ved in this place. But with the furzels healed, maybe we can use them to open a single path out.*

And how, Eden asked, *are we going to get past Mara, the guards?*

You pretend to put me under. I can put myself into a deep enough trance to muddle the med-sensors. Mara and her assistant will be focused on the operation and, with me unconscious, won't consider us a physical threat. Then you say there's a problem, something to bring Nando leaning over me. I'll grab him. You handle Mara. I'm guessing they'll be armed. We take their weapons and make a run for it, using the furzels to clear the way.

Jace. Eden's tone was firm. *So many things could go wrong. Not the least being I'm no expert in hand-to-hand combat.*

If we can get to my old ship, we'll make it. All you have to do is knock Mara down. There must be some piece of medical equipment in here you can use. He felt her confidence waver. *I can take Nando out easily. And I'll be there to help you. You can do it, Eden. You have to.* He touched her in a ritual blessing: forehead, cheek, chin, and then brought her and the furzels out of Novalis. *It's our only chance.*

THE *WINDBLADE*

Sass woke, her internal alarm opening her eyes at the forty-five-minute mark. A small smile touched her lips and, stretching, she turned toward him. He wasn't there. She levered up on her elbow, shot a quick glance around Angel's cabin. The sanifac door was open. No light from within, no sound of water splashing in the sink.

"Hey," she said softly to the quiet room. "Kel-Paten?"

No answer. Damn. She sat up fully. Her clothes were on the floor. His weren't. Had she dreamed making love to him? Or had Bad Thing struck again, transporting her somewhere, some*when* else?

She threw off the blanket, then grabbed for her clothes. "Kel-Paten?" Her voice was stronger. But not strong enough to drown out the damning thoughts racing through her head or the small ache growing around her heart. She'd been too aggressive; some men didn't like that. He needed to make the first move and she'd taken away that prerogative. She scared him off.

Kel-Paten? Scared? another part of her mind argued.

Yeah, well. She had no idea he was a virgin. She would have done things differently. Been ... what? Gentler? She gave a soft snort at her own ruminations as she sealed her shirt and tucked it into her pants. There was a comm panel on the wall by the door to the corridor. She headed for it, keyed it to intraship. "Captain's on duty. Status."

There was a moment of silence, then: "Twenty-six minutes forty-one seconds to the jumpgate. All systems green."

He was alive. He was in the cockpit. More than that she couldn't tell from his voice. Damned emo-inhibitors. And damn her own stupidity for not reading the signals of his inexperience. No doubt he'd envisioned making love to the well-bred, top-of-her-class Tasha Sebastian. He ended up with Lady Sass, raft rat and fugitive.

So much for dreams. His and hers.

She missed Tank. If nothing else, she'd get her fidget back on HV-1.

She palmed open the cabin door and headed for the bridge.

The hatchway was open. He swiveled in the pilot's seat when she was halfway down the corridor, and even at this distance she saw his eyes were luminous. Powered up. Habit or precaution?

"Trouble?" she asked, stepping through the hatchway.

He frowned for a moment. "You could have stayed in bed longer."

"So could you," she said pointedly, because if he thought making love to her was a mistake, she wanted to hear it now.

"I don't need as much rest—"

"I'm not talking about sleeping."

He stared at her. She rested one hand on the back of the copilot's chair, swiveling it around, but didn't sit.

"You wanted me there when you woke up?"

She nodded slowly. "Uh-huh."

"May I take you up on that offer at a later date?"

He looked so sincerely chastised that she had to laugh, the ache fading from around her heart. The *trock*-brained idiot did care about her, about Lady Sass. "You damned well better," she told him as she sat.

"Sass, I'm sorry," he said as she turned toward the console. "I didn't want to bother you. You needed the sleep."

Sass. More and more, he called her that. She glanced at him. "I needed you," she said softly, and was rewarded by his small, crooked smile of surprise.

"You damned well better," he said, echoing her retort.

"Aye, sir. Now tell me why being here was preferable to being in bed with me. Trouble?"

"Preventive measures." He clasped her hand briefly, then tapped at the console's monitors, bringing up data. His gloves were off, and she wondered if he'd found a way to spike in. "I've been thinking about those fighters that chased us into the jumpgate at Panperra. I'm hoping they came from here."

"From the void? So you're thinking there is some charted way in and out, that this isn't a parallel universe?"

"It can't be parallel or our being here would violate the law of physics," Kel-Paten said.

"But that wasn't Zanorian or Angel, not as I know them. What else—"

"A dimension of its own, based on what data I've been able to collect. How much is tailored to the observer and how much is externally controlled, I'm not sure. But if those fighters can move in and out, so can we."

"And if they can't?" Sass asked, with a strong feeling she wasn't going to like his answer.

"Then we can't use this ship, or anything created in here, to get home. It would cease to exist once we crossed through the gate. We'd die."

"But there are options," Kel-Paten told her, as Sass's stomach executed a few flip-flops. She did not want to spend the rest of her life in the void being emotionally tortured by blue glowing psi-creatures. Dealing with her feelings for the admiral was tough enough without adding Bad Thing's influence into the mix.

"Assuming this is another dimension," Kel-Paten continued.

"Can't you tell?"

"I've narrowed it down to two hypotheses."

She knew that. But she didn't realize they might be conflicting and said so.

"We've been here a relatively short period of time, with malfunctioning equipment and no correlative database to work with. What's here," and he tapped the *Blade*'s console, "is the first functional system I've had at my disposal. But I don't know if it's reliable."

"The data could be part of the illusion." Garbage in, garbage out.

"Exactly."

"There must be some way to differentiate—" A question surfaced. "How do you know I'm real?"

He glanced down for a moment, and she had a feeling her question wasn't one he wanted asked. "I imprinted your biosignature years ago," he said when he looked back at her.

"Imprinted?"

"Dr. Fynn reads auras. I read biosignatures."

"Like a datalyzer?"

He gave a short, curt nod.

His 'cybe functions again. Something he wasn't comfortable with around her. "That's why you've stayed powered up?" The glow in his eyes made sense now.

"If it bothers you—"

"Hell, no!" She was relieved there was at least one thread of sanity in all this lunacy. "So I'm me. How do I know you're you?"

"Objectively, you don't."

So much for sanity. She pinned him with a hard gaze. "I'm overjoyed to hear that." She thought for a moment. "Did Zanorian's biosignature match?"

"His isn't one I have on fi—memorized. And I don't have the *Vax*'s databases to work with. But his appearance was different, and you noted there were associational inaccuracies. That's one of the reasons I question if this is a parallel universe."

"A parallel universe doesn't preclude variations of the original."

His eyes narrowed slightly, but a small smile

played over his mouth. "I do love the fact you punch holes in every hypothesis I come up with. But nothing so far confirms the parallel hypothesis. I do need to determine if we have to find another means of transportation. If the *Galaxus* was in better shape, we could use her, since we brought her into this dimension with us. But she's not, and I don't know what would happen if we repaired her with components created here."

She did not want to die in jump. Or, worse, be stranded in stasis, the ship in a kind of hyperspace paralysis. Given that, she'd opt for the void. At least the scenery was better. And she was sure she could find a bar. Unless...

"The *Mystic Traveler*," she said carefully, because her mind was just now grasping the idea, "might have come from our existence. Maybe Andgarran didn't disappear after he stole the ship—"

"He *stole* it?"

She shot him a narrow-eyed look of disbelief. "I bet Serafino told you he sold it, right?" She laughed. "Andgarran stole it, embarrassing the hell out of 'Fino, which is why we all thought he took off. But maybe he didn't. Maybe he was caught in the same kind of jump we were. And ended up here."

"Or else this place created the ship out of Serafino's memories."

"Except that getting the *Traveler* back wouldn't be a negative memory. And so far that's all I've seen here—Bad Things creating bad things."

"But we can't be sure."

She shook her head. "Serafino would know. Just as I can tell you that this ship," and she ran her hand over the edge of the console, "isn't the real *Windblade*. And I can't tell you why, other than I've been in the real one and this isn't it." Like Zanorian and Angel.

Kel-Paten leaned back in his chair, steepling his fingers together. "That would mean abandoning this ship, hijacking the *Traveler,* locating Fynn, Serafino, and the furzels, locking them in a transbeam, and getting everyone on board, off planet, and through the jumpgate. Without anyone at the outpost taking retaliatory action. And without any more enemy fighters waiting to blow us out of the space lanes when we arrive."

Hell of a list. And a hundred things that could go wrong. A hundred ways to die. "Piece o' cake. Anything else?"

"Yes." The perimeter warning chimed. He turned to it, then slanted her a quick glance. "Don't forget you still need me when we get home."

The *Blade* flowed out the jumpgate, a flawless machine of speed and stealth, weapons hot, scanner array parsing the starfield for anything that could remotely be considered a threat. Which encompassed, as far as Sass was concerned, everything. It had been more than three hours since their last Bad Thing-induced episode. They were not only overdue but she had a strong suspicion the void was collecting interest on it. She wanted to be long gone when it presented the invoice.

"Nice to know no one's moved the planet while we

were away," she said, seeing HV-1's data on the nav comp.

"Let's confirm the *Galaxus* and the outpost before we celebrate."

An hour before they could do that. Another twenty minutes before they made orbit. The *Blade* had considerably more speed than the damaged shuttle and, thanks to Kel-Paten, had exited the gate on the proper axis.

Sass brought the sublights to max, then coaxed them a bit more. It had been only a few hours since they were dumped on the raft; the outpost was still in the dark of night. But the worry she'd held in abeyance now rushed to the forefront of her mind. Eden. Tank and Reilly. And 'Fino, that damned Nasyry pirate.

A lot could happen in a few hours. A lot had happened already.

Kel-Paten was running his simulations, data streaming down one screen, charts and schematics revolving on another. Tension hung in the air like a storm cloud riding the horizon. She thought of Lethant again. The storms there were fierce, violent.

No. She pushed the thought away. Don't draw it to you. Don't give the void anything to work with. Even though Kel-Paten had confirmed there were no Bad Things slithering through the corners of the ship, Sass was nervous. She didn't know how big one would have to be to grab them, sending them reeling again. A little one could be tucked inside a conduit on board.

She focused on HV-1's data, now coming in more detail. Fifteen minutes later she whooped in joy. "Got her!" The *Galaxus* was a mere pinprick of data at this distance but recognizable. Kel-Paten confirmed her finding with a nod.

But they were too far for the *Blade* to scan for biosignatures at this distance. The Strafer-class ship wasn't the *Vax*.

Minutes later they confirmed the outpost and then, surprisingly or perhaps not so, a few other scattered small settlements, no apparent threat. Illusions? Reality?

"We're in a void-based ship," Kel-Paten grumbled, double-checking all data. Sass understood: garbage in, garbage out.

But they had nothing else to go on.

They crossed out of geosynchronous orbit and into the low planetary orbit zone. Then the *Blade*'s scanner erupted with warnings. Weapons came online automatically. Heart pounding, Sass brought the data to her console with brisk precision.

"Bogies, six—"

"Eight," Kel-Paten corrected. "Closing fast, port and starboard."

"Got 'em. Shields at max."

"Initiating evasive programs two and six. If I don't like them, I'm going manual."

"Agreed," Sass said tersely as the first barrage of laser fire peppered the shields. "Shields holding."

"Returning fire. Launching seeker." Kel-Paten released the first of three long-range tracking torpedoes the ship carried. "Two minutes to impact."

"Cutting it a little close, aren't we?" A seeker could easily destroy the attacking and defending ship if it wasn't detonated at a safe distance.

"Right at perimeter of the danger zone, not to worry. We'll just get some chaff."

Hell. And Eden thought Sass took crazy risks.

"We need to let our friends know we're serious," he added.

"Our friends look familiar," Sass said as she shifted shield calibration to manual and keyed in a pattern.

"Affirmative. Same hull configuration as those at Panperra."

She played with the pattern again, then let the computer take over. Just a little something to cause a *mullytrock* in the attackers' targeting systems.

The fighter targeted by the seeker veered violently. The missile corrected and closed the distance.

"Ten seconds to impact," Kel-Paten said. "My compliments to Zanorian. His ship handles well."

"Actually, he'd be flattered as hell—"

"Impact. One down."

"—to hear that," she finished, bracing for the onslaught of ship fragments that would pepper the *Blade*'s shields for the next few moments. That *was* close.

"Noted. But he's not getting you back. Launching seeker two."

The target was much farther away this time. "Noted," she answered, and caught him quirking an eyebrow at her. She grinned in spite of the tension. The *Blade* shuddered slightly, the fragments acting as infinitesimal missiles stressing the shields. "Reworking shields." She tapped them over to manual again, keyed in another series of illogical patterns.

"Three minutes to impact."

"We only have one more of those," she warned. She was in her element, working a ship in the heat of battle, coaxing more out of the systems, countering the attackers' moves. But she was also practical and scared. Only a fool would feel otherwise.

"Noted. I want to use them now because we can't once we hit heavy air."

Kel-Paten angled the ship toward HV-1 again, thrusters firing, the fighters following. For a moment she tensed. His heavy-air, lower-atmosphere experience was limited. Why would he . . . ? "I take it I'm flying once we hit blue sky?"

"You know this ship, Lady Sass. I know your profile. That, too, is a compliment," he added. Then a few minutes later: "Impact. Two down."

He launched the third seeker, and four minutes after that it was five against one. Not great odds, Sass knew, but the *Blade* was designed for combat and, unlike the *Galaxus,* handled heavy air with skill. There would be a few risky moments when she switched to the heavy-air engines. But the fighters—if they pursued—would have the same problem. She sucked in a breath, prepped her console for the change from copilot and pilot. They were descending more rapidly now. Shield structure would have to change too, to compensate for the superheating upon entry.

Sweat beaded on her brow, as if she could already feel the increase in temperature. It had been years since she'd taken a Strafer dirtside in a wild dive. Landing the *Galaxus* with Serafino was a joyride compared to this.

"Three minutes to changeover," she told Kel-Paten, whose aggressive actions with the ship's lasers had caused one more attacker to wheel off. They were down to four. But shields were down to seventy-five percent. A portside scanner flickered out, creating a large blind spot. Not good. "We'll be coming in nightside. I need my eyes."

"On it," Kel-Paten said. "Compensating." He worked diligently at his console, then turned abruptly to a smaller engineering station on his left. Sass glanced at weapons, now on autodefense.

"Best I can do right now." Kel-Paten turned back to the main console as the port scanner monitor blinked on again. But there were gaps in the datastream.

"I can work with it," Sass told him. "One minute thirty seconds to changeover."

"Shifting command console to manual," he said over the sound of the starboard lasers firing. "Bogies are pulling back."

"Praise the gods and pass the peanut butter. Blue sky boundary forty-five seconds." She focused on the dataflow as the sublights segued over to the heavy airs, the ship shuddering. The checklist flowed through her mind and she automatically adjusted the power grid and fuel mixture. "Fifteen seconds to primary wing extension."

"Thrusters—"

"Hold off, flyboy. We're coming in hotter than I like." But the bogies gave them no choice. They still followed, though at a greater distance. She prayed they'd pull off. She had other problems now.

"On your mark."

"Extending wings, twenty percent." The *Blade*

bucked, slipping, a feed-valve rupture alarm blaring. Damn! This was not the way you took a Strafer dirt-side. Zanorian would kick her ass all over Kesh Valirr if he saw what she was doing to his ship.

"Must be jelly..." Kel-Paten intoned, and in spite of her growing case of nerves, she laughed.

" 'Cause jam doesn't shake like this. Okay, flyboy. Give me a bit of back burn. Heavy airs"—and a long vibration rattled through the ship—"online. It's blue-sky time."

And then she was hand-flying the ship, putting her through her S-curves to bleed off speed, watching hull temperature as she did so. The shields held, but just barely. The bogies behind them stopped firing. Maybe they knew shield failure at this point would do the job for them.

Data came in from the port scanners intermittently. Whatever fix Kel-Paten had applied was failing. He tried another patch, but this wasn't the *Vax*. He couldn't spike in and become part of the system.

Then shield strength dropped another ten percent, and the port scanner died.

He clicked off his straps. "I can work through a datalink below—"

"Don't," she told him, teeth clenched, "even think about it."

"Damn it, Sebastian—"

"Damn *you*, Kel-Paten! No."

"And how do you intend to find the outpost, the landing strip?"

"The old-fashioned way. Looking out the forward viewport." She shot him a quick, narrow-eyed glance. "I've done it before."

"At night?"

"That's where you come in."

He stared at her for a moment, then sat and raked his straps back across his chest. And not happily.

"If we crash," she told him, "I'll buy you a beer in hell. Now, where are those bogies?"

"They pulled off three minutes ago. They're not heavy-air capable. That gives me time to go below-decks and—"

"No. It's a simple word. Learn it. They probably have skimmers—Interceptors—heading for us from dirtside. I need you here." Another S-curve, the last as the Strafer was starting to fly now, its wings out at fifty percent. She began a controlled descent as stars winked around her in the night sky.

Kel-Paten went back to working his console, silently, patching damaged systems. Sass flew the *Blade* through the blackness, grateful for a cloudless night and two bright moons, grateful he wasn't going to try to kill himself again to save her.

Wind buffeted the ship, a small bit of air turbulence. She reduced the shields; they were creating unneeded drag. If Interceptors showed up, the shields would come up automatically again. As much as they could. They were below fifty percent now. And all they had to fight back with were lasers, creativity, and luck.

Then she had to land this thing, get to the *Traveler*—

Or maybe they didn't have to land this thing at all. There was a shortcut. And it would make one *mully-trock* of a diversion. "Branden," she said, and he looked over at her with a questioning glance. "Did the transbeam generators take any damage?"

"None."

"I think I like your idea of crashing this ship."

One dark eyebrow rose. She waited. Then he nodded. She knew he would catch on, once she gave him the two major components.

"It'll be a tight transfer," he cautioned. "This isn't a long-range unit. But I have the coordinates for the *Traveler*. It'll take me only a few seconds to program them—"

The remaining working scanner blared in alarm. Sass flashed a glance at her console, adrenaline spiking. Interceptors, three of them. Coming in hot, firing.

"Make it quick," she told him as he swore out loud. Laser fire hit their shields, breaking through at Port Bulkhead 46 aft. She sealed the compartment with quick, tense moves. "We're not going to have much time."

THE OUTPOST

He looks so damned vulnerable. In her nervousness over their impending escape plans, Doc Eden Fynn forgot that Jace Serafino was not unconscious on the surgery table, even though his damned kissable mouth was slack and his damned twinkling eyes were closed.

Appearances are deceiving, he whispered in her mind, his tone playful and seductive.

Stop it! she told him, flashing an image of a rectal thermometer. Next to her, Mara finished laying out the instruments, including three different levels of

sonic scalpels and two medical lasers. Mara and
Nando seemed far more concerned with the instruments that would touch the implant than with Jace's
condition. They barely checked his life signs on the
diag panel.

Both wore, as Jace surmised, small but deadly laser
pistols clipped to their belts. *Cure 'Em then Kill 'Em,
at your service,* she thought with disgust as she ran
her medicorder over Jace's head and chest. She took a
deep breath. Time to start the show. Gods, Sass was
so much better at this than she was. But Sass wasn't
here.

"Hmm." She made that worried-medical-doctor
sigh. Mara was a med-tech. She knew what it meant.

But Mara, it seemed, wasn't interested in anything
the medicorder said about Jace.

"Hmm," Eden said louder, and tapped at the
medicorder. "I seem to have a possible equipment
malfunction." She glanced from Mara to Nando.
"Do you have another medicorder handy?"

At Mara's nod, Nando unclipped one from his belt
and handed it to Eden.

"Thanks." She flipped it on and stared at it a moment, foot tapping. "Hmm," she said again.

"Doctor Fynn." Mara was clearly not pleased.
"Delaying the procedure—"

"Assures the implant won't be damaged," Eden
cut in brusquely. Her anger wasn't feigned. "I
thought I was getting an incorrect reading. I'm not.
See for yourself." She thrust the medicorder's screen
almost to Mara's nose.

The woman stepped back, then frowned. "Abnormal brain waves around the harness. He didn't have that earlier. We ran full scans on him."

"He has it now." She turned and shoved the medicorder toward Nando, who stood on the other side of the surgery bed. "Maybe you can explain it."

Nando had to lean over Jace to see the screen. Which is exactly what Jace wanted him to do. *Now,* he told Eden.

He lunged upward. Eden swung the medicorder and smashed it against the side of Mara's face. The woman stumbled backward, one arm coming up to shield her face, the other reaching for her pistol.

Eden struck again with the medicorder, grabbed the woman's arm, and pushed her backward, giving the med-tech no room to raise her weapon. But Mara was strong. She kicked out, catching Eden in the shin. Pain shot up her leg as grunts and thuds sounded behind her. She momentarily lost her balance. Mara shoved her back toward the bed.

Eden tried for another blow with the medicorder, but Mara was quicker this time and, blood streaming from her nose, caught Eden's arm as it swung inches from her face.

"Nando!" Mara bellowed, locking Eden's wrist in a paralyzing grip.

A screeching yowl filled the room. Reilly, launching himself from his hiding place on a supply shelf, latched on to Mara's thigh, claws slicing through her uniform.

She jerked sideways but didn't let go of Eden's arm.

Laser fire sliced the air. Eden wrenched around,

dragging Mara with her, her arm numb, her leg spasming. Bianca stood in the doorway.

"Stop this now!" She held a pistol in both hands, switching her target from Eden to Jace, now pulling himself off the floor. Two guards were behind her, rifles at the ready.

Fuck. Jace's desolation filled Eden's senses as his voice sounded harsh in her mind.

"Against the wall, both of you, hands out!" Bianca ordered.

Eden, sweetling, I'm sorry.

It's okay. Her voice trembled, tears pricking at the back of her eyes. *We had to try.* She glanced surreptitiously around as she limped toward the back wall. Reilly and Tank were nowhere to be seen. *Go Blink,* she told them. *Be safe. Please, go Blink.*

Reilly help! came back the small voice.

No! She leaned wearily against the wall and stared at Bianca. *Be safe. Mommy loves you. Mommy will always love you. Now go Blink!*

I'll always love you, Jace told her softly.

Bianca moved swiftly into the room, guards flanking her. Mara, her face still smeared with blood, had her pistol out and aimed it at Eden.

"Kill me," Eden said, "and you'll never get the codes for the implant."

"I don't have to kill you," Bianca replied. She jerked her chin at Nando, whose left eye was battered shut. "Hand me a scalpel. I'm going to do a little surgery on my brother. Not enough to kill him, Doctor," she told Eden, "but enough to make him wish he was dead. Let's see how long you can listen to him scream."

THE *WINDBLADE*

"Ten thousand feet and descending," Sass called out over the din as she seesawed the *Blade* through the night sky in a final attempt to avoid the Interceptor's lasers. They'd taken six more direct hits aft. Compartments 52 and 47 were blown. Shield-failure alarms blared, engine-temperature alarms wailed, incoming-craft-advisory alarms trilled. At least the cockpit-pressure alarms ceased screaming in her ears.

Small reassurance, that.

"Almost there," Kel-Paten called back. They needed a secure lock on the *Traveler* in order to transport to the ship, or else they would shortly share a beer in hell. Starboard laser banks were depleted. The weapons comp targeted the Interceptors, returning fire with the port banks, but wouldn't last much longer.

Zanorian would be really, really pissed if he saw the holes in his beloved ship right now.

A console behind her sparked. Cockpit lights—already on emergency greens—flickered ominously. "Shit."

"Got. A. Lock." Kel-Paten spaced his words in between his frantic actions on his console, his hands moving rapidly from one screen to another. He'd removed his safety straps, hooking one leg around the base of his chair to keep from being thrown to the cockpit floor. "Got it!"

"Go!" Sass shouted hoarsely. "Program a four-minute lag. I'll be right behind you."

He grabbed her shoulder. "You go. I'll follow."

"You need to be first on scene. We've been over

this." He was far better equipped than she was to take out any guards on board and get the ship online. "Damn you, go!"

"Sass—"

She spared ten seconds to glance at him. The desolate look in his eyes tore at her. "I love you, Branden. Remember that, no matter what. I love you. Now go! That's an order."

He kissed her quickly, not much more than a glancing brush of lips, his fingers fumbling in his shirt pocket. His admiral's insignia—five stars cresting a slash of lightning, set in gold and diamonds. The *Blade* dipped as he pinned it to her shirt. "Keep this part of me with you forever." His voice broke. "I love you, Sass." She leveled the wings as he stepped away.

She bit her lip to keep from crying and, hands trembling on the console keypads, listened to the muted whine of a transbeam kicking on behind her.

Five thousand feet. Four thousand. She had to make sure the *Blade*—so heavily damaged it strained her ability to control it—didn't take out the outpost or, worse, the *Traveler*. She had to hold her on course to a crash scene just south. Enough to pull the guards from the buildings. Enough that no one would be watching the *Traveler*. Enough to give them time to find Jace, Eden, and the furzels and get off planet.

They'd be pursued. They expected that. But they'd have a fresh ship and full laser banks.

She hoped. She prayed. Or else it was all for nothing.

Three thousand feet, flying in the dark with no instruments. Not even Kel-Paten's night sight to guide her. Flying by feel, by gut instinct. Kel-Paten would be on the *Traveler* by now, taking care of any guards, powering up ship's systems. She thought of that. Not how she had no idea how she was going to release the controls two and a half minutes from now and make it to the back of the cabin in time. The Interceptors behind her still raked the ship with laser fire.

A red light glared bright on the console, a new alarm adding its funereal dirge to the din.

The transbeam generator had died.

For a moment she sat frozen, staring at the information on the screen. Then a cry—primal, angry, and harsh—rose in her throat. Wordless, pained, she let it out as she desperately shunted any remaining power to the unit. Engines, lights, guidance, weapons comps went black and died. Life support, air recyclers went silent. The transbeam generator never came back on. She was trapped.

Twenty-eight hundred feet. Two thousand. In the bright moonlight Sass could see the faint outlines of the treetops below. It was past four minutes. Branden was listening for a transbeam signal that would never chime.

But the crash, the crash he would hear.

Her fingers found the diamond insignia. "I love you," she whispered, tears trailing down her face as the Interceptors attacked again. The *Blade*'s starboard wing sheared off from enemy fire, rendering the controls useless. But she was clear of the outpost, clear of the *Traveler*. That was one of the last bits of data she'd seen before the console went dark.

Now it was only the moonlight and the stars and the oncoming treetops. And a part of Branden with her, forever.

Captain Tasha Sebastian forcibly leaned back in her seat, ship shuddering and yawing beneath her, and rested her hands on the armrests. If she was going to die in the captain's chair, she was damned sure she was going to look like a captain when she did so.

She brought the image of the blue-purple Bad Thing deliberately into her mind. "Fuck you and the equinnard you rode in on," she told it.

MommyMommy! said a small voice in her mind as something warm and furry suddenly thudded into her lap. *Go Blink!*

THE *MYSTIC TRAVELER*

The roar of Interceptor engines overhead was almost deafening, even from inside Serafino's ship.

It was minuscule compared to the pain lancing Kel-Paten's heart. The four-minute mark had elapsed. He knew immediately that something was very wrong.

He worked with intense, methodical precision at the transbeam controls of the *Traveler*, his 'cybe functions at max, his emo-inhibitors on triple duty, every Psy-Serv-designed control program in his system activated. Yet his hands shook as he stood as he keyed search after search. He couldn't get a lock on Sass. There was too much interference from the Interceptors and the wild spikes from the *Blade*'s failing systems.

With each passing second, his chest tightened unbearably, but he didn't stop trying. Three times he glimpsed her biosignature, made a grab for her, and lost it. At six minutes forty-one seconds, when the scanners showed the *Blade*'s battered outline, starboard wing gone, the ship careening wildly out of control, he had to look away. Tremors racked his body.

Not like this. Gods, please. Pull up. Fly!

He altered parameters again, rekeyed the search. At eight minutes twenty-seven seconds the ground under the *Traveler* shuddered violently, sending vibrations into his boots. The sound of the explosion followed.

His legs buckled. He locked his knees, locked his arms, pushing heavily against the transbeam console. His stomach heaved. He couldn't stop trembling.

A siren wailed in the distance. He turned to stare out the viewport, and his night vision, now blurred by tears, showed square land vehicles racing down the tarmac toward the plume of smoke, the tips of orange flames licking into the dark sky.

He wanted to cover his face with his hands. But he knew if he let go of the console he'd collapse.

"Branden!"

He went rigid for a second, then spun to his right so quickly he lost his balance. He grabbed the back of the copilot's chair, stumbling because there was the sound of hurried footsteps in the short corridor that led to the bridge and a voice, her voice, even though there was no way, she couldn't possibly be—

"Tasha!" He gasped her name and surged forward, closing the distance between himself and the woman coming toward him, a black and white fidget under one arm, two backpacks looped over the other, a twinkling insignia on her shirt.

He yanked her against him, Tank squirming between them then plopping to the floor along with the backpacks.

Oof! BrandenFriend!

"Tasha!" He buried his face in her hair, felt her arms wrap tightly around him. "Gods, Tasha." His voice wasn't much more than a whisper, and sobs—his and hers—punctuated the words.

He framed her wet face in his hands and kissed her hard, tasting her tears, life flowing back into him.

"The transbeam failed," she said against his mouth, but he kissed her again, not letting her talk. They could talk about what had happened later. Tomorrow. Next month. Next year.

"We don't," she managed, turning her face, but his mouth followed, covering hers again. "Have time," she added, breaking that kiss too.

"I know. I know," he breathed into her ear, but he couldn't let go.

She angled back and ran her fingers down his wet face. "It's okay, flyboy," she said softly.

He could only nod, his throat closing.

"Jace and Eden," she said. "Reilly can't Blink both of them here. Here's Eden's biosignature." She grabbed her datalyzer from her belt. "Get her via transbeam. Reilly will bring Jace."

Go Blink! JaceFriend go Blink!

"Now," she said, shoving him toward the rear console.

He moved, reading Fynn's numerical code from the handheld. He keyed it into the transbeam access module, hit wide scan, locked on to her with no trouble.

"Got her!" he said over the low whine of a transfer in progress.

"How in hell?"

He heard Serafino's surprised exclamation, shot a quick glance over his shoulder, and for a split second didn't recognize the hairless man, shirt torn, blood running down his left arm. Sass grabbed Serafino as he wobbled dangerously. "Sit, 'Fino, here. You look like hell."

"Jace?" Eden Fynn was a blur off the transbeam platform, shoving past Kel-Paten, almost tripping over Reilly, who darted out of her path with a yowl.

"Let's go!" Sass waved Kel-Paten forward with a jerk of her hand. "Get those engines hot. I've got weapons, nav. Eden, secure 'Fino and the furzels."

"Got them all," Eden replied, but her voice shook.

Kel-Paten slid into the pilot's seat as Sass, in the copilot's, raked the straps over her chest. He permitted himself one long glimpse of her—hair ruffled, face smudgy, furzel fur streaking the front of her black jacket, five diamond stars glistening. She was alive.

"Guess we don't give traffic control a courtesy warning," he intoned.

She shot him a sly glance, then looked over her shoulder at Fynn and Serafino. "Brace for emergency takeoff. This is not going to be pleasant."

Pleasant? No. It was going to be godsdamned wonderful.

Lady Sass was alive.

*   *   *

A pair of Interceptors was on their tail within minutes, but those few minutes were enough to create a slim margin of safety. Plus the Interceptors were heavy-air fighters, and the *Traveler* was heading far out of their range and at a speed they couldn't match.

Serafino's old ship was Triad-built. Kel-Paten recreated a spike port easily in the pilot's armrest, in spite of being flattened into his seat by the pull of gravity. That made piloting—though Sass handled that at the moment—navigation and defense more a thought process and less a physical one.

The Interceptors swung away and regrouped for another attack, but he and the weapons comp were on them. Aft shields took the worst of the hits, dropped down to seventy percent at one point, but between his fixes and Sass's wild revisions, they held.

Sass. He couldn't stop sneaking glances at her. Losing her had been unbearable. Finding her was indescribable.

Loooove Mommy, trilled a small voice in his mind.

For a moment, Kel-Paten tensed and was about to shoot a less-than-kind comment back at Serafino. Except Serafino wasn't on the bridge—he was in the ship's small sick bay with Fynn. And that wasn't Serafino's voice.

They cleared the planet's lower atmosphere. Artificial gravity kicked on. Sass sighed and wiggled a bit, adjusting her straps. "One problem gone, but more to come, no doubt."

The Interceptors had pulled off. But the deep-space fightercraft were very likely out there, waiting.

Love BrandenFriend, the voice cooed.

Branden friend?

"Branden friend?" he repeated aloud.

"What?" Sass frowned.

Tank jumped into his lap and sat. *BrandenFriend!*

Oh, sweet gods. "I think your fidget is talking to me," he said slowly, automatically adjusting shields to counter deep-space effects. "I'm hearing...this is crazy." He shook his head.

Sass chuckled. "You can hear Tank?"

Mommy! BrandenFriend! Safe. Reilly hunt. Tank hunt. Safe.

"He said—"

"I heard him that time." She reached over and ruffled the fidget's ears. "Safe? Did you check for Bad Thing here on the ship?"

Look. Hunt. Small Bad Thing. Very small. Dying now. I Blinked it. I did! I did! Want to see?

"You get that?" she asked him.

The fidget's nonsensical chatter could easily make his head spin. "He blinked at a bad thing."

"The furzels found a small psi-creature on board and neutralized it. They call it Blinking. I tried to explain this before."

She had. It made no sense then. It made even less now.

"Don't try to analyze it, Kel-Paten. Just listen and accept. It gets easier the more you talk to him."

He wasn't sure he wanted to talk to a fidget. "Why am I able to hear him?"

She shrugged. "Ask Serafino, not me. But first we need to ask him if this is the real *Traveler*." She tapped a few commands into her console. "Approaching geosynch. You have the con."

He accepted full control of the ship with a coded thought.

Want to see? Want to see? Tank pawed Kel-Paten's arm.

"BrandenFriend and I can't leave the bridge right now, sweet baby," Sass said. "There might be bad ships out there. As soon as we're in jump, we will." She nodded at Kel-Paten. "Pet his head and tell him he did a good job."

"What?"

She mimicked a stroking motion with her hand. "Pet him. Say, 'Good furzel.'"

"Sass—" He paused, deliberately.

"Branden." She pursed her lips, eyes narrowed. Definitely sassy. "Do it."

He touched Tank's soft head, rubbing the place between his ears. "Good furzel."

Tank leaned against his hand and purred. *Branden-Friend.*

A warning chime pinged. "Right on time," Sass intoned. "Five unfriendly friends. Tank, go to sick bay. Go to Eden and Reilly. Be safe."

O-kay. Safe. Go Blink!

The fidget vanished. Kel-Paten started slightly. Sass had evidently caught his uncharacteristic flinch and grinned. Sweet gods, how he loved her smile. "Time to get to work," he told her. "Hour twenty to the gate."

"We'll make it."

He took a moment to squeeze her hand. Then it was coded thought and physical action.

"Seeker launched," he said. The *Traveler*—a larger ship than the *Blade*—carried four. A good defense against their unfriendly friends, who, because of their small size, were appearently armed only with lasers.

Their small size gave them speed and agility, though.

Sass played with the shields. "Three bogies coming in hard portside—"

"Got 'em." His response was faster than weapons comp's, and he raked the pair of attackers with laser fire—not seekers, because the ships were now too close. The pair quickly split apart but not quickly enough; debris trailed behind one of them as it slowed, tumbling. Two down. Three to go.

"Got problems with shields, starboard aft," Sass told him. "Can you tweak it?"

"Take the con." He shifted command functions to her console. "I'll work weapons and see what I can do."

Starboard shields did have a problem. His first patch took, then failed. He worked a more detailed one, taking longer than he liked because he had to split his attention between the repair and the attacking fighters. Sublights were again beyond max capabilities, and the *Traveler* dipped and wove as it streaked for the gate. An hour to go.

He launched another seeker at a fighter that had pulled back, then caught Sass's concerned frown.

"Have two more," he reminded her. "And, yes, I'm worried what will greet us on the other side too." He needed something to work with until the Triad Fleet showed up to defend one of their own. Of that he had no doubt.

"Those are Psy-Serv ships," she said.

He nodded as he watched the seeker gain on its

target—this one more wily than the others. It might well evade the seeker, but it would also be far off their tail by the time it did so. "These psi-creatures must be some kind of mutant experiment of theirs."

"They're not. They're mine," said Serafino's voice from behind them.

Kel-Paten and Sass turned almost in unison. Serafino, leaning on Fynn, walked slowly through the bridge hatchway. Tank and Reilly trailed behind.

"Yours?" Sass asked before Kel-Paten could.

"Not personally. They're Nasyry." He eased down into the seat at navigation behind Sass and ran a hand self-consciously over his shaved head. "Thought you might need my help, Kel-Paten."

There was something different about the man, and it wasn't just his appearance.

"You need to be in sick bay." Fynn took the chair next to Serafino but left one hand on his arm.

"We'll nap in jump, sweetling." He turned back to Kel-Paten. "The Ved'eskhar are a Nasyry mistake."

It took a moment for Kel-Paten to recognize the name. Ved'eskhar. Vampirelike energy beings. He'd found only a few odd, chilling references in Psy-Serv files over the years but nothing definitive.

"The furzels killed the one that had been left on this ship to guard it," Serafino was saying. "They're the Veds only known natural predator."

"What is Psy-Serv doing with them?" Kel-Paten asked.

"It's not what Psy-Serv's doing with them," Serafino answered ominously. "It's what they're doing with Psy-Serv. The pet has become the master."

The *Traveler* shimmied as the shields absorbed incoming fire from the two remaining fighters.

"On it," Kel-Paten said, tripping weapons command codes in his mind, shoring up the starboard shield again.

"I know what's wrong with the shields," Serafino said, swiveling around to the nav-station controls. "I'll handle them. You keep those bastards off our tail."

Kel-Paten hesitated. Psy-Serv was telepaths. The Nasyry was a telepath. He wasn't sure if he trusted the man—

"Admiral Kel-Paten." Serafino angled back around. "Eden can confirm I'm not the enemy. But I need to apologize first. My lack of respect toward you was wrong. I was fed a lot of misinformation," and he tapped his head, "by Psy-Serv."

"The implant," Kel-Paten said, a little stunned at the change in the man.

"That implant also recorded things, damning things that Psy-Serv can't afford to have known, including what we've just been through. We don't have time to go into it now," Serafino added as the ship dipped again. "I'm asking you to trust me. I understand if you can't."

"Do it, Branden." Sass nodded at him, but he was already transferring control of the shields to Serafino. Serafino wasn't the only one who'd changed. The console in front of the Nasyry lit up, flowing with data.

"Thank you," Serafino said. "And by the way, congratulations on your promotion, Sebastian." Grinning, he pointed to the insignia on Sass's shirt.

"Fix the shields, 'Fino," she said. Blushing.

Kel-Paten caught her eye as Serafino swiveled to his console and she was turning toward hers. Her smile was soft, but it faded as she looked at the scanners. "Here they come again."

"Got 'em," he said, segueing into the weapons comp and targeting with all laser banks. "Forty minutes to the gate. Serafino, shields look good. Keep it up. Dr. Fynn, please keep Captain Serafino alive. We need those shields. Sass, I'll take the con back now."

"Shunting command codes to you in five," she said. "Four, three, two—she's yours."

"Affirmative." He plucked the datalyzer from his belt and handed it to her. "Download that to the computers, send a copy to Serafino's station. I need to know before we hit the gate what we're dealing with. Is this your real ship, Serafino?"

The fighters launched another barrage. Kel-Paten countered, answering with a barrage of his own. He was saving the seekers, for now. Serafino's information worried him.

"Real?" Serafino asked.

"Your Ved dropped us on a raft off Kesh," Sass said before Kel-Paten could. "We met up with Zanorian and Angel. Without Suki. Drund was there."

"But Drund died on—" Serafino stopped as if suddenly realizing he said too much.

"Lethant," Sass filled in. "The admiral knows who I am, 'Fino."

"That explains the promotion," Serafino quipped.

"I'm glad you approve," Kel-Paten said, but it was an easy exchange, as was Serafino's answering grin.

"It may be," he continued, "we're dealing with a dimension that can copy things from our minds. Like this ship. Or it could be something else altogether. I need to know before we hit that gate. Because I'm not sure if anything created here can cross it without disintegrating."

"This ship looks real, but let me run some checks," Serafino said. "And, yes, that's exactly what we're dealing with: a dimension manipulated by the Ved." Starboard shields flickered. Serafino was on the problem before Kel-Paten could mention it. "They operate within the observer's paradox—that is, the observer influences the outcome. The Ved extract a memory that's highly emotional, magnify that for the host body. What my people realized too late was that the symbiont wasn't the only one having the experiences. And when the Ved hungered for more, it went seeking more experiences and more hosts. It learned to control both."

The pair of fighters had pulled back. Kel-Paten didn't know if that was a good sign or an omen of a new tactic. He considered using a seeker, opted against it. He didn't know what trouble they yet faced ahead.

Fynn left her seat and hovered over Serafino, medicorder beeping and clicking in her hand.

"Psy-Serv, running experiments to recreate the Nasyry dimension of Novalis, found the Ved about thirty years ago," Serafino continued. "And now the Ved control Psy-Serv."

"This ship, Serafino," Kel-Paten intoned. "I'm not going to chance the gate—"

"No risk. She's real, not an emulation. Looks like Rej paid for his sins," Serafino added with a grin.

"Here they come again," Sass warned.

Kel-Paten knew that. He watched them even as he talked to Serafino and, as always, kept Sass in his line of sight. He quickly brought up three evasive-action patterns, chose two, and then realized neither would work. The fighters weren't moving in to attack. They were moving in to suicide—and at an unbelievable rate of speed. They were already too close to use the seekers.

"Serafino! I need aft shields at max." Even as Kel-Paten shouted the command, he rerouted the power grid. "They're going to ram us."

"Shit." That was Sass. "Eden, grab the furzels, strap in. Hang on!"

"No," Serafino shouted back. "I can take us into jump now!"

"There's no gate here," Sass argued before Kel-Paten could state the same concern.

"Nasyry don't use them. And I'm *nas garra*. A pilot guide, remember?"

"Jace." Fynn sounded angry and scared.

"I know what went wrong last time, Eden. Kel-Paten, give me the con."

Kel-Paten had no choice. Blind jump or death. "You damned well better know what went wrong last time," he said, shunting the command codes to navigation. He subverted all the fail-safes and engaged the hyperspace engines. The *Traveler* shuddered violently, as if from the center outward.

"I never make the same mistake twice. Spike out,

Kel-Paten," Serafino advised. "Thirty seconds to jump."

"Forty-five seconds to impact," Kel-Paten answered back. He withdrew the feeds in his wrist and reached for Sass's hand. But she was already reaching for his. The fighters were closing fast.

Alarms blared on the *Traveler*'s bridge, set off by the incoming fighters and the hyperspace engines being pushed beyond specs and capacity.

Kel-Paten tightened his grip on Sass's hand and felt the first twinge of disorientation.

The *Traveler* jumped.

The starfield outside the bridge viewports disappeared, replaced by a blackness streaked with colors. The shuddering stopped, hyperspace engines dropping into sync. Incoming alarms fell silent.

"Hot damn," Serafino said. "I actually did it." Then he slumped forward in his chair, his arms hanging limp at his sides.

Kel-Paten swiveled his chair around at the sound of footsteps coming down the short corridor leading to the bridge and watched Sass approach. To say she looked tired was an understatement. She looked exhausted. Barring another crisis, he would order her off duty as soon as he heard her report on Serafino's condition. A ship in the sterility of jumpspace needed minimal human attention.

"Don't scowl, Kel-Paten." She stepped through the hatchway. "Eden has him sedated. Tank and Reilly are perched on his chest like two furry med-broches. He'll make it."

He assumed as much. If Serafino was at death's door, he would have been called to sick bay a half hour ago. "I should have her sedate you next. You're off duty as of right now."

"Lady Sass thanks you and will take a nap," she said, settling into her seat at the copilot's console.

"But Captain Sebastian has too many things to worry about." She cocked her head. "Don't you want to know what happened in the outpost?"

He'd figured her delay in returning from sick bay was because she was chatting with Fynn—something that would have very much worried him two weeks ago. He did wonder, however, if Sass had told the CMO about what happened on the *Windblade*. How would the CMO—whose determinations could justify filing a Section 46 on an officer—view his role as Sass's lover?

"You're scowling again."

He reached toward her, curling the fingers of his right hand into hers. His left was spiked in to the ship through thin cables trailing from the armrest. Her hand was warm and reassuring, even through his gloves. It still amazed him how willingly she touched him when he was under full 'cybe power. "Tell me about the outpost."

"They ran into 'Fino's sister, who not only cut off all his hair but decided to slice up his body with surgical lasers. All because Eden had rigged that implant in his head so she was the only one who could remove it."

"The implant that shut off his telepathy."

"And sent him instructions from Psy-Serv and recorded everything he did so that Psy-Serv could retrieve it later."

"Was his sister a simulation, like Zanorian?" He still played with hypotheses in regard to what had happened on the raft.

Sass shook her head. "Eden said her aura showed

she was real-time. She's Bianca Kel-Rea. Recognize the name?"

He ran it through his memory banks. "An Officer Galen Kel-Rea was an evaluator on a Psy-Serv training project fourteen years ago. The *Vax* transported the team to their meet-point on Fendantun. That's the only reference I have for a Kel-Rea. Other than that he was a pompous bastard."

"That pompous bastard married Serafino's sister shortly after you met him, brought her under the influence of these Ved creatures, and together they set out to control Serafino—one of the few rogue Nasyry around—for Psy-Serv. They twisted your transporting Kel-Rea on that mission to you being the matchmaker who put them together so that Psy-Serv could pretend to hold Bianca hostage. It was close enough to the truth—Kel-Rea was on the *Vax* and Bianca was part of Psy-Serv—that it registered as true to 'Fino. He underwent the surgery believing he was saving his sister's life, when in fact she didn't care if he lived or died. She's an *oullum*; she hates all telepaths. And, yes, Officer Kel-Rea has an implant too. That's how Psy-Serv used —or misused—the Intergalactic Psychic Concordance and Protection Statutes. The high suicide rate they quoted for telepaths as proof that the talent drove them insane was a ploy. The suicides were due to failed implants. Telepathy itself is completely benign."

He nodded, seeing the facts fall into place. "But telepaths sense the Ved. So restricting those talents is the only way the Ved and Psy-Serv can ensure their own survival."

"Brilliant deduction. No wonder I love you."

He squeezed her fingers, because her words of affection tended to make his own catch in his throat. It was all too new, too tenuous. And he'd wanted her so very badly for so very long.

"Did Dr. Fynn have any explanation why I can hear Tank?" he asked when he found his voice again.

"The furzels were injured in the outpost. That's something else I need to tell you. To heal them, 'Fino and Eden took them into Novalis—the place, not his ship. The furzels became stronger. 'Fino told Eden he thought they accessed the old knowledge, so maybe their telepathic range expanded too. That's how Tank was able to transport me off the *Windblade* and back to the forest after the transbeam failed. And how Reilly brought Jace to this ship. They weren't capable of anything like that before."

The *Windblade*. When he closed his eyes he could still see the ship's battered image on the scanner. Could still see the curl of smoke, the harsh glow of flames.

"I couldn't get a lock on you," Kel-Paten rasped. "You don't know how—"

"It's okay." She leaned forward and brushed her lips over his.

It wasn't. He had failed her—something else he'd never forget. He cleared his throat. "Back to Serafino's implant. You told me on HV-One it contains proof of Psy-Serv activity. Now we know it has Ved activity as well. If that's intact—"

"Eden says it is."

"—they're going to want it. Is he functional enough to give us a list of agents controlled by the Ved?"

"He will be, in a little while." Her fingers tightened around his. "Branden, what we know will tear the Triad apart. It could well end the Alliance, since Psy-Serv was involved in the treaty negotiations. The U-Cees will balk at what they see as psi-manipulation."

Those issues had hovered in the back of his mind ever since he saw the guard at the outpost with a Zonn-X, and he told her that.

"If the treaty fails, we could be enemies again," she said.

"Never." He caressed her fingers with his thumb. "I know the Triad. Once our ministers realize what's happened, they will immediately act. I promise you. The Alliance will stand."

"But just in case..." She sucked in a breath. "I have no authority to make this offer. But I need you to know that you, your crew, and the *Vaxxar* are welcome on my side of the Zone and as part of our Fleet."

His thumb stilled. She was talking as if another war was a certainty and the Triad was in the wrong. "My existence has been far from perfect," he said slowly, "but one thing I've never regretted is serving the Triad as an officer. It is who and what I am. I would fail in my duties if I let the actions of a small faction in Psy-Serv alter that."

"The Faction may not be that small. They've been involved with Psy-Serv for over two decades."

"Psy-Serv is not the Triad. Our code of honor is strong. There could be a few rough spots when we get back, but then everything will proceed as before. Trust me."

"You're the only one I trust," she said. "And I hope you're right."

"I am." He brought her fingers to his lips, brushed a kiss across her knuckles. "Now. I'm ordering Captain Sebastian off duty. No arguments. I have a randomizer search program running, gathering jump-gate fixes. If Serafino wakes and can help, fine. But if he doesn't, I can still get us home in about two hours."

Standing, she pulled her hand out of his. "If you get bored being brilliant, you know where to find me. Cabin two, starboard side."

He watched her leave, indulging himself with the sway of her hips, and then turned back to his calculations. The program already defined three strong possibilities for gate exits. If he concentrated on those for the next fifteen minutes, he might just find himself not only bored but with forty-five minutes to spare before he had to be back on the bridge.

He did it in twelve.

"Five minutes to gate perimeter," Kel-Paten said, wishing it was Sass sitting in the copilot's seat and not Serafino. But even though he felt sure his calculations for the Tygaris gate were flawless, their entry into jumpspace was at Serafino's hands. If something went wrong on exit, he wanted those same hands in the best position to get them out.

"Five minutes," Serafino echoed. "Looks good. Feel free to drop me off at the casinos, come back in a few days. I should have at least a sweet million credits by then. I really need to upgrade this ship, now that I have her back."

Sass's light laughter from the nav station made him smile. Actually, he'd had a difficult time keeping a silly, idiotic grin from his face ever since he left her cabin ten minutes before. The woman was amazing. Wonderful. Incredible. And he was finally taking her to Tygaris.

Well, almost. First they had to get Serafino safely ensconced on a Triad Fleet ship and—according to Dr. Fynn—back in sick bay for at least another three hours. Which was also why he chose the Tygaris gate from those the randomizer search had offered. This was Captain Ralland Kel-Tyra's sector.

"And," Serafino drawled, glancing over his shoulder to where Fynn was seated next to Sass, "Doc Eden and I have to do some very special jewelry shopping. So make that a sweet two million."

"I'm glad to know you're willing to spend as much on me as you are on your ship," Eden retorted with a laugh.

"Sweetling!"

JaceFriend looooves EdenFriend. Tank was on the bridge, probably near the nav station. *BrandenFriend looooves Mommy!*

"Two minutes," Kel-Paten said over the din. "Doctor, secure the furzels, in case we hit any problems on exit."

"Aye, sir," Fynn answered. "I have them."

"We're going to exit weapons hot—I don't know who those Psy-Serv fighters might have talked to by now. But this ship will broadcast my personal ID. The *Dalkerris* or any one of Captain Kel-Tyra's fleet will recognize that immediately. That doesn't mean there won't be confusion. But that does mean I do all the talking until I give the order otherwise."

"One minute and it's still sweet," Serafino said. "Damn, but I'm good."

"Have a clear fix," Kel-Paten announced, tripping codes in his mind as the ship edged toward the gate. "Locking fix. We have a lock. Integrating."

The *Traveler* shimmied slightly.

"Not to worry." Serafino made adjustments. "Disconnecting hyperspace engine."

"Deep-space sensors online. Scanners on," Sass announced. "We have live data."

"Sublights coming on in three, two..." Serafino tapped at his console. "We're on sublight."

"Confirming position," Sass said. There was a moment of silence. "Position confirmed. Tygaris jump-gate."

Through the viewport, the first twinkle of the star-field glistened in the vanishing color-streaked haze of jumpspace.

"Confirming with Tygaris jumpgate," Kel-Paten said, monitoring sublights, scanners, sensors, life support. And Sass. He could still feel the slick heat of her skin against his as he opened the *Traveler*'s communications ports. He needed to establish contact with the Triad quickly. He'd just come through a jumpgate in a ship on the Triad's known-enemy list, weapons showing hot.

He sent out a sequence of codes that every computer in the Triad would immediately acknowledge far more quickly than any spoken identification. Some *trock*-brained ensign might not remember his face, his name, but no Triad computer would permit its system to fire a weapon on a ship broadcasting Admiral Branden Kel-Paten's personal codes.

But a Psy-Serv ship might.

So he intended to obliterate anything that fired on them. He had two seekers left.

He saw the huntership just as Sass did. "Triad huntership, diamond class, forty minutes out," she said, relaying coordinates.

Diamond class. He had the coordinates before she did. He knew the ship well. Very well. Thank you, sweet gods.

He opened the voice comm and didn't even try to keep the smile off his face. "*Dalkerris,* this is Admiral Branden Kel-Paten. Put me through to Captain Kel-Tyra, priority one."

The wait was less than three minutes. He didn't know if Rall was asleep or in a meeting or simply filling his coffee cup in the wardroom. But when the visual link came on, it was Ralland's typically messy office—stacks of files, a discarded jacket, a holo-album, a racquetlob helmet—in the background. And Rall, uniform shirtsleeves rolled up to his elbows. Three diamond stars sat crookedly over his breast pocket.

"Admiral Kel-Paten." Ralland Kel-Tyra sat ramrod straight in his chair. "May I say it's very good to see you, sir. I—we were worried."

"You should know better than to worry about me, Rall." Kel-Paten leaned back. "You're among friends. You can drop rank."

Kel-Tyra's shoulders relaxed. He crossed his arms on top of his desk, his lean face creased with concern. "What in hell happened?" His gaze darted, taking in

the rest of the bridge. "Captain Sebastian. Serafino."
That rated a quirked eyebrow. "And...ma'am, I
apologize, but I don't know you. Doctor, I assume?"

Fynn wore a blue med coat. "Eden Fynn, CMO on
the *Vaxxar*, Captain. No reason you should know
me. You look far too healthy."

"Dr. Fynn. Of course." Kel-Tyra nodded, then
looked back at Kel-Paten. "The old man's planning
your funeral arrangements. You have no idea how
godsdamned glad I am to see you, Branden."

"The feeling is mutual, Rall. We'll be alongside in
thirty-one minutes, seventeen seconds. Would you be
so kind as to provide a secure docking port? And I do
mean secure. This is priority one. The Illithians are
not our only problem."

"I want Serafino and Eden to stay on the *Traveler* for
now," Sass said, fiddling with the clasp on Kel-Paten's
insignia. They had docked without incident at an airlock on the command tower, two decks down from
the bridge on the *Dalkerris*'s port side, clamps locking on with a clang that reverberated through the
Traveler. Serafino and Kel-Paten were working the
shutdown checklist on the command console.
Through the viewport, the hatchway tube's lights ro-
tated red. Air pressure had yet to equalize in the extended rampway.

Sass pushed out of her seat at navigation. "Here."
She handed the insignia to Kel-Paten, who turned to
her with a questioning frown. "Let's not complicate
matters for poor Ralland Kel-Tyra. He's had enough

to worry about without wondering why I'm wearing that."

"Actually, no, he wouldn't wonder at all," Kel-Paten said softly, with a quick glance at Serafino. But he took the gold and diamond stars and slipped them into his pocket.

Serafino turned. "Sending me back to sick bay?"

"Eden wants you there," Sass answered. "It would be embarrassing to our cause to have you pass out cold in Kel-Tyra's ready room."

"Eden just wants me naked," Serafino replied, grinning. He ducked as a lightpen sailed past his head and clanked against the viewport. "And that's exactly how I want her. But, honestly, Sass. I'm fine." He shoved himself out of the seat. "And I think if Rowdy Rall hears it from my own—"

Serafino's legs buckled. Kel-Paten caught him under the armpits, then lowered him back to the chair.

"This *is* embarrassing," Serafino rasped as Eden waved her medicorder in his face.

"The things you do to get my CMO's attention." Kel-Paten stepped toward Sass. "Doctor, can you get him to sick bay or do you need me to carry him?"

"I'll manage," Eden and Serafino said in unison.

"I'm sure you will," Kel-Paten put in smoothly as Sass chuckled. "Sebastian?" He looked down at her.

"Kel-Paten." She caught a sparkle in his eyes. He'd powered down. A good sign, she thought, as they headed down the corridor for the airlock. A very good sign. This might not be the *Vax*, but they were home. They were safe.

Mommy! Mommy! Tank go with!

She picked him up. "Sweet baby," she started.

She was sure Kel-Tyra wouldn't appreciate—or understand—a fidget in his ready room. But she owed her life to the furry creature. And she hadn't had time to spend with him with all that happened. What little free time she'd had in jump, she and Kel-Paten spent exploring each other's bodies, making incredible love.

She ruffled the fidget's head. "Tank go with," she told him, tucking him in the crook of her arm. "But behave. And don't steal anyone's food."

Food? Food?

Kel-Paten stroked the fidget's nose with one black-clad finger. "We'll see if Captain Kel-Tyra can find a dish of cream for you."

"You still hear him?" Sass asked as the lights on the airlock panel went green.

"Not always. Loud and clear just now."

Cream. Sweet!

Sass reached for the hatchway release, but Kel-Paten grabbed her hand. "One second." He brushed his mouth over hers, then caught her lips in a deep kiss that warmed her all the way to her toes. "Now we're ready."

Sass trotted down the short rampway a step behind Kel-Paten, through the shipside airlock, then down a flight of four stairs to a well-lit waiting room with a row of cushioned gray chairs and a small viewport that showed the *Traveler*'s hull. A man and a woman entered the room from a corridor door as she reached the last stair tread. Both were in Triad black, but the woman stayed by the door, hand on one hip. Security. The tall man kept walking toward them.

Ralland Kel-Tyra. Drop-dead gorgeous, as Eden often noted. He'd unrolled his sleeves, straightened his captain's insignia and uniform collar. He quickened his pace, and his smile, as he held one hand out toward Kel-Paten, was genuine.

"Branden." He clasped Kel-Paten's hand in a firm grip.

The resemblance between the two men, standing so close together, was immediate and unmistakable. Sass had thought she saw a similarity in the way Kel-Tyra quirked an eyebrow earlier. But that was on the vidscreen. It wasn't the same as seeing him in person.

Her instinct told her they were brothers. She wondered if Kel-Paten knew and, if he did, if he'd ever feel comfortable enough admitting that to her.

Friend? Tank asked her.

Friend, she told him. *Friend of BrandenFriend. Safe here.*

Kel-Tyra turned to her. "Captain Sebastian. A pleasure. And this is . . . ?" He noticed the fidget.

"Tank," she said, shifting the fidget's bulk so she could accept Kel-Tyra's hand. "I hope you don't mind."

A quick glance from Kel-Tyra to Kel-Paten. One quirk of an eyebrow answered by an identical one.

"Not at all," Kel-Tyra answered. "Please." He indicated the doorway with a sweep of his hand. "I know you have something important to tell us."

The security officer fell into step as they exited into the corridor. Sass let Tank trot along beside her, his plumy tail flicking left and right, his small voice making singsong comments in her mind.

Big ship! Friends! Fun!

Conversation in the corridor was innocuous. Yes, they were safe. No major injuries, though Serafino was confined to sick bay for a few more hours. The *Vaxxar* was updated on their status, as was Admiral Roderick Kel-Tyra.

Sass picked up Tank when they entered the lift and was still holding him when they stepped into the ready room just aft of the *Dalkerris*'s bridge. A gray-haired man stood at the far end of the wide viewport, his back to them. It took a moment for her to register he was in civilian clothing. Kel-Paten didn't appear to notice him but walked to the long table, his focus on his hushed conversation with Kel-Tyra. He stopped, hand on the back of one chair and motioned for her to come by his side. She heard the ready-room doors slide closed and the security lock click on.

"Would you like some coffee?" Kel-Paten asked, looking down at her. Kel-Tyra held up one hand.

"Admiral, Captain, excuse me. I know you asked for a closed meeting, but we have someone on board who can be a great help. Minister Kel-Sennarin, of course you know Admiral Kel-Paten. But have you met Captain Tasha Sebastian?"

The man in the dark suit smiled easily as he strode to the table. His thick gray hair framed a long face with a slightly bulbous nose.

"I don't recall having the pleasure. Captain?"

Defense Minister Kel-Sennarin. Kel-Paten's former CO and now his superior at Triad Strategic Command. And, according to Serafino, an assassin for Psy-Serv.

The door behind her was locked and—damn it!—she was unarmed. Sass wound her fingers into Tank's fur. "Minister," she said, her smile far less easy than his. *Not a friend, Tank.*

Bad man?

I think so. Tell BrandenFriend.

O-kay.

Beside her, Kel-Paten twitched ever so slightly. If Sass hadn't watched for it, she never would have noticed. Tank was talking to him, she hoped. She couldn't hear the conversation.

"Have a seat, please," Kel-Tyra was saying. "I'll have an ensign bring coffee. How do you take yours, Captain Sebastian?"

"Black," she answered automatically, sitting gingerly. She shoved Tank down into her lap. *Stay.*

O-kay. BrandenFriend question. Question. Not understand. Sorry. Try.

She ruffled his ears, her whole body tense, adrenaline coursing through her veins. Kel-Sennarin here on the *Dalkerris*. He was the Defense Minister. He had a right to be here. But why now?

She tried again. *Tank tell Reilly. Reilly tell JaceFriend. Bad man. Kel-Sennarin. You understand?*

O-kay.

Kel-Sennarin was talking while Ralland Kel-Tyra ordered coffee through a comm panel on the far wall. The Fleet was so concerned, Panperra in an uproar. The ships that had attacked the *Galaxus* had unfortunately been destroyed. No, he had no idea of their origin. Perhaps Admiral Kel-Paten knew more?

Sass could see something warring inside Kel-Paten. It was the minutest of things, a slight tension around his eyes and mouth. But she *knew* him. He was struggling. Because of what she had Tank tell him? Or because—like the last time she brought up Kel-Sennarin's name as part of the Faction—he refused to believe her?

Could Jace be wrong?

Damn it! They needed Eden or Serafino here. Someone to read Kel-Sennarin's thoughts.

Kel-Paten clasped his hands on the table. "We think an alien entity may have infiltrated Psy-Serv."

"The Illithians?" Kel-Tyra asked.

"You have proof?" This from Kel-Sennarin.

"What do you know about the Ved'eskhar?" Kel-Paten asked pointedly.

Sass almost kicked him in the leg under the table. She wasn't sure what side Kel-Sennarin was on. Admitting they knew about the Ved could well seal their death warrants. Or maybe only hers, Eden's, and Jace's. Kel-Paten had cost the Triad too much money. Him, they'd reprogram.

Kel-Tyra looked puzzled, but the minister nodded. "I remember the name from a class in my university days. A Rebashee legend. No." He made a small aimless motion with his fingers. "Nasyry. Yes, I believe that was it."

"They're not legend," Kel-Paten said. "They're real."

"You have proof?" Kel-Sennarin asked again, but then coffee arrived, served graciously by a young ensign who brought a dish of cream for Tank. Sass put it on the chair next to her. She didn't want Kel-Sennarin's attention on the fidget. She didn't know if he knew what furzels could do.

Almost unconsciously, she slipped from being Tasha to Lady Sass, her outward demeanor relaxed but every nerve taut, ready, waiting. She sipped her coffee, watched, and listened.

Watched Kel-Sennarin's concern. Kel-Tyra's surprise. Listened as Kel-Paten took them minute by minute through the blind jump, the crash landing of the *Galaxus,* the disappearance of Serafino and Dr. Fynn.

But not the mining raft. Zanorian, Angel, and Drund were left unsaid. The *Windblade* was never mentioned. Neither were the furzels' strange abilities or the name Bianca Kel-Rea. It was the *Galaxus* they'd managed to get airborne and crash as a diversion so they could use the *Traveler*'s transbeam to grab Fynn and Serafino.

And it was the Ved, only the Ved, who were the enemy, controlling a few misguided Psy-Serv agents.

Was he editing what happened because he didn't trust Kel-Sennarin? Or because he was protecting her identity as Lady Sass, rim runner and mercenary? Student of Gund'jalar. Enemy of the Triad.

Or was Kel-Paten's loyalty to the Triad so strong that he honestly didn't see that the Triad was part of the problem?

Kel-Sennarin rubbed his hands over his face. "Branden, this is devastating news, if true."

"Unfortunately, Max, it's fact."

"Captain Sebastian." Kel-Sennarin turned to her. "The Triad is in debt to you, to the United Coalition. We will take immediate action on this."

"The United Coalition will offer every assistance," she said perfunctorily as something registered in the back of her mind. Max. A common name, but Eden had said Serafino's sister was waiting for someone named Max and—

"And poor Captain Serafino, with that deadly

device in his head. I'll make sure our best neurologist, Dr. Kel-Novaco, personally takes his case at Sellarmaris Medical."

Kel-Novaco. Max and Kel-Novaco. Those were the names Eden told her Bianca had mentioned.

Gods.

For a moment she froze, then: "That won't be necessary. Doctor Fynn already handled the matter."

She saw it. The slight tension in Kel-Sennarin's eyes. The almost unnoticeable dip of his mouth. Kel-Sennarin and Kel-Novaco wanted that implant. They wanted Serafino dead because he was Nasyry. And they knew she knew that.

"Sebastian." Kel-Paten touched her arm lightly. "Dr. Fynn didn't—"

"While we were in jump." She stiffened her spine, as she had on Lethant when lives depended on her answers. "That's why he almost passed out on the bridge. He was just out of surgery."

"He obviously still needs medical care," Kel-Sennarin said. "Captain Kel-Tyra, can you arrange for emergency medical transportation to Sellarmaris immediately?"

"No." The word was out of Sass's mouth before she could stop it.

"Excuse me?" the Minister asked.

"Sebastian." Kel-Paten's voice was a low growl of warning.

"Admiral Kel-Paten." She gave him a hard look. *Read between the lines, damn you!* "Transporting Serafino and the implant is not advisable at this time."

"That's not your decision to make," he shot back,

then turned to Kel-Sennarin. "Max, I apologize. Captain Sebastian has had—we've all had a very difficult time. But she's U-Cee and doesn't understand that Psy-Serv is not the Fleet. It's not the Triad."

Kel-Sennarin smiled at her. A chill ran up her spine. "We'll take very good care of Captain Serafino. I can even arrange for you to accompany him, if you like."

Like hell he would! This time she did kick Kel-Paten's leg under the table. He had the presence of mind not to flinch. Or else she didn't kick him hard enough.

"Minister. Captain Kel-Tyra," Kel-Paten said tightly. "May I speak to Captain Sebastian alone for ten minutes?"

"Absolutely." Kel-Sennarin rose. "Captain Kel-Tyra, if I may borrow your office, I'll alert Sellarmaris Medical that Serafino will shortly be on his way."

Sass rose swiftly and spun on Kel-Paten the moment the doors closed behind the two men. "Are you out of your fucking mind?"

He stared at her, his face a stony mask. Then he stood, towering over her. "Captain."

"He's one of them. Eden heard Bianca say that Max—which has to be Max Kel-Sennarin—and a Dr. Kel-Novaco were waiting for Serafino's implant. And Serafino has proof Kel-Sennarin's a murderer. I *told* you this."

"Have you seen this proof?"

"I wasn't in the outpost. But Serafino—"

"Has had a malfunctioning implant in his head for several years and has admitted there are errors in his memory. I strongly suggest you consider that before you accuse Max of treason."

Sass realized her breath was coming in short, hard gasps. She was suddenly afraid. "You're Psy-Serv, aren't you? Serafino said they programmed you—"

"Gods, no." He thrust one hand through his hair, and when he turned back to her, his face was pained. "Tasha, you're not thinking straight. I should have let you sleep instead of—"

"Making love to a U-Cee who doesn't understand the difference between Psy-Serv and the Triadian Fleet? I know the difference, Branden. The question is, do you?"

"I've known Max Kel-Sennarin for twenty years," he replied forcefully, eyes narrowing again. "He is not a Psy-Serv agent." He pointed to Tank, who crouched on all fours in the chair. "If there was a Ved on this ship, he would have warned you, wouldn't he?"

"The Ved don't have to—"

"Wouldn't he?" Kel-Paten stepped closer, a vein pulsing in his jaw.

"Yes, but—"

"Exactly. You trust Tank. I trust Tank. Serafino is wrong. Fynn misheard the names. Kel-Sennarin is not the enemy. He's as loyal to the Triad as I am and will help us stop the Ved. That means you will work with him and you will let him take Serafino to Sellarmaris. Do you understand?"

She glanced behind her. "Door's not locked. We can be in jumpspace before they know we're gone. I can contact Ace—"

"Sit *down*, Captain. That's an order."

Sass stared at Kel-Paten for a long moment, then

slowly folded down into her chair, drawing Tank into her lap. She bowed her head over his soft, furry body, her heart breaking. *Tank, sweet baby.*

Mommy? Mommy sad.

Very sad. Help Mommy. Tell Reilly and JaceFriend exactly what I say. Now listen.

I listen.

Tell JaceFriend. Flash out. Burn bulkhead. Thirty seconds. Repeat that.

The fidget trembled under her fingers. He knew something was very wrong. *I tell Reilly, JaceFriend. Flash. Out. Burn. Bulk. Head. Thirty. Seconds. Flash. Out.*

Good furzel. Tell him. Now, she added emphatically, praying Jace was well enough to function.

O-kay.

"Do you understand, Captain Sebastian?" Kel-Paten repeated.

She raised her face. "I love you, Branden," she said softly. "Never forget that." She closed her eyes because she couldn't bear to see his pain. But she couldn't risk Serafino's life, the lives of every empath and telepath in the Alliance, just because her heart was breaking.

Tank. Take Mommy with. Go Blink back to JaceFriend. Now!

Tank and Mommy! Go Blink!

Silence.

She fell on her ass in the corridor just aft of the *Traveler*'s bridge. The decking trembled under her, sublight drives roaring.

"Flash out, 'Fino," she screamed as Tank raced ahead of her through the hatchway.

"Docking clamps—"

"Shear 'em." She raked the straps over her chest, locking herself into the copilot's seat, and brought her console online. Eden was wide-eyed at navigation. "The minute we clear the ship, we jump. Can you do it?"

Serafino fired the starboard laser cannons, the intense glow flaring white-hot across the *Dalkerris*'s hull plating. "Absolutely, Lady Sass." He was grinning. "Destination?"

"The hell of your choice," she said, wiping the tears from her eyes as the thrusters jettisoned them hard away from the Triad huntership. From Branden Kel-Paten. "I need a beer."

UNITED COALITION
HUNTERSHIP *REGALIA*

It was too quiet at the edge of the Zone. Captain Tasha Sebastian hated quiet. It left space for thoughts to intrude as she paced the curved apex of the *Regalia*'s bridge, hands shoved in her pockets, heart empty. Six months and counting since the *Traveler* had burned bulkheads in Tygaris. Five months since the Alliance fell apart. One month, three days, and fourteen hours since—

She turned abruptly, paced back toward the command sling, her gaze taking in the various data cascading over the huntership's screens: sublights at optimum, sensors on full sweep, scanners parsing the starfield in all directions.

Last week there were three refugee ships to keep her and her crew busy, including an ore freighter filled not with sharvonite but people. Triad citizens, afraid, hungry, desperate; their leader—trained captains were scarce now—not sure if the U-Cee huntership with its security skimmers circling him were real... or another Ved-induced nightmare.

The man's uncertainty had continued until he saw Tank by Sass's side on the viewscreen and—twenty minutes later—another furzel at the heels of the armed security team that efficiently boarded his ship under Commander Cisco Garrick's watchful eye. Word had spread. The Ved could emulate many things, but not a furzel.

Furzels had been banned in the Triad. Telepaths were slaughtered. Kel-Sennarin had kept his word— Psy-Serv was disbanded. The Faction, the Ved, were now the Triad.

That Alliance was no more, but a new one had emerged—the Rebashee and the Tsarii joining with the U-Cees to seal the Triad borders.

The Illithians wisely kept their distance.

"Captain." Lieutenant Lucari, the communications officer, turned at her station. "Incoming message from Doctor Serafino."

Ah, Eden. "I'll take it in my office."

She headed off the bridge, then palmed open the second door on the right. The comm screen slanting out of her desk showed the triangular U-Cee logo. She plucked Tank out of her chair, planted a kiss on his head, and tapped on the deep-space link. The furzel sprawled across a long printout with a sigh and closed his eyes. *Love Mommy.*

Love you too, sweet baby.

"Doctor." Sass smiled as Eden's face appeared on the screen, a white furzel draped over the back of her chair. Four others in various colors and sizes sauntered or stalked across the credenza behind her. "How goes the furzel farm?"

"Five new litters this week, including these." Eden tapped at her desk, bringing up an image that both she and Sass could see.

Three tiny but plump black and white bundles curled in a soft blanket. A small sigh of pleasure escaped Sass's lips.

"Tank's cloning was successful," Eden said. "Thought you'd want to know."

"Copy me on the image?"

"Sending. Jace is very excited."

Sass motioned to the sleeping fidget on her left. "Tank, as you can see, is beside himself with joy."

"When are you coming through Glitterkiln?"

"Probably within ten days. We're just about at the end of this tour. Ace said she might have us swap with Fourth Fleet and take the Staceyan Belt after that."

"Wise decision. You need to get away from the Zone."

Get away from the Triad border, Sass knew Eden meant. Away from memories of a certain Triad admiral and their encounters in the Zone when he'd been a mere captain. "Eden, I'm okay."

"Grief takes time," Eden said softly. "A month isn't always long enough."

Not a month. One month, three days, and fourteen and a half hours since she'd found out Branden was dead.

Killed in the line of duty. She had no idea what that meant in the Triad, where the only news came from refugees, who heard it from other refugees. She only knew what it meant to her—an empty ache that had yet to fade. And when there were no refugees to rescue, no Ved-controlled Triad cruisers to deflect, far too much quiet.

"Tell 'Fino I'll see him at the Starfield Doubles tables in ten days." She pasted a smile on her face.

Eden shook her head knowingly. "Aye, Captain. It's a date."

The screen blanked, the U-Cee logo winking back on.

Her fingers hovered over a small star-shaped icon. A touch and she could bring up the logs. Sometimes it lessened the pain. Most times it did not.

She knew them all by heart anyway.

I don't know where you found that No, No, Bad Captain shirt. Nor do I know where you found those pink sweatpants. But sweet holy gods, Tasha, you don't know how close I came to totally losing it and making more of a fool of myself than I already have.

It seems all I'm able to do in your presence is stare at you like some stupid schoolboy. I just want to talk to you. I've been trying so hard to reach you, but I'm so afraid, and the gods know if you found out you'd probably think it hysterically funny . . . but I'm so afraid of losing you. I don't know how close I can get. I tell myself all the time that you're here with me on the *Vax* and I should be thankful for that! It's more than I ever thought I deserved. I know where you are, I know you're safe, I know I can protect you.

She closed the file, closed her eyes, sat in the office's deafening silence, her head against the tall back of her chair, willing herself to feel nothing, knowing she felt too much.

Mommy sad? Don't be sad.

Tank's innocent love washed over her. She leaned forward and rubbed his belly fur. Then she sighed. "Mommy has to get back to work, sweet baby."

She stood. Red-alert sirens erupted.

Shit! Sass flicked on intraship as Tank bolted off the desk into the safety kennel in the corner of the office. "Sebastian to bridge. Status, Mister Rembert!"

"Incoming interstellar thermal wave," her First Officer told her. "Five-point-two on the Graslan scale. McAbian-residue readings—"

"On my way! Sebastian out."

The bridge was a flurry of frenzied activity, U-Cee officers moving efficiently from station to station, specialists glued to their chairs but swiveling quickly as new information downloaded to nearby screens. Voices were tense, commands clipped. Every screen streamed with data.

She stopped behind Rembert and in less than fifteen seconds knew what they had.

"McAbian levels increasing at the rate of twelve parts per nanosecond," she called out as she darted for the command sling. "Chances of a vortex in the next ten minutes is eighty percent and rising."

She slapped at intraship as she sat. "This is the captain. Secure all decks. We're on a rift horizon. Sebastian out." She raked the straps across her, grabbed the arm-pad console, and swung it into place. "Switching helm control to manual, ten seconds ... nine ... eight ... Hang on, boys and girls, it's going to be a rough ride."

The vortex's primary flare came in a blinding flash on the forward viewscreens. The *Regalia* lurched, buffeted by the energy spiraling outward. Bridge lights flickered as Sass, heart pounding, coaxed the huntership through a series of countermoves.

"Remy, watch those vanes."

"On it, Captain."

"I'm retracting forward vanes ... now. Advise on any structural slippage."

"Hull's holding, Captain."

"Inverting aft vanes, ten percent."

The ship shimmied, jerking. Alarms wailed again. She altered vane pitch. The shimmying lessened though didn't stop completely. One alarm, blessedly, fell silent.

"Status, Remy," she called out.

"Almost through the wave, Captain. Two minutes, eight seconds ..."

Another hard shimmy. More lights flickered. Voices were still clipped, but Sass could feel some of the tension abate. The *Regalia,* trooper that she was, held tight. The last alarm ceased and, at a heartbeat past the two-minute mark, she allowed herself a long breath.

Tank?

Ooh, bumpy jumpy time. Tank o-kay. Food now?

She bit back a small grin. *Few minutes.*

She tapped intraship, opening the link to sick bay. "Cal, how's my crew?"

"Two broken arms, one concussion, one broken

furzel tail. All under control," Dr. Monterro reported easily.

"And the gods smile on the U-Cees once again," she intoned, cutting the link. "Remy?"

"Minimal damage. Repair crews are already reporting to stations."

She unhooked her straps. "Find out where in hell that thermal wave came from," she told him as she stood. "I'll be—"

A short-range-scanner alarm trilled discordantly.

"Huntership, Captain," Rembert called out. "Attempting to acquire configuration and ident now."

She sprinted to his station, scanning the data as it streamed down his screens.

Her heart stopped.

Rembert locked in the information. "Ship is—"

"The *Vaxxar*." She breathed the name. Sweet holy gods.

"Get me all images on forward screens," she ordered, swinging around, heart pounding again, throat dry. Her hands went cold, clammy.

The *Vaxxar*. His flagship.

"Confirming Triad huntership *Vaxxar*," Rembert said. "Going to full shields, weapons online. We have visual on screens one and three forward."

She saw. Her breath caught in her throat. The one-time pride of the Triadian Fleet hung in the star-filled blackness of space like a triangular dark void. No lights dotted most of her hull. Those few lights she saw were dim, sparsely scattered. The command tower was dark. Sensor dishes and comm arrays were little more than twisted wreckage.

"Remy, get me life signs!"

"Scanning, Captain, but we're having problems getting past her shield configurations. She's spiking off the scale."

Wild, erratic power surges. A ship in the throes of death. Plays hell with the sensors. Nullifies any transbeams.

"Drop our shields. Helm, bring us alongside."

"Captain?"

"Do it! She can't hurt us. And that's one less level of interference you'll have to compensate for."

A moment of silence. Her bridge crew probably thought she was crazy. But her crew—save for Perrin Rembert, Cisco Garrick, and Cal Monterro—didn't know she was his Lady Sass. And he was her flyboy.

"Lowering shields."

"Engaging thrusters."

She walked back to her command sling, surprised her knees didn't buckle. She tapped open the link to the shuttle bays. The transbeams were useless. But a shuttle at close range could use lasers to punch a hole in the shields. "This is the captain. Prep the *Liberty*." She had to get on board. She had to know. She had to see. Even if it tore her heart in half.

Rembert stepped away from his console. "I strongly advise against—"

"Noted."

"I'll go with you."

"I go alone, Remy. But thank you."

"At least take Tank."

She nodded. That she would do. He had a right to know too. Days after they left the *Dalkerris*, Serafino had explained that the furzel's link to Kel-Paten was

because she and the admiral had made love. Bonded.
Tank was grieving too.

"Captain, wait." Not Rembert's voice but
Lieutenant Lucari at communications. "I'm picking
up a voice signal. No. Lost it." Her fingers moved
rapidly across her console. "Got it. Voice and visual.
It's coming in on an old Alliance stream we used to
synch our datalyzers."

Sass grabbed for the back of her chair, waved
Rembert off as he stepped toward her. "Center screen,
now."

Something flashed below her. Tank, Blinking into
her seat. *Mommy!*

Her fingers trembled as she touched his head.

The *Regalia*'s center screen flickered, shifting from
the starfield to a green-tinged bridge. Upper tier. She
recognized it, recognized the U-shaped command
center, the double-command sling, and, in front of
that, the curve of the railing.

And a tall dark-haired man, gloved hands braced
against it.

"Branden." She breathed his name.

He raised his face as if he heard her. "United
Coalition huntership *Regalia*, this is Branden Kel-
Paten. I don't know if you can hear me. Our comm
array is down. Life support is failing. We can't control the shields, though we're trying." He glanced
over his left shoulder at a man sitting at a nearby station.

Gods. Ralland Kel-Tyra, nodding. It was then she
realized no one on the *Vaxxar*'s bridge was in Triad
uniform. Kel-Tyra's shirt was light-colored. Kel-
Paten's was collarless, slightly darker. Freighter grays.

"I repeat. Our comm array is down. Weapons banks, life support depleted. We're not a threat. We are...we are all that's left. The Triad is no more."

"Lucari! Get me a voice link, anything, with the *Vaxxar*!" Sass ordered.

"Working on it, Captain."

"*Regalia,* if Tash—if Captain Sebastian is on board or anywhere in your Fleet, reach her. Please. Tell her I...tell her Branden Kel-Paten hopes—prays—her offer still stands. If you can hear me, *Regalia,* send us a signal. We have only two hours of air left—"

"Remy, alert Monterro, prep the shuttles." She spun back to communications. "Lucari!"

"Still trying!"

Damn it! Branden...She wanted to scream in frustration.

BrandenFriend! Tank go Blink!

"Tank!" The seat in front of her was empty. She stared back up at the center screen and suddenly the furzel was there, balancing on the wide railing in the green-tinged darkness, plumy tail flicking back and forth.

Kel-Paten flinched, Ralland Kel-Tyra behind him rising swiftly from his seat. Then, in a blur of movement, Kel-Paten grabbed the furzel, clasping him tightly against his chest as, head bowed, he dropped slowly on his knees to the floor.

The *Liberty*—the first of the three shuttles to launch—glided easily under Perrin Rembert's touch, with only a few small thumps as she aligned with an exterior docking port on the *Vaxxar*'s command tower. Sass was at the shuttle's airlock hatchway; she'd spent the entire five-minute trip there, boots set wide for balance, fingers grasping a handhold. She couldn't sit. She sure as hell couldn't be strapped into a seat like Dr. Monterro and his assistant were. Regulations be damned.

"We may have to manually engage the lock," Rembert was saying. "Sensors show widespread outages in her power grid."

Something thunked, clanked. Whirred.

"Negative that. Receiving signal from the airlock. Synchronizing." Rembert keyed in the codes.

Sass sucked in a long, shuddering breath. She had died a hundred deaths on the way over, would die a hundred more until they got that godsdamned *mullytrocked* hatchway—

The airlock panel light blinked from red to green, air quality and structural data flashing on. She slapped at the release button with a sweaty hand and squeezed sideways through the sliding hatchway door as it groaned open, wiggling as her utility belt momentarily snagged on something.

Then she was free, running down the short rampway tube, her boots clanging sharply against the metal grid plates. The shipside airlock was already open, but she saw him before she cleared it, saw him moving toward her, his eyes luminous, his lips parted as if in uncertainty.

She surged through the airlock hatch tread and he grabbed her, arms tight as metal bands circling her back and waist as he spun her around. His face— rough, unshaven, wet—rasped against hers until their mouths met, fusing in a kiss of blinding passion, of reckless desperation. Of surrender.

She raked her hands up his neck and through his hair. It was longer, felt thick and wavy to her fingers. She grasped a handful and kissed him harder.

He groaned, his hands caressing, kneading her back, her hips, skewing her utility belt, then traveling back up and over her shoulders, splaying against the nape of her neck.

She broke the kiss and framed his face with her hands. In the white glow of the only working overhead light, she saw silver sprinkled through his temples, deeper lines at the corners of his pale eyes. He'd lost weight. She felt it when her hands explored him, saw it in the hard planes of his face.

"Damn you, flyboy," she whispered.

"I love you, Sass," he whispered back. "I need you. I'm sorry—"

She kissed him gently, halting his apology. His breath shuddered against her mouth.

Footsteps came up behind her.

"Admiral Kel-Paten," Rembert said as Sass stepped away. Kel-Paten, arm around her waist, drew her back against his side. Remy, gods love him, was saluting. "Glad you made it, sir."

Kel-Paten nodded but didn't return the salute. "Thank you. It's not admiral anymore. Just Kel-Paten. Or Branden."

"Sir, you will always be Admiral Kel-Paten."

Kel-Paten drew a breath, then stopped. Sass knew he hadn't expected Rembert's earnest reply.

"I need to start with your most seriously injured," Cal Monterro said as Sasha, his orange-striped furzel, sat down at the CMO's feet to lick a spot on his haunch.

Kel-Paten nodded. "Timm Kel-Faray. My First Officer. Sick bay's gone, but we rigged a stasis chamber in my office. He's been on basic regen for four months. Tank's in there with him and Rissa. If you could—"

"On our way." Monterro waved his med-tech forward, the furzel trotting briskly behind.

"We have two more shuttles en route," Rembert said. "They're waiting for clearance from you to dock. Then we can start with the evacuations. How many on board, sir?"

"Besides Timm and Rissa, twenty-six others, plus Rall—Captain Kel-Tyra and ten of his crew." He drew in a deep breath. "Thirty-nine. And me. That's all that's left of the one hundred eighty-two who stood by me when we mutinied against the Triad, against the Ved. Four months ago. They're on the bridge or in the ready room."

"And working airlocks?" Rembert asked.

"Just these two." Kel-Paten indicated them with a wave of his hand.

"I'll get the shuttles in position, sir. If you'll bring your officers and crew?"

Kel-Paten hugged Sass tightly against his side again, then stepped back, slipping his hand through hers. "We'll go now."

She followed him down the darkened corridor, remembering he didn't need light to see. Remembering what he just said. "Four months ago? Why in hell didn't you contact me?"

He guided her around a broken pylon. "We were

dragged into the void. When I finally got us out, they grabbed Ralland's pinnace from the *Dalkerris*, on his way to meet me on the *Vax*. Eight top crew and officers and Ralland. He's my brother, Sass. I couldn't leave them—I couldn't leave *him* in there. So I went back in. Three hours ago we managed to get out. To here."

Suddenly she knew how. "The vortex—"

"Using a vortex is an idea I've worked on for a few years. I told you and Eden that after we captured Serafino. It's not perfect yet. I had to bastardize the weapons system and the shields to do it, but it works. No jumpgate, no Nasyry pilot required. And oddly, any Ved on the ship perish in transit, even though they survive through a normal jumpgate. I thought the U-Cees—the Alliance—might find it useful."

Useful? How about the gods' gift—no. The Tin Soldier's. She followed him up two flights of greentinged stairs to the upper tier of the bridge. The damage she saw to the once magnificent command center appalled her. The sight of thirty-seven people standing in unison and saluting her when Kel-Paten announced, "Captain is on the bridge," made her throat close up and tears come to her eyes.

"At ease. Thank you," she managed, then, "Welcome home. Now let's get you to safety—and to hot coffee and cold beer."

Ralland Kel-Tyra, the last to leave the bridge, brushed her cheek with a kiss as he filed by.

Kel-Paten cuffed him lightly on the shoulder, then slipped his hand back in hers, tucking something between her fingers.

She pulled her hand away to examine the object,

knowing by touch what it was before she even held it up in the dim light. Five diamond-studded stars riding a slash of gold lightning.

"Keep it this time. Please." He secured it to her shirt, just over her captain's bars.

She knew she would never let it go again. A part of him, a part of Branden Kel-Paten. And a promise of forever.

She threaded her hand back through his and let him lead her through his ship's dark and dying corridors to the airlock's hatchway. A fat, long-furred black and white furzel sat patiently waiting for them in the bright glow of the only working overhead light. Guardian of their safety. A beacon to guide them home.

about the author

A former news reporter and retired private detective, Linnea Sinclair has managed to use all her college degrees (journalism and criminology) but hasn't soothed the yearning in her soul to travel the galaxy. To that end she's authored several award-winning science fiction and fantasy novels, including *Finders Keepers, Gabriel's Ghost, An Accidental Goddess, Games of Command,* and, coming in 2007–2008, *The Down Home Zombie Blues* and *Chasidah's Choice.* When not on duty with some intergalactic fleet she resides in Naples, Florida, with her husband and their two thoroughly spoiled cats. Readers can find her perched on the third barstool from the left in her Intergalactic Bar and Grille at www.linneasinclair.com.

Be sure not to miss

THE
DOWN HOME
ZOMBIE
BLUES

the next sexy, action-packed adventure
from multi-award-winning author

LINNEA SINCLAIR

On sale fall 2007

Here's a special preview:

ᏖᎮᏋ ᎠᎣᏯᏁ ᎮᎣᎷᏋ
ᏃᎣᎷᏰᎥᏋ ᏰᏞᏌᏋᏚ

On sale fall 2007

Another dark, humid, stinking alley. Another nil-tech planet. What a surprise.

Commander Jorie Mikkalah automatically cataloged her surroundings as she absently rubbed her bare arm. Thousands of needle-pricks danced across her skin. Only her vision was unaffected by the dispersing and reassembling of her molecules, courtesy of the Personnel Matter Transporter—her means of arrival in the alley only moments before.

The ocular over her right eye eradicated the alley's murky gloom, enhancing the moonlight so she could clearly see the shards of broken glass and small rusted metal cylinders strewn in a haphazard trail across the hard surface under her and her team's boots.

Another dark, humid, stinking, filthy alley. Jorie amended her initial appraisal of her location as a breeze filtered past, sending one of the metal cylinders tumbling, clanking hollowly.

She checked her scanner even though no alarm had sounded. But it would take a few more seconds yet for her body to adjust to the aftereffects of the PMaT, and for her equilibrium to segue from the lighter gravity of an intergalactic battle cruiser to the heavier gravity of a Class-F5 world. It wouldn't do to fall flat on her face trying to defend her team if a zombie appeared.

She swiveled toward them. "You two all right?"

Tamlynne Herryck's sharp features relaxed under her short cap of dark red curls as she managed a nod. "Fine, sir."

Low mechanical rumblings echoed behind Jorie. She shot a quick glance over her shoulder, saw nothing threatening at the alleyway opening. Only the expected metallic land vehicles, lighted front and aft, moving slowly past.

Herryck was scrubbing at her face with the side of her hand when Jorie turned back. The ever-efficient lieutenant had been under Jorie's command for four years; she knew how to work through the PMaT experience.

Ensign Jacare Trenat, however, was as green as the *liaso* hedges on Paroo's lush southern islands, and looked more than a bit dazed from the transit.

"Optimum," replied Trenat when Jorie turned to him, straightening his shoulders, trying hard not to twitch. Or fall over.

Jorie bit back an amused snort of disbelief and caught Herryck's eye. A corner of Herryck's mouth quirked up in response. They both knew this was Trenat's third dirtside mission; perhaps his sixth PMaT experience.

After eight years with the Guardian Force, Jorie had lost track of how much time she'd logged through the PMaT, having her molecules haphazardly spewed through some planet's atmosphere. She'd seen stronger officers than the broad-shouldered ensign leave their lunch on the ground after a transit. The itching and disorientation would drive him crazy for a few more trips.

At least it was a standard transit and not an emergency one. Even she was known to land on her rump after one of those.

"Are we where we're supposed to be, Lieutenant?" she asked as Herryck flipped open her scanner. The screen blinked to life with a greenish-yellow glow.

"Confirming location now, sir."

Jorie glanced again at the scanner she'd kept in her left hand through the entire transport, power on, shielding at full. If it beeped, her laser would be in her right hand, set for hard-terminate. Recent intelligence reported the chilling fact that some zombies had acquired the ability to sense a Guardian's tech, even through shields.

That's why she and her team were in this stinking, filthy alleyway, on this backward, nil-tech planet the natives aptly named after dirt.

They were hunting zombies.

Because zombies were hunting them.

"Confirmed, Commander." Herryck squinted at the screen with her unshielded eye. Trenat stepped closer to her, viewing the data as she did. "Bahia Vista, Florida state. Nation of American States United."

A subtropical area, according to the Guardian agent who was on active hunt status here for three planetary months. An agent whose reports had ceased without explanation two days ago. Jorie knew from experience what that could portend. She'd seen it before with agents and trackers who thought they could solve a rogue herd situation alone. One tracker against one zombie had a chance. An agent with basic tracker training might live long enough to escape. But if there was more than one zombie or if the agent was caught unawares . . . It was the latter she feared.

She'd known Danjay Wain for more than a dozen years—he was a friend of her older brother's—and she'd worked with him as a Mission Agent for almost three. In spite of his teasing prankster ways—he and Galin were so much alike—he was a conscientious agent with a quick mind and an insatiable curiosity about tracker procedures.

She dreaded now that during their many sessions over a wedge and brew in the crew lounge, she'd either taught him too much about her job—or not enough.

"Think he's alive, sir?" Herryck's quiet question echoed her thoughts. No surprise, that. Danjay Wain was her teammate as well. His sudden silence bothered Herryck as much as it bothered Jorie.

She huffed out a short breath. "I hope so. Any response from his transcomm yet?"

Herryck squinted at her screen, tapped the query code again, then shook her head. "Still no answer."

Damn. She so wanted the problem to be one of distance, of the ship in orbit, atmospheric interference . . . anything. Anything but what her gut told her was true. Galin would not take any bad news about his longtime friend well. "How far are we from his last signal?"

"Twelve point two marks, sir."

Twelve marks? Jorie directed a scowl upward, even though there was no way the PMaT chief on board the *Sakanah* could see her. *All right. I can deal with one stinking alley after another,* she railed silently at the chief. *I know we can't just materialize anywhere we want without setting the native nil-techs on edge. But, damn your hide, Ronna, twelve marks! On foot. Let's forget the fact that this is a time-critical mission. Let's forget the fact that we have an agent missing. Do I look like I'm dressed for sightseeing?*

She was in standard hot-weather tracker gear: sleeveless shirt, shorts, knee-high duraboots, socks, and a right arm technosleeve so she could multitask her units if she had to. Two G-1 laser pistols were shoulder-holstered left and right. A Hazer micro-rifle slanted across her back. In the side of her right boot rested a sonic-blade. Not to mention her utility belt with her MOD-tech—her Mech-Organic Data scanner—and transcomm. Her headset with its ocular and mouth-mike striped her hair like a dark band. She'd need that to target the zombies once a warning sounded.

Hot-weather gear notwithstanding, she was definitely not dressed for a leisurely twelve-mark sightseeing stroll.

"Sir?"

"We have to acquire transportation," she told Herryck,

taking a few steps toward the alley's entrance, then stopping. And Ronna needed to recalibrate her tiny seeker 'droids to provide landing coordinates better suited to humanoids.

As for Trenat...she turned back to him. "Relax, Ensign." In the light of the almost full moon overhead, she could see the stiff tension in the young man's shoulders under his tracker shirt. He hadn't taken his hand off his laser pistol since they arrived. "There's not a zombie within fifty marks of this place."

Yet. But there would be. There were close to three hundred on planet, per Danjay's last report. It was the largest herd the Guardians had found to date. The zombies' Controller, their C-Prime, had to be straining its capabilities to direct all the drones.

That also meant the zombie's sensenet was large. They'd probably already detected the energy from her team's PMaT and were alerted to an off-world transport. But PMaT trails faded quickly. As long as her team's MOD-tech stayed shielded, they were safe.

"Transportation," Herryck thumbed down Danjay's data on her scanner screen. "Land vehicles powered by combustion engines. Fossil-petroleum fueled. Local term is *car*."

Jorie had read the reports. No personal air transits; at least, not for internal city use. Damn nil-techs. A four-seater gravripper would be very convenient right now. Pure bliss. She resumed her trek toward the alley's entrance, waving her team to follow. "Let's go find one of those cars."

"City population is less than three hundred thousand humans." Herryck dutifully read as she came up behind Jorie. "The surrounding region contains approximately one million."

In her eight years as a Guardian, Jorie had worked cities larger and smaller. Six months ago Kohrkin, a medium-sized city on Delos-5, held seven hundred thousand humanoids. A herd of eighty zombies had reduced the population to three hundred fifty thousand by the time the *Sakanah* was alerted. Jorie, Herryck, and two other commanders went dirtside with a full battle squadron. Their mission was successful. But the lives of those she couldn't save always haunted her.

She thought she'd seen death as a pilot in the Kedrian Marines fighting in the Tresh Border Wars, ten years past. That was civilized warfare compared to what the Guardians faced with the zombies.

Unless you were a pilot taken prisoner by the Tresh. Her fingers automatically rose to the long, bumpy scar just below her collarbone as Herryck continued to recite the facts Danjay had provided. And, as always, Jorie's stomach clenched. A memento—a very special one she couldn't afford to think about now. She had other problems. Serious ones, if something had happened to Danjay.

The stickiness of the air and the sharp stench of rotting garbage faded. Jorie paused cautiously at the darkened alley entrance, assessing the landscape—the street dotted with silent land vehicles, all pointing in the same direction, lights extinguished; black shadows of thin trees jutting now and then in between; the uneven rows of low buildings, two-story, five-story, a few taller. Two much taller ones—twenty stories or more—glowed with a few uneven rectangles of light far down to her right.

Judging from the brief flashes of light between the buildings, and tinny echoes of sound, most of the city's activity appeared to be a street or so in front of her. At least Ronna's seeker 'droid analyzed that correctly. Materializing in the midst of a crowd of nil-techs while dressed in full tracker gear had proven to be patently counterproductive.

A bell clanged hollowly to her left. Trenat, beside her, stiffened. She didn't, but tilted her head toward the sound, curious. As the third gong pealed she guessed it wasn't a warning system and remembered reading about a nil-tech method of announcing the time.

She didn't know local time, didn't care. Unlike the Tresh, humanoids here had no naturally enhanced night sight. It was only important that it was dark and would continue to be dark for a while yet. She and her team needed that, dressed as they were, if they were going to find out what had happened to Agent Wain.

The bell pealed eight more times then fell silent. A fresh breeze drifted over her skin. She caught a salty tang in the air.

"...is situated on a peninsula that is bordered on one side by a large body of water known as Bay Tampa." Herryck was still reading. "On the other..."

Gulf of Mexico, Jorie knew, tuning her out. Data was Herryck's passion.

Zombie hunting was Jorie's.

But first, she had to appropriate a car and find her agent and her brother's longtime friend, Danjay Wain.

"Weird, huh?" Antonio Martinez's voice held an unusual note of amazement.

Homicide Detective Sergeant Theo Petrakos shoved his hands into the pockets of his slacks and nodded mutely in answer to his former partner's comment. There definitely was something weird about the dead, withered body of the man sprawled faceup on the floor. His skin looked like crisp parchment that had been shrink-wrapped over his bones. His T-shirt lay loosely on his frame; his sweat pants seemed overlarge. His red hair, though, was thick, full, healthy. Not sparse, like the hair of the mummy the dead man resembled.

Worse, his eyeballs were still, well, moist. They bulged from his face like two large, wet dimple-less golf balls.

Theo had never heard of a mummy with wet eyeballs. But then, this man was no ancient mummy. Mummification of a body took at least a year under normal circumstances. The landlord had last seen the deceased—one Dan

J. Wayne, according to the documents Martinez and Detective Amy Holloway had found in the bungalow—alive and well two days ago.

Theo had heard of spontaneous combustion. But spontaneous mummification?

Crime scene technicians in protective overalls prowled around the small apartment's living room, photographing, dusting for prints, snagging samples. Judging from their comments, they were as puzzled as he, Martinez, and Holloway were.

They couldn't even definitively say that this was a homicide.

All they did know was what the landlord—a wizened old *mejicano* who lived next door—had told Martinez and Holloway: he was walking his poodle after the six o'clock news when he noticed the broken front window on his rental property. When his knock on the door brought no response, he peered in. Then, voice shaking, Señor Santiago had called the police on his cell phone. First officers to arrive on scene found clear signs of a struggle in the overturned, broken furniture and torn draperies.

But the struggle didn't seem to leave any corresponding injuries on the dead man on the floor. And there was no evidence of who—or what—he had struggled with. If anything.

For all Theo knew, the dead man was running around like a whirling dervish, demolishing his own living room before falling to the floor in a mummified state.

That would fit with the pattern of shattered glass from the window. Fragments were scattered outside onto the bushes. Not inside, onto the floor. The window wasn't broken by someone coming in, but by something—which included a portion of a wooden end table, from all appearances—going out.

The other half of the table was sticking out from under the sagging blue couch.

Theo hunkered down on his heels next to the body and

snagged a pair of plastic gloves from a nearby evidence kit. Carefully, he plucked at the neck of the man's T-shirt, then the sleeves.

"Maybe you shouldn't get too close to Mr. Crunchy." Martinez, still standing, leaned back as if Theo's touching the corpse might cause it to burst, sending lethal chunks flying in his direction. "Might be some kind of virus. Contagious. A new SARS strain or something."

In the fifteen years that he and Martinez had worked for the Bahia Vista PD, Theo had seen the wiry man fearlessly dodge any number of flying fists, speeding cars, and even, a few times, bullets. Diseases, however, were another issue entirely. Martinez was probably the sole reason local vitamin stores made any profits. And how he stayed married to a doctor was a source of continual speculation.

Theo continued his examination. "SARS is respiratory, not dermatological."

"So what we got? Some Satanic cult who thinks the Christmas holidays are Halloween, killing people by draining their blood?"

"Not sure." He frowned, then looked up. "Hey, Liza, you see this?"

The stocky blond crime-scene photographer squatted down next to him with a grunt. "You mean those marks on the side of his head?" she asked. "Yeah. Got those when Holloway rolled him."

"They line up. Almost like a large pronged vise grabbed him."

"Like this?" She pulled off her hair clip and clicked it in his face. It was a plastic half-moon curve, spring-loaded with rows of teeth.

He took it, turning it over in his hand. "Like this, but big enough to cover his head."

"Saw that happen on a construction site, once." She retrieved the clip from his fingers, twisted her long hair into a bun at the back of her head, and clamped the clip over it.

"Guy's skull was crushed. Lots of blood, gray matter. Don't have that here."

No, they didn't. Not even a puncture. Just some barely discernible bruises.

"So, how are your holidays so far, Theo?" Liza was still squatting next to him.

He shrugged. "Fine," he lied. "Yours?"

"Kids are up to their eyes in toys they don't need, as usual. And they can't even get to the ones under the tree for three days yet." She nudged him with her elbow and grinned. "My husband's cousin Bonnie is in town through the holidays. She's a couple years younger than you, thirty-four or thirty-five, single. Real cute. Like you." She winked. "You're clocking out for a week's vacation, right?"

He nodded, reluctantly. He had wondered why she asked about his schedule earlier. Now, he had a feeling he knew.

"Why don't you come by the house tomorrow night, say hi to Mark and the kids, meet Bonnie?"

He rose. She stood with him. Liza Walters was, as his mother used to say, good people. She meant well. He didn't want to hurt her feelings. But ever since he'd divorced Camille last year, Liza had joined the ranks of friends and coworkers trying to make sure Theo Petrakos didn't spend his nights alone.

"Thanks. I mean that. But I've got some things to do."

"How about the day after, then? I'm sure you'll like her. Then you could come with us to the New Year's fireworks at Bayshore Park." She raised her chin toward Martinez. "You too, Tony. Unless Suzanne has other plans?"

"New Year's Eve is always at her sister's house." Martinez splayed his hands outward in a gesture of helplessness. "One of those things where I don't have a choice."

Liza briefly laid her hand on Theo's arm. "Think about it. You need to have some fun. Forget about the bitch."

He smiled grimly. Forgetting about the bitch wasn't the problem. Trusting another woman was. "I'll let you know."

"That Bonnie sounds real nice," Martinez intoned innocently as Liza went back to photographing a splintered bookcase. "Thirty-five's not too young for you. I mean, you're not even fifty."

Theo shot a narrow-eyed glance at the shorter man. "Forty-three. And don't you start on me, too."

Martinez grinned affably. "So what *are* your plans for tomorrow night, old man?"

"I'm restringing my guitar."

"Alone?"

Theo only glared at him.

Martinez shook his head. "Still singing the Down Home Divorced Guy Blues? *Amigo*, you gotta change your tune."

"I like my life just the way it is."

"When's the last time you got laid?"

"If you focus that fine investigative mind of yours on our dead friend's problems, and not mine, we just might get out of here by midnight."

"That long ago, eh?"

"I'm going to go see what I can find in the bedroom," he said, ignoring Martinez's leering grin at his choice of destination. "You take the kitchen."

Martinez's good-natured snort of laughter sounded behind him as he left.

"Nice work, Trenat." Jorie laid both hands on the vehicle's round plastic guidance wheel and, looking over her shoulder, offered the young ensign an appreciative smile along with her words. He had done *very* nice work locating a well-concealed storage area of land vehicles and using a combination of mechanical and technical skills to override a series of locks and security devices. All in under ten minutes. Hopefully, determining Danjay's status and returning him and his critical T-MOD unit to the ship would go as smoothly.

Trenat all but beamed at her from the rear seat, most of his earlier unease gone. "This power pack," he said, handing her a thin box slightly smaller than her hand, "will create an ignition sequence and activate the engine."

She followed his instructions as to placement, tabbed on the power. The vehicle vibrated to life, a grumbling noise sounding from its front. "No aft propulsion?"

"No sir."

No antigravs, either. Well, damn. When in Vekris, one must do as the Vekrisians do. She slipped off her headset, draping it around her neck, and studied the control panel with its round numbered gauges. Other gauges had symbols like those she saw on signs as they'd walked the short distance to A-1 Rental Cars. Danjay's reports noted that the local language was similar to Vekran, which Jorie spoke along with three other galactic tongues. The two languages shared a similar alphabet—though not completely—which explained why many of the signs she saw didn't made sense.

Herryck, rummaging through the vehicle's small storage compartment on the control panel, produced a short paperbound book. "Aw-nortz Min-o-al," she read in the tight glow of her wristbeam on her technosleeve.

Jorie leaned toward her. Herryck's Vekran was, at best, rudimentary. "Ow-ner's Min-u-al," she corrected. She took the book, tapped on her wristbeam, and scanned the first few pages. It would be too much to ask, she supposed, that the entire universe be civilized enough—and considerate enough—to speak Alarsh. "Operating instructions for the vehicle's pilot." As the engine continued to chug quietly, she found a page depicting the gauges and read in silence for a few moments. "Okay, I think I have the basics." She tapped off her wristbeam, then caught Trenat's smile in the rectangular mirror over her head.

"Never met a ship I couldn't fly, Ensign. That's what six years in the marines will teach you."

The vehicle's control stick was between the two front seats. She depressed the small buttons, eased it until it clicked once.

The vehicle lurched backward, crashing into the one parked behind it.

"Damn!" She shoved the stick forward and only missed a head-on impact with another parked vehicle because she grabbed the wheel and yanked it to the left.

Herryck bounced against the door. "Sir!"

"I got it, I got it. It's okay." Damn, damn. Give her a nice antigrav hopper any day.

Her feet played with the two pedals, the vehicle seesawing as it jerked toward the open gate.

"I think," Herryck said, bracing herself with her right hand against the front control panel, "those are some kind of throttle and braking system. Sir."

"Thank you, Lieutenant. I know that. I'm just trying to determine their sensitivity ranges."

"Of course, sir." Herryck's head jerked back and forth, but whether she was nodding or reacting to the vehicle's movement, Jorie didn't know. "Good idea."

By the time they exited onto the street, Jorie felt she had the nil-tech land vehicle under control. "Which direction?"

"We need to take a heading of two-four-oh-point-eight, sir." Herryck glanced from her scanner over at the gauges in front of Jorie, none of which functioned as guidance or directional. "Oh." She pulled her palm off the control panel and pointed out the window. "That way."

They went that way, this way, then that way again. Jorie noticed that Trenat had found some kind of safety webbing and flattened himself against the cushions of the rear seat.

"What do you think those colored lights on their structures mean?" Herryck asked as Jorie was forced to swerve, for the fifth time, to avoid impact with another vehicle whose driver was obviously not adept at the proper usage of airspace.

Jorie shrugged. "A religious custom. Wain mentioned that locals hang colored lights on their residences, even the foliage this time of the year. Nil-techs can be very supersti—hey!" A dark land vehicle appeared on her right, seemingly out of nowhere. Jorie pushed her foot down on the throttle, barely escaping being rammed broadside. There was a loud screeching noise, then the discordant blare of a horn. A pair of oncoming vehicles added their horns to the noise as she sped by them.

"Another religious custom," she told Herryck, who sank down in her seat and planted her boots against the front console. "Their vehicles play music as they pass. And they're blessing us."

"Blessing us?"

Jorie nodded as she negotiated her vehicle between two others that seemed to want to travel at an unreasonably slow rate of speed. "They put one hand out the window, middle finger pointing upward. Wain's reports stated many natives worship a god they believe lives in the sky. So I think that raised finger is a gesture of blessing."

"How kind of them. We need to go that way again, sir."

"I'm coming up to an intersection now. How much farther?"

"We should be within walking distance in a few minutes."

"Praise be," Trenat croaked from the rear seat.

Jorie snickered softly. "You'd never survive in the marines, Ensign."

Martinez let out a low whistle as Theo led him and Liza into the bedroom. "Damn. Looks like some kind of minicomputer you'd find in a sci-fi flick. It was behind that dresser?"

"The dresser's a fake." Theo shoved the chest-high piece of furniture farther away from the wall. Liza moved in front of him, digital camera whirring. "Drawer fronts are glued on. Inside's hollow."

"Looks like Mr. Wayne didn't want just anyone to find this," Liza said, adjusting the camera's telephoto, zooming in on the object on the floor. The blinking unit resembled an overlarge black metallic mouse pad with a thin lime-green monitor.

"Maybe it's a new kind of laptop?" Martinez asked.

"Not sure," Theo answered honestly. "The screen's a strange color. And the keyboard"—if that's what that long, dark area was—"doesn't have keys."

"Touch pad system?" Liza ventured.

Theo shook his head. "Maybe." He knelt in front of the greenish-yellow screen, pointed to the symbols splattered across it. "That's not ASCII and it's not HTML. But it looks somewhat like both."

Martinez squinted. "Hey, it's all Greek to me." He smacked Theo playfully on his shoulder. "Get it, Petrakos? Greek."

"It's not Greek. You know damn well I can speak—"

"I know, I know. I just thought it was a good line."

"Suzanne can't possibly love you for your personality."

Martinez arched one eyebrow. "Actually, I'll tell you what my little *mamacita* loves about me."

"Spare me, *amigo*." Theo shoved himself to his feet as Liza headed back to the living room to find a tech to dust the unit for prints. "I put a call in to the techno squad. One of their geeks should be here in about," he glanced at his watch, "thirty minutes to pick this up. Maybe there are e-mails or documents, an Internet trail. Something that will tell us what happened to Mr. Wayne out there." Noises behind him made him turn toward the living room. The body snatchers had arrived with gurney and body bag.

"Come on." He tapped Martinez on the arm. "Let's go see what the ME can tell us."